a single

Kiss

GRACE
BURROWES

Published by Sourcebooks Casablanca, an imprint of Sourcebooks, Inc.
P.O. Box 4410, Naperville, Illinois 60567-4410
(630) 961-3900
Fax: (630) 961-2168
www.sourcebooks.com

Printed and bound in Canada.
MBP 10 9 8 7 6 5 4 3 2 1

To the child welfare professionals and foster families who bail against a tide of misery with a teaspoon of hope and buckets of heart, thank you. You make all the difference.

Chapter 1

"SHE HAD THAT TWITCHY, NOTHING-GETS-BY-HER quality." MacKenzie Knightley flipped a fountain pen through his fingers in a slow, thoughtful rhythm. "I liked her."

Trenton Knightley left off doodling Celtic knots on his legal pad to peer at his older brother. "You liked her? You *liked* this woman? You don't like anybody, particularly females."

"I respected her," Mac said, "which, because you were once upon a time a husband, you ought to know is more important to the ladies than whether I like them."

"Has judge written all over him," James, their younger brother, muttered. "The criminals in this town would howl to lose their best defense counsel, though. I liked the lady's résumé, and I respected it too."

Gail Russo, the law firm's head of human resources, thwacked a file onto the conference table.

"Don't start, gentlemen. Mac has a great idea. Hannah Stark interviewed very well, better than any other candidate we've considered in the past six months. She's temped with all the big boys in Baltimore, has sterling academic credentials, and—are you listening?—is available."

"The best kind," James murmured.

Trent used Gail's folder to smack James on the shoulder, though James talked a better game of tomcat than he strutted.

"You weren't even here to interview her, James, and she's under consideration for your department."

"The press of business..." James waved a languid hand. "My time isn't always my own."

"You were pressing business all afternoon?" Mac asked from beyond retaliatory smacking range.

"The client needed attention," James replied. "Alas for poor, hardworking me, she likes a hands-on approach. Was this Hannah Stark young, pretty, and single, and can she bill sixty hours a week?"

"We have a decision to make," Gail said. "Do we dragoon Hannah Stark into six months in domestic relations then let her have the corporate law slot, or do we hire her for corporate when the need is greater in family law? Or do we start all over and this time advertise for a domestic relations associate?"

Domestic law was Trent's bailiwick, but because certain Child In Need of Assistance attorneys could not keep their closing arguments to less than twenty minutes per case, Trent hadn't interviewed the Stark woman either.

"Mac, you really liked her?" Trent asked.

"She won't tolerate loose ends," Mac said. "She'll work her ass off before she goes to court. The judges and opposing counsel will respect that, and anybody who can't get along with you for their boss for six months doesn't deserve to be in the profession."

"I agree with Mac." James dropped his chair forward, so the front legs hit the carpet. "I'm shorthanded, true, but not that shorthanded. Let's ask her to pitch in for six months in domestic, then let her have the first shot at corporate if we're still swamped in the spring."

"Do it, Trent," Mac said, rising. "Nobody had a bad thing to say about her, and you'll be a better mentor for her first six months in practice than Lance Romance would be. And speaking of domestic relations, shouldn't you be getting home?"

———

Grace Stark bounded into the house ahead of her mother, while Hannah brought up the rear with two grocery bags and a shoulder-bag-cum-purse. Whenever possible, for the sake of the domestic tranquility and the budget, Hannah did her shopping without her daughter's company.

Hannah's little log house sat on the shoulder of a rolling western Maryland valley, snug between the cultivated fields and the wooded mountains. She took a minute to stand beside the car and appreciate the sight of her own house—hers and the bank's—and to draw in a fortifying breath of chipper air scented with wood smoke.

The Appalachians rose up around the house like benevolent geological dowagers, surrounding Hannah's home with maternal protectiveness. Farther out across the valley, subdivisions encroached on the family farms, but up here much of the land wouldn't perc, and the roads were little more than widened logging trails.

The property was quiet, unless the farm dogs across the lane took exception to the roosters, and the roosters on the next farm over took exception to the barking dogs, and so on.

Still, it was a good spot to raise a daughter who enjoyed a busy imagination and an appreciation for nature. Damson Valley had a reputation as a peaceful, friendly community, a good place to set down roots. Hannah's little house wasn't that far from the Y, the park, and the craft shops that called to her restricted budget like so many sirens.

The shoulder bag dropped down to Hannah's elbow as she wrestled the door open while juggling grocery bags.

"Hey, Mom. Would you make cheese shells again? I promise I'll eat most of mine."

"Most?" Hannah asked as she put the milk in the fridge. The amount she'd spent was appalling, considering how tight money was. Thank heavens Grace thought pasta and cheese sauce was a delicacy.

"A few might fall on the floor," Grace said, petting a sleek tuxedo cat taking its bath in the old-fashioned dry sink.

"How would they get on the floor?"

"They might fall off my plate." Grace cuddled the cat, who bore up begrudgingly for about three seconds, then vaulted to the floor. Grace took a piece of purple yarn from a drawer, trailing an end around the cat's ears.

"Cats have to eat too, you know," Grace said. "They love cheese. It says so on TV, and Henry says his mom lets him feed cheese to Ginger."

"Ginger is a dog. She'd eat kittens if she got hungry enough." The groceries put away, Hannah set out place mats and cutlery for two on the kitchen table. "You wouldn't eat kittens just because Henry let Ginger eat kittens, would you?"

Did all parents make that same dumb argument?

And did all parents put just a few cheesy pieces of pasta in the cat dish? Did all parents try to assuage guilt by buying *fancy 100 percent beef wieners* instead of hot dogs?

"Time to wash your hands, Grace," Hannah said twenty minutes later. "Hot dogs are ready, so is your cat food."

"But, Mom," Grace said, looping the string around the drawer pull on the dry sink, "all I did was pet Geeves, and she's just taken a whole bath. Why do I always have to wash my hands?"

"Because Geeves used the same tongue to wash her butt as she did to wash her paws, and because I'm telling you to."

Grace tried to frown mightily at her mother but burst out giggling. "You said butt, and you're supposed to ask."

"Butt, butt, butt," Hannah chorused. "Grace, would you please wash your hands before Geeves and I gobble up all your cheesy shells?"

They sat down to their mac and cheese, hot dogs, and salad, a time Hannah treasured—she treasured any time with her daughter—and dreaded. Grace could be stubborn when tired or when her day had gone badly.

"Grace, please don't wipe your hands on your shirt. Ketchup stains, and you like that shirt."

"When you were a kid, did you wipe your hands on your shirt?" Grace asked while chewing a bite of hot dog.

"Of course, and I got reminded not to, unless I was wearing a ketchup-colored shirt, in which case I could sneak a small smear."

Grace started to laugh with her mouth full, and Hannah was trying to concoct a *request* that would encourage the child to desist, when her cell phone rang. This far into the country, the expense of a landline was necessary because cell reception was spotty, though tonight the signal was apparently strong enough.

"Hello, Stark's."

"Hi, this is Gail Russo from Hartman and Whitney. Is this Hannah?"

The three bites of cheesy shells Hannah had snitched while preparing dinner went on a tumbling run in her tummy. "This is Hannah."

"I hope I'm not interrupting your dinner, Hannah, but most people like to hear something as soon as possible after an interview. I have good news, I think."

"I'm listening."

Grace used her fork to draw a cat in her ketchup.

"You interviewed with two department heads and a partner," Gail said, "which is our in-house rule before a new hire, and they all liked you."

Hannah had liked the two department heads. The partner, Mr. MacKenzie Knightley, had been charm-free, to put it charitably. Still, he'd been civil, and when he'd asked if she had any questions, Hannah had the sense he'd answer with absolute honesty.

The guy had been good-looking, in a six-foot-four, dark-haired, blue-eyed way that did not matter in the least.

"I'm glad they were favorably impressed," Hannah said as Grace finished her mac and cheese.

"Unfortunately for you, we also had a little excitement in the office today. The chief associate in our domestic relations department came down with persistent light-headedness. She went to her obstetrician just to make sure all was well with her pregnancy and was summarily sent home and put on complete bed rest."

"I'm sorry to hear that." *Not domestic relations.* If there were a merciful God, Hannah would never again set foot in the same courtroom with a family law case. Never.

"She's seven months along, so we're looking at another two months without her, then she'll be out on maternity leave. It changed the complexion of the offer we'd like to make you."

"An offer is good." An offer would become an absolute necessity in about one-and-a-half house payments.

Grace was disappearing her hot dog with as much dispatch as she'd scarfed up her mac and cheese.

"We'd like you to start as soon as possible, but put you in the domestic relations department until Janelle can come back in the spring. We'll hire somebody for domestic in addition to her, but you're qualified, and the need, as they say, is now."

"Domestic relations?" Prisoners sentenced to life-plus-thirty probably used that same tone of voice.

"Family law. Our domestic partner is another Knightley brother, but he's willing to take any help he can get. He was in court today when Janelle packed up and went home, otherwise you might have interviewed with him."

"I see."

What Hannah saw was Grace, helping herself to her mother's unfinished pasta.

"You'd be in domestic for only a few months, Hannah, and Trent Knightley is the nicest guy you'd ever want to work for. He takes care of his people, and you might find you don't want to leave domestic in the spring, though James Knightley is also a great boss."

Gail went on to list benefits that included a signing bonus. Not a big one, but by Hannah's standards, it would clear off all the bills, allow for a few extravagances, and maybe even the start of a savings account.

God in heaven, a savings account.

"Mom, can I have another hot dog?" Grace stage-whispered her request, clearly trying to be good.

Except there wasn't another hot dog. Hannah had toted up her grocery bill as she'd filled her cart, and there wasn't another damned hot dog.

Thank God my child is safe for another day... But how safe was Grace in a household where even hot dogs were carefully rationed?

Hannah covered the phone. "You may have mine, Grace."

"Thanks!"

"Hannah? Are you there?"

A beat of silence, while Hannah weighed her daughter's need for a second hot dog against six months of practicing law in a specialty Hannah loathed, dreaded, and despised.

"I accept the job, Gail, though be warned I will transfer to corporate law as soon as I can."

"You haven't met Trent. You're going to love him."

No, Hannah would not.

Gail went on to explain details—starting day, parking sticker, county bar identification badge—and all the while, Hannah watched her hot dog disappear and knew she was making a terrible mistake.

"Trent Knightley is a fine man, and his people love him," Gail said, passing Hannah's signing bonus check across the desk. "The only folks who don't like to see him coming are opposing counsel, and even they respect him."

"He sounds like an ideal first boss."

What kind of fine man wanted to spend his days breaking up families and needed the head of HR singing his praises at every turn?

The entire first morning was spent with Gail, filling out forms—and leaving some spaces on those forms blank. Gail took Hannah to lunch, calling it de rigueur for a new hire.

"In fact," Gail said between bites of a chicken Caesar, "you will likely be taken out to lunch by each of the three partners, though Mac tends to be less social than his brothers. You ordering dessert?"

People who could afford gym memberships ordered dessert.

"I'd like to get back to work if you don't mind, Gail. I have yet to meet the elusive Trent Knightley, and if he should appear in the office this afternoon, I don't want to be accused of stretching lunch on my first day."

Not on any day. If Hannah had learned anything temping for the Baltimore firms, it was that law firms were OCD about time sheets and billable hours.

"Hannah, you are not bagging groceries. No one, and I mean no one, will watch your time as long as your work is getting done, your time sheet is accurate, and most of your clients aren't complaining. Get over the convenience-store galley slave mentality."

Gail paid the bill with a corporate card, and no doubt the cost of lunch would have bought many packages of fancy 100 percent beef wieners.

"Don't sweat the occasional long lunch," Gail said as they drove back to the office. "Trent takes as many as anyone else, and the way he eats, he'd better."

Gail's comment had Hannah picturing Mr. Wonderful Boss, Esq., as a pudgy middle-aged fellow who put nervous clients at ease and probably used a cart and a caddy when he played golf with the judges.

―――

Hannah finished arranging the fresh flowers that had just been delivered to her office, her sole extravagance as the proud recipient of a signing bonus. The florist had recommended the purple glads, and for good reason, for they were splendid specimens. Hannah pulled out one long, magenta-lavender blossom to share with Grace.

Gino, the beefy Italian facility manager, had delivered a banker's box piled high with every imaginable office supply and promised Hannah he'd have her computer installed by tomorrow morning. Her office was a tidy, impersonal space but for the flower arrangement, and she liked it that way—even when temping, a lawyer learned that clients got nosy. She wrapped the gladiolus in a wet paper towel, then spotted a volume of *Maryland Family Law* on her credenza.

A poo-poo brown book for a poo-poo brown subject, Grace would say.

Still, it was a reference book that belonged in the boss's shelves. Hannah had taken a moment to assess Trenton Knightley's private office, and found it cozy, like a den or study, more baronial than palatial. The Oriental rug and upholstered furniture went with her well-fed, middle-aged, avuncular image of him. Then too, if he kept the firm's family law library in printed book form, maybe he was a bit of a cyberphobe.

Some of the older attorneys were.

Hannah approached the door to the boss's office, book in one hand, flower in the other. A man's voice coming from within stopped her before she would have barged through the slightly open door.

"So what are you doing tonight?" the guy asked, voice pitched intimately, the inflection lazy and personal. A beautiful, sexy voice completely inappropriate for a law office during business hours.

"Do you think he could stand to part with you for an hour?" the man asked.

Hannah told herself to put the damned book back another time, but curiosity held her in place.

"I'm in the mood for a ride." *A ride? How crude was that?* "I was stuck all day on a nasty case, and I need to change gears. The best way I know to do that is spend some time with my favorite girl."

Oh, for cryin' in a bucket. Hannah turned to go, but some flicker of light or shadow must have given her away. The door swung open.

"I'll be there in less than an hour," he said into a cell phone. "Go ahead and eat something—you'll need your energy." He slipped the phone into his pocket and smiled at Hannah. His jacket was off, his shirt sleeves cuffed back, and his tie—a stylized image of a white horse galloping out of a crashing blue surf—was loosened.

The informality of the guy's attire only emphasized

that fact that he was drop-dead-of-an-estrogen-coronary gorgeous. Tall, dark, and handsome, three for three. His sable hair was a tad long, his facial architecture a touch dramatic. Even white teeth arranged in a shark-smile, and blue, blue eyes finished off a walking assault to a woman's composure.

Hannah stood in the doorway, *Family Law* in one hand, a perfectly phallic flower in the other.

Her mouth snapped shut.

"Hello," he said, still exuding the air of happy anticipation he'd had on the phone. "Is that flower for me?"

"You got some nerve, buddy." Hannah plowed past him. "If you must arrange your assignations on company time, then at least do it someplace other than the boss's office, and no, this flower is not for you."

Those bachelor-button blue eyes began to dance. "Perhaps we'd best introduce ourselves before we're handing out citations for unprofessional conduct. Trent Knightley, director, Domestic Relations. And you would be?"

Unemployed. *Again.*

"Toast," Hannah muttered, setting the book on the pale oak coffee table and seeing her new, improved grocery budget evaporate before her eyes. "I would be utter toast."

"You're my new hire," he said, the smile dipping into a frown. "Heather? Helen? No…"

Was it a good thing that he couldn't recall the name of the associate he probably intended to work to death?

She dutifully extended a hand. "Hannah Stark."

"Hannah," he said, taking her hand in his and not shaking it, but holding it as he studied her. "Have a seat.

I am remiss for not greeting you in person, but depositions wait for no man or lady. How was your first day?"

Lawyers could be remiss; other people dropped the ball or screwed up.

The mischief in his gaze was gone, which was a relief. Everybody had said he was nice; nobody had said he was a gorgeous, womanizing, flirting—

She took a seat while he folded his length into a wing chair, stretched out long legs, and crossed them at the ankle.

"My *assignation* isn't for an hour," he reminded her. "Spare me five minutes and tell me about your day."

Cross-examination, of course.

"Busy," Hannah said, "but unremarkable. My forms are executed for HR, my office is outfitted, I did lunch with Gail. I spent some time this afternoon trying to track down a case for another associate—I forget the gentleman's name."

"Viking blond? Toothpaste-commercial smile?"

"He has the child support docket." Hannah had seen no toothpaste-commercial smiles outside present company. "Matthew?"

"Gerald Matthews."

"Right. Gerald. His client can prove he had a vasectomy prior to the child's birth—the client, not Gerald—and the procedure hasn't reversed itself since. Gerald thinks there's some relevant case law."

"If the case is coming up Friday and Gerald hasn't started his research, then perhaps you'd like to handle it?"

A silence spread, with Hannah eyeing her flower, while her boss eyed her. This was the price of fancy

100 percent beef wieners. She didn't want to touch the child support docket, neither did she want to admit her reluctance to Mr. Divorces-Are-Us.

"How about not quite yet?" Hannah hedged.

"Fair enough. Why the flower, Hannah Stark?"

Damned lawyer. He'd dropped back into that sexy, conspiring, you-can-trust-me tone he'd used on the phone.

"They're pretty."

"You sent them to yourself?"

She fingered the last blossom, feeling foolish and angry, because a good lawyer could do this. Lead the witness down one path of inquiry, then ambush them from an entirely different direction.

"I like flowers."

She liked signing bonuses, too, and making her mortgage payments on time.

"How about you plan to observe Gerald on happy pappy day?"

"I beg your pardon?"

"We hear all child support matters on Friday in Damson County. It's payday for a lot of people, so it maximizes the chance of some money coming in against arrearages. A Friday docket also gives the folks who are locked up for nonsupport the weekend to come up with the money so they don't miss as much work getting processed out."

The science of lives coming unraveled was part of the reason Hannah loathed family law. "You want me to handle child support cases?"

"Gerald has the docket well in hand, but, yes, I'll want you trained for it, because we should all be able to back each other up. You and I did not get a chance to interview each other, Hannah. My philosophy with the people working for me is to give them what they need to do a good job, then leave them alone to do it. With you, I'll have to be more hands on."

Not a hint of an innuendo of a possibility of flirtation underlay the words *hands on*.

"Because?"

"Because you have no courtroom experience, and family law is litigation intensive."

She'd been in courtrooms since she'd turned three years old. "You and the other three associates can't do the courtroom cases?"

He rose and took the flower from her, poured a glass of water from a pitcher on the windowsill, and balanced the gladiolus in its makeshift vase. The long stem leaned precariously against a thriving rhododendron, but was at least spared death-by-wilting before Hannah even got it home.

"Most new associates are chomping at the bit to get on their white chargers and be God's gift to the courtroom," he said. "I gather you're not."

The problem was not litigation—Hannah was as willing to go to court as the next attorney—the problem was family law.

"I will be honest," Hannah said, because honesty was expedient in this case, and because he'd looked after Grace's flower. "I want to pull my share of the load until I can safely slide over to corporate services. In a divorcing family, the children can't be in two different households at the same time. It's a zero-sum game that isn't a game at all."

"Gail warned me you were reluctant. Not too reluctant, I trust?"

"No, sir," Hannah said, getting to her feet.

"No, Trent."

"I beg your pardon?"

"Hannah, before you let my little brother work your fanny off this spring, you and I will be eating cold pepperoni with black olives out of the same pizza box. We'll get into yelling matches about litigation strategy. We'll drive to and from the courthouse together at least once a week. I might pick up your dry cleaning. You might share your worst professional fears with me or pass off to me the client who couldn't keep his hands to himself. Call. Me. Trent."

What to say? Yes, sir? "Yes, Trent, but I draw the line at anchovies and pineapple."

"Sit down for one more minute, and let me explain something to you." He did not make it a question. Grace would have told him so.

Hannah dropped into her seat, though the clock on the wall said if she didn't want to be late to pick up Grace—with all the misery that would cause—then she couldn't afford any protracted lectures.

"Mac handles criminal law, but he's never committed a crime. James does corporate and property, though he's never owned a business except for this one, and he owns exactly one piece of ground. I, however, practice family law and was raised in a family. So were you—good, bad, indifferent, or wonderful, every family law attorney has family, and baggage as a result."

After nearly two decades with the most overworked therapists the taxpayer could inflict on foster children,

Hannah still had to get the baggage lecture from her new boss.

"What's your point?"

"You'll get your buttons pushed in this business, Hannah Stark, by the cases, the clients, opposing counsel, the judges. We aren't like the social workers and counselors who have a built-in chain of command to support them when they're losing their emotional balance, but we do have common sense. When you're in over your head, you come to me, and we'll address it. When I have a tough case, we staff it and get the benefit of everybody's wisdom. The point is you will not be in the deep end alone with the sharks. I'll be there with you, if I'm doing my job."

Family law *was* the deep end, and she was already in it and late to pick up her kid.

"This is what Gail meant when she said you were good to work for, isn't it?"

"She said that?"

"Said everybody loves to work for you."

"Probably because I'm off at court so much." He smiled, the corners of his eyes crinkling. This curving of his lips was more charming than his "Hi, I'm your new boss" version. "I'll tell Gerald to expect you to shadow him this week, but for tomorrow, why not watch my deposition?"

"May I take the case file home with me tonight?" And leave in the next six minutes?

"You may not," he said, his smile broadening. "You're already doing research for Gerald he ought to do himself. If he's swamped, he also has a paralegal to help him, or he could have come to me. Pace yourself for the long haul, Hannah. Enough cases go home with you whether you want them to or not. Now get your things, and I'll walk you to your car. I'm scheduled to freeze my backside off trail riding under the full moon tonight."

That kind of ride? Well, then, maybe it was OK to like the guy, even if he was down-to-earth, good-looking, and willing to brave the full moon on a weeknight.

"No need to walk me to my car, thank you," Hannah said, getting to her feet. Her answer might have been different if he'd made it a question.

"Suit yourself," he said, rising as well. "Deposition starts at nine. We'll leave here around eight thirty, and, Hannah?"

"Sir?"

He raised an eyebrow.

"Trent?"

"Welcome aboard." He shook her hand again, then let her go.

Because he had to freeze his backside off under the full moon, while Hannah had to pick up her daughter.

———

"I cannot for the life of me figure out why you let me have Hannah Stark," Trent said, leaning on the jamb of James's office door.

"You needed somebody." James had his feet up on the corner of his desk, a book on merger law open in his lap. "Mac liked her. Besides, curvaceous, twitchy redheads in sensible shoes aren't my type."

Any female in need of a shoulder to cry on was James's type. "You have plans tonight?"

"I always have plans. Think Hannah will be a keeper?"

Hannah was a mystery. "Mac called it right: she's the sort who will never, ever let her hair down. She won't be caught unprepared, won't color outside the lines, won't pop off at opposing counsel, won't neglect a matter in her care."

James was the family golden boy, long-limbed and broad-shouldered like a swimmer. He had the right smile for a corporate attorney, confident and competent without being calculating, but he was also—according to Merle—better than Trent or Mac at making popcorn and watching princess movies.

"Do I hear a 'but' after praise like that?" James asked.

"But good lawyers get sued all the time because they're short on warm-and-fuzzy charm." Or because they worked themselves to a frazzle and screwed their brains out in the mistaken belief that qualified as fun.

"Your warm and fuzzies are not short," James said. "Which is why you have to turn away business. If you can talk Miss Hannah into it, go ahead and keep her on the domestic law team. I'll just bill more hours."

James never fudged on a time sheet—nobody at Hartman and Whitney did—but he surely didn't get enough sleep either. Trent had decided long ago that being a brother trumped being a law partner, and he suspected James and Mac had come to the same conclusion.

"How will you keep up with your social calendar if you're billing seventy hours a week?"

"Neither the socializing nor the law particularly challenges me anymore. I can do both with my eyes closed."

"I do worry about you," Trent said, not even half in jest.

James was reading a fifty-year-old case, for mercy's sake. "I did want to thank you for Hannah. She'll be a workhorse."

"Don't work her so hard she quits and goes to massage school."

Massage school, feng shui, medical coding: the temptations wooing good lawyers from the courtroom were treacherous and myriad.

"You sure you have plans tonight?"

"Shoo." James gave his characteristic hand wave. "Genius thrives in solitude."

"I'm leaving, but I have a question for you as the familial authority on the fairer sex."

James crossed his arms, his expression curious.

"Is it now rude to offer to escort a female employee to her car?"

James glanced out the window, as if Peahen v. Piracy Unlimited—corporate cases had the dumbest captions—was so fascinating, he hadn't realized darkness had fallen.

"Walking a woman to her car is gallant, particularly after dark on her first day. My rule of thumb is to figure how I would want somebody treating Merle when she grows up, and that's how I behave. Mostly."

"Good rule. Don't work too late."

"Said the pot to the kettle."

Trent let James have the last word, though with all the hours James had billed lately, James's legendary velocity with the ladies had to be suffering—or taking a breather. Mac's light was still on too, but Trent left his older brother undisturbed. Thanks to Mac's peculiar insights regarding Hannah, Trent's department had a prayer of making it through until spring.

Though Trent wished somebody—a devoted brother, perhaps?—had warned him his new hire was stunningly pretty. Dark auburn hair swept up on a coiled bun gave her a classic appeal, accentuating a lovely profile, big brown eyes, and a full, mobile mouth.

A kissable mouth, if Trent were honest.

She wasn't attractive, though. Hannah Stark had No Trespassing signs posted at every property line, which was puzzling.

Trent got into his late-model Beemer, tucked a disc of Vera Winston playing Scarlatti into the CD player, and let his day's quotient of tension and drama drift away on strains of baroque beauty. As he reached his own property line, though, a question plagued him:

For whom had Hannah Stark taken home that single, lonely, lovely flower?

Some nights, good enough had to be good enough, even for the most devoted single mom.

In that spirit, Hannah used eight of her ten spare minutes on the way home to hit the fast-food drive-through and pick up a kiddie meal and a tuna salad. When she got to Eliza's, she took the gladiolus from among the flotsam in the backseat and headed for Eliza's kitchen door.

"Mom! You were almost late, but not quite, Eliza said. That's a pretty flower, is it for me?" Grace slammed into Hannah, throwing her arms around her mother in a seven-year-old's version of a bear hug.

Thank God my child is safe for another day.

"It is for you. It's called a gladiolus, from the Latin word for sword, like a gladiator might use. This flower wants to bloom in a little girl's bedroom, so she can wake up and see something as wonderful as she is."

Abruptly shy, Grace mashed her nose against her mother's waist. "Thanks, Mom."

"There's a kiddie meal for you in the car, Grace. Please don't open the ketchup." Not quite a request, but a polite command.

"No fair," Eliza's oldest, Henry, moaned from the kitchen sink, where he washed his hands. "We never get kiddie meals."

"You have a dog, Henry," Grace said, shoving her arms into the sleeves of her coat. "Ginger is better than a kiddie meal." She galloped out the door, holding up her flower like an Olympic torch. "C'mon, Bronco!"

"First day go OK?" Eliza asked, passing Henry a tea towel.

Hannah ran a finger down little Adam's cheek. He gurgled happily against his mother's shoulder and beamed a perfect baby smile at Hannah.

"Everyone was very nice, Eliza." Which had been unnerving as hell.

"That's how first days are supposed to go. Get home, have a glass of white wine, and congratulate yourself."

"Except now they'll expect me to be nice right back, and sooner or later, I'll screw that up. I didn't get the gene for corporate pleasantries."

For any pleasantries.

At the sink, Henry ran the taps full out and started the garbage disposal.

"Henry Aaron Moser, you stop that or you'll go without supper," Eliza snapped. Henry shut off the taps and the disposal, grinned an all-boy grin, and scampered out of the kitchen. "I could argue about those genes, Hannah, but I know better than to argue with a lawyer. Do you suppose the car is covered with ketchup yet?"

"Bye, Eliza."

The goddess of commuting families had smiled, though, and Grace was sitting serenely in the passenger's seat, consuming her fries one at a time.

"Mom, do you think I'm little?"

What on earth was this about?

"Compared to what? Compared to me you are little now, but you'll likely be taller than I am before you're all grown up. You will never be as big, say, as Pedro." He'd been a source of fascination ever since he'd moved in across the lane.

"Pedro is a Brahma bull. I know I won't ever be as big as he is, but do you think I'm small?"

"I guess so, for now, for a human."

A pause ensued, lasting two whole fries. "Do you think I'm teensy?"

Hannah looked over at her daughter, searching for a clue, finding none. "I do not think you are teensy. You were not even teensy as a newborn, but you were absolutely adorable."

Also scary as hell.

"I don't want to be teensy."

"Why not?"

Another pause, one fry in duration.

"We learned about the teensy fly in school today. It can kill you, and it's teensy. The flies in our house are really small, don't you think? Are you laughing at me?" A fry poised in the air punctuated the question.

"I am not laughing at you. Your teacher made a silly mistake, that's all." Hannah tried to explain the "mistake" to Grace, of confusing tsetse with teensy, but second-grade spelling made the translation slow. Once Grace got the joke, though, she howled.

"Mrs. Corner forgot tsetse sounds like teensy, like teensy-weensy. Gee, Mom, even I know that."

Grace bounced out of the car in great good spirits, which set the tone for a pleasant evening, so pleasant in fact, the child was in bed twenty minutes early.

The extra few minutes should have been a treat, a chance to have that glass of wine Eliza mentioned fairly frequently.

Except Hannah would never risk it.

What if she had to drive Grace to the emergency room?

What if she had to call 911 when Grace complained of a sudden severe bellyache, and the EMTs arrived to find "the mother had been drinking"?

What if the relaxation alcohol afforded became too seductive?

What if somebody made a referral to Child Protective Services, and the state's eyes and ears popped by unannounced at the end of some difficult week to find the wine bottle was the only thing in the fridge?

"That won't happen," Hannah said, putting the teakettle on. Even Child Protective Services needed a referral before they came knocking on doors in the dead of night—though that was pretty much all they needed before putting a child into foster care.

Hannah brewed up a cup of chamomile tea, dosed it with honey, and put in an old Richard Gere–Julia Roberts movie, a romance. The tale had once been one of her favorites, but in the past year the *Pygmalion* story line had seemed pathetic.

Sometimes, a lady got too empty to dream. Those times were scary, but Hannah had survived them. She might lack the nice-nice gene, but she had a blazingly good memory, an eye for detail, and an excellent grasp of the law. That was enough to sustain a dream of a good job in the field of corporate law.

And hopefully, enough to sustain Hannah for a short, uneventful detour through the legal dungeon known as family law.

———

Trent lay back on an old quilt under the full moon. A few yards away, horses munched deep fall grass, and one lonely cricket sang a slow aria to the crisp night air. The nip in the air, the pitch and tempo of that cricket's song, confirmed that this would be the last such outing for months.

"Daddy?" came a small voice from the other side of the blanket.

"Sweetie?"

"Is there really such a thing as a teensy fly, and can it really kill you? Do they live around here?"

Chapter 2

HANNAH DROPPED A SMILING, BOUNCY GRACE OFF AT school by 7:20 a.m., and spent the commute through the western Maryland hills fretting.

What if she said something inappropriate at today's deposition? What if she failed to say something appropriate? What *was* appropriate? And that paternity law she was researching—was Trent Knightley unhappy she'd taken it on without his say so? Or was he unhappy with Gerald?

By the time Hannah reached the office, a tidy little headache at the base of her skull was threatening to go rogue and climb up the left side of her neck. She got out of her Prius, put on the bolero jacket that went with her A-line dress, and bent to gather up her shoulder bag, briefcase, umbrella, and thermos from the back of the car.

"Good morning, Hannah! May I carry something in for you?"

Trent Knightley's voice so startled Hannah she bumped her head hard on the car's roof.

"That sounded like a pretty ferocious conk on the noggin." He reached toward her face, as if to brush her hair back and inspect the damage, and Hannah flinched away, her forearm coming up to block him.

Which knocked Trent's hand against the car door.

Which bumped the car door into Hannah's elbow hard.

Which sent her belongings flying in all directions.

And dumped the contents of her purse on the black-top at her feet.

"Oliver Wendell Holmes on a pogo stick, Stark." Trent tucked his hand under his opposite arm, much as a kid might have done at a sandlot ball game. "Ouch."

"I'm…sorry. I wasn't… I thought… You startled me."

She tried to get her breath and failed.

Knightley's eyes narrowed. "Down you go." His hands were on her shoulders, pushing her to sit sideways in her own driver's seat. "Head down, take little breaths, like the air is too cold to breathe easily."

She popped back up. "I'm not about to…"

Her ears started to roar from standing too quickly, from rapping her head, from being surprised, from… him, standing too close, and *handling* her.

"Spare me your motion to dismiss." His tone was grouchy as his arms came around her and eased her back down onto her car seat. "You're pale as a blank page, and this qualifies as a workplace injury."

Did not.

Hannah couldn't correct him, because she was not quite steady on her pins and his voice sounded far away. As she struggled for breath, she caught a strong whiff of sandalwood and spices—from him, from the wonderfully soft wool of his jacket.

That scent, that softness, calmed her.

"I'm fine," she said, meaning to sound authoritative and failing spectacularly.

"You're stubborn as hell," he retorted, worry in his voice blending with exasperation. "How about you please don't squander your breath arguing with me?"

"You made it a question." The car prevented her from scooting any farther away, and he—damn him to the lawyers' special reserved section of hell—did not step back. He hung over her in the open car door, his expression disgruntled.

"Did you skip breakfast? That's two questions."

She did not admit she'd skipped breakfast and had eaten only a few bites of last night's tuna salad. Yesterday had been all smiles and new job protocol; today the lawyering began.

"Your color's better," Trent said, still hovering like a mother cat. "Catch your breath, and I'll retrieve"—he went down on one knee and reached under Hannah's car—"your worldly goods."

Hannah watched in sheer mortification as he stashed her birth control pills, tampon holder, moisturizer, headache prescription, wallet, lavender lip balm, and brush back into her purse, then set the thing in her lap.

"You carry this. I will carry the rest of your plunder, and you will allow me to escort you to your office without a peep of protest."

"But—" When was the last time anybody had fussed at her this way, part scold, part concern, and more than a little dear?

"That meets the legal definition of a peep. No peeps, Hannah Stark. I need to recover from my ordeal." He braced himself with one hand on the roof of the car, while Hannah tried not to laugh.

"Your ordeal?"

"Bruised knuckles, bruised ego. Did you really think I was about to wallop my only chance of covering my caseload for the next six months?"

Whose idea was it to turn this guy loose with the questions? "I startle easily, and badly."

"You do." He eyed his hand, then extended it down to her. "Let's get you out of this cold before Gail pulls up and accuses me of committing actionable torts in the parking lot."

A nanosecond of awkwardness blossomed. Hannah was supposed to put her hand in his. The term "poorly socialized" jumped from Hannah's past into her present. She gave Trent her hand, because poorly socialized did not mean entirely clueless.

Trent's grasp was wonderfully warm, at variance with his expression. He drew her to her feet and treated her to an even closer perusal. "You all right, Stark?"

"I'm fine. Mortified, but fine." Mortification should be an actionable tort, the scent of his aftershave and the warmth of his hand the required restitution.

"Mortified is part of the profession," he said, lifting the strap of her purse from her elbow to her shoulder. "No land-speed records if you please."

"In deference to the trauma you've experienced?"

"You catch on, Stark. You startle easily, but you do catch on. You also smell good."

After that peculiar complaint—for he was griping about lily of the valley-scented moisturizer, clearly—he walked her to her office in blessed silence. Hannah's headache still crouched at the base of her skull, but something in this bumpy start to her day was *nice*.

Nice was not always bad, though it was seldom long term, and yet, Hannah liked that her boss could cluck and fuss—and pout.

"Stay right here," he said when they reached her office. "No, don't get your knickers in a twist. I'm your boss, not your playground buddy, and occasionally when I give an order, I'm entitled to be humored."

He disappeared after depositing Hannah's personal effects on her desk. She'd just changed from sneakers to pumps—what would Trenton Knightley know about playground buddies?—when he came back.

"I can send Gino out for something more substantial." He put a folded napkin down before her and a steaming cup of tea. "Strike that. I will send Gino out for something more substantial if you don't eat every cookie."

He was a little too attached to that peremptory tone, but Hannah brought the teacup to her nose. More spices, cinnamon, clove, citrus, scents of comfort.

"Thank you."

"I keep the shortbread in my credenza, right side. It's a communal stash, from The Sweetest Things down on Frederick Douglass Drive. The tea is in the kitchen."

"Decaf?" The taste was too good to be decaf.

"Decaf, though I debated. You get migraines?"

Hannah hadn't had a true migraine since finishing law school. "What makes you ask?"

"You have the same prescription James does."

"James?"

Trent settled a hip on the corner of her desk. "My brother James, the guy you're supposed to go work for when you desert me like a low-down, faithless traitor this spring." He was teasing, or maybe still pouting.

"The tea is quite good."

And like a slow, happy sunrise, Trent smiled. The smile started with his lips, a gentle, sweet curving of humor, then spread to the grooves on either side of his mouth, and up to his eyes, to finish out with crow's-feet.

"Atta girl, Stark. The tea is very good. Mac picks it out, and he doesn't let me push him around either. I'm on to you tea-drinking types."

Still teasing. Hannah longed to return his smile. She took another sip of warm, spicy heaven. "When do we leave for the deposition?"

"When you've eaten your breakfast and I've had a few minutes to glance over my notes from yesterday's festivities. We'll take my car."

Hannah munched a cookie in silence—a rich, buttery cookie such as would earn a bossy-boss a modicum more tolerance for his tendency to use the imperative voice.

"I won't fit in that glorified lawn mower you drive," he said, heading for her door, "and I like my heated seats, Stark. We can take separate cars, if you'd rather, but that's bad for your carbon footprint, and there is no explaining how to find a parking space within two blocks of the courthouse, not even if you're admitted to practice before the Sue-preme Court."

He was gone with a wiggle of his dark eyebrows and a piratical smile, and all Hannah could think about—despite the fact that he'd seen her female unmentionables—was his smile, his scent, and his warm hands.

<center>~~~</center>

Trent made his way to the Human Resources suite while trying to recall the last time he'd been intimate with a woman.

After some corporate Fourth of July picnic two...no,

three…maybe *four* years ago, though the name of his patriotic moment escaped him, not that he could recall fireworks of any variety accompanying it either.

He pushed the memory aside and attributed the flare of interest he'd felt in Hannah Stark to protracted deprivation. As a younger man, he'd expected inconvenient and harmless commentary from his mating urges with cheerful frequency. Somewhere between passing his thirtieth birthday, enduring a divorce, and acquiring sole legal and physical custody of a child, those comments had slowed to a trickle, then gone silent.

Until this morning.

Until he'd had a lithe, fragrant female momentarily warm and pliant in his arms.

Until Hannah's hair had tickled his nose, and her blush had warmed his soul.

He hadn't known women still blushed over something as simple as feminine hygiene products.

Mercy.

He sat at Gail Russo's desk and found Hannah's file sitting on the right-hand corner, a file he was obligated to review as her immediate superior. The file was like the lady: it raised more questions than it answered. Her age was right where he'd estimated it, twenty-eight, and yet the form had blanks in peculiar places—like marital status.

Who left that blank? Under Maryland law, nobody could compel that information on a job application, but why conceal it? Her insurance forms listed benefits for self plus dependents, but the person to notify in case of emergency was Eliza Moser.

A married sister, perhaps?

And the life insurance beneficiary was L. Grace Stark. The relation given was "relative." Very funny.

A mother? An unmarried sister? Trent had six months to find out. Between his own cross-examination skills, the magic of shared pizza, and private investigators kept on retainer, Trent would unearth those answers sooner or later.

Though the more interesting inquiry was why he'd want to.

———

Hannah's law school curriculum had missed a few classes, like Chitchat 101, though Hannah probably would have flunked that one. Her boss wanted to gently grill her, and all she wanted was to let his magic heated car seat soothe away her headache.

Where did she go to law school? A patently stupid question when he would have read her application line by line.

How about undergraduate?

Did she follow the Ravens or the Orioles, or—"Say it ain't so, Stark"—the Pirates?

Did she have any team *at all*?

And then, blast him, he slipped in a CD and turned the volume down low. He'd chosen the Brahms clarinet sonatas, as lush, lyrical, and gorgeous a pair of works as Hannah had ever fallen asleep to time after time in college.

"Hope you don't mind a dash of something classical," he said, turning the volume down even further. "Helps me change gears on the way home, usually."

His expression was a study in handsome innocence—

if there were such a thing—but Hannah had the sense it was a test.

"I don't think Brahms wrote anything ugly, ever," she said. "He is proof of romance in the German soul."

"As if Bach and Beethoven weren't?"

"Bach was more of a passionate mathematician…" Hannah caught herself. "What should I expect from this morning's deposition?"

"Uncomfortable chairs," Trent said, adopting ominous tones. "Terrible coffee. Elvin Gregory is old school, which means this is all very serious business. He doesn't break role, and he's always got one eye on the clock."

"He's in a hurry?"

"If it's billable work, he's never in a hurry. How's your head?"

"The tea and cookies helped, thank you for asking." Nice try, Boss. "What are the issues?"

Trent glanced over at her, his expression amused. Nice try, Stark?

"One child, so custody is the big issue, and where there is a custody battle, there will also be tussling over use and possession of the family home, and child support. If you need a chocolate energy bar, they're in my briefcase."

Points for tenacity and chocolate energy bars. "Alimony?"

"Now that is a fine line. Mister wants to prove Missus is right next door to an incompetent parent, but somehow, she's completely capable of supporting herself."

"Is she?"

"She hasn't during the marriage, but she held some jobs out of college."

"College doesn't go as far as it used to. How does Mister expect to prove she's a bad parent?"

"She has bipolar disorder. Had to go off the meds to get pregnant, and has some inpatient history."

"Yikes."

"You're familiar with the condition?" Trent was driving now, no longer chatting up the help, thank God.

"Bipolar disorder can mean a family history of suicides and addiction, because it wasn't a well-understood malady years ago. That diagnosis is no cakewalk."

"Still isn't, according to Mrs. Loomis, but she seems together enough to me."

Hannah asked the only question that would ever matter to her. "What does the kid want?"

"He loves both parents, but wants to live with mom."

Because Hannah was with her boss, who expected her to have her lawyer-head in the game that was never a game, she asked the next question:

"What do we want?"

"We want our client to win," Trent said, smiling as he turned the car into a cobbled alley near the courthouse. "We always want our client to win."

Hannah kept further questions to herself, such as how the kid was supposed to cope if mom's condition didn't respond to treatment, and why custody was an either-or question in this case.

Hannah followed Trent into a handsome old brick row house converted to office space. The hallways were narrow, the ceilings high, and the hardwood floors uneven, creaky, and springy.

Old money for Damson County, such as it was.

Trent introduced Hannah as his associate, sitting

second chair on the case. Mr. Elvin Gregory, counsel for Husband, did not shake Hannah's hand and did not appear pleased. But then, his saturnine features looked like smiling was a biennial event, coinciding with the near occasion of intestinal regularity.

The morning was interesting. Trent's style was less like an interrogator and more like an investigator soliciting assistance from the opposing spouse. Several times, Gregory interrupted and tried to amend what his client had answered, and each time, Trent let Gregory ramble at length.

Mrs. Loomis, however, became increasingly agitated as the morning wore on, trying to correct her spouse's answers or answer for him.

Trent asked the court stenographer to go off the record, then turned to his client.

"I have only a few more questions for Mr. Loomis, but we've been at this for nearly three hours. If you'd like, Hannah can take you down to the courthouse café and get you a cup of coffee."

He was up to something.

"I did park at the courthouse garage," Mrs. Loomis said, "and it has been a long morning." She shot a gratuitously cranky look at her spouse, whose great offenses had been to sit in his chair and answer questions Trent had put to him.

Trent glanced at Hannah, a passing nothing of a glance. "If you'd be so kind?"

She was being dismissed, and more particularly, the client was being dismissed into her keeping.

"I'm happy to stretch my legs," she said. "Mr. Loomis, Mr. Gregory, my thanks for allowing me to observe."

She *was* happy to stretch her legs, happy to escape the cramped pretentiousness of Gregory's law offices, happy to breathe the cold autumn air.

"So tell me, dear," Mrs. Loomis said as she trundled along beside Hannah. "What ever made you want to practice family law?"

An hour later, Hannah was on her third cup of weak decaf tea and wondering when in the name of God Almighty her boss would rescue her from the client's clutches.

"And this is Dubbie when he was just two." Mrs. Loomis pushed another color print across the table. "I made that costume myself. I have an old Touch and Sew that was my mother's—she made all my clothes growing up. Did your mother sew? No? So few women do anymore, though we have the best fabric shop out by the high school, right next to the bakery. Where do you suppose Mr. Knightley has got off to?"

Answering the petite brunette wasn't necessary. She babbled along like a human white-noise generator, her speech gaining momentum when it should have been winding down.

"Hello, ladies." Trent sauntered into the courthouse café—The Lunch Bar—and sat at their table. "My apologies if I kept you waiting. I think the depositions went well."

"Do you?" Mrs. Loomis paused for two nanoseconds. "I'm not sure I agree, Mr. Knightley. *That man* has a way of twisting his words to hide the truth, and it just makes me *so mad*. He never raises his voice, but he can have me shouting in no time, he's so *annoying*."

Trent jumped in smoothly. "He'd better not twist his words. All those answers this morning were under oath. If he doesn't give me the same responses when he's on the witness stand, he'll look like a liar."

"Which he is, he definitely is, and if he thinks he's a fit influence to have the exclusive raising of *my son*—"

"Now, we talked about that." Trent patted her hand and rose. "He's the boy's father, and he loves his son, and we're not out to ruin his relationship with Dubbie."

"He'll do that all on his own, if he hasn't already," Mrs. Loomis muttered, getting to her feet as well. Trent held her chair, then held her coat for her, and the whole time, the woman chattered on.

Hannah wanted to sprint for the door, but Mrs. Loomis would not be hurried, and neither, it seemed, would Trent Knightley.

"Mrs. Loomis, I'll call you as soon as we have the transcripts," Trent said as they reached the sidewalk. "It may take a few weeks, but that will give us all time to recover from depositions."

"Recover, yes, well. I'll wait to hear from you, Mr. Knightley. Ms. Stark, you have a nice day, and maybe I'll see you at the fabric store."

Maybe not.

She bustled off, muttering about *that man*, the *poor boy*, the shortcomings of the American legal system today, and a preholiday sale on velvet.

"Not one word," Trent said, turning Hannah by the arm to head in the opposite direction. "Let's savor the quiet."

—〜〜—

Hannah Stark was not a people person, which Trent considered a strength in a family law practitioner. He, however, was a people person, and it made his job at once harder and easier.

"Do you think she's cycling up?" Hannah asked.

"Beg pardon?" He would have been happy to saunter along in the crisp air, Hannah at his side, but after three hours of watching him and Elvin go at it, Hannah was entitled to ask questions.

"Do you think Mrs. Loomis was starting a manic episode?"

Well, crap. Trent stopped walking and eyed Hannah balefully. "Why do you say that?"

"The pressured speech, the hyperbolic thinking, the lack of continuity in her conversation, the perhaps grandiose idea that she's the only competent parent Dubbie will ever have?"

Hannah was cataloging the behaviors that had caused Trent to figuratively toss his client from the room. He treated himself to a few more muttered curses—no seven-year-old lurked in the hedges to be the Cussing Police—and then flipped open his briefcase on the hood of a parked car.

"Here." He passed Hannah the first folder of the Loomis file. "You have your cell phone with you?"

"In my purse," she said as they resumed their progress up the uneven sidewalk.

"Somewhere in that file is her primary care doctor's information. She insisted we have it in case Gregory wanted to depose the man or call him as a witness."

"You want me to call him?"

"Either that, or you back my Beemer out of the alley it's parked in."

She considered it. He could see that by the way she frowned and knit her brow, the way her full lips pursed. This was not a woman who dodged a challenge—any challenge.

"Heaven forfend your Beemer should come to harm on my watch. What am I supposed to say to this doctor?"

"Exactly what you said to me, what you observed."

"What's the real reason I'm the one calling?" She stepped back while Trent unlocked and opened the car door for her. It was a courtesy he enjoyed performing, and to hell with those tricky little keyless entry systems that were contributing to the death of chivalry.

He slid into his side of the car.

"If I call, and Mrs. Loomis goes on some spectacular spree this afternoon," he said, "I could be put in the position of having to testify against my client, which would really make me look bad and force Mrs. Loomis to find another lawyer. That's an unneeded expense and a delay for her."

He also simply did not want to have to tattle on his client.

Assistant counsel leafed through the file. "And a misery for you. You honestly want to win this case for her."

"Why shouldn't I? She's saddled with a mental illness, that kid means the world to her, and if she loses him, she might very well lose her grip entirely."

"It isn't a six-year-old's job to be the guardian of his mother's mental health, or her sobriety, or her moral fitness."

Hannah made that pronouncement, fastened her seat belt, then buried her nose—a good, determined nose—back in the file.

"I expect that sort of harassment from my brothers," Trent said two blocks later. "Mrs. Loomis is decent people, and I will tell you the rest of it over lunch."

He fell silent as Hannah dialed on her cell. He resented mightily that unlike with his brothers, he couldn't shift the argument with Hannah to some tussling on the rug until the third brother declared the match over *and* a draw.

Of course, his brothers didn't smell half so good, and they probably would not have zeroed in on the client's symptoms, either.

"Doctor Simmons, please."

Trent was tempted to tell Hannah what to say, what not to say. He shut up and drove instead—talking on a hand held while driving was against the law, after all.

"Hello, Dr. Simmons, my name is Hannah Stark. I'm an attorney with the firm of Hartman and Whitney. One of our clients is your patient, Mrs. Sandra Loomis. I do not expect you to verify you're treating her, but I want to report some behaviors I observed this morning."

She recited what she'd seen, her voice neither hurried nor confiding. The doc was listening, apparently finding a dispassionate accounting more credible than any drama.

"I understand confidentiality, of course. No, she wasn't talking about traveling anywhere in particular, and yes, Dubbie should be in school all day. Thank you. Of course." She gave him the office number, repeated her name, and closed her phone.

"You handled that well." Better than Trent could have.

"With an untreated bipolar disorder in the neighbor-hood, everybody's sense of drama usually goes up," Hannah said. "The mental health folks get numb to it, though they call it having boundaries."

As Hannah sounded numb.

"You've been around somebody with this diagnosis?"

She looked out the window so he couldn't assess what she was hiding.

"Roommate," she said. "A long time ago, but the dis-ease doesn't change. She'd get to feeling a little better, either because the meds were working or because they weren't, and then she'd think she didn't need them, and the wild rumpus would begin again."

Wild rumpus was a term from a children's classic. Coming from Hannah it might have been funny, except her tone was flat, weary, and clearly signaled a need for a change in topic.

"I'm exercising my prerogative as your boss and taking you out to lunch."

She swung her gaze to his, her expression unflatter-ingly disgruntled.

"You must practice making your imperial decrees into questions," she said. "It's really a very useful skill."

Trent's daughter had told him more or less the same thing, not two days ago.

—⁓—

Lunch was a good idea, just not lunch with the boss. Hannah was hungry as a penguin in springtime, and Trent would no doubt want to chitchat, socialize, and otherwise invade her privacy.

He helped her off with her coat, when she'd been dressing and undressing herself since the age of three.

He held her chair.

He offered to order for her.

No matter that coming from him, these old-fashioned courtesies were oddly appealing, Hannah was determined to set the man straight.

"This isn't a date. Why would you order for me? Even if it were a date, how would you feel if I offered to order for you?"

"If you knew the menu better than I did, if you were particularly enthusiastic about one of the entrées, would you order for me?" His question was both genuinely curious and challenging.

"I'm not sure. I haven't been in a position… That is, nobody has ever… I don't date." Or make small talk, or practice family law.

Oops. He was smiling again, that warm, flirty, I-know-what-you're-thinking smile. "You were about to say nobody has offered."

"A sit-down meal hasn't been included in the offers," she admitted. "Not on any of the three outings I can honestly call dates, though farm-team baseball games and paintball competitions probably don't give a guy a chance to show off his manners."

Trent pretended to study his menu. Hannah suspected he wanted to laugh—out loud, at length, while she endured a pang of protectiveness toward her younger, lonelier self.

"You must have been a very serious student," he observed.

Safer territory. "Phi Beta Kappa, Mensa, the usual."

Motherhood, motherhood, and motherhood had also played role. "Nobody will invest in my future but me, hence the focus."

"Then why did you go in-state undergrad? You probably had the credentials to go anywhere."

This too was a legacy from foster care, the gentle probing that never ended, and often became outright rudeness. Who are your parents? Where are you from? Why did you switch schools? Why do you wear the same clothes all the time? *Did your mother teach you to sew?*

Except from Trent, Hannah sensed she was safe from the worst questions. She had only to tell him to mind his own business, and he would, at least temporarily.

"Scholarships were more plentiful in-state." That was the truth—a truth. Their salads arrived, artful little concoctions appropriate to a place with linen tablecloths and leather-bound menus.

A nice place, when Trent could have swung past some drive-through. Nice—again. He used his fork to move purple circles of onion to his bread plate.

"Why not send it back?" Hannah asked. "You ordered it without onions. I heard you."

"Probably a new sous-chef. You want them?"

"No, thank you." She'd chosen her salad for its lack of onions.

Trent gestured with his fork. "How is it?"

"Interesting. Crunchy, not as sweet as I was afraid it would be."

Hannah could see him making a list: does not share onions, thinks paintball qualifies as a date, doesn't get out much.

"Ask me a question, Hannah Stark."

Was that trail ride a serious date? "About?"

"About the depositions, about my last date, about my salad. I'll answer honestly, but not too honestly."

Are you married? He could be—he was nice enough. "Why did you go stag at this morning's depositions? You said you were almost done, and Mrs. Loomis might have resented being excused."

He arranged his discarded onions in the shape of the interlocking Olympic circles, something Grace might do. "Did you resent being asked to leave?"

"By the third cup of tea and umpteenth picture of the prodigy, yes. I signed up to practice law, not provide hospice care to dying marriages."

"You're articulate, Hannah Stark, and you have my thanks for taking your cues graciously this morning. Had you said you wanted to stay, Mrs. Loomis could have found her own way back to her car."

"But you wanted boys only."

"I did. Most people gravitate toward lawyers with whom they get along. Sometimes, the cream puff will hire a shark, but for the most part, when that happens, the client is a wolf in cream-puff clothing, and that costume comes off in litigation. A wolf doesn't hire a cream puff, though, or if he does, he quickly fires him or her, gets his entire retainer back no matter how hard the attorney has worked, and moves on to more aggressive counsel."

Trent's observations jived with Hannah's experience, though she'd never connected the dots.

"You're not a cream puff or a wolf." Though he seemed capable of impersonating either. "Your theory suggests if Elvin Gregory is an old-fashioned chauvinist, then his client has the same tendencies?"

"Got it in one." He set his empty salad plate aside. "As it turns out, I was right. When the missus left, mister began to unload on me. 'You see what I have to put up with?' and so forth."

As missus had unloaded on Hannah. "Is that ethical? To encourage confidences that way?"

"His lawyer was sitting right beside him the whole time, and the very best material came at the end of the morning."

"Best material?" Whatever it was, the best material would signal misery for someone. Such were the pleasures of family law.

"I asked how Mrs. Loomis was as a disciplinarian, and Dad waxed eloquent about sparing the belt and spoiling the child. Said all he had to do was ask Dubbie to hand Dad his belt, and Dubbie would straighten right up."

In her heart, Hannah hadn't ducked fast enough. This was why she loathed family law—her emotional reflexes were just too damn slow, the synapses exhausted from too many years in foster care.

"Trent, that boy is six years old."

"He would have been five when he last lived with his father."

"You're *pleased* with this?"

"I'm pleased Dad will learn some parenting skills in a hurry if he doesn't want to be visiting his kid in the blue room at the Department of Social Services."

Hannah knew the blue rooms, with their tired toys, sagging vinyl sofas, easily disinfected surfaces, and—most common characteristic of all—their one-way mirrors. Anybody's kid could end up there with a single phone call, though most people lived in blissful ignorance of this aspect of the state's power.

She gave up on her salad despite the many benefits of fiber and phytonutrients.

"What did the doc say about Sandra's condition?" Trent asked.

This was a more cheerful topic? "He said privacy laws required that he not even confirm he was treating her, but patients with this diagnosis often have family on alert, blah, blah. He'll call her sister, which is her agreed-upon safety net when she's symptomatic. She has a tendency to skip meds to save money, though I didn't hear the doctor say that."

Trent's eyebrows came down. The kid getting smacked with a belt hadn't provoked a scowl like that.

"What's bothering you?" Hannah asked.

"I'll talk to her about a payment plan, that's what."

Hannah had ordered a steak in a misguided attempt to do battle with creeping, tight-budget anemia, but the cut that arrived was both the shape and nearly the size of Madagascar.

"You can get a doggie bag," Trent said. "Unless you want some help with that?"

Trent was offering to eat food off Hannah's plate. A perfectly functional and even clean fridge waited back at the office, so Hannah could save every leftover morsel if she chose to. She passed him her plate and watched as he moved his knife over a very generous cut of sirloin.

"There." She stopped him when he'd sectioned the steak into unequal halves. Geeves would thank her.

"You're about to tell me I've ruined your appetite with my legal strategizing," Trent said as he transferred about a third of the meat onto his plate. "Would you like some of my ravioli?"

Pasta was comfort food, and seeing it on his plate delicately drizzled with a fragrant marinara made Hannah's mouth water. "Just a little."

Hannah wasn't *having* lunch with her boss. She was *sharing* lunch with him. To take her mind off that novelty, she fished mentally for a question.

Did you freeze your butt off under the full moon? "What else did you find out from the depositions?"

Trent paused with a bite of steak halfway to his mouth, tines down, Continental fashion.

"I learned it was emphatically Mr. Loomis's idea that they have a child, and Missus made no effort to hide her mental health history, or the effect going untreated for months might have."

"You didn't believe her when she told you that?"

"I am ethically obligated to believe my client. I'd be a damned fool not to verify her version of events when I'm procedurally able to do so. Were there any questions you wanted to ask?"

Hannah paused in the consumption of a very good cut of steak.

"After Dad had trashed the daylights out of Mom's ability to discipline the child, I would have asked him if he respected anything about her as a parent or a spouse."

"Good strategy. Would you like some more ravioli?"

To go with Hannah's compromised life plan? "Two bites."

Trent forked them across the table onto her plate.

"I purposely did not ask about the Loomis's intimate

relations," he said, and Hannah about choked on her pasta.

"Why on earth would you ask such a thing?"

He sprinkled more cheese over his pasta, something else Grace would do. "To rattle him, to see if the parental carping and carrying on is a proxy for sexual frustration, or worse."

Five months and twenty-nine days to go in family law, no matter how much Hannah liked her lunch companion. "What's worse?"

"He can't satisfy her, that's worse for a guy—or it damned well should be—and yet things go wrong for most couples in the bedroom long before anybody sees a lawyer."

Trenton Knightley was undeniably a guy. "I don't want to hear this."

He munched on his steak. "Nobody wants to hear it. If we were told in law school what domestic practice is really like, nobody would do family law. This isn't even a case involving overt claims of adultery."

"May we change the subject?"

"You're blushing, Stark."

"That doesn't qualify as changing the subject."

He regarded her over a very good meal, and Hannah wanted to slide under the table, though Geeves would never forgive her for abandoning her steak.

"Your blush is endearing, Stark. Because you blush, I will order dessert for you, and we will share it."

He hadn't made that a question either, but Hannah didn't chide him for it. Dessert was a change of subject. She'd take what she could get.

Chapter 3

INSTEAD OF HERBAL TEA, TRENT ORDERED A HOT
chocolate for Hannah—unspiked—and a chocolate
mousse "for the table." The hot chocolate came first,
a frothy, creamy concoction with cinnamon sticks for
garnish and multicolored sugar swirled over a fat dollop
of whipped cream.

"My goodness."

For Hannah that was probably tantamount to swear-
ing with glee.

Very serious, Miss Hannah Stark. Serious and careful, but capable of blushing when teased—an interesting combination.

When the mousse came, Trent slid it across the table
to Hannah, sensing she'd want first crack. If this were
a date, he'd sit beside her, they'd eat off each other's
plates, and they'd attack the mousse at the same time.

This was *not* a date.

Something was wrong with the male population of
the University of Maryland if they thought paintball
and farm-team baseball were adequate dates for Hannah
Stark. If Trent had been in her poli sci 101 class, he'd
have taken her to the symphony when the program
included Brahms or Rachmaninoff.

Lush, passionate music for prim Hannah Stark.

"Works better if you eat it," he said.

She peered at her hot chocolate, though it sported a

perfectly obvious long-handled gold spoon in addition to the cinnamon sticks.

"I hate to disturb a work of art."

"The colored sugar is a nice touch." He appropriated a cinnamon stick, licking off the whipped cream. Merle would have scolded him for that.

"Larceny at high noon," she said with a ghost of a smile. She took the other cinnamon stick and licked the whipped cream off as Trent had, but more delicately.

Did James order hot chocolate for his dates? He damned well should.

"Delicious," Hannah murmured. "Real whipped cream, and not too sweet."

"We believe in our dairy out here in the country. You going to try to the mousse?"

"I ought to try it." Her expression was almost comical, so covetous was her regard for her hot chocolate.

"I will not steal your drink, Hannah. I'm having coffee." He lifted his cup to remind her, and she pulled the mousse closer.

"This looks very good."

She looked good. The hot food had put a touch of color in her cheeks, and as the meal had progressed, she'd relaxed. Trent had the completely inappropriate thought that Hannah Stark with a couple of glasses of wine under her belt would be adorable.

And in bed—

He took another sip of strong black coffee.

"There," she said, putting down her spoon a few moments later. "That's all I can eat."

"Liar, liar, pants on fire." He appropriated the mousse

and set about doing justice to it. "What do you have planned for the afternoon?"

Stupid question. Trent wanted to kick himself. Back to business, and he was just getting a peek beneath the professional veneer at the real Hannah.

"I want to dig into the child support files. Gerald said the docket moves quickly, and if you don't know the cases well, they can all run together."

"A hazard of the profession. Whatever you do, don't let Gerald intimidate you. Six months ago, he was right where you are. He'd never set foot in a courtroom, never interviewed a client, never negotiated an outcome with opposing counsel. Don't rush that hot chocolate. We're not in a hurry."

He'd lied, of course. Phone messages were probably piling up hip deep on his desk.

"You might not be. You could do child support cases in your sleep."

"You'll be able to too, sooner than you think."

Hannah pushed the hot chocolate away, the drink only half-finished. Why had he turned the discussion back to work?

"Hey there, Trent Knightley!" A pretty brunette hailed him from several feet away.

"Darla, always a pleasure." He got to his feet and kissed her cheek, accepting the hand she held out to him. "How is my favorite five-year-old?"

"Tommy is loving kindergarten, thank God. He asks about you from time to time."

"Bring him by the office, and we'll make paper airplanes again."

"How 'bout not," she said, smiling a mom's smile,

the sight of which did a divorce attorney's heart good. Darla had gone for months without a smile, once upon a time.

"Hannah, let me introduce you to Darla Carstairs. Darla, Hannah is a new associate in the family law department."

"Hannah." Darla stuck out a hand, which Hannah shook. "Don't let Trent work you too hard, and don't let Trent work too hard." She gave him a pointed look and, with a kiss to his cheek, went on her way.

"Stark, why are you looking at me like that?"

"Do you kiss everybody?"

She seemed genuinely puzzled, and some devil urged him to befuddle her just a little bit more. He leaned over, close enough to get a hint of lily of the valley and shampoo, and whispered in her ear.

"No, I do not kiss everybody."

Though, if she'd shown the least hint of receptivity, he might very well have kissed *her*.

"I'm not sure why we're having this conversation. Hannah's your employee." James tapped a golf ball into a practice cup. The door to his office was closed or he'd never have indulged, though in Trent's experience, when the putter came out, James was working through some maze of subrogation or indemnity language.

"We're having this conversation because I very nearly kissed an employee. You're pulling to the left."

James nodded, ever serious about his play. "Because I'm the office Lothario, you're coming to me for what? Pointers? Absolution? Both?"

"How about moral support?"

James missed again, by a whisker. "Is this serious?"

"I don't know." Trent sat back in James's ergonomically ingenious chair and propped his feet on the corner of the desk. "It's something."

"You've known the woman two days, and you're hitting on her? Mac won't approve."

"Mac doesn't approve of anything except Thin Mints in moderation and regularly annihilating the state's attorney's case."

"He's getting worse." James moved back a couple of feet and squinted down the handle of his putter. "Needs to get his wick trimmed."

"Your answer to everything."

"When has a good old-fashioned bout of sweaty sex ever hurt a guy's outlook on life?"

"It ain't world peace, James."

"A little not-quite kiss on the cheek in public is hardly World War III. Did she slap you?"

"She's the quiet type."

"Did she quietly ask you to desist? Threaten *legal* action?" He wiggled swooping golden brows.

"She did not." Not yet.

"What did she do?"

This was what Trent had sought from his brother, analysis and reflection rather than interrogation. "She blushed."

James straightened, expression puzzled. "A grown woman admitted to the bar in the great State of Maryland, practitioner of family law, wearer of sensible shoes—all you did was *not* kiss her on the cheek and she blushed? *Blushed?*"

"Very becomingly, and gave me a Mona Lisa smile."

"Are we going to be uncles again?"

"I've known her two days, James."

"My record is about twenty minutes. Names are optional when the sap rises."

"A brain is optional with you. A pulse and an orifice will do."

James took a few practices swings, smooth, controlled, even graceful. "I'm loyal to my team too, you mustn't forget that."

"Mac swears you went through an awkward phase in college."

"Mac means I tried monogamous dating and about blew a gasket."

"I worry about you, James."

"Well, I don't worry about you. It's time you shuffled off your monk's robes and rejoined the living. There's more to life than handing hankies to jilted housewives and cheating dentists—and raising my niece."

"Yeah," Trent said, opening a drawer and finding every single paper clip and pen neatly arranged. "Like being so bored with your job you're working on your short game—your real short game—at three in the afternoon in the dead of winter."

"It's not the dead of winter."

Not yet, but outside, flurries were thickening into a squall. Trent rose, took the putter from his brother, and tapped the ball down the length of the carpet into the waiting cup.

—∿∿—

Some people should wear signs—scarlet letters—saying, "Likes to touch and be touched."

Hannah would have worn a sign, "Do not touch." She made exceptions of course—she was affectionate with her daughter, and could be with Eliza and Eliza's boys too. The cats strutted under her radar, and Ginger the dog had a few privileges.

But now Hannah worked for a hands-on man. Driving back to the office to the soft strains of Vivaldi, Trent had remained quiet. The deposition had been both interesting and tedious.

Lunch had been interesting and *not* tedious. Also delicious. Maybe even—the word hardly felt like part of Hannah's vocabulary—*fun*.

They'd been stopped on the way to the restaurant's door by two of the waitstaff, both of whom were on hugging, cheek-kissing terms with Trent. At the table, he'd acted as if his hand brushing Hannah's passing the plates was of no moment, and when Hannah had reached for her winter coat, he'd taken it from her, held it, and then given her shoulders a pat. He held the car door for her and took her elbow when she stepped up on the curb.

Sadly judgmental of her, but she did not associate consideration like that with such a good-looking, successful man.

With any man of her acquaintance.

She shouldn't find his old-fashioned manners appealing, shouldn't have found that whisper in her ear charming, but she did, which made no sense whatsoever. Lunch distracted her for the balance of the afternoon and made drafting the memo to the Loomis file more time-consuming than it should have been.

No time to lose. Her homeward itinerary called for a stop at the bank before picking Grace up from Eliza's by six. Hannah had just laced up her running shoes when a handsome blond head presented itself around her partially closed office door.

What was his name? Matthew? Micah? Something biblical.

"You weren't leaving already, were you, Hannah? We should spend some time going over the child support case files. If you're not doing anything this evening, we could grab a bite, maybe take a few of the files with us. I know some decent places to eat around here."

And then go to your place and work on the finer points of litigation strategy?

She didn't need to recall his name—Gerald Matthews, that was it—to know this guy and a hundred others like him. She'd met them in pre-law; they'd gotten worse in law school. Once in practice, they were an occupational hazard at the larger firms. They made all the really decent guy lawyers stand out in higher relief.

"How about if I look the files over first, Gerald, and only bother you with questions about the ones I don't understand? I get in early and can make a good start on them tomorrow."

He sidled into her office, smiling with more teeth than graciousness.

"You're supposed to observe court on Friday. You'll have questions after court, so dinner together would be a good idea."

"I have plans, but lunch on Friday might be an option." Particularly if Hannah was stuck at the courthouse between morning and afternoon dockets.

"Fine, then, lunch on Friday." He settled into one of her guest chairs and crossed an ankle over his knee.

"I'll look forward to having the intricacies of the case law explained to me," she said, shrugging into her coat. As she passed him, Matthews remained sitting right where he was.

"In child support law, we refer to the ins and outs, not the intricacies, if you get my drift, Hannah."

"Inappropriate humor in a professional environment, Gerald." She kept her tone light, while Matthews's smile turned bratty. "Good night, and I'll be done with the files by midmorning."

Trent Knightley could take her arm, hold her coat, and whisper in her ear, and Hannah liked it a lot more than she should.

Gerald Matthews smiled at her, and she felt dirty.

———

"You want half my PBJ?" Merle made the offer hesitantly. Sharing food was against the rules, but the lunch aide was yelling at Larry Smithson for spilling his milk again.

"I have a PBJ too!" Grace said, holding up half a sandwich with a bite taken out of the soft middle. They shared a smile, delighting in yet another aspect of life they had in common. The differences were cool too, though.

"Mine's cut longways, yours is on the diagonal," Merle said, holding her half sandwich up next to Grace's. "They're both on whole wheat, though."

"Bronco likes whole wheat better than the other stuff," Grace said, which made sense. Horses loved grain. Wheat was a grain, and unicorns were related to horses. "Do you ever have cream cheese and raspberry jam?"

Blech. Merle was too new to having a friend to be that honest. "Sounds grown-up. What about fluffernut and peanut butter?"

Grace took another bite. She ate from the middle out, leaving the crust last. Merle ate the crust first, like doing chores before having fun.

"What's fluggernut?"

Merle laughed with her mouth full—and did not choke, neener-neener—and then Grace was laughing, and at the next table over, Estella Popper tried to give them the dork-repellent look, but she ended up smiling too, until Henry Moser tried to steal something from her tray.

"Fluf-fer-nut, like fluffy clouds," Merle clarified, taking a sip of her milk. "It's like marshmallows but spreadable, or almost spreadable. Have you ever toasted marshmallows?"

"The first time my mom lit the fire in the woodstove," Grace said, getting a smear of jam on her cheek. "She had a hard time getting the fire to catch, then we figured out about the things you turn at the front of the stove that let in air. We made s'mores, but I cheated and had two marshmallows without the s'more."

"S'mores are the best. My uncle James makes really good s'mores. Dad says they're messy."

"Most of the good stuff is. Does your dad make brownies?"

Eventually, all of their conversations got around to the fascinating business of comparing a mom with a dad. Merle had a mom. Uncle Mac had shown her on the globe where Australia was, because Merle hadn't wanted to ask Dad. Grace probably had a dad too.

"I don't think Dad knows how to make brownies," Merle said, "but we sometimes get a brownie from The Sweetest Things and split it." Nothing like a warm brownie and a cold glass of milk.

"So what if your dad doesn't make brownies? You have horses," Grace said, because Grace was the nicest person Merle had met, nicer even than the uncles. Horses made up for a lot, and Grace didn't have any.

"I'll ask Dad if you can come over to play. Pasha's all white because he's so old." Merle lowered her voice. "We could paint spots on his butt so he'd look more like Bronco."

Oh, the utter glee of giggling at lunch, of galloping around the playground, of saying "butt" out loud and having somebody to enjoy it with.

"You almost done?" Grace asked, folding her napkin up in a perfect square. Merle did likewise, though she'd never be as naturally tidy as Grace.

"Pasture time," Merle said, closing her lunch box. "I'll ask Dad to pack me some carrot sticks tomorrow so we can share them with the unicorns at recess."

Grace passed over a carrot stick. "Mom says carrots are good for your eyes. Looks like Larry's staying in again."

Larry stayed in a lot, which was a heck of a way to avoid the fifth graders who loved to pick on the dumb kid. Larry had suffered the worst fate possible in elementary school: he'd been *held back*. As if that wasn't bad enough, he was already big to begin with.

"Larry needs a unicorn," Merle said. They trooped out to the hallway, retrieved coats and hats and scarves from their assigned hooks, and went galloping out across the chilly playground.

Merle followed Grace, skipping because that was the closest they could come to a canter. Unicorns were wonderful, a friend was even wonderful-er, but Merle knew Grace thought about the same thing Merle did: How wonderful would it be to have both a dad *and* a mom?

———

"Hey, Mommy, I have a new friend at school. You said I would too, make some friends in second grade I didn't have in first or kindergarten. Those kindergarteners looks so shrimpy. I like to watch them on the playground. Was I ever that small?"

Thank God my child has come safely—and even happily—through another day.

Grace rummaged in the taco meal bag as she chattered away beside Hannah. Two fast food raids in the space of a week used up the entire month's quota, but Hannah had become absorbed in the child support cases and lost track of time.

"You may have one," Hannah said as they tooled toward home.

"Thanks, Mom." Grace set about comparing every nacho in the bag to ensure the one she ate was the largest.

"Who's your new friend?"

"She's real, not a unicorn. Unicorns are real, but this friend is a person. She has a unicorn too, and she knew what I meant when I told her Bronco was a uniloosa, not an apicorn—she knew what an Appaloosa horse was, and said she wished she'd thought of having a spotted unicorn with wings. Should I tell you her real name, or her Unicorn Club name?"

A friend, indeed. "Either or both, if the Club rules allow it."

"You're allowed to know the Club names, Mom, as long as you don't tell anybody. My friend's name is Falcon, her unicorn is Trailclimber."

A rabbit dodged out of the headlights and into the undergrowth along the lane. "How does Bronco get along with Trailclimber?"

"We let them meet by touching noses over the fence in the Cloud Pasture. They like each another fine, and me and Falcon do too."

"Each other, honey. They like each other fine— and it's Falcon and I. First grade was a little lonely, wasn't it?"

Hannah held her breath for the reply. Grace did not express feelings often in response to a prompt. They came out, if at all, in casual asides, behaviors, or projections onto the ever-faithful Bronco.

"Mom, don't be silly. I'm never lonely when Bronco is with me." Grace held up two nachos side by side that appeared to be the exact same dimensions. "Can I have both?"

"May I. Not until we get home." Hannah's mind was not on nachos.

Was Grace a loner because her mother was so lacking in social skills? Was Grace a normally social if shy kid with a great imagination? Something in between?

Hannah's upbringing was the last yardstick she could use to get her bearings as Grace's mother. Children in foster care were either loners, hell-raisers, or pleasers. They clung to approval or shunned it, depending on the circumstances and individual chemistry. Hannah was essentially a loner, though she gave herself points for being a fairly functional one.

But loneliness wasn't what she wanted for Grace. Safety, yes. Above all, Grace had to be kept safe from the people and events in Hannah's past that might cause harm to Grace, but did that mean Grace wasn't to have joy as well?

When Hannah pulled into her driveway, Grace exploded from the car with a happy yelp.

"C'mon, Bronco! I'll let you have two nachos if you wash your hooves before I ask you to." She held the door for her imaginary friend, then let it slam shut.

Hannah, moving more slowly, gathered her plunder—Trent Knightley's word—and followed her daughter into the house.

"We live in a door-slam house," Hannah softly quoted her daughter. The house was very old, and the doors didn't latch unless they were closed quite soundly.

Thanks to whatever deity oversaw weeknights in the households of single parents, the take-home folder in Grace's backpack was empty. The early, easy night might have contributed to Grace's gracious mood the next morning, or perhaps she looked forward to finding her new friend at the beginning of the school day.

As Hannah pulled into the office parking lot, she was pleased to see she'd beaten the estimable Mr. Trenton Knightley to work and felt some relief—*not* disappointment—to have avoided him first thing in the day. When she'd brewed herself a cup of Earl Grey and heated a cheese danish in the office microwave, she sat down with the child support files.

The tea was lovely, the danish was scrumptious, the child support files were miserable.

Hartman and Whitney represented both moms and dads, because either could be the noncustodial parent. The State of Maryland took on responsibility for the case, as if it were a criminal matter. The custodial parents might be witnesses for the State, but they weren't parties, and neither were the children on whose behalf the money was collected.

"Great system," Hannah muttered around a mouthful of danish. "Criminalize one parent, marginalize the other, and ignore the children."

She put her distaste for the whole business aside and plowed through the files, soon forgetting her tea and danish. One case in particular had already caught her attention: Rory Cavanaugh could document that he'd had a vasectomy prior to the child's conception, and had further proof that the procedure hadn't reversed itself since. He'd begun paying child support eight years ago, after he and the mom had split, because he'd felt sorry for the lady and for the baby. The State sought an increase after a routine review of the case by the Support Enforcement office, with the mom's hearty endorsement.

A note in the file indicated Cavanaugh had rescheduled his appointment because he couldn't miss chemotherapy again.

Ah, geez.

———

Trent Knightley stood in Hannah's office doorway for a good five minutes, watching her nibble her lip, mutter, and jot down notes. She was lost to the world, utterly absorbed in her files, and that pleased him. Detachment had a place in the practice of law—and so did passion.

"Good morning?" He rapped his knuckles on her door, but in deference to his daughter's patient tutelage, made his greeting a question. "You look fierce, Hannah Stark. What has you going nineteen to the dozen so early in the day?"

She sat back and blinked at him.

Earth to Stark.

"Why does the State of Maryland value money over truth?"

"Give me the facts of the case." Where any legal brief was supposed to start. While Hannah marshaled those facts, Trent noted that her tea was no longer steaming, and five stems of lavender gladiolus enjoyed pride of place on her credenza.

Because he'd collected her effects from the pavement yesterday morning, he knew she used lavender lip balm. *Would her kisses taste like lavender?*

"Rory Cavanaugh has medical proof he cannot be the child's father," she recited, "but because he felt sorry for the mom, he started paying when the kid was born. He's been paying for eight years, but now that he's *out of remission* the State is seeking an increase."

"This does not sit well with you?" Trent settled into a chair and prepared to have a lawyer's version of fun.

"Since when did paternity mean the obligation to pay for children you're not related to? You're a guy, doesn't that bother you?"

"Since when did being a kid mean you had no need for food, clothing, and shelter?"

She slammed the file shut, the way a pissed-off judge might whack a gavel to bring the courtroom to order.

"The State can and does provide necessities for children in need, regularly," she said. "In this case, the State has abdicated its responsibility to the child in favor of having old Rory foot the bills."

"So all this righteous indignation is for your new best friend Rory?" Trent kept his tone goading, because this was the first sign of a legal vocation he'd seen in Hannah Stark.

"Don't be an ass." She rose and put her hands on her hips. "My indignation is for the *child*. What good does tapping Rory out financially do the child when she needs to know her medical history, and half her family tree is a lie or unavailable to her because of the State's moral complaisance? What good will Rory's money be when she needs a bone marrow or kidney transplant and half her probable donors are a mystery, because the State never had a long talk with Mom about who the real dad is?"

She was pacing now, tearing into a fine Court of Appeals closing argument.

"And what does it signal to the child that half of her identity, *half of who she is*, doesn't matter to the society she's raised in? How would you like to be told the identity of your father means nothing, and shouldn't mean anything to you? How do you think every kid feels whose fate was sealed by a private adoption? She waits eighteen years to look on the adoption registries—now that we finally *have* adoption registries—and of all the children in all the families in all the world, she's the one without a dad."

"But illegitimacy is stigmatizing…" Trent began, only to be cut off with a slice of Hannah's hand—no nail polish, and she didn't bite her nails either.

"Mom wasn't married to Rory. Even if the State were clinging to the old-fashioned doctrine that it can protect a fiction of legitimacy at the cost of truth, that fig leaf wouldn't fit here."

"So what will you do, counselor? Your client has been wronged, the law needs to be changed or enforced differently, and you feel strongly about the outcome. And yet, you also know that the child's father could be a mother's worst nightmare—a criminal, a child abuser, a disgrace to his gender, a threat to the child. Will you decide the girl needs to make *his* acquaintance in the name of your almighty truth?"

At Trent's rhetorical question, Hannah collapsed into the other guest chair like a marionette whose strings had been cut. Something skipped across her features. Chagrin, maybe, or bewilderment.

This argument was personal to her, or to somebody close to her. Family law was like that. Hypotheticals had a way of ending up sitting next to your daughter in art class or dating your brother.

"Every case is different," Hannah said wearily, "though your point about a father who's a danger to the child is valid. I'll discuss the matter—I would discuss the matter—thoroughly with my client, *if* he were my client, and then craft a litigation strategy consistent with his goal."

"You'll hate it if he tells you to accept what the State offers."

She turned big brown eyes on him, troubled eyes. "I will hate it to smithereens. If he loves that kid, he ought to try to establish the truth for her, provided the real dad's not a horror."

Trent agreed, and nearly told her so.

"That truth could come at the cost of the kid's material needs, if it creates bad feeling between Rory and Mom. Insisting on the truth could mean Rory never gets to see the kid again, when she could be enjoying Rory's last years and building happy memories of him."

Hannah peered into her cup of cold tea. The mug was plain, white, sturdy, and out of place somehow in her office.

"This isn't a game to me, Trent. I can't enjoy it as a game."

Trent. He liked that part. "You're not supposed to." And because she looked so dejected and bewildered, he patted her shoulder. The last of the fight went out of her posture at the contact, and she didn't draw away.

"You get the brass ring, Hannah. You advocate zealously for your client within the bounds of the law. Repeat that mantra, and you'll keep your balance."

"I'll keep my balance," she said, gaze going to the stack of pink-and-blue child support files, "but I might lose my mind." She ran a hand over her hair, patting the tidy bun at the back, where literally not a hair was out of place. "I left you a draft of the Loomis memo to file."

As changes of subject went, it wasn't smooth, but Trent understood the need for breathing room.

"You write well, Stark, as well as most lawyers wish they could."

"But?"

"But nothing. That was a compliment. Com-pli-ment. C-o-m-p—"

"I understand the term. Thank you."

Her thank-yous bore an interesting hint of that No

Trespassing quality. "Have you considered a career as a writer?"

Her eyebrows went up, and Trent was pleased to think he'd distracted her from her frustration with Rory Cavanaugh's situation, the State of Maryland, and the law.

And possibly, her frustration with her boss.

"Not seriously, though writing has always been easy for me and even enjoyable—any writing. Too bad there's the small matter of needing to eat regularly."

"Hmm." He resisted the urge to lawyer her, or tried to.

"What, hmm?" She tidied the stack of files. "Just say it."

"You and the State of Maryland would both seem to place a certain emphasis on the importance of meeting basic needs, on the bottom line, so to speak, even at the cost of higher values."

Her jaw dropped then snapped shut. She pointed at the door.

"Out," she said, getting to her feet. "You, out of this office right now, before I do something a lady would regret but a lawyer would find tremendously gratifying."

He got to his feet s-l-o-w-l-y, put his hands in his pockets, and sauntered out.

Chapter 4

"GOOD MORNING, HANNAH-BOFANNA-BANANA-BABY."
Gerald Matthews strolled into Hannah's office, and her
temper, barely cooled from the last exchange with her
boss, rocketed right back up.

Hannah remained at her desk, when what she wanted
to do was put a toilet seat protector down on her guest
chairs before Gerald got comfortable.

"How about we go over these files in your office?"
Hannah asked, rising and pretending to make sure her
flowers had water. Why did she have the sense Gerald
was checking out her ass? "Give me a minute to wash
out my cup. I'll be along directly."

He left at that suggestion, while Hannah's foul mood
stayed with her.

She did wash out her cup, then grabbed the files
and made her way to Gerald's office. Trent Knightley
would have carried the files for her or taken at least
half on general principles, whether he was meeting
with her or Gerald. The contrast wasn't lost on Hannah,
but she was soon listening to Gerald's end of a tele-
phone conversation.

"I pity you, buddy," he said. "If they'd spring me
here, I could jump in for you on that DUI." Why would
Gerald want to deal with cases other than the ones
Hartman and Whitney gave him? "See you at the gym."

He hung up and grinned at Hannah.

"Solo practice has its challenges, apparently." He eyed the stack of files. "We have Judge Linker on Friday. You want to take the docket?"

Baby? His question was a little power play, a dare, a taunt—also a failure, because Trent would not allow Gerald to reassign cases for which the firm was responsible.

"I am by no means ready or able to competently handle an entire docket of child support cases. My job Friday is to learn from your expert example."

Hannah crossed her arms over her chest, which he'd been ogling—of course.

"Let's get to it, shall we?" Gerald shifted again, putting his feet up on the desk as if he were a partner, not the last new hire before Hannah.

He rattled off the factual posture of each case as Hannah jotted down whatever she hadn't noticed on her perusal of the file. Gerald was in constant motion, getting up and down, blowing his nose, mutilating paper clips, playing wastebasket basketball with balled-up printer paper.

"The kid isn't his," Gerald said when they'd reached the last case, "but Callahan will end up paying because he was stupid enough to feel sorry for the randy bitch eight years ago."

An odd dart of gratitude deflated some of Hannah's distaste, because Gerald Matthews was what she never wanted to become—cold, self-centered, and probably terrified by the misery and disorder of his clients' lives. His example would provide Hannah a benchmark of how not to practice law, and clear guidelines were good to have.

"I believe the client's name is Cavanaugh," she said, "and *the kid* is named Marlena."

Gerald started clicking some silver-barreled designer pen repeatedly.

"He's a client. I'll do a good job for him, but I am not his friend, nor do I want to be. I mean this as kindly as I ever mean anything: if you don't adopt a business-like attitude in your legal practice, you won't have a life. You'll be like all the other associates around here, obsessing on cases and taking all this 'pro bono publico' shit for free because your bleeding heart can't turn anybody down."

He bounced to his feet, tossing the pen onto his desk blotter and checking his appearance in a mirror hanging on the back of his door.

"Don't do it, Hannah. Not for poor old Cavanaugh, who was free, white, and twenty-two when he dropped trou with the tramp. Don't do it for him, not for points in the partner poker stakes, not for anybody. Look out for Number One, or there won't be anything left of you in five years."

He would have lasted about two weeks in foster care before the group homes got hold of him. Gerald was vain and arrogant, and neither the vain ones nor the arrogant ones fared well in the tough placements.

"So what will you do for the client?" she asked, because somewhere in even Gerald's hierarchy, client satisfaction was part of keeping Number One in fancy 100 percent all-beef designer pens.

Hannah was spared the tedium of Gerald's reply by a soft rap on the closed door. Trent Knightley did not wait to be permitted entrance.

"Hannah, if you're through here," he said, "I'd like to introduce you to someone."

Rescue. Hannah was on her feet the next instant, only to see Gerald bristling behind a fixed smile. *Note to self*: meet with Gerald only in the conference room, which had a glass wall visible from the reception area and the main corridor.

"We were on our last case," Hannah said. "I've discussed it in some detail with you, so Gerald and I would likely be covering the same ground."

The paper clip Gerald had been torturing snapped in two. "Don't let me hold you up, Hannah."

Peachy. The guy responsible for showing her the ropes was now in a Warp Nine pout.

"My thanks for your time, Gerald. I look forward to seeing you in action on Friday." Hannah followed Trent to his office, nearly running into him when he paused outside the door.

"I forget you are mine for only a few months," he said, regarding her with a slight frown. "I hope you aren't bored to tears by the child support guidelines."

Hannah had lost the habit of crying years ago.

"I like the idea of helping people with real, significant problems. I'm not so keen on those problems being as personal as they are in family law." Gerald's point was valid, if self-serving and overstated.

"When you handle your family law cases well, you help me with a real, significant problem, and the clients and entire firm benefit. Thank you for that."

Well, hell. Hannah had apparently not lost the habit of appreciating a sincere thank-you.

Trent opened his office door, and behind his desk,

a tall, white-haired gentleman closed a book of what looked like Supreme Court opinions and set it near the rhododendron.

Hannah tried to put out of her mind Trent's earlier words: *You are mine for only a few months*. She'd been a sister or a daughter in some fashion for a few months over and over again, and she still—seven years into the mommy gig—expected Grace to be snatched away with no notice.

"Hannah, I'd like you to meet Judge Daniel Halverston," Trent said, "absent without leave from his post on the appellate bench. Judge, Miss Hannah Stark, our newest family law associate."

"Hannah." The judge struck Hannah as an affable old polar bear, but a keen light in his blue eyes warned her she'd best stay on her toes.

"Judge Halverston." She stuck out her hand, because this guy was probably old enough he would wait for a lady to make the first overture.

"Pleased to make your acquaintance, Hannah Stark. You don't come across that name often in this area, but I could swear I've met you before." He kept her hand in his callused paw another moment.

The legal profession apparently boasted unsuspected reserves of men who were touchers.

"I'm an only child. My family's not from around here." For all Hannah knew, it was the truth.

He relinquished her hand. "So why do you want to practice family law?"

"I don't, actually," she said, shooting a look at her boss. Trent was smiling as he leaned against his desk, which told her nothing. "I'm headed for the slot in corporate in the spring, but domestic was shorthanded, so I'm doing a tour here first."

"You don't like all the drama and excitement of families in disarray?"

She wished now she'd given the judge some smarmy platitude about Why She Loved Family Law, except Trent was standing right there, and lying in front of him—even a socially acceptable lie—didn't sit well.

"I probably have as many zealous advocacy genes as the next lawyer, Judge, but I don't like being an undertaker to anybody's relationships. If a family is in court, then the family has pretty much given up on itself in its natural form. In corporate law, you have a chance to do a lot of preventive lawyering, and the worst thing someone suffers is a money judgment."

"You're right," Halverston said. "Corporations don't fall in love or get each other with child, at least not quite like people do."

Hannah did not lapse into a panegyric over the populated joint venture, lest some buffoon leaning against the desk snort unprofessionally.

"Nobody in law school warns you it isn't enough to be smart, prepared, and knowledgeable," Hannah went on. "You also have to keep your balance, and even in my first few days here, I'm seeing that's the greater challenge."

Take that, Ye Smirking Boss.

"You should be clerking for us down in Annapolis," Halverston said. "You ever want to make that contribution, you let Trent know, and he'll probably spring you for the duration."

"It won't be my call," Trent said, pushing off his

desk. "Hannah is technically James's employee, but he's not the jealous type."

Judges were political creatures, and appellate judges were shrewd political creatures. Hannah did not for a moment believe Halverston was making an overture—to her.

"Before you leave the profession in disgust," the judge said, "you call me, Hannah. I'd hate to see you turn into a real estate agent or insurance broker because the Knightley boys didn't take good care of you."

He peered at her again, and Hannah knew he was still convinced he'd seen her before. She didn't think he'd ever heard her foster care case. She recalled the judges who'd asked her their few perfunctory questions:

"Anything you want to tell me, young lady?"

"Everything going fine in your foster home?"

"How are you doing in school?"

The questions, though no doubt intended to make her feel included in the legal process, had hurt like dull knives. She'd answered with courtroom honesty, not with honesty of the heart.

"Good morning, Your Honor." *My name is not young lady.*

"Everything in the foster home is fine, sir." *Nothing goes right in my foster homes for very long.*

"School is OK. I should make honor roll again this marking period." *School is lonely and grueling but it helps me forget, though I'm never in any one school long enough to be anything more than the foster kid.*

The judges who didn't talk to her, who didn't meet her eyes, were even more painful. Hannah had hated going to her hearings, but had decided by the time she

A SINGLE KISS   77

was ten years old she wouldn't give the social workers, judges, or attorneys the relief of not having to acknowledge her.

So she went to her hearings and looked them all in the eye every time.

Just as Judge Halverston was still regarding her directly.

"I have a good memory for faces," Halverston said, "much to the dismay of some of my criminal defendants, who prefer to travel under a nom de guerre. I have either seen you before or met your double—and I hope to see you again."

———

Trent looped an arm across Hannah's shoulders and walked her to his conversational grouping. She'd smiled at the judge, really, truly smiled, and the older man had been charmed.

Trent had too.

"Talk to me, Stark. I introduce all of my associates to any judges I bump into, and Dan's a good egg."

She plopped down in one of the comfortable chairs, her expression puzzled. Maybe she wondered how a good egg could enforce the death penalty, though Maryland at least had stepped back from capital punishment.

"I don't expect a judge to be such a nice guy," she said. "Judges should be tough enough to make life and death decisions, and to have everybody second-guess them, including the appellate courts. You can't do that if you're a wimp."

Oh, to be so innocent. "The hell you can't, and please recall, I clerked for a circuit court judge at one point.

Wimps are impersonating judges in every state of the union. It's the wimpy guys and gals who put on those black robes and think they're somehow infallible as a result. The nice guys and gals—the real judges—do their jobs because they genuinely care about the people in their courtrooms and the society they're part of."

"I know," Hannah said, leaning her head back and closing her eyes. "You can tell the judges who are human from the ones who are scared to be human."

Something in the remoteness of Hannah's voice caught Trent's ear. She was away again, focused inwardly, parsing some profundity known only to her. With her eyes closed she looked younger than when she was in her usual cannon-at-the-ready mode. She was, in fact, a pretty woman, particularly in her more contemplative moods.

Also hopelessly honest, which might not be a good thing.

"You think Halverston is a nice guy?" Trent prompted.

"I think he is a wise, kind guy, and I've had that same impression upon meeting someone, that I know them from somewhere." She opened her eyes and directed a frown at Trent. "I had it when I first saw you, but you're a stranger to me. I think Judge Halverston has seen a lot of grief, personal as well as from the bench, but he's keeping on as best he can anyway."

"Why do you say that?"

"The look in his eyes, maybe. Just a feeling. I get them sometimes—stronger than a hunch. Intuition, I suppose."

Or keen insight. "His wife died a year and a half ago. She was quite a bit younger than he, and they'd been trying to have a child for years. She got pregnant just about when they realized she was ill, the cancer went on for years, and this is not common knowledge."

"And the baby?" Hannah studied her hands.

Not every lawyer would have asked. "No baby, not with all the chemo and radiation and God knows what else. I don't know what hurt the judge worse, losing his wife or not having a child to remember her by."

"Sad," Hannah said, rising and rolling her shoulders.

"Hannah?" Trent remained sitting, and did not take her slender, graceful wrist to prevent her from leaving. "I have a serious question."

She glanced down at him, her expression unreadable. "Ask."

"What do you think of Gerald?"

She wrinkled her nose and took a few steps to lean against Trent's desk, arms crossed—the same posture he often took when he, Mac, and James were arguing their way through some partnership decision.

"That is a trick question," Hannah said. "One of those, 'when did you stop beating your wife?' questions. If I find fault with a coworker, then I am petty and conniving. If I ignore fault in a coworker, then I am superficial and dishonest."

Lawyers. "This isn't moot court, Hannah. Help me decide whether to give Gerald the Loomis case." Because something had to be done about Gerald. Either he rose to the challenges before him and found the work meaningful, or he'd be consigned to the ranks of the ambulance chasers eking out a living in solo practice.

"Why are you asking me?"

"Maybe because you intuitively scoped out

Halverston's life story so easily, maybe because I am thinking of teaming you with Gerald on the case."

Maybe because Trent liked simply looking at her, watching her mind parse through a problem, and that was…that was not entirely a bad thing.

"I just got here, Trent. Gerald's ego would not take kindly to my getting a taste of a contested case the first week on the job, while he's had to toil away with deadbeat dads for months. You're the attorney Mrs. Loomis trusts, and you know the case best. What is your real agenda?"

His brothers might have gotten around to asking that question—eventually.

And he probably should not be discussing one employee with another in any other terms than, "How well could you work with…?"

"Gerald may be hard to take sometimes—good litigators often are, to wit, my brothers Mac and James—but Gerald has done a yeoman's job with the support cases for months. The clients don't complain, the judges don't complain, and in fairness to Gerald, he'll be more valuable to the company if he branches out. We'll lose him otherwise."

To wit? Since when did he make closing arguments to his employees?

"You really worry about losing an employee, don't you?"

Hannah inspected his shelves, which bore the usual collection of textbooks, casebooks, and dated photos of various Knightleys signing the bar registry.

"It's my job to check on the chickens and keep them happy," Trent said. "Turnover is expensive and bad for client relations." Because she was studying a sunflower drawing Merle had done in first grade, Trent tossed out another question he shouldn't be asking. "Why are you so set on going to corporate in the spring, Hannah? James will let me keep you, if that's the problem."

He hoped James would let him keep her. For all James wasn't the least bit possessive, he could be protective, and James had a healthy disgust of family law despite his stance of casual generosity a few days earlier.

She studied the sunflowers—yellow with purple, green, and red centers, then set the drawing down a few inches to the left of where Trent had positioned it.

"Why do you want me in family law, Trent? You've had me less than week, and I have no relevant experience. All of my temping was in corporate. I am not pawing and snorting to be in any courtroom. I am not looking to make partner in five years. I don't care to bill eighty hours a week. I'm too lazy for family law. I think it can take too much out of you."

"Have you been through a bad divorce?" His question was a shot in the dark, but Hannah's objection to his field was personal.

She scooted back onto his desk, exposing a length of shapely thigh. "I have not been through a bad divorce. Why do you ask?"

"Maybe because I have been through a bad divorce?" He hadn't meant to disclose that, but his admission stopped Hannah from twitching at her hem. She wore purple well.

"I'm sorry, Trent. Is there such a thing as a good divorce?"

Trent settled in beside her, shoulder to shoulder,

though the desk creaked, and should anybody—say a nosy brother or two—come through the door, Trent's proximity might inspire Hannah to more blushes.

"I stay with family law because it can also give back a lot more than other kinds of law," he said. "You can look after kids and old people, help a family get reorganized, settle questions that are tearing a family apart."

She let the heel of one shoe dangle loose, so her black pump hung by her toes.

"Right, you're just a bootleg member of the helping professions with an extra row of teeth."

She had cute knees.

While Trent had a problem, the like of which hadn't plagued him since before he'd been married. "That sounds like Gerald Matthews talking."

Her shoe came off, and she shoved off the desk to wiggle her foot back into it.

"That's why you won't put Gerald on the Loomis divorce. Mrs. Loomis needs someone who can think about her son, and about her best interests while listening to her immediate desires. Gerald would be better off with a divorce that involves a lot of property, no kids, and maybe some sticky pension issues. He'd do better with clients who honestly want a predatory attorney."

Trent tugged her back to the desk by the wrist. She frowned from her perch beside him, looking like Merle when Dad was being dense about something obvious to any seven-year-old.

"The judge was right, Hannah Stark, Esq. You have a lot of skills that will make you a very good attorney. I know what I'll do with Gerald, and it won't be the Loomis case."

She'd solved a puzzle for him, even as she herself remained one.

"You're coming halfway undone," she said, dipping her head and swinging the right shoe again, a bashful posture, and charming.

Did she mean his fly was…?

"I mean your tie. You're coming loose." She hopped off the desk and unknotted his tie. Merle liked the tie, one of about ten she'd given him with horses on it. Trent did not like it, because it came undone, which was doubtless why Mac and James had helped Merle buy it.

Hannah measured the ends against each other and deftly re-knotted a plain Windsor.

When she was through, she brushed his hair back over his left ear, a thoroughly maternal gesture. "You are blessed with thick hair, but it's also fine."

"From my mother, who was rumored to have some Cherokee genes." He enjoyed the feel of a woman's hands in his hair, even though the moment should have been mundane. Hannah's touch was feminine and yet competent to the point of disinterested.

"There," she said, patting his shoulder. "You're presentable."

"And you're blushing." He resisted the urge to make some kind of fuss about the first time she'd put her hands on him. His heart rate was making a fuss, though, and so was the retired soldier in his briefs.

"You know, Hannah Stark, if you really want to go to corporate, I will be the first to boost you into that pumpkin patch, come spring. But you're right about family law, it takes special people to do it well, and you're a special person. I would be proud to have you working with us on whatever terms it takes to get you to join us, and you wouldn't be coping by yourself. I'd be responsible for making sure the job never got to be too much for you."

Hannah's expression shuttered. She gave his tie one more pat and headed for the door.

Scared her off. Or maybe she'd scared herself off. She stopped at the door and kept her back to him as he followed her across the room.

"I'll think about what you're offering, Trent, but don't pressure me. I need to make the decision for myself."

"Of course you do." She startled so slightly, Trent could feel it but not see it when he put his hand on her shoulder. "You think about what I've said—what I've promised—and next week over lunch we'll talk again. For now, keep an eye on Gerald, get up to speed on paternity and support law, and consider your options."

She left his office and closed his door behind her, which was fortunate, because Trent had liked the look of her at ease on his desk all too much. A rap on the door a few moments later signaled the appearance of his brother Mac, who sported a bemused expression.

"Tell me what case you were discussing with Hannah Stark, because it put the oddest smile on the woman's face."

Mac went to the window, beyond which the wind swirled a dusting of snow across sidewalks and pavement.

"We talked about my stealing her from James," Trent said, careful to keep his poker face in place. This was Mac, after all.

"You want to steal her already?" Mac nudged

Merle's sunflower drawing back to its former location. "She's brilliant, then? God's gift to deadbeat dads and jilted moms?"

"She's smart enough. More to the point she has integrity to go with her brains, and will do her best for each client."

"Unlike that idiot Matthews."

"He does an adequate job," Trent said, crossing his arms. "You try six months of wheedling and cajoling with the Support Enforcement Office, see what it does to your microscopic store of joie de vivre."

"I have plenty of joie de vivre," Mac said in tones that invited Trent to go best out of three falls. Mac was a seriously good-looking man, but his seriously grouchy attitude usually made the stronger impression. "I save it for what matters, like my niece."

"She loves you too."

"C'mon, Trent. Christmas is coming. Deal."

Comprehension had Trent grinning. "You don't know what to get Merle for Christmas."

"Clearly, I got all the brains in this family, and James got the looks. You, however, got Merle, so we'll consider you adequately compensated for your short suits."

"Talk like that will get you a free trip to the toy store," Trent said, "where you will wander in lonely bewilderment until some single mother of five takes pity on you."

"I can still beat you up, and I will take Merle shopping for your birthday if you don't see the light of sweet reason."

Visions of Winnie the Pooh boxers danced in Trent's head.

"Anything to do with horses or unicorns or zebras or donkeys," Trent said. "Anything equine, anything at all, provided it's not another goddamned tie for me." Or a bathrobe or bath towel or shower curtain or bath mat. Trent heard the pounding of little hooves every time he took a shower.

"I thought horses were a phase, like weddings in second grade."

That Mac knew second grade was a year prone to playground weddings surprised Trent, but then, Mac took being an uncle as seriously as he took everything else.

"She draws horses on all her book covers, has horses as her screen saver and cell phone wallpaper, collects stuffed horses and model horses. It's getting worse, not better."

"Don't you dare tell James," Mac said, his expression fierce. "I asked first."

"James is threatening to get her a miniature horse. We already have enough livestock, so if he follows through, you will referee the fight."

"Damned straight I will. Minis are like short people, there's no trusting them." Mac was a part-time farrier, and this was not a casual opinion, though neither was it rational.

"To think you're admitted to the Federal bar. It boggles the mind."

"Licensed to practice before the Sue-preme Court of the U-nited States, unlike the peasants I call my brothers." Mac sauntered out, then poked his head back in the door.

"Did you know Dan Halverston's carrying a torch for Louise Merriman?"

Gossip, from Mac? "How do you know that?"

"He was meeting her for lunch, and he asked me where to pick up flowers."

"What did you tell him?" Why hadn't he asked Trent?

"I had my secretary get on the Internet and have the flowers delivered to the restaurant. I know how to treat a sitting appellate judge, for chrissakes. James would have sent him to the grocery store."

But Mac did not know how to treat a date.

"James would get to the grocery store by way of the drugstore," Trent said, which provoked another small smile from his brother. Two in one day.

"Quite a force of nature, our James," Mac said, sounding almost proud and easing around the door back into Trent's office. "Which reminds me. In my capacity as managing partner and your older brother, do not give Hannah Stark grounds to sue us for sexual harassment."

"James is a force of nature, and I'm litigation waiting to happen?"

"James has a certain forthright charm, which we may both envy, but we do not possess. That, and virtuosic skills in the bedroom, make him nearly suit proof. You've been on the shelf so long you forget what your equipment is for, and you could bungle any attempt at office romance as a result."

"Bungle?"

"Bungle." Mac's expression was somber. He nodded in agreement with himself once. "Badly. Don't bungle it with Hannah. Get it right or go home. I'm tempted to give her the same warning."

"I see." Trent saw that Mac meant well, for a protective older brother with a death wish. "I'll tell James his niece is pining away for a nice fluffy, cuddly bunny, complete with a wiggly little nose and the cutest ears God ever put on a rabbit. Maybe I'll let him get her a Flemish Giant, and we'll name him Duke and train him to attack Supreme Court bar members on sight."

"A were-rabbit. I'm quaking in my Johnston and Murphys. All I'm saying is don't rush into anything with the new associate. Take it slowly. You're out of practice."

"Always thinking of me," Trent said, pointing to the door. "Get out while you still can, old man, and hope Merle doesn't move on to bunnies between now and Christmas, or kittens."

Mac left, and this time he stayed gone. Trent waited a few minutes in case James wanted to come by and dispense his version of fraternal advice. There had been a time during Trent's divorce when Mac had kept him going, bullying, teasing, and lecturing his younger brother by turns. James had played a role as well, pitching the idea of buying the law firm and supporting Trent vociferously when most other brothers would have sent a pair of tickets to an Orioles game and beat feet.

A man did not forget to whom he owed his present happiness.

But Hannah Stark had been smiling, and Mac had noticed and jumped to certain conclusions. This was not a bad thing. In fact, the longer Trent considered it, the more it seemed like a good thing. A very good thing indeed.

—⁓—

"This is awful." Hannah muttered. She closed her office door, reached for a tissue, and sat at her desk.

In foster care, she'd learned what it was to be unwanted. She'd watched as time after time, younger, cuter, more charming children had been chosen for adoption, until she'd seen the writing on the wall: you have been weighed in the scales and found unadoptable.

She was a spare part no family needed.

Then survival became a matter of rejecting before she was rejected, and the group home placements had started. Glorified orphanages, they had provided a measure of emotional relief from the closeness of family.

As she'd outgrown her adolescent behaviors, some well-meaning social worker had placed Hannah in yet another foster home. Then Hannah had learned what it meant to be an object of lust, which was not at all the same thing as being wanted.

Valued.

She'd been fussing with Trent's hair before she'd thought twice about it, the mom in her unable to tolerate untidiness. He hadn't made any big deal out of it, hadn't called her on her presumption.

But the words he'd said after that were a big deal indeed. *"I'd be proud..."*

Nobody had been proud of her, except for the pride she took in herself. The only person to come to her college graduation had been Joe, the old foster care court bailiff, the same guy whose signature had appeared as guarantor on her very first apartment lease. She had been so grateful to the man, she still sent him a Christmas card each year.

And God help her, Trent Knightley meant what he said. She would not, *would not*, let him entice her into joining his department permanently.

Not now, not in six months, and that was what she would tell him the next time they met for lunch.

Chapter 5

"I HAVE TO COMMEND YOU," SAID A VOICE AT Trent's elbow.

He looked up from the learning computer in his hands and found James peering over his shoulder in the toy store's electronics section.

"Because I can spell 'giraffe'?"

"That too, but mostly because you've paired Hannah Stark with Gerald Matthews on the child support docket. She'll bust his microscopic balls but good. Let me try that thing."

Trent passed over the demo model. "She's understudying Gerald on the happy pappy docket, but I haven't paired her with him, nor will I."

"Is there an *e* in 'horny bastard'?"

"James, that toy did not ask you to spell horny bastard."

A skinny, teenaged boy stocking the shelves halfway down the aisle tried to hide a smirk.

"You know Matthews is banging our head of HR? I think this thing is broken." The toy made an odd noise and the stock clerk snickered.

Trent glared at the kid, who climbed off his stepladder and sauntered away.

"Gail and Gerald occasionally bang each other," Trent said, "not that it's any of my business, or yours. I suspect on Gerald's part, the attraction has waned."

"Until he wants something from Gail again. Here, see if you can get it to work."

"What could Gerald want from Gail that she's in a position to give?" Trent turned the toy off and turned it back on.

"Besides the obvious? Hannah Stark's starting salary, perhaps her home phone number, her marital status. The partner draws."

"He won't find anything useful on Hannah's application." The machine beeped cheerfully.

"You fixed it. Must be a dad thing." James seized the computer again and punched some keys. "I looked over Hannah's application myself, seeing as we hired her for my department, and I noticed the same gaps in her data. I conclude the lady is protective of her privacy."

"You thinking of buying this thing for Merle?"

James wrinkled his nose. "Should I be?"

"No. It doesn't have horses on it."

"Here, then, you break it." James handed it back. "If I were you, I'd keep a close eye on old Matthews. I've heard some rumors."

"You've heard rumors. Do you know what rumors I've heard about you and the twins in the office of the clerk of the court in Wicks County?"

"That was months ago, and between consenting adults, and did not involve controlled dangerous substances beyond chocolate syrup." James wasn't joking, and his motions were always walked straight up to judge's chambers, not just in Wicks County.

"What are you accusing my employee of, James?"

"Nothing, just telling you to keep your ear to the

ground, and don't leave my Hannah alone with him for very long."

"Your Hannah?"

James regarded him for a long moment. "Our Hannah," he said. "Or *your* Hannah?"

Trent picked up another beeping, blinking digital toy.

"Maybe my Hannah. The choice of area of practice is ultimately up to the associate."

"Right." James patted his arm, his smile turning devilish. "You're calling dibs, aren't you?"

"She isn't some leftover dessert that I'd call dibs before you or Mac can scarf her up."

An image of Hannah and a hot chocolate with whipped cream, sprinkles, cinnamon sticks, and a long-handled gold spoon came to mind.

A can of chocolate syrup threatened to add itself to that scene in Trent's head.

Rather than teasing, which is what James ought to have done, James's grin faded to an expression both knowing and sweet.

"Spring has come early to the domestic relations department," he said. "I'm off to buy my niece a large, fierce, furry rabbit."

"You wouldn't dare."

"Mac promised me you'd suggested it."

―⁓―

Being in a courtroom—any courtroom at all—had Hannah's breakfast roiling in her stomach and her breath hitching. She was here only to observe, and these were not foster care cases, but the feeling—the anxious, tense, hopeless feeling of the room—was all too familiar. She ducked down the hallway to the ladies room and ran cold water on her wrists.

Which helped not at all, except that it delayed dealing with Gerald for a few minutes. He'd appropriated the counsel table on the left side of the courtroom, spreading his files around like a tomcat marking his territory with scent.

When Hannah returned to the courtroom, the state's attorney was lounging in the jury box beside a tall, dark-haired young deputy sheriff. They both looked amused at something, while Gerald stood at the defense counsel table, his blond head bent toward a short, scruffy guy in flannel shirt, combat boots, and jeans.

Hannah approached the jury box, not particularly eager to introduce herself, but truly reluctant to join Gerald.

"That's Rory Cavanaugh," the deputy was saying—Deputy Moreland, according to his silver badge. "I saw his name on the docket. What's he doing here?"

The state's attorney, a compact strawberry blond in sensible shoes, pawed through her stack of files and opened one.

"Getting screwed, it looks like," she muttered. "He is the dad of record to a little girl, but not the bio dad."

"You ring the bell, you get the prize," the deputy said.

Hannah sidled closer, though the state's attorney's brusque demeanor, blunt cut, and thick-soled shoes struck Hannah as another incarnation of Miss Wallingford, Esq., Counsel for the Douglas County DSS—a key figure in Hannah's worst nightmares, both waking and sleeping.

"But Mr. Cavanaugh didn't ring that bell," Hannah

said, knowing she should keep her mouth shut. "He has plenty of medical documentation to prove he isn't the dad."

The attorney let the file fall closed. "Who are you, and what do you want to do about it? There's precedent saying the kid is entitled to rely on him because he's been paying for years."

"I'm Hannah Stark, the new associate from Hartman and Whitney, here to observe. I don't think Mr. Cavanaugh has any problem with continuing to pay, but Mom, through the State, is asking for three hundred dollars per month more. Did Gerald tell you Mr. Cavanaugh is out of remission?"

The attorney winced, and the deputy swore.

"He hasn't been to the bowling league since summer," the deputy said. "He doesn't look too good now that you mention it."

The state's attorney chewed her lip and reopened the file.

"You could probably get a continuance on the basis of medical hardship, at least buy the guy some time to get back on his feet or die. Margaret Jenson, by the way. Assistant state's attorney until I hit the lottery." She stuck out a hand. Short fingernails, no polish, what looked like a man's watch strapped around one wrist.

Hannah shook. "You're all heart, Margaret."

"If it were Gerald asking, I wouldn't even offer a six-month reprieve."

"You'd hold Rory's choice of counsel against him, then?"

The deputy smiled—a smile so full of mischief it ought to be illegal—and so did Margaret, but hers wasn't a nice expression.

"I tell myself I shouldn't hold it against these guys if they hire a turkey for their lawyer, but my weak, feminine nature gets the better of me, and I react subjectively." Margaret fluttered her eyelashes comically.

"My thanks in any case, and I'll relay your offer to Gerald."

Gerald now stood very close to a blowsy blond whose generous curves threatened to overrun her slinky top. The woman's age was hard to tell, as either time or hard living might have put the grooves beside her mouth and the cynicism in her eyes. Hannah crossed the room and waited while Gerald and the woman continued to whisper.

Gerald shot Hannah a peevish look. "Mrs. Smithson and I are discussing her case. Did you want something, Hannah?"

In the stack of cases Hannah had reviewed earlier in the week, no party or witness had been named Mrs. Smithson.

"You're in a sweet mood," Hannah said.

"C'mon, Hannah. The judge will be on the bench any minute, and if you're a good girl, I'll introduce you to him at the recess."

And why hadn't Gerald performed that courtesy already?

"Margaret is willing to continue the Cavanaugh case generally for six months," Hannah said. "She'll put off any kind of trial asking for an increase until then."

Gerald's expression shifted, suggesting Hannah at least had his attention.

He slapped a file down on the table loud enough to cut through the hum and buzz of the courtroom. "When did you go behind my back to cut this deal, Hannah?"

Where was a hat pin when a woman needed to deflate a hot air balloon?

"I went over to that jury box right there, where Madam State's Attorney is hanging out with Deputy Moreland. I did not go behind your back. The deputy knows Rory, and Margaret was willing to cut the guy a break. You had only to ask her."

Mrs. Smithson took a step back.

"So you think you're ready to start handling cases, Hannah?" Gerald hissed. "Think you can show me how to do my job? Well, listen to me, Hannah Stark. You don't go pulling shit like this with *my* cases on *my* docket in *my* courtroom—" He was winding up to make a scene, while Mrs. Smithson found it imperative to examine designer nails with the American flag lacquered onto them.

"All rise! The Circuit Court for Damson County is now in session, the Honorable John D. Linker presiding. Hear ye, hear ye, and give your attention to this honorable court." The bailiff's voice had everyone in the courtroom scrambling to find a place, Margaret hustling over to her counsel table, and Hannah—her belly full of butterflies—taking a seat on one of the back pews.

Linker, wearing black judicial robes, appeared from between the heavy folds of a red velvet curtain hung behind the judge's bench, like something out of *The Wizard of Oz*. He was a sandy-haired man of medium height, sporting professorial horn-rimmed glasses and a grim expression.

"Thank you, you may be seated," he muttered, picking up the first file.

Margaret, as state's attorney or prosecutor, called the

cases and stated the facts. Gerald would rebut what could be rebutted, and admit what his clients were willing to admit. The procedure wasn't legally complicated—both sides were proffering their cases rather than putting on sworn testimony—but the fact patterns could be complicated.

Trent had explained to Hannah that contempt of court cases were called first. Three dads and a mom who'd had multiple opportunities to pay down arrearages were hauled off in handcuffs and leg shackles. As each defendant was committed to the Damson County Detention Center, a small stir at the back of the courtroom indicated that—as intended—upcoming defendants were inspired to hustle out to the hallway in hopes last-minute phone calls could scare up cash.

Defendant number five, who looked about three years past high school, took his place beside Gerald, and Margaret read the facts of the case: five children under the age of three, four different moms, none of them married to Dad.

Judge Linker made a show of perusing the thick file then shifting back in his chair.

"Sir, would you oblige the court by turning around, please?"

The Defendant looked confused by the request but turned in a slow circle.

"Is that a wallet in your back pocket?"

Gerald nudged his client.

"Yes, sir. Yes, Your Honor, I mean, sir," the man said.

"Would you mind removing that wallet from your pocket?"

Super-dad complied, looking more and more nervous,

though Hannah's constitutional instincts were yipping about warrantless searches and invasion of privacy.

"Could you empty your wallet, please?" the judge bade him with implacable courtesy.

Gerald's client stacked fifty one-dollar bills beside the wallet, then a driver's license and some receipts.

"Anything else in the wallet, sir?"

"No, Your Honor."

This was why Hannah hated courtrooms. People could be mean in courtrooms and call it the pursuit of justice.

"What about the other pocket?" His Honor asked.

A pack of cigarettes appeared on the table beside the wallet, while Hannah looked on, perplexed as hell. Why wasn't Gerald objecting? The money and cigarettes sat on the table as some sort of symbolic sacrificial offering, and Hannah's nausea spiked toward real pain. The judge was up to something; that much was obvious.

"Sir," His Honor said quietly, "you come into my courtroom, having left five children without a father to speak of. You show up here with enough cash to feed them all for quite a while, and yet you tell me you want your support reduced—support, I might add, you haven't paid for months. Then I see that you smoke."

An ominous silence spread, though Hannah had the sense this was a rehearsed drama, Jurisprudence for the Overly Reproductive.

"How much do you smoke, sir?"

"About a pack a day, Judge. Been trying to quit for years."

Hannah was ready to bounce out of her seat. This was

surely objectionable on the grounds of relevance. What did smoking have to do with child support payments?

"I didn't hear you."

Hannah had heard him, and she was clear in the back of the room.

"I said, about a pack a day, Your Honor."

"How much do you spend on a habit that's likely to kill you while your children go hungry?"

The silence grew until the judge slammed the file shut.

"Mr. Matthews, I find your client in contempt of my order. Deputies, you will take this man to the lock up, there to be transported to the county detention center to serve a sentence of thirty days. Said contempt can be purged by paying all arrearages and remaining current on all other payments. Madam State's Attorney, call your next case."

Hannah winced, and an older woman beside her snorted.

"Don't you feel sorry for that one, honey. He's got two more on the way, and one of them will be my grand-baby. If the judge really wanted to fix this situation, he'd cut the balls off half the guys in this room."

Or put a chastity belt on half the women? A trickle of sympathy for Gerald dripped through the unease in Hannah's belly. The court focused on the practicalities—children needed to eat—without examining cause, effect, or cure beyond that. What attorney wouldn't sour on such fare week after week?

What judge wouldn't sour?

Margaret kept the cases coming, and not all of them were Gerald's, though he had more than any other two attorneys put together. They kept at it for almost two hours before the judge called for the morning recess.

"All rise! Circuit Court for Damson County is now in recess. Court will reconvene in ten minutes."

Hannah flinched at the bailiff's command, a reflex she hated. She was pondering a career of flinching when Gerald came over to stand beside her pew.

"Look, Hannah, I get a little tense before a docket. Don't take anything I said seriously, OK?" He flashed a megawatt smile, and Hannah mentally fished for the air sickness bag. Bullshit was bullshit was bullshit, whether it came with a serving of intimidation or a side of charm.

"It's a lot to keep straight, Gerald. I know that. Do you think we'll finish at a reasonable hour?"

If the judge started out cranky, how much civility— much less justice—would be left for the poor schmucks at the end of the day?

"I don't know. The last few cases are the ones requiring testimony, but we usually run a few minutes over if that will finish the docket in the morning. I'll be back in a few minutes—gotta go, you know?"

Mrs. Smithson left the courtroom at the same time Gerald did, hustling past Margaret, who was coming back in.

"Like what you see so far?" Margaret asked. "Justice through intimidation and incarceration? It's the stuff of great parental relationships."

Margaret's comments were oddly reassuring, though her cavalier attitude was not. "You don't like what you do, Margaret?"

"For God's sake, Hannah, take a look around you. That last Romeo of the Center City Projects is hardly the worst of the lot. I've done cases with guys with a dozen kids, and more on the way. As far as I know, that boy wasn't giving anybody AIDS—though I'm sure the next time Judge Linker does a wallet check, there will be a condom in there."

Hannah's jaw dropped. "That's what he was looking for?"

"It varies. One guy had a condom, and the judge told him to keep it because he might need it where he was going. That was a particularly bad docket, though this stuff gets old fast."

"Somebody has to keep these people from welshing on their kids," Hannah said. That was the point, wasn't it?

"Hannah, you see who's here today. The average deadbeat parent is less than twenty-five years old, and he or she has at least three kids to support. These people don't finish high school, and what they have to give their children is a pittance. I've often wondered how much it costs the State—in my time, the judge's time, the deputies and bailiffs, the support enforcements staff, much less the cost of incarcerating these people—compared to the money we collect."

Margaret looked as if she wanted to say more, but her head whipped around as the bailiff took up his post.

"Showtime," she muttered. "Where's Gerald?"

"Don't know," Hannah whispered as the bailiff called the room to order and the judge reappeared from behind his magic curtain. He gave everybody permission to sit, and like good doggies, sit they did.

"Madam State, call your next case."

"Your Honor," Margaret said, standing to address the

court, "I see Mr. Matthews is not yet back from recess, and his are the only cases left."

The judge scowled mightily at a courtroom considerably less crowded than it had been two hours earlier. "Mr. Matthews indicated to me before we started this morning that we have another representative of Hartman and Whitney present in the courtroom, Madam State, one whose responsibilities lie in the child support arena. *Call your next case.*"

Margaret shrugged at Hannah and pulled a file out of the middle of a stack.

"The State calls case number CS 42.446.15, State of Maryland v. Rory Cavanaugh. Mr. Cavanaugh, come forward please if you're in the courtroom."

Hannah made her way to defendant's counsel table as Mr. Cavanaugh shuffled along beside her. Her bowels turned to water, and at the base of her neck, the Timpani of Agony went into a frenzy.

Her usual reaction to being before a judge. The realization steadied her.

Margaret had at least pulled the one case Hannah knew cold, though nowhere had the nice law school professors offered advice about what to do with a judge who was pissed off to the point of disregarding courtroom protocol.

"Ms. Stark, is it? Please enter your appearance for the record," the judge said.

"Hannah Stark, Your Honor, and the firm of Hartman and Whitney for your defendant, Rory Cavanaugh."

"Thank you. Madam State?"

"Your Honor," Margaret began, "the parties have agreed to join in a motion to continue this matter generally for the next six months. The defendant's circumstances are extenuating, and the matter at issue is strictly a routine request for increase. Mr. Cavanaugh has been scrupulous about making his support payments since the inception of the case."

I owe Margaret, I owe Margaret, I owe Margaret.

"Ms. Stark?" The judge turned an impatient expression on Hannah.

What? What does he want me to say?

"Your Honor, Madam State's Attorney has accurately represented that Mr. Cavanaugh is requesting a continuance at this time." Hannah turned to the client, whose ruddy features betrayed a welter of confusion. "Mr. Cavanaugh, could you explain why an increase in payments would be especially hard for you right now?"

Mr. Cavanaugh hitched up his blue jeans, shuffled his steel-toed boots, and squared his shoulders as he met the judge's eye.

"I was diagnosed with cancer six years ago, Y'Honor. We went through the chemo and radiation and the whole bit, and I thought I had it licked when I went five years clean. I guess I don't quite have it licked yet, because they tell me I done come outta remission."

"Do you have extra medical bills?" Hannah asked.

"Oh, Lord. Last time it took four years just to get 'em paid off. They can't do the radiation again, I know that, but them bills are murder."

What else should she ask? What else mattered? "Are you able to report for work?"

"The treatments make you tired," he said. "But I work for a good man, and I can usually get in a few days a week. The guys cover for me when they can."

Hannah glanced at the judge, who looked bemused—the turkey. "Is Marlena your daughter?"

"Objection!" Margaret was on her feet immediately. "That is hardly relevant when he's held himself out to be the father for years."

The judge folded his arms across his chest. "Overruled. The man is not under oath. He may answer, Ms. Stark."

"Marlena isn't my blood kin," Cavanaugh said. "But I love her like she was, and she comes to visit all the time. I just can't pay no more money right now."

"Ms. Stark?" the judge prompted.

"This is an honorable man, Judge. Please grant his request for a six-month continuance."

My maiden closing argument. All two sentences of it.

And the judge looked irritated again.

"Sir, this is what I am going to do," the judge said. "The order requiring support will be kept in place, but the amount owed will be reduced to one hundred dollar per month. You can pay more than that if you choose, but for the next six months your obligation is reduced to one hundred dollars per month. At the end of six months, we'll take another look at the case, and perhaps by then your health won't be such a con- straining factor. Get well, and we'll see you back here next spring."

Cavanaugh dropped to his seat beside Hannah, and she nearly fell into the chair beside him.

"Mr. Cavanaugh, can you get yourself home, or do you need to rest a bit first?" she asked.

"Madam State," the judge said as he shuffled files, "call your next case."

Hannah's head came up, but the judge's expression was unreadable. He was hustling her, though. Hustling her and the client, probably so he could practice his putt or meet some good old boy for lunch.

"Your Honor, Mr. Cavanaugh may need some assistance." She remembered to stand when she addressed the court, but she did not even try to make her tone ingratiating.

Cavanaugh was still in his seat, shoulders jerking. The guy was trying not to cry, though whether he was moved by relief, humiliation, or sorrow, she could not tell.

"Bailiff," the judge barked, "get Mr. Cavanaugh a cab. His counsel will no doubt provide the fare if necessary."

Cavanaugh stood and leveled a look at Hannah.

"I don't know where you come from, but that other fella said I might have to pay the increase, plus a few months back, and there was nothing I could do about it. I got the cab fare, thank you just the same."

Hannah watched him shuffle out, Deputy Moreland at his side, while Margaret called the next case.

Fortunato. Hannah grabbed for the file. Dad was alleging Mom made a lot more money than she admitted, and the children were with Dad most of the time. A deadbeat mom.

Hannah nodded to Margaret, who looked faintly amused.

"Madam State, a recitation of the facts, please." The judge's expression was bored, and Hannah saw his gaze go to the clock hanging on the side wall. Before Margaret could launch into her patter, the rear door to the courtroom swung open with a bang.

"Your Honor, my apologies." Gerald Matthews bustled up the aisle, a placatory smile directed at the judge. "I was detained by the matter of, shall we say, adequate public facilities?"

"We're on the Fortunato case, Mr. Matthews."

Just that, no scolding? Not a word of castigation for being AWOL? Hannah passed Gerald the file and took a seat at the counsel table rather than give him the satisfaction of entirely yielding her post.

Gerald opened the file and ran a finger down the top page.

"I'll deal with you later, bitch." He didn't even look at Hannah as he fired that poison dart, his tone vicious. Had Gerald forgotten that every word spoken in the courtroom was recorded when the judge was on the bench?

"You're welcome," Hannah murmured.

Margaret recited her facts, and the next few cases went quickly, because the payors were agreeing to the increases called for by the child support guidelines. At 11:45 a.m., Margaret closed her last file.

"This concludes the morning docket, Your Honor," she said. "Permission to step back?"

"Thank you, Madam State, counsel. Court is adjourned until one thirty this afternoon."

"All rise!" the bailiff called. "Circuit Court for Damson County is now adjourned."

The judge had no sooner disappeared behind his Mr. Wizard curtain than Gerald was looming over Hannah, or doing his best to loom. Hannah had worn heels in honor of her first visit to the courthouse.

"I don't know what the hell you were trying to pull, Hannah Stark, but making me look like an ass before the judge in whose courtroom I work was the dumbest move of your short and doomed legal career. You messed with the wrong guy, this time. Find your own way back to the office."

He stuffed files into his briefcase, while Hannah caught Margaret frowning at them from the other counsel table. She'd heard every word, and that was something at least.

"Juliet? Juliet Randall?"

An elderly man in a gray suit stood in the door. He sported a courthouse employee's badge, and a smile wreathed his *American Gothic* face. "I knew that was you, I just knew it!"

"Joe?" Hannah moved away from the table rather than be anywhere near Gerald. "Mr. Jones?"

"Of course it's old Joe." The guy held his arms wide, and Hannah permitted him an old man's hug—careful and enthusiastic at the same time. "My goodness, you have grown up, lady. Just look at you."

Joe, who'd heard every word of every one of her foster care hearings.

Joe, who'd brought flowers to her college graduation.

Joe, whose name had mysteriously appeared next to hers on the very first lease she'd ever signed.

"It's good to see you, Joe." Good to recall not everybody at the courthouse was a grouch or a cynic. "Have you transferred from Douglas County?" And wouldn't that just be awkward as heck?

"Nah. I just get called in when somebody's on leave or gone hunting. I might work a couple days a month, mostly over in Douglas County. Don't tell me you're a lawyer now?"

She'd sent him Christmas cards signed Juliet Randall and without a return address. Most years, his was the only one she sent. She told herself she cut ties to keep Grace safe, but that wasn't the entire reason.

She'd had precious few ties to cut.

They small talked for a few minutes, until another bailiff came along and claimed Joe for lunch. Margaret stood a few feet away, files piled up in her arms, and Gerald was nowhere to be seen.

"You need a ride back to the office?" Margaret asked.

"I guess so. Thanks." Hannah would walk back to the office before she'd wander around the courthouse, looking for a Knightley brother.

Margaret dumped her files into a double-sized briefcase on rollers. "Does your first day in court leave you awed by the great Gerald Matthews, God's Gift to Litigation?"

"Impressed, not in a good way." Horrified was a sort of impressed. Hannah sank onto the front pew, her stomach in knots, her headache prowling around the base of her skull, and weariness dragging at her soul.

While Margaret took a call on a cell phone, Hannah surveyed the scene of the morning's various disasters. Late morning sun poured through the courtroom's cathedral windows and slanted onto the wooden pews, while velvet curtains added both elegance and color to an otherwise austere stage. Now that the room was empty, it exuded a sort of worn peacefulness.

"Don't turn your back on Gerald," Margaret said as she tucked her phone away. "I want to tell you he's just another arrogant son of a bitch with a little pee-pee, but Gerald plays with some bad actors."

Was this the lawyer version of girl talk? "What do you mean?"

"I saw Gerald leaving the courthouse with that Smithson woman. She has connections with a number of convicted felons, and solicitation ain't the half of it."

Soliciting, as in a prostitute drumming up business.

Hannah rose, abruptly glad to be leaving. "Gack. Hasn't he heard of AIDS?" Or the attorney grievance commission?

"Don't spare him the concern. The practice of law would be a better place without him. You want to do fast food?"

"No, thank you. My appetite took a hit this morning. I could do with a soft drink though, so maybe just a drive-through."

Margaret clicked the latches closed on her black briefcase, smiling that same cynical smile Hannah had seen on her earlier. "Sugar and caffeine for lunch. How quickly the practice of law corrupts us."

Chapter 6

"WE'LL MAKE THIS QUICK, BECAUSE WE HATE TO SEE A grown man cry unless we're the ones who rearranged his nose."

James closed Trent's door behind him as he delivered that opening line. Mac merely folded his arms and stood silently by the window.

"You've been missing me," Trent suggested. "Missing those fraternal lunches Mac tried to impose on us when he was first in practice."

"I do not miss watching grown men pitch linen napkins at each other across the table," Mac said. "This is serious, Trent."

When Mac said something was serious, particularly with that ominous, gentle note in his voice...

Trent rose from his desk and came around to sit on the front of it. "I'm listening."

"You won't like it," James said, "but we decided we had to tell you."

"So quit toying with your prey. Spill."

Mac spoke from his place by the window, his gaze on the parking lot, a manila folder in his right hand. "You recall Harold Niederland had a heart attack earlier this fall?"

"Yes, I do." Harold's heart attack had substantially increased the county bar association's representation at the local Y. Harold was a laid-back guy, not an ounce of fat on him, and not quite forty-five years under his belt.

"You probably don't recall that the Douglas County courthouse, in a display of well-meant humanitarian accommodation, continued every single one of his cases to the same day."

"I do remember hearing about that," Trent said. "That was likely a day long enough to put the man back in the hospital."

"Not quite," James said, taking over the narrative. "The rest of the criminal defense bar pitched in, and they each took on a case or two for Hal and waived the fee. Mac took a couple of cases."

"Decent of you."

"A lapse," Mac said. "Don't go having any heart attacks, because family law isn't my area of expertise."

"Point noted."

"Nor mine," James said. "Hal stopped Mac last night at the feed store and asked him since when did Hartman poach on the criminal dockets in Wicks County?"

"I wasn't aware we practiced criminal law in Wicks County, though I've heard rumors regarding a certain Hartman and Whitney partner's social habits with the employees in the clerk's office—note the plural."

"This isn't a rumor, Trent." Mac's tone was almost sad, and the uh-oh feeling started up in Trent's belly.

Mac didn't do overt displays of emotion any more than he did family law.

"It's Gerald Matthews," James said. "Mac and I spent this morning over in the Wicks County courthouse, nosing around the files, and Gerald has been regularly appearing on their Tuesday morning traffic docket. He dated some gal in the state's attorney's office there who passed him a few quiet referrals for DUIs, and we're sure if you look at his time sheets, he's been ill, out seeing clients, down at the courthouse doing research, and otherwise lying to and cheating on his employers about his whereabouts."

"Well, hell." Trent pinched the bridge of his nose and mentally added a quarter to the Bad Words Pay Back jar sitting on top of the fridge at home. "You're sure?"

Mac passed Trent a manila folder. Certified copies of Gerald's entries of appearance as counsel for the defendant in a dozen different cases were neatly arranged by date in the file. Driving Under the Influence, Driving While Intoxicated, Driving on Suspended Tags, Driving Without a License… Gerald had a regular full-service traffic practice going two counties over.

"This has been happening almost since he started with us," Trent said. "For crap's sake, we pay him enough. Why moonlight when you know it will cost you your job?"

"He's a litigating attorney," Mac said, twisting off a wilted rhododendron leaf and pitching it into the wastebasket. "The only people with more testosterone than litigating attorneys are convicted murderers, and neither group is known for its humility."

"He's a greedy little turd," James paraphrased. "He likely has expensive taste in recreation."

"What does that mean?" Though Trent knew—drugs, gambling, expensive toys. All manner of vices beckoned when the job was stressful, the ego inflated, and the coping skills few.

"It means I don't want him in my department," James said. "Mac?"

"Not if he were the last law school graduate admitted to the Maryland bar and voluntarily surrendered both balls."

"That's clear enough," Trent said as more quarters silently flung themselves at that jar on the fridge. Shit, damn, hell, and shit. He'd chosen Gerald from the pool of applicants, thinking a hard-nosed slant on the occasional case would give the department balance.

"You have another problem," Mac said, gaze on the snow-dusted parking lot.

"Besides a breach of ethics on my staff?"

"Your breach of ethics is coming back from the happy pappy docket now, but I don't see your newest associate with him. Better hope he didn't run her off in her very first week, because I will not under any circumstances take on a family law case to bail your ass out."

"I can't take on any," James said. "I have federal depositions coming up in December, and my Christmas shopping isn't done yet."

It was an attempt at humor. A lame attempt.

"I'll handle this," Trent said. But if Gerald had sent Hannah packing on her first day at the courthouse, the guy had a lot more trouble to deal with than the mere loss of his job.

"It's good to be the king."

Gerald addressed the interior of his Beemer, where he did, indeed, feel like the king. The lease payments were killing him, but oh, the pleasure… He'd spent a few minutes of his lunch break in the backseat with the estimable Joan Smithson, and between her enthusiastic attentions and the goodies she'd brought to the party, Gerald's mood was confident and expansive.

Maybe he wouldn't snitch to Trent Knightley about Hannah's head-bitch-in-charge behavior in court. What could the girl have been thinking, to just stand up and start handling cases when she hadn't the first hour of courtroom experience? Of course, Gerald had told Judge Linker she was pawing and snorting to take on cases, and the results had been lovely. Throw a bored judge a chew toy, and he'll entertain himself every time.

Then that bit with the zillion-year-old bailiff calling her Juliet Randall…

Gerald switched off the ignition, adjusted his dick in his boxers, and made a mental note to see if Gail's HR files held any clues to the Hannah-Juliet Stark-Randall mystery.

He'd parked in an empty slot at least two spaces away from other vehicles, positioned so that any partners staring out of their office windows could see him hustling into the building. The receptionist—upon whom Gerald had long since ceased hitting—told him Trent wanted to see him ASAP.

Trent's summons likely involved nothing more pressing than a rehash of the morning docket, so Gerald ducked into the bathroom to blow his nose and address the damage Joan's busy fingers had done to a ninety-five-dollar haircut.

To snitch on Hannah, or not snitch on Hannah?

He hung up his coat, stowed his briefcase, and ambled down the hall, both hands in his pockets: A partner-schmoozing smile affixed to his features, he tapped on the door and let himself into the office.

"You wanted to see me, Trent?"

Knightley was probably about to offer him one of the contested divorces, like it was some big deal to be given honest-to-God litigation. If the Knightley boys only knew.

"Close the door, please." Trent's tone was serious, no doubt trying to make an impression. He came around the front of his desk and leaned against it while Gerald took a wing chair.

"Gerald, I am going to ask this question only once: Where were you last Tuesday morning?"

"I wasn't here, if that's what you're asking." *I was making enough in fifteen minutes for a few days worth of blow.* "That was the morning I took my car in for some work. An oxygen sensor had the check engine light coming on. I got here around noon or so, but I put in the OT to make up for the time, Trent. What's this about?"

Spend enough time with defendants, and the lying came easily. The Loomis divorce would be a good place to start. Elvin Gregory wasn't exactly the sharpest letter opener in the—

"You are fired, for cause. These entries of appearance from Wicks County prove that you've violated the terms of your employment agreement." Trent dropped a file in Gerald's lap. "Gino will escort you to your desk, where you will pack your personal possessions and leave. You will not return to this office under any circumstances. Do I make myself clear?"

Gerald shot to his feet, propelled by equal parts amusement, rage, and sheer disbelief as the paperwork fluttered to the carpet.

"For crap's sake, Knightley." Six months of hard work, ass kissing, and shit cases, and *this* was his thanks? "Are you too petty to let anyone else take some initiative? So what if I handled a few DUIs on the side? That's no skin off the nose of this uptight, holier-than-thou, shithole of a law firm. You can't share the pie, can you? Well, you don't have to fire me, Knightley. I'll happily move aside so you and your brothers can diddle each other in peace. I am so sick of working here I could—"

Gino's hirsute form appeared in the doorway.

"Mr. Trent, you gotta problem for Gino to fix?"

"Gerald is leaving the firm, Gino, effective immediately. Please see him to his office and assist him with his packing, then help him get his effects out to his car. Confiscate his badge before he leaves the premises. If he needs anything off his hard drive, have him request it by letter within fifteen days, per company policy."

Gino stepped away from the door, and Gerald moved quickly enough that the office cretin wouldn't think of taking him by the arm.

No more ass kissing, no more having to represent every dickhead and ho-bag with a mind to stiff their dickhead, ho-bag exes, no more putting up with the Knightley mafia running his life, no more moony-eyed Gail Russo, who couldn't cut loose if she were knee-crawling drunk...

This would work out, and work out well. Gerald flipped Saint Trenton the bird and headed for his office.

In a corner of Gerald's brain, close to where the survival instinct resided, he admitted some of his optimism—his bravado—was a function of the drugs. Self-preservation required he acknowledge anxiety as well.

That he'd left Hartman and Whitney to go solo would raise a few eyebrows in itself. Hartman and Whitney as a firm would say nothing incriminating, but their silence would speak loudly.

Though they might sue him for breach of his employment contract.

Or Hartman and Whitney could notify the State's bar counsel and start an ethical inquiry.

"Deal with that shit tomorrow," Gerald muttered, tossing his office toy collection of interlocking metal puzzles into a box. As he came upon the package of condoms in his bottom drawer, he realized Trent Knightley was elbowing him out so Hannah Stark could be elbowed in faster. *Damned uppity bitch.*

"You say something, Mr. Gerald?" Gino set one banker's box on top of the other.

"Not to you, asshole." Gerald dumped out two more drawers, thinking how much easier Hannah Stark made it for Knightley to screw him. Hannah Stark or Juliet Randall or whoever the hell she was. The bitch had cost him his job, meaning at the very least, he would cost her hers.

"You about done, Mr. Gerald?"

Gerald tossed the French ticklers in the trash. "Yeah, I'm done."

For now.

As Hannah passed the Human Resources suite, both Mac and James were heading into Gail's office, and for once, James looked as grim as Mac.

Bad day at Flat Rock.

Hannah had just gotten her coat off and her notes from the

morning out of her briefcase when Trent Knightley appeared in her doorway, looking as unhappy as Mac and James.

"I need to speak to you." No how-was-the-morning or did-you-learn-anything?

No asking if Gerald tried to crap all over her, then blame her when his tactic backfired?

"Have a seat," Hannah said.

"My office." He turned and left Hannah to trail him across the hall, her anxiety growing with each step. Was she really to be called to the principal's office her very first week on the job?

"We have a problem," Trent said, closing his door as soon as Hannah entered his office.

"Lawyers are good at solving problems," she said, but she didn't take a seat, not even when he took up his characteristic position leaning against his desk.

"Sometimes we excel at creating them. Effective the first Friday in December, you'll handle the child support docket."

Hannah repeated Trent's pronouncement in her head, looking for another meaning, for humor, for any interpretation other than the obvious. When it became clear he was waiting for a response, all she could muster was a disbelieving monosyllabic squeak.

"*Me?*"

"Come here." Trent pushed away from his desk and steered her by the arm to the sofa. "You have an affirmative talent for going pale right before my very eyes. We'll find a way to use that before a jury. Sit down and don't fuss me for giving an order."

"I'm not fussing." Not fussing, not thinking, and *not* handling that damned docket.

Trent sat beside her and kept a hand on her neck, brushing his thumb along her nape, a peculiarly soothing touch.

"I should not have sprung it on you like this, but we'll be shorthanded for a while, and I don't see an alternative."

Neither did Hannah, though the timing was a surprise. She'd taken this job, knowing courtrooms would be part of it someday. Someday-in-two-weeks would be a challenge.

"Are you doing this to me because of what happened in court this morning?" she asked.

"What haven't you told me, Hannah?" The hand on her neck slowed but didn't disappear, and for that Hannah was grateful. She'd done well in court, at least in the client's opinion.

She took courage from that. "Gerald and I had a little, um, situation. Nothing worth mentioning."

"I'll be the judge of that. Out with it, Stark."

She focused on the soft green leaves of the rhododendron on the windowsill, while Trent's hand rested at the back of her neck.

She'd been called tactile avoidant for much of her childhood, but she had the peculiar notion that if Trent stopped touching her, she'd be unable to give him the report he sought.

Unable to tell him one of his associates had tried to betray another.

And failed.

"We were in recess," Hannah said. "The judge came back on the bench and told Margaret to call her case, but Gerald had ducked out to use the facilities. The judge said a representative of Hartman and Whitney was in the courtroom, and directed Margaret again to call a case. I'd discussed Rory Cavanaugh's situation with her, so we put a joint motion to continue on the record, and the judge granted it. No big deal."

To Rory, it had been a very big deal.

"You entered your appearance?" Trent asked.

"And the firm's, though the firm's appearance was a matter of record."

"Did your client say anything?"

He'd said thank you, more or less. "I asked him a few questions demonstrating hardship, but he wasn't under oath."

"Linker was on the bench?"

While Knightley was on cross-examination. "Gerald had apparently told him I'd be in the courtroom as an observer. He seemed impatient, the judge that is."

"They all hate the child support docket. It's tedious as hell, the same facts over and over, but you got your boy a much-needed continuance. Linker gets quirky when his blood sugar's low. I'm proud of you, Hannah Stark. Job well done."

Trent hugged her. A quick, friendly, one-armed squeeze around her shoulders Hannah had not seen coming. That embrace—the equivalent of a high five, a towel snap, or a fist bump—was nearly as disconcerting as his announcement about the child support docket.

But a whole lot nicer. Trent's arm fell away, and he rose to resume his position leaning against his desk. "What did Gerald have to say about his absence?"

How long had it been since Hannah had been hugged by an adult male and enjoyed it?

"Gerald apologized to the court and let me know he didn't appreciate my interference." *I'll deal with you later, bitch.*

Trent regarded her steadily, as if he could hear the words replaying in Hannah's head. She stood rather than endure that stare. Dads had stares like that, like they could see right into your soul's backpack to the C minus on your small talk quiz.

Dads did not, however, hug like that.

"I don't think Gerald is in the habit of censoring himself," Hannah said rather than endure more silence. "He's not the first bully I've met."

"He's gone."

"Gone where?"

"Gone from the firm, perhaps from the practice of law. I have to calm down before I decide whether to report him or not."

"For going to the bathroom?" Hannah asked.

"For moonlighting. The specific details of his discharge will remain confidential, but it's public record that he entered his appearance on behalf of private clients in Wick's County. He was tending to his own clients on Tuesday mornings and God knows when else, while we were paying him to tend to ours, and that will soon be all over every bar association in the circuit."

"I see." Out in the parking lot, flurries danced down from a leaden sky while Hannah battled longing for another hug. "Actually, I don't see. Salaries here are generous, benefits good, and Gerald had no trouble with the work. Why would he screw up a good thing?"

And why had she worn heels? Her calves were aching, and the Very Sugary Irradiated Berry-Colored

Smoothie she'd had for lunch wasn't sitting well. A hug might help with that too.

"Maybe Gerald suffered from champagne tastes on a white zin budget," Trent said. "Maybe the problem was sheer arrogance. In any case, Gerald is gone, and my department is back to square one in terms of workload. Next week is Thanksgiving, so there won't be a Friday docket, but the first week in December, you're the new whiz-bang child support associate at Hartman and Whitney."

He came to stand beside her at the window, sounding like he himself could use a hug.

"I wish I could say I'll be with you every step of the way, Hannah, but I have a contested trial next week and another the week after. You'll have to take on the Loomis divorce, and your next target after you get all that under control will be domestic violence emergency hearings."

She'd never wanted to touch so much as a single family law file. Contracts, leases, partnership agreements, those had been her objective. Business law, not this morass of competing needs and inadequate resources.

Hannah did want to touch her boss. She also wanted to take off her damned shoes, especially the right one.

"Child support, the Loomis divorce, and domestic violence restraining orders. Anything else?" What did that leave? Pre-nups, maybe? She wasn't doing adoptions. Nope-ity, nope, nope, nope.

Trent frowned at her for a long moment. "You're used to managing on your own, aren't you?"

She thought of Grace, without whom she couldn't manage anything. "Most of the time, yes. I temped a lot right out of law school and learned to eat what was on my plate." Another foster care lesson, in truth. "I didn't expect being a lawyer would mean somebody led me around by the hand for the first five years."

Trent took her hand in his.

"It shouldn't mean you never have a hand to hold either. This is my hand." He laced his fingers with hers. "You grab it when you need it, and don't wait until you're going under for the third time."

He squeezed her fingers and let their hands drop.

"What if you're in court?" Hannah asked, pushing aside the simple, disconcerting pleasure of having clasped hands with him. "We'll all be busy, apparently, including Lee and Ann."

"They haven't been on board much longer than you, though Lee had years of paralegal experience up in Pennsylvania before she went to law school." He was back at his command position, leaning on his desk, pinching the bridge of his nose.

"As much as I hate to do it," he went on, "if you have questions and I'm not here, go to James or Mac. They avoid family law like it is recurring chicken pox, but they will not be able to deny a damsel in distress."

"Bat my eyes, simper, and look helpless?"

"Do you know how?"

"I do not."

He looked relieved, which was intriguing. "You'd distract James if you did, and probably terrify Mac. If they can't help you and it's an end-of-the-world emergency, Aaron Glover is another attorney with whom I sometimes kick cases around—when I'm not opposing him. Jane DeLuca is very good, and Dunstan Cromarty would be regarded as judge material, but for his Scottish burr. What are you doing this weekend?"

Mr. Here's-A-Hug, Job-Well-Done was about to "ask" her to put in some overtime her very first weekend on the job. If Hannah begged and wheedled, Eliza might spring her for an afternoon, but Grace would be mortally disappointed.

As would Hannah. "I like my weekends at home," Hannah said, chin coming up.

"So do I. I need them, in fact. Here's my number. If you want to join us for a trail ride, give me a call."

Trail ride? "I beg your pardon?"

"My daughter, Merle, is horse crazy. I have enough land, and I'm sentimental enough to cave to her wheedling. We have a guest horse, if you're ever so inclined."

Holy unicorns, Trent Knightley had a daughter. That made so much sense, connected so many dots, Hannah nearly kicked herself.

"I took some lessons once." A therapeutic riding program Hannah had been enrolled in at the age of thirteen. She'd loved it, absolutely loved the horses, the scent of the barn, the feel of a furry pony on a cold day. Then the foster parents had decided to divorce, and with two days' notice, every kid in that home had been moved.

"I'll need your number as well, Stark. Your home number."

"Why?" Hannah hadn't even put the landline number on her employee forms.

"Because we live in western Maryland, where the hills are high and the cell towers are few, and some fine day I'll go home with a file you need, or you'll get snowed in, or I'll have a question for you when I'm stuck here in the office on a weekend. Because somebody should know how to get in touch with you if you ever no-call-no-show. Because I'm asking."

Because he was her boss, but he didn't say that, another little puzzle. Maybe being a dad had taught him not to pull rank unless the situation was dire.

"You can't give it out," Hannah said, because she would grant Trent this *request*. "Not to HR or the clients, not to nobody, not no how."

"*Wizard of Oz.*"

"I beg your pardon?"

"When they get to the Emerald City and ask to see the wizard and are refused because the wizard sees no one. Not nobody, not no how. I know my kid flicks. I won't give your number out to your own mother."

Hannah made a production out of jotting down her number on a sticky, giving herself time to recover from the thought that her mother was nobody.

"Here." She passed him the sticky. "I mean nobody."

Trent folded it and put it in his breast pocket. "My English comprehension is pretty good, Stark. I will literally memorize it and destroy the evidence. Now I'll bet you can't wait to see what your first docket looks like, so scoot. Debbie will have the particulars, and she'll show you how we schedule appointments and annotate the files."

"I am flattered, you know."

"I have faith in you, Hannah Stark, now get back to work."

She regarded him propped against the prow of his desk, smiling, arms crossed, every inch the corporate conqueror—almost.

Hannah crossed the room and snugged his tie back up to a tidy knot—a pattern of abstract horse heads in brown and silver. She finger combed his hair into order and kissed his cheek.

He had faith in her. Nobody save Hannah herself had had faith in her previously—and possibly Grace and Bronco. That Trenton Knightley might have wedged a foot into the very small circle of Hannah's supporters pleased her far more than it ought to, and didn't scare her nearly as much as it should.

"I have faith in you too, Trent Knightley." Trent Knightley, who did not have a wife but who did have a daughter. For whom he kept horses, and whom he took on trail rides.

Having indulged the shamelessly unprofessional urge to get her hands on that very same Trenton Knightly, Hannah assembled the December child support files and got back to work.

—⁓—

"I need your keen insight and unflinching honesty," Trent informed his older brother.

Mac remained staring at his monitor, his mouse moving in a small ballet on a pad that said: Old lawyers never die, they just lose their appeal.

"You want me to tell you you're an idiot, or should I be nice about it?"

"James is being nice." Unnerving, when James was nice. Trent sank onto Mac's black leather sofa, which was a mistake, because the sofa was a lot cushier than it looked.

"Does this have to do with that prick Matthews?"

"No. I asked the clerk's office in Wicks County to do a search, and Gerald was taking drug court cases as well."

"The drug cases often pay cash, hence his ability to afford a new Beemer on a first-year salary. You'd better be glad he's gone, Trent, or I will have to pound you."

"You'd be forced to give up your standing date with Merle if you put a mark on me, and she's the only female who breaks bread with you these days."

The mouse moved at the same efficient, controlled speed. "I sometimes share an apple with Kanga."

"A horse? I thought the rumors about James were bad." A lame horse at that, and one old enough to have secured a berth on Noah's ark.

"You're stalling, and I have an appellate brief to write."

"I am losing my balance over Hannah Stark." Trent heaved himself away from the leather cushions and went to stand at Mac's window, just as Mac did on his rare visits to Trent's office.

"You hardly know the woman."

"I have a child, Mac. I cannot afford to be stupid about women, and I admit I hardly know Hannah, but I like what I know in a way I thought I'd left behind when I divorced Sheila. I thought I was done being ass-over-teakettle about a woman."

Though with Hannah, that wasn't quite a fair description. She interested him, yes, but it wasn't strictly a mating interest.

"Sheila divorced *you*." Mac shoved away from his keyboard, revealing an appellate brief that looked suspiciously like a game of solitaire. "If it's any consolation, Hannah isn't Sheila."

No, Hannah was tenderhearted, honorable, sweet, and very private, while Sheila, once she'd decided to dump Trent, had been as sentimental, kind, and self-contained as a rabid wolverine.

"Have I ever thanked you for advising me to go for sole custody?" Trent asked.

Mac's screen saver came on, an endless progression of kittens, chicks, puppies, and the occasional perky-eared fox kit.

"Merle thanks me when she takes me out for pancakes the first Saturday of each month. Are you about to put moves on Hannah Stark?"

"I think I already have." She might have a put a few on Trent too. He kept that delectable detail to himself.

"I was afraid you'd bungle it, but I have to say I'm relieved."

So, in an odd way, was Trent. Also horny as hell. "Why?"

Mac rose and stretched. "Being Merle's dad brought you back from the complete oblivion That Woman left you in, but it isn't Merle's job to be your whole life."

How often had Trent cautioned his clients not to smother their kids as a way to weather a divorce? "Is that why you and James spring me every other Saturday?"

"Part of the reason, yes."

Trent had suspected that, had suspected doting uncle behavior wasn't all that motivated those precious, quiet Saturdays when he could ride by himself, get some reading done, shut the damned TV off for a change, or pick up a hard, fast game or two of racquetball.

"What's the rest of the reason?"

"You can't have her all to yourself," Mac said, fishing a

box of mint cookies out of a desk drawer, helping himself to three and extending the box to Trent. "The child will grow up warped, spouting family law of all the godforsaken wastes of talent. Was there something else you wanted?"

Trent took a cookie, because when was a cookie a bad idea? "You aren't being any help regarding Hannah."

"I explained the facts of life to you when you were seven," Mac said around a mouthful of cookie. "You offend the lady at your peril—but you disappoint her, and James and I will both beat your ass. We'll also beat your ass if you get us sued. If she's interested in you, and you're interested in her, then nobody will file any suits. Most of the Fortune 500s have no corporate policy on casual dating, so why should we? That's as much help as I'm going to be."

Two more cookies disappeared as Mac sat and started a fresh game of solitaire.

"She works for me, Mac."

"For now."

Trent still didn't leave, because the conversation wasn't at all what he'd envisioned. Mac was a consummate criminal attorney and dealt in black and white very well: guilty or not guilty, admissible or inadmissible, convicted or acquitted. An attraction to Hannah didn't feel wrong, but it felt like it should be wrong.

Or at least tricky. Very tricky.

"You are still here." On the screen, cards went flying in all directions, suggesting Mac had won his game. "You want Merle to grow up knowing what's what, don't you?"

"You are not winding up for your That Child Needs A Mother speech, are you?"

"All right, I won't, but what about my Trent Knightley Is Eaten Up With Loneliness speech? I know the difference between randy—which malady afflicts James sorely—and lonely, which is your cross to bear. You were so happy to shackle yourself to That Woman, and then so devastated when she dumped you, that you're incapable of seeing a good woman clearly. That constitutes bungling if you let it cost you a chance with Hannah."

"You're saying I'm afraid?" This from the guy who hadn't dated for nearly a decade?

"But not stupid." Mac leaned back in his chair and put his feet up, his posture an exact replica of James's. "Let's agree you're not stupid. You're attracted to a perfectly lovely, available female for the first time in years, and even if she's attracted to you right back, you have to look for ways to deny yourself the pleasure. You work with your brothers every day, Trent. You could work with a fiancée or a wife if you wanted badly enough to make it succeed. This is a family business, and we all chose to make it one."

"I couldn't work with a wife. Company policy."

"The policy is you can't be in a boss-subordinate relationship with a spouse, which means you'd have to marry the woman before the policy even kicks in. There is no policy on dating per se. As much time as you're wasting thinking this to death, Hannah will be running James's department before you get your priorities straight. Now get out. I have an appellate brief to write."

In spades, clubs, diamonds, and hearts. "You're coming by to get Merle this weekend?"

"Eight o'clock sharp, and we're picking out names for the rabbits Uncle James is getting her for Christmas."

"Rabbits, plural?"

"Rabbits are always plural. They have their poli-
cies too."

Chapter 7

HANNAH HADN'T SEEN TRENT FOR THE REST OF THE day. He'd been closeted with Lee, Ann, Debbie, then Gail Russo, and finally, he'd wandered off in the direction of the criminal department—Mac Knightley's bailiwick.

James was handsome—gorgeous, more like—and Mac would be the most stunning of the three, except his every gesture, silence, and expression managed to be quietly forbidding.

Trent was *attractive*. His subtle expressions were the most dangerous Hannah had seen in a long time: You Can Trust Me. Come A Little Closer. Lean On Me.

We're In This Together.

If other men had directed those messages to her, she'd been blind to them and glad of it. Raising Grace was challenge enough without the god-awful complications of a dating relationship, and Hannah had no intention of letting a man get close enough to start asking the wrong questions.

But close enough to share a little warmth? To kiss her cheek, touch her hair? Pass along a few sincere compliments? Hold her?

She'd certainly kissed *his* cheek.

Why not? The question plagued her as she drove home from Eliza's and the very last of the light vanished from the sky. She'd read her employee handbook from front to back. Hartman and Whitney had no policy on dating, though spouses were not permitted to directly report to each other, nor work in the same department.

A casual, discreet, exclusive arrangement would be nice. So nice.

Hannah wasn't in the market for marriage. That would require a great deal more trust and commitment than she was capable of. Marriage would require risking Grace's safety too, and that Hannah could not do.

But maybe with the right man—with Trent Knightley—under the right circumstances, Hannah could date a little. Flirt a little. Share a little comfort.

She let her imagination go one more step, far enough to admit that with Trent Knightley, that kind of comfort would be *lovely*.

"Mommy, why do some people have headlights?"

Grace occupied the passenger seat, her backpack stowed in the backseat. A glistening wet thumb went right back into Grace's maw when she finished asking her question.

"Thumb, Grace. Headlights are so you can see better at night."

"Are they like flashlights, then?"

"In a way," Hannah said, maneuvering her car down the single paved lane leading from Eliza's house.

"I think I might have to go to the eye doctor." Grace was almost whispering now.

Also puzzling her mother. "You went over the summer, and your eyes are fine."

"But I can't see 'em," Grace said, a catch in her voice.

"What can't you see?"

"The headlights. I know what they look like because George has them, but Miss Grayson—our school nurse—she said Larry had headlights and had to go home to get rid of them. But, Mommy, I couldn't see any headlights on Larry. He looked just the same to me."

Grace was crying now, clearly distraught over her terrible inability to see…what? George was Grace's name for the car, and fortunately "he" did have two functional headlights. Hannah had a spare set of bulbs in the glove compartment too, because the last thing she wanted was to be pulled over for a safety citation.

But headlights? On a child?

A foster care memory assailed her, of a new kid sitting on a stool in the middle of the foster mom's kitchen, an odd, disinfectant smell permeating the air.

"Grace, what Larry had are head lice, little bugs that think it's nice and warm and safe in your hair. They crawl around on your scalp, setting up housekeeping and making baby bugs. The whole business can get pretty itchy, but it's no big deal, really. You just use a special shampoo, and it makes the bugs go away."

Grace turned abruptly to look at her mother, her little girl face screwed up in a combination of distaste, fascination, and relief.

"Eeeeeww! Bugs in his hair—yuck! Poor Larry. So that's what Miss Grayson was looking for. She checked me too, but I guess those bugs don't like me, because I smell a lot better than old Larry."

"I'm sure the bugs think you smell much too nice to make a good bug home," Hannah said. "Did anyone else have to go home?"

If ADHD was the common cold of foster care, head lice were not far behind, and Hannah had assisted several of her foster moms with nitpicking, shampooing, bagging and disinfecting toys, and sterilizing bedding. The whole process was revolting, except she'd felt awful for the smaller children who'd suffered the infestations.

"Nobody else had to go home," Grace said. "Just Larry. If I had to go home with those headlights, would you come get me?"

Just making sure, again.

"Yes. No matter what, if you need me I will come and I will keep you safe and I will love you forever. No matter what."

―――∿∿∿―――

"I will hate Trenton Knightley forever, no matter what, and you may tell him I said so. I will also kill Gerald Matthews and anybody else who thinks I deserve to get stuck with this."

Ten o'clock Monday morning, and Hannah was ready to toss her license to practice law—firmly tied to a large rock—into the Potomac River. She'd spent the last hour once again reviewing the first December child support docket with Debbie, the paralegal formerly assigned to Gerald.

"How could Gerald meet with his clients only at court?" Hannah asked. "How can you represent somebody you've never met?"

Of the twenty cases, not a one was ready, and court was less than two weeks away.

"I'd meet the clients, Hannah," Debbie said, tossing back professionally streaked blond hair. "I'd run the child support guidelines, tell the client what the court's options were, tell them what Gerald looked like, and that would be that."

"What about what the clients want? Didn't Gerald even ask them that?"

"They want to have kids and not pay for it," Debbie said, opening another file and running a designer nail down the case log. "That's the impression I got."

She exhibited about as much compassion as some of the born charmers Hannah had had as foster care caseworkers. Real assets to the community.

"Look, Deb, whatever you did, it was enough so Gerald could breeze into the courtroom, open the file, and sound like he'd prepared the case from scratch. I saw him do it all morning on Friday. But clients have to have a chance to tell us what their priorities are, what their worst and best cases would be. We should be asking them what they think the judge needs to know to make a fair decision."

"Whatever you say."

Right. Fair was not a useful concept in most legal contexts. "If you think I'm about to make a first-class jackass out of myself, Deb, please tell me now."

Deb smiled, albeit sardonically. "If you sat in court all morning on Friday, then you know making a jackass of yourself for the cause is part of it."

By lunch time, using two phones, they had scheduled appointments for every client, this time all dads. Hannah took several of the case files back to her office to review in detail later that day, springing Deb for a lunch appointment that had been distracting her for the past half hour.

Gino? Matthews? Her nail stylist?

Hannah was just tearing into the first four-inch-thick folder when Trent appeared in her doorway.

"I'm here to see if you've quit. I haven't quit yet myself, in case you were wondering." He sounded half-serious.

"You're tempted?"

"I'd miss the Christmas party, and it's the only time we get to see Mac truly socialize. How was your morning?" He slid into a chair and crossed an ankle over one knee.

"Did you know Gerald never met with his clients except at court?"

"Sometimes the clients don't want to take time off from work to come in. Deb could get the information over the phone."

"Oh, no. They came in here, every one of them, and the hours are on Deb's time sheet to prove it, but she told them what Gerald looked like, and he met them when their cases were called."

"I don't like it," Trent said, frowning. "I like less that it became standard operating procedure in my own department and I hadn't noticed. I'll take another look at Gerald's time sheets, too, but you didn't hear me say that." He hated it, in fact, if the bleakness in his eyes was any indication.

"When was the last time you had a vacation?" Hannah asked.

Trent flipped his tie, an image Grace would have loved of a charging, winged unicorn done in silver on a blue background.

"Where did that question come from?"

"You look tired, and it's Monday morning." He looked in need of a hug and nap—or something.

"Late nights, looking over files when the moon is full, and I can't burn the candle at both ends quite like I could fifteen years ago."

"You're not old." Though Hannah had known seven-year-olds who'd been old.

"I'm over thirty, and sometimes that feels old. So who's on your docket?" He took up the nearest file and opened it. "Rene Fontaineau. I know this guy. Mac defended him on a subsequent DWI and some assault charges. He's a tough hombre, but he doesn't seem to have trouble attracting the ladies."

Hannah was reminded of Deputy Moreland's familiarity with Rory Cavanaugh. "The joys of small-town practice. I bet Mr. Fontaineau is short."

Trent looked up from the file. "He makes up for it with attitude, which can be useful."

Hannah stood and came around the desk to take the other guest chair. "Are you sure I'm the best person for this job?"

He tossed the file back on the desk. "Why do you ask?"

"Because these guys—ninety percent of them are guys—don't think enough of their own womenfolk to send along child support. Many of them aren't making the smallest effort. These are men who can't distinguish between their responsibilities as a dad and their hurt feelings or arrogance as jilted or disenchanted lovers, and they don't care if their own children are doing without because of it. How can I relate to them when I'm starting out as a member of the lesser, troublesome gender to begin with?"

How could she respect them, when they were every parent she'd ever seen go shuffling, kid-less and relieved to be so, out of foster care court?

"Mac has a whole sermon about this," Trent said. "It

boils down to this, Hannah: everybody in the helping
professions, lawyers included, has a tendency to take on
the characteristics of their clients, especially if they deal
with one particular kind of client steadily. You might
want to ask yourself if you're doing it already."

A hug and a nap, this was *not*. "I haven't even met
these guys, and if I had child support obligations, by
God, I would pay them."

"I'm sure you would, as would I, but you're very
close to deciding every guy in these files is a misogynist
and a deadbeat with a defeatist attitude."

Oh, hell. Not more cleverness from the boss.

"Defeatist," Hannah said. "As in, how can I possibly
do a good job with this docket?"

He smiled, more sympathetic than judgmental.

"You jumped to unflattering conclusions about your
clients just as they jump to conclusions about their
lawyers and the custodial parents: she doesn't use the
money for the kids; she left me to make me start giving
her money; she doesn't need the money as much as I
do. The suspicion and disrespect are commonplace, and
if you have that attitude toward your clients, at least be
aware of it."

"You don't pull any punches, Knightley." She wanted
to lean on him as he dispensed his brand of wisdom,
lean physically.

"I would not be this honest, this soon, if I didn't think
you would appreciate my point."

"Oh, that makes me feel loads better." Except it did,
that and the way he was looking at her so steadily. "What
about Rene Fontaineau?" Hannah tapped the file on her
desk. "Are you telling me I shouldn't be suspicious of

the information he gives me, if he even shows up for his appointment?"

"I am not suggesting you abandon all caution and take Rene to your favorite watering hole on Friday night. I'm telling you to make sure your caution is your own, and not the dysfunctional miasma of your client population."

Were there miasmas down the hall in the corporate law department? "Now you make me feel like I need a gas mask."

Trent said nothing, while Hannah wished he'd take her hand. Just that, just a hand to hold.

"What am I supposed to do differently, then?" she asked. "I don't want to antagonize these guys, and I don't want to end up like Margaret Jenson."

"Most people like and respect Margaret, as far as I know."

"I like and respect her as well," Hannah said. Whose hand did Margaret hold? "What I know of her, but if succeeding in this profession means I am constantly subjected to the petty slights of the Gerald Matthews and John Linkers and Elvin Gregorys of the world, and the only way I can cope is to pretend—as Margaret pretends—that her skin is so thick she doesn't feel it, then I don't really want to be a part of this profession. You guys play too rough for something that isn't a game."

Though the student loan collections folks could play pretty rough too.

Another silence, and Trent's expression mirrored Grace's when Hannah threatened to serve boiled spinach for dinner.

"I can dish it out," he said. "I suppose that means

I have to take it, but I want you to be honest with me, always, and that was honest. Margaret can be casual, about some things. We all can."

"Sorry." Hannah felt as if she'd disappointed him, or shown him something disappointing. "Seems to me if you don't treat people generally in a condescending, insulting manner, then why should your profession make it acceptable to treat them that way?"

"A fair question."

"You won't give me the lecture about toughening up?" Hannah tried a small smile, but Trent wasn't smiling back.

"I don't want you to toughen up," he said, and she had the sense he meant it. "Just because you're good at something, that doesn't necessarily equate with it being good for you."

"You speak from experience?"

"I was a good law clerk," he said, his expression bleak. "It about gutted me. I was a good husband too."

"Isn't this a cheery topic?" James Knightley strolled in, exuding sex appeal and something else—something restless and unlawyerly. "Hannah doesn't have to give back the signing bonus if you put her in a clinical depression first, Trent. I know you family law types go in for soap opera, but Hannah isn't like you. Come, Hannah, my love. I'm taking you away from all this."

He drew her to her feet and kept his hand in hers, sheer silliness on his part.

"Trent will work you right through your lunch hour, and I'm here on my white horse to prevent such a tragedy. You want us to bring you back anything, Trent?"

"You're being invited to lunch, Hannah," Trent said, rising. "You may decline, but your knight in Savile Row armor will only pester you that much more intensely, until Mac and I have to beat him away for you."

"I'm to go quietly to my fate?"

"She catches on quickly," James said, putting Hannah's hand on his arm as if they were at some cotillion. "Must be destined for the corporate law. Ta, Trent. Don't work too late on an empty stomach."

Hannah just had time to grab her purse and coat, and James had her out the door.

Submitting to her fate.

It was an interesting fate. James took her to the same restaurant Trent had, but he got them a quiet booth in the back and slid in beside her on the seat.

Right beside her.

And where Trent had a kind of warmth to him, James gave off heat, flirtatious, naughty-man, not-quite-pandering heat. More silliness.

He stole from her plate, and he tried to feed her a bite off his fork, but she took the fork from his hand and set it back on his plate. He ordered them dessert with two spoons, as if women were supposed to prefer sharing with him to having both halves of a chocolate mousse.

"That's enough, James."

He was James to her after a meal like that.

"Enough?"

"You've been flirting your eyelashes off, and fine eyelashes they are too, but we're not sharing a damned dessert."

He sat back. "That's your final word? I didn't get the impression you were seeing anybody, Hannah, and I know how to treat a lady." He reached for her hand and rubbed his thumb across her knuckles. "I don't kiss and tell. Ever."

For all his innuendo, she knew exactly what his comments could turn into. Maybe not this very day, but soon, when he'd decided he'd had enough of enjoying the chase: a detour on the way back to the office, probably to his place, because James Knightley wasn't a hotel room kinda guy, and maybe a few sheepish grins from Hannah's coworkers when she rolled into work after a three-and-a-half-hour lunch, but otherwise, there wouldn't be a ripple on the pond.

He'd see to it.

"James Knightley, you are an idiot."

She should have been offended, but for all he was doing a great imitation of the opening moves to an irresistible fling—or a sexual harassment lawsuit—she had the sense it was just that, an imitation.

"I'm a good-looking, talented idiot who could show you a very good time."

"You're going to be my boss."

"Not for six months, and Hartman is a family firm, Hannah. We're used to dealing with overlapping roles on staff. We've never been sued by an employee, and we never will be."

"Even with your cruising the new hires so shamelessly?"

The flirtatious light in his blue, blue eyes died, and Hannah caught a glimpse of ruthlessness.

"For your information," James said, "my actions are far more circumspect than my reputation suggests. Trent and Mac are a couple of monks, and it amuses them to play up my every peccadillo and flirtation. Then too, in the legal community, being a cross on my fuselage seems to have acquired a certain cachet I did nothing to promote."

"Let me see if I know the next verse. You haven't been with anybody for months, right? Who knows where things might lead, after all? You're very attracted to me."

He frowned and looked very much like his oldest brother.

"Things would lead nowhere. All I offer is a diversion. I don't flirt under false pretenses."

The real James Knightley had just joined the discussion.

"I don't flirt with *you* under any pretenses at all. You will be an interesting boss to watch, James, but I won't be sharing your dessert spoon."

Hannah took a bite of mousse and slid her spoon very slowly out of her mouth.

He smiled at her, really truly smiled, and for the first time since they'd sat down, Hannah was dazzled.

"You're OK, Stark," he said, digging in with his own spoon. "You want me to order you another one of those?"

"May I get it to go?"

"Sweetie, you can have whatever you want."

She'd meant the second mousse for Trent, but he was behind a closed door, getting ready for a two-day trial that kept him out of the office on Tuesday and Wednesday. James poked his head into Hannah's office a couple of times, asking her if she needed anything and putting as much innuendo into the question as possible.

Sweet *and* silly. Hannah looked forward to working for him, because whatever test she'd passed at lunch, he'd passed a test with her too.

She moved through her appointments, developed a position on each case, and started trading calls with Margaret Jenson to prepare for the next docket. Anxiety became a constant gnawing ache low in her gut, and Hannah was reminded of the many, many times she'd felt the same thing in a new foster home, a new school, a new minimum-wage student job.

Beginnings were hard for her. She knew that, and she knew why: beginnings invariably preceded unhappy endings.

—◦◦◦—

Trent stood in the doorway to his own office, his enormous courthouse briefcase at his feet, his coat slung over his shoulder while Hannah Stark shelved reference books, each going back to its exact, proper location. She handled every tome as if merely touching a bound volume of Maryland law was a privilege.

The way he'd like to handle her.

Maybe he'd sighed a little too loudly.

"How long have you been standing there?" She peered at *Courts and Judicial Proceedings* as he moved into the room and closed the door.

"Long enough to know you borrowed half my library."

"Just the child support references, and I wanted to check the most recent decisions from Annapolis. You don't look so good, Trent Knightley."

She put the book away and turned to lean against his desk as he often did. She was welcome to the damned desk, which sported half a ream of pink message notes. Trent tossed his coat in the direction of the coat stand and plunked his tired ass down in a guest chair.

"My guy won," he said, because small talk and even boss talk was beyond him. "Sole physical custody, use and possession of the family home, child support, and mortgage assistance from Mom. He won."

"Why aren't you doing the end zone dance?"

Why did he *never* do the end zone dance? "Judge Merriman is terrific at talking to kids. She keeps crayons and stuffed animals in her office, gets down on the floor with the little ones so they can make up stories with her. Even she couldn't get anything out of these two. Mom and Dad are good people, they love their kids, they simply can't both live with them anymore."

"Sometimes, every available option stinks." Hannah pushed his hair back over his ear, her touch as comforting as her words.

Trent hated wearing a tie, and as soon as he'd left the courthouse, he'd taken off the one Merle had picked out for him that morning. "I'm not exactly ready for inspection."

"The grooming police have the day off. You're in your own office, and it's only me."

A sign of trust, that Hannah would promote herself to "only me" status so soon. Trent used a foot to shove his briefcase away.

"My guy had the decency to leave the kids with the mom for this weekend, and the judge made Mom and Dad write down phone numbers for the children and exchange them while the kids looked on, all the micro-ritual bullshit."

Because it was bullshit. Band-Aids concocted by adults to deal with arterial bleeding from the hearts of children.

Hannah scooted back onto the desk and toed off one shoe. "You're sad for the kids, the parents, and maybe even the judge."

Ouch. Merle could coldcock him with pronouncements like that.

"I'm sad, tired, and ready for the weekend." He leaned forward so his crown was against Hannah's midriff. He closed his eyes and felt the weight of a very long, difficult two days.

Maybe mashing on his new hire would get him sued; maybe his radar had malfunctioned completely when it suggested she wouldn't be offended. Still, Trent did not move, but remained leaning against her.

Hannah's hands settled on his hair, her touch tentative. "It's a wonder you don't have one hell of headache."

She slid her fingers over his scalp and massaged the base of his neck. A glorious warmth spread from his nape to his shoulders and down into his body, and he was reluctant to breathe lest he give her an excuse to stop.

"That feels—I might fall asleep right where I'm sitting." Oh, the dreams he could dream, with Hannah easing away all of the day's stress and exhaustion.

Her touch shifted, to a slow, rhythmic stroke over his hair. "You have such beautiful hair."

"I used to have longer hair, but it's tidier this way, and when you're a parent, you have to set the kind of example you want your children to follow." Trent was thinking of shifting in closer, or nuzzling her belly or pulling her into his lap, for God's sake, when her hands went still then disappeared.

"I've been meaning to ask you about that. You're a dad."

A carefully neutral statement, which told him his next words mattered. Trent sat up, and abruptly, the lovely moment faded.

"Merle is seven, or almost eight as she constantly reminds me."

A smart woman knew that if she had to compete with a child for a guy's attention, the relationship would proceed slowly, if at all.

Too bad he wasn't interested in being anybody's booty call.

"How much do you see her?"

"Have a seat." Trent patted the chair beside him. "I will regale you with the details of my parental privileges. I am Merle's sole custodian, and she hasn't seen her mother for three years, except for the occasional visit by webcam."

Hannah stayed right where she was and crossed her legs. "Three years?"

"You'll hear the details around the water cooler at some point. I was approached by members of the judicial nominating committee, and I would have been one of the youngest sitting judges in the history of the state. My career seemed set. I was bound to work my way into the appellate ranks, the state supreme court, even a federal judgeship was possible if I wrote smart opinions and stayed out of trouble."

"There's a but coming."

Better that she hear it from him. "I thought the big career was what Sheila wanted for me. We met in law school, worked together on the law review. She was pretty, smart, poised, and ambitious. I was smitten."

Hannah nudged his briefcase with her stockinged toe. "Old-fashioned word, smitten."

"Knightleys are essentially old-fashioned men, James's reputation notwithstanding."

"We will talk about your baby brother later." She didn't seem mad, but neither was she intrigued with James. *Neener-neener, baby brother.*

"I am such an old-fashioned man that when my wife started having an affair, I told myself it would pass. We had a child together, one whom I thought we both loved to distraction."

"Then you were approached about a judgeship?"

She made it sound as if an F-5 tornado had swept into his life, which, in essence, it had. Enduring a divorce had been invaluable for understanding what domestic relations clients went through—also stinking miserable.

"Sheila was all for the judgeship. I realize now she thought it would enhance her own shot at the bench, but at the time, I loved my wife and was determined to keep her married to me."

Even then, though, he'd known he wasn't *in love* with Sheila.

Hannah's big toe flipped the handle of his briefcase over, then back—dexterous toes. "I can see the deter-mined part, and yet, she's not your wife now."

"James and Mac had hatched the idea of buying this firm, but I declined. They probably knew exactly what was afoot long before I did, but they said nothing. All I could think was I'd lose Merle if Sheila and I divorced. I'd become one of those pathetic every-other-weekend dads whose kids treat him like a glorified au pair."

Hannah was frowning, and he could see her lawyer's mind putting together the facts of the Knightley case.

"So you doubled down on the parenting? Wrapped

yourself around the kid, took the day care drop-off and pick-up duty, handled the pediatrician visits, and tried to make it so Sheila had all the mom creds and none of the work? All while you're trying to keep up with a busy practice?"

"The cases don't stop coming because somebody got knocked up."

"Don't use that term," Hannah snapped, scooting back onto his desk. "You and Sheila conceived a child you both had every intention of loving. That isn't knocking up your wife."

"To Sheila, it was exactly that, and she told me so before it was all over. She was more ambitious than I knew and thought the image of me as a family man would make me easier to promote. It didn't hurt her appearances either."

Hannah's stocking-clad foot started swinging. "So what happened? She fell out of love with you?"

"She had never been in love with me." The unkindest cut in a protracted duel of attrition. Most spouses enjoyed at least a few years of infatuation, but from the start, Sheila had been playing him.

"In hindsight," Hannah said, "it can often seem as if we never—"

In hindsight, the entire marriage was all pretty sad, except Trent had Merle, and that was wonderful.

"Sheila is gay," he said. "Or at least bisexual. When I was stuck in the office late at night, trying to prepare for the next day's docket, she stashed Merle with the nanny and hung out online. She said she was dying in the marriage and didn't care what it cost her to get out of it. Told me I was never going to make an appellate judge, my brothers were troglodytes, and—I feel no compunction to forgive her for this—told me she had never wanted a baby."

"Geezopete, that's just plain mean. Merle was how old?"

"Toddling when the whole thing began. Sheila had me served with divorce papers between cases at the courthouse."

"Charming."

Pathetic. Or as Hannah had put it, just plain mean. "She moved out with Merle, and I about lost my mind. I wasn't humiliated, exactly, though that was part of it. I was devastated, shot right off my horse. I love my daughter, Hannah. I hadn't realized how much and how much she's a part of me. And as for her mother, I did not see the real Sheila."

Hannah's second shoe came off, landing on the first. "The real Sheila sounds like everything that ever gave lawyers, women, or exes a bad name."

"Mac and James sat me down one day as the litigation was dragging on and told me they didn't want to see their niece raised by a ruthless, manipulative barracuda when the girl had a perfectly competent and loving dad ready, willing, and able to step up. They pooled their resources and offered to lend me the money to buy Sheila out."

"They love you."

"They love me, and they love Merle, and they are not guys you want to mess with."

"My favorite kind of guy. Sheila took the money?"

"I didn't think her pride would allow it. I thought she'd want the cachet of having a little girl to raise, want the pleasures of parenthood while she set down roots somewhere else."

"Guessed wrong again?"

Yes, he had, thank a merciful God. "She lives in Sydney, which suits me fine. I offered the cash, thinking it was one of Mac's crazier strategies. No mother worth the name would turn her back on her child for money. I made the terms draconian, probably trying to sabotage the deal so Merle wouldn't lose her mother."

"What do you consider draconian?"

Trent considered this conversation encouraging, because Hannah's questions were insightful, and she had the knack of offering understanding without turning him, Merle, or Sheila into a victim.

"I am Merle's sole legal and physical custodian, and Sheila's visitation is subject to my reasonable convenience."

"You're not a jerk."

"Sheila hasn't asked for any visitation."

Hannah stared at the plain black pumps laying side by side near his left shoe. "You did the right thing, Trent. Better to be with one loving parent than forced to shuttle between that and a bewildering alternative."

"There are scholarly articles to that effect, but there's just as much literature to the contrary, saying better to know a bad parent than to have no second parent at all. When Sheila sets up a web visit, I never deny her."

Her foot twitched. "You know it's stupid to blame yourself?"

"When you have the brothers I do, you hear how stupid on a regular basis." God love 'em both.

"As if lecturing them gets anywhere?"

"Don't say that to Mac."

"He lectures because his mind works that way," she said. "He thinks in opening and closing arguments and cross- and direct examinations. Will your brothers join you for Thanksgiving?"

To shift the topic to something as mundane as weekend plans was a relief, though Trent was also relieved to have his past on the table between them. A lot of women thought a man with custody of his child was a great bet, until they tried to fit themselves into his life between the kid and his career.

"The uncles, as Merle calls them, make her a part of their every holiday. They each take her out to breakfast one Saturday a month so I get a little time to myself, and they regularly kidnap her at odd moments when they think I'm getting overwhelmed."

"Or when their own lives feel a little too empty and meaningless?"

Damn, Hannah was quick. "If I said that to their faces—"

"Right, they'd beat you up. You're a very violent family, you Knightleys."

"Utter barbarians." Trent picked up her left shoe, took her foot in his hand, and slipped her pump back on over her sheer stockings. When she didn't protest, he put the second one on as well.

They remained in that posture, him sitting before her, her perched on the desk, and abruptly, Trent forgot the name of the client whose case he'd won not an hour earlier. He'd handled Hannah's *foot*.

And she'd let him.

She stood, and Trent did as well, mentally flailing

for something innocuous to stuff into a silence that had all too many possibilities. "What are your plans for the weekend, Hannah?"

He should have called her Stark.

She gave his rhodie a drink from the pitcher on the credenza. "Probably a lot like yours. Some cleaning and cooking, a dead bird, a few hungry people, the cats circling in relentless hope of scraps."

Was that a scold or a tease or a recitation of fact? "I wish you could join us. Judge Halverston will be there."

"Merle will have you gentlemen all to herself?"

"Debbie is bringing her five-year-old, and there'll be a few more to round out the numbers."

"You invite children so Merle won't feel so isolated. That's smart."

"It's chaos," he said, pleased Hannah could grasp parental strategy. James and Mac weren't that quick on the uptake when it came to managing a kid.

Hannah put the pitcher back on its tray and moved toward the door. "You can still smile. You're looking forward to a weekend with family, and all's right with the world. I'll just wish you a happy Thanks—"

"Hannah?"

She stopped at the door but didn't turn, which allowed Trent to come up behind her and slide his arms around her waist. She simply stood in his embrace as if waiting for him to realize he'd hugged her by accident. He turned her by the shoulders.

"I like talking to you," he said, closing his arms around her. He also liked her grass-and-flowers scent, a fragrance bearing a promise of both spring and clean, sweet woman.

"I haven't held a lady in my arms in forever," he said, though the sorry truth was he hadn't wanted to hold a woman in his arms. "I forget how grand and simple a pleasure it can be."

She dropped her forehead to his shoulder, and he could feel her blushing, though she wasn't pulling away. She slipped her arms around his waist, and God in heaven, was the fit ever sweet.

"I was attracted to you before you listened to my tale, Hannah." Lest she think this was some sort of platonic office-buddy hug.

A nod, and no maybe about it, she burrowed closer.

"You haven't been held in a while either, have you?"

She shook her head, and something light and lovely coursed through Trent, part arousal but also hope and warmth and peace. Still, Hannah was female, so he asked the obligatory question.

"Do we need to talk about this, Hannah?"

A big sigh, and she took one step away. "I need to think about it. You're a lovely man, but I've never done an office—an office whatever. I'm not at all sure... I'm just not sure."

"Fair enough." He should probably think too, *later*. "You need to know one thing, though: I am not after an office fling. If we decide to do something about what I hope is a mutual attraction, then sooner or later, I'll be looking for a relationship, Hannah. I'm too old, too much a dad, and too old-fashioned to pretend I'm nineteen anymore."

Trent was looking for a relationship that very instant, which would probably surprise Hannah as much as it surprised him. While he didn't begrudge her time to think, to consider her preferences and terms, he was also too much a strategist not to give her something to think *about*.

He closed the distance between them, glad somebody had had the sense to shut the damned door.

Chapter 8

"WHEN YOU'RE CONSIDERING THE EVIDENCE, HANNAH Stark, consider this." Trent leaned in and brushed a kiss to her cheek—a warning shot. She stood her ground, so he did it again. Her breath hitched, and she seemed to have developed a fascination with the rhododendron.

For a procession of instants, Trent savored sensations he hadn't felt in years. Arousal and anticipation, for this was a woman he could desire. Gratitude, that he was still capable of a healthy response to a willing woman, and determination.

Hannah hadn't been kissed in a while, he'd bet his membership in the Maryland Bar Association on that, and he wanted Brahms, Rachmaninoff, and chocolate mousse for her, not paintball and farm team baseball.

He wrapped one arm around her shoulders and anchored the second low on her back. Everything lined up wonderfully, and Hannah wasn't shy about holding onto him, either. She slid her arm under his coat and used her free hand to cup his jaw.

"Bristly," she said. "I like it."

He liked *her*, and he liked kissing her. She let a guy lead, let him start with a soft press of mouths, a slide and tease of lips, another press. She scooted closer, and Trent thought of Mac's big cushy couch and the elegant arch of Hannah's foot.

The longer they kissed, the more closely he held her,

until tongues got involved—two of them—and sighs and moans—lots of those—and an inevitable heating of Trent's blood.

"I want to see you with your hair down," he whispered. He wanted to screw her on the desk too, or a part of him was advocating for that plan.

She eased back but kept her arms around him. "I need to think. You're too good at this."

"I'll get better, though it will take some practice." A lot of practice, but when Hannah said she needed to think, what she meant was she needed privacy to do it. James's rule of thumb came to mind, about treating the ladies as he'd want Merle to be treated. "May I walk you to your car?"

"You made it a question."

Apparently the right question, because Hannah allowed it, and when Trent held her coat for her and held the doors and carried her briefcase, she allowed that too. Though it about killed him, when they reached her car, he closed the door for her without kissing her again and without standing around in the parking lot like a half-frozen, love-struck idiot for more than a solid minute.

~~~

James stood beside Mac at the window in Mac's office, watching the head of the domestic relations department escort his newest associate to her car.

"Why isn't that idiot sneaking in a little kiss here and there?" James asked. "He's not even touching her. Didn't offer his arm, hasn't got his hand on her back."

"Some of us appreciate a more subtle approach," Mac said. "Some of us with a little discretion and tact."

"I about sat her in my lap at lunch earlier this week. She said I was flirting my eyelashes off, and laughed at me."

"Laughed?" By a little blue Prius, Trent handed Hannah her briefcase. "You have my condolences, James. You must be losing your touch. We depend on you to carry the Knightley standard into the bedrooms of western Maryland, but it looks as if at long last—well, one hopes it's *long* last—"

"Shut up." James smacked Mac's shoulder for good measure. "It's just as long and lasting as it ever was, but Hannah Stark has been inoculated against my devastating charms by the only thing that has ever protected a female from falling for me."

"Common sense?" Mac drawled. "A functioning brain? A sense of humor? An accurately calibrated *ruler*?"

"She's fallen for him," James said, gesturing toward the parking lot. "We have reason to hope, Mac. You'd better give him your don't-fuck-it-up speech."

"I already have."

"He wasn't listening."

"Yes, James, I think he was. I think he was listening as well as he ever has."

"Then again"—James's expression became thoughtful—"if he breaks her heart, I can always console her, or you could."

"You've succeeded in literally screwing your brains out if you think I'd lay a hand on that woman."

"I haven't yet—literally screwed my brains out, that is—but a guy needs a worthy goal."

—∿—

"But, Eliza, he doesn't want just a fling."

Hannah sat on a bar stool in Eliza's kitchen while Eliza poured boiling water off a big pot of macaroni, and in the next room Henry and Grace played a game of slapjack that consisted mostly of arguing and smacking each other's hands.

"He told you he doesn't want just a fling?" Eliza asked as she took off her kitchen mitts.

"In those exact words."

"So where's the problem? You like this guy or you wouldn't have let him lay a hand on you."

Hannah didn't merely like Trenton Knightley, she respected him, and she liked *kissing* him. "How do you know I let him lay his hands on me?"

Eliza mixed two piles of grated cheese into the pasta with a big wooden spoon, while Henry bellowed that the winner did so have to clean up all messes.

"Trenton Knightly has you flustered," Eliza said while the kitchen filled with the scent of cheesy domesticity. "All those guys in law school couldn't get you to give them the time of day, the associates and even the partners at the temp jobs couldn't get you to go out to lunch. You've been to lunch with Mr. Domestic Relations, Esq., and you haven't known him a month. You must trust him in some regard, or he'd get the same polite brush-off you gave all those other legal beagles."

"They *were* beagles too, right down to the pawing and sniffing."

"This Trent guy, you see him differently."

Hannah saw him in her dreams. "That smells good."

"You're welcome to stay. Who wouldn't want to watch Adam smear macaroni in his hair while Henry laughs so hard he snorks at the table?"

"I think I'll pass." Then too, Hannah wanted to go home, where she'd have the peace and quiet she needed to think—and recall every detail of a kiss that had left her wanting to take off more than her shoes or Trent's tie.

"Maybe I should send some macaroni home with you, and I'll even throw in Henry for no extra charge." Eliza sprinkled Italian spices on the macaroni and cheese, oregano and garlic joining the kitchen fragrances.

"Trent's a dad, Eliza," Hannah admitted softly, forlornly, while Eliza dusted her hands over the pasta.

"A custodial dad?"

The worst kind, a loving, conscientious custodial dad. "His daughter is almost the same age as Grace, and when he talks about her, you'd think he was describing—I don't know. I get the sense she's what keeps all three brothers together as a family somehow."

"Children do that. They connect us."

"That's why I can't indulge in any romantic nonsense with Trent Knightley. What if he thinks all dads should have access to their children? What if he thinks Grace's dad should have regular unsupervised visits? What if Grace gets attached to Trent, only to have Trent start drawing lines in the sand?"

Eliza set the bowl of macaroni on the dining table and faced Hannah, hands on hips.

"We aren't in foster care anymore, Toto. Miss Wallingford, Esq., isn't going to lumber into the courtroom and blather your private business to the world.

You can tell Trent any damned thing you want about Grace's dad, or draw your own line in the sand and tell him that topic is off-limits. If he's as interested as I think he is, he won't let it come between you."

The very mention of the Miss Wallingford, attorney for the Douglas County DSS, made Hannah wince.

"But, Eliza, what sort of relationship is built on lies and secrets?"

"Privacy is not lies and secrets. You want some of this to take home?"

"No thanks. Well, maybe a little." Geeves would thank her. "I don't think Trent would stand for anything less than the truth. He's that kind of man."

"An honest man who's a loving father and happily employed in a worthwhile career. What is so blessedly wonderful about chronic loneliness that you'd pass him up without even a look, Hannah?"

Eliza cut off the possibility of a reply—thank heavens—by hollering for Henry to come wash his hands. That mercy meant Hannah wrestled with the answer to Eliza's question for all of the next four days.

―∾∾―

Gerald let himself into Joan Smithson's apartment with the key she'd given him, even though she'd asked him to wait outside for her to come home.

If she hadn't wanted him coming and going as he pleased, she shouldn't have given him a key. For a street-smart girl, Joan Smithson could be blindingly naive.

She was like this apartment: shopworn, comfortable, and possessed of odd domestic touches. A spray of dried flowers in an old glass bottle, a dream catcher hanging from the kitchen light, a picture of her dumb-as-a-box-of-rocks nephew on the refrigerator.

"You were supposed to wait in the car," Joan said, pitching her keys into a ceramic bowl on a stand near the front door. She was bottle blond, probably five-foot-one in her bare feet, and she liked to dress loud and tight. "I specifically asked you to wait outside, Gerald."

"Did you bring the stuff?"

She smiled at him, the smile of a forgiving woman who'd learned too early in life to keep her expectations low.

"Here's your toot, but don't do it too fast." She held up a tiny white paper envelope. "I need some attention too."

Stupid bitch, though useful, in a well-worn way. Joan wasn't thirty, and she liked to party. Besides, they all looked the same in the dark, she could suck the chrome off a ball hitch, and she wasn't stingy with the goodies.

Where she got the drugs, or how she was able to afford them, was none of Gerald's business. Their liaison had begun when she'd retained him to defend her for a DUI. It was her first offense, and of all people, Joan Smithson had a perfect driving record.

In her peculiar ignorance of criminal process, Joan hadn't realized a first offender would be offered some sort of break based on her spotless record. She'd been desperate to ensure she was getting the best representation money—or any other inducement—could buy. He'd caught her at a point where money was tight, and she'd been pleased as hell to trade in those other inducements.

Even Gerald was amazed that Joan could traffic in all manner of vice and never run afoul of the law. She probably whored as often as she dealt, and whored for her drugs, but she had no arrests, no convictions, no charges, nothing.

She had her rules, and they pretty much assured she wouldn't get caught: never buy, sell, or hustle a stranger; never use or transact business in a public place; never transact more than you can use; and always deal in cash at the time of sale.

Gerald snatched the drugs from Joan, noting that her bright-red nail polish had chipped on two fingers.

Like Joan herself. Painted, but not carefully enough to hide the wear. Still, Joan had a fun-loving sort of enthusiasm about her, and she liked to screw.

A fine quality in a woman. He tucked the snowsuit into the pocket of his jeans, swatted Joan's tight little butt, and gave her a solid shove toward the bedroom.

—⁓—

"Dad, am I a bastard?"

Trent paused in the middle of mucking Bishop's stall, wondering if he'd heard correctly. Merle was in the next stall over with Pasha, her very own horse, grooming the old duffer within an inch of his lazy life.

"What makes you ask that?"

"Joey Hinlicky said Grace is a bastard, and Grace told him he better not call her that or she'd tell Mrs. Corner, but then Grace told me Joey was right, and Grace really is a bastard. She's not supposed to make a big deal over it, because some people aren't very nice about it."

Merle paused to scratch her horse's neck.

"What did Joey mean when he used the word?" Trent asked.

"Grace told me what it means. It means her mom got a baby but she didn't get married. You have me and you're not married anymore, so I just wondered. Grace said she doesn't mind being a bastard because she gets her mom all to herself."

Grace? Merle never mentioned friends at school by name. Trent wasn't sure she even had friends among her classmates.

"Come sit beside me minute, Merle. We need to have a talk."

He waited for her to obey—Merle was nothing if not obedient—and collected his thoughts. Closing arguments were nothing compared to the talks a dad had with his kid.

Merle joined him on the hay bale and budged up to his side in a manner an older daughter would disdain.

"The word bastard used to mean somebody whose parents weren't married when the child was born," Trent said. "A long, long time ago, this was serious because it meant you had a real hard time inheriting anything from your dad if your mom wasn't ever married to him. Now, you can inherit from anybody who wants to leave you something, so being this kind of bastard is no big deal."

Merle twirled the end of her dark braid over her finger, clearly marshaling her patience for dear old Dad.

"Nowadays," Trent went on, "people use the word bastard to mean somebody nobody respects, like people used to not respect a child who couldn't inherit from a dad. If somebody calls me a bastard now, it's like saying I'm a real bear, or a…"

"A horse's ass?" Merle put in helpfully. "Or a son of a bitch? A butthead?"

Trent grabbed her around the middle and tickled her until she was giggling heartily.

"Yes, twerp, and a bastard is like all those other names you aren't supposed to hear me use. It's a nasty thing to call somebody, and Joey was being mean if he called your friend Grace a bastard."

Merle wrinkled her nose. "Joey is a boy. Can I finish grooming Pasha now?"

"In a minute. I have a question for you: Did Joey mean Grace was a nasty person, or did he mean Grace's mom and dad never married?"

Merle tied a knot in her braid. "Why does it matter?"

"Because, if Grace really doesn't have a dad of her own, she might be able to ask you questions about having a dad. If she's that kind of bastard, you have something she doesn't."

Merle untied the knot. "Grace is really nice. Everybody likes her because she's so nice, even the boys, but Grace said her mom and dad never married, so it's that kind. She said her dad is a very handsome man, but she's never seen him. I told her you were handsome too." She drew her braid across her top lip. "Are we done yet?"

"Yes, but I bet you have more than one thing Grace doesn't have, even if he's a little old and slow."

"You're not that old," Merle said, hopping down.

Ouch. "I meant Pasha. Does Grace like to ride?"

Merle's smile became mysterious. "I promised Grace I wouldn't tell. It's club stuff, Dad. You wouldn't understand."

Club stuff? Pony Club? Or some second-grade precursor to a gang?

Trent had clearly exhausted Merle's tolerance for the subject of Miss Grace the Bastard, so he took himself back into the house and got ready to serve the largest midday meal of the year.

Wondering all the while what secrets his daughter was having such a good time keeping from her only custodial parent.

———

"Mom?" Grace stood beside her mother at the kitchen sink, drying the Thanksgiving dinner dishes, or swiping at them with a damp towel before arranging them in stacks on the counter.

"Yes?"

"Why don't we ever have cousins and uncles and grandmas over for a big dinner? Or we could go to their house, like 'over the river and through the woods'?"

"We don't have those folks to visit us, Grace, because we're not related to anybody. I was an only child, as far as I know, and my parents died in a car accident."

"I know," Grace chirped wistfully. "You were only three years old, and they 'dopted you, and your mom and dad died, and you can't really remember them but you think the smell of lilacs reminds you of your mom. You own this house partly because of all the lilacs in the yard."

"I make payments on this house." Oral tradition was alive and well in the Stark family, however small that family was.

"I like lilacs too, Mom. Is that your favorite flower?"

Hannah pulled the stopper from the drain. She was about to list all her favorites when the phone rang.

"You think up your favorite while I get the phone."

Telemarketers wouldn't call on a holiday, would they? And yet the phone rang so rarely, who else could it be?

"Hannah Stark."

"How'd your turkey day go? This is Trent."

Trenton Knightley? Hannah was abruptly catapulted back to adolescence, when the phone might ring for every other girl in the house, but never, ever for her.

"This is a nice surprise," she managed. "We're finishing up in the kitchen and looking forward to turkey pancakes for breakfast tomorrow." Across the kitchen, Grace made a yuck face, proof positive she was eavesdropping.

Of course.

"I require my guests to take home leftovers so we're spared tryptophan overdose. Do you have a few minutes, Hannah, or did I call at an awkward time?"

"I'm almost done cleaning up, the cats are in a turkey-induced coma and it's a good time to chat a bit. Did you cook for a gang?"

"For enough people that we had to clean as much as we cooked. Merle has dragged Judge Halverston out for the ritual visit to the barn, so I'm stealing a little peace and quiet in the kitchen."

What to say? This conversation was like dancing without music. It took focus and didn't feel smooth. "Merle enjoys having company?"

"She does," he said, sounding a little perplexed. "She's very shy, very serious, but now that you mention it, she does seem to light up when we have people over. She was particularly pleased when Tommie got caught sucking the pimentos out of the olives and putting the olives back in the dish."

"How old is Tommie?"

"Five. I introduced you to his mom when we went out to lunch. Her boyfriend is a cop who had to work, so we got the honor of hosting Tommie the Terror. He gets on well with both of my brothers."

And with Trent. Hannah was speaking to a man who would have liked to have a son. Sons, daughters, more children of either stripe.

"You love that pimento-sucking terror," Hannah said, certain it was true.

Cue seventh awkward micro-pause.

"Tommie laughs a lot. He leaps into life, he doesn't hang back and sort through a cost-benefit analysis. In other words, he is the exact opposite of my very dear daughter. Sometimes, I wish Merle would bust a gut laughing, bellow at the top of her lungs, have a complete meltdown, anything spontaneous and passionate. But she's so disciplined."

While Grace's sole coping mechanism seemed to be her imagination. "Something wrong with being disciplined?"

"What? You were serious as a kid and you turned out all right? I won't argue that, if you say so."

This pause was a tad less strained.

"For as long as I can remember, I've wanted to be on top of my game," Hannah said. "I could not stand the sense of my world being out of control, and I loathed the humiliation of failure. That fearfulness has abated as I've withstood a few of life's dings and dents, but I still have to work hard not to see every confrontation as a threat, and every failure as a comment on my value as a person."

Something about the anonymity of talking on the phone—the privacy of it—permitted the near occasion of confidences, apparently.

Though enough was enough. "You had both your brothers over too?"

"Merle insists, and they enjoy it. Did you cook a big bird?"

"Big enough, but the size of the mess can vary independently from the size of the bird. This is scientific fact." Across the kitchen, Grace was silently counting each stack of plates—and they were short stacks. "How many did you cook for?"

"Me—I do recall sitting down to eat—Merle, James, Debbie, Tommie and his mom, Mac, His Honor. Eight I guess, except Tommie should count double, and Mac and James can eat an entire pie between them."

"That's a lot of dishes. How does the judge get along with the children?"

"Interesting question. He dotes on Merle. He's her Uncle Judge, and he seemed to delight in Tommie too, much to Merle's consternation. She takes the doting fellows in her life pretty much for granted, which brings me to the rest of the reason I called."

"The rest of the reason?" Grace was wandering around the kitchen as if deciding what mischief to get into next.

"I called simply to visit, of course, but also in honor of the day. It's Thanksgiving, and you are one of the blessings I've been most grateful for lately. My department would have fallen on its sword by spring were you not willing to roll up your sleeves and wade in the way you have been, so you have my heartfelt thanks."

"You're welcome." Hannah had to swallow around a lump in her throat though. Was this what all those cousins and uncles and grandmas Grace longed for would say to each other on Thanksgiving?

"Hannah, you there?"

No, she was in the Children's Haven group home, helping Eliza get ready for the junior prom. "I said you're welcome."

"Maybe sometime over the holidays we can get you here for a meal, and I can show my appreciation in more than just words."

"Maybe. My cleanup crew needs some direction. It was sweet of you to call, and I'll see you at the office."

"Not for three more days, you won't. Have a good weekend, and go sleep off your turkey."

"Good night, Trent."

She hung up, reached for a tissue, and stared at the phone.

What on earth had that whole phone call been about?

———

"You ever do something you still regret years later?"

Dan Halverston lounged against the jamb of Trent's kitchen door, though no question from a judge should be considered idle. James and Mac had been shanghaied by Merle into doing the evening barn chores, and from thence would be chained to her DVD player watching an old Garfield video.

While His Honor wanted a tête-à-tête, and Trent

wanted to know why Hannah Stark had sounded near tears at the end of their phone call.

"Have a seat, Daniel. This sounds like a discussion to have over some spiked hot chocolate."

"Hot chocolate sounds good, but it's dark out there, and my night vision isn't what it used to be, so easy on the spiking for me."

"Feeling old?" Trent asked as he got out the fixings and opened a cupboard over the refrigerator. "A few years ago I went on a liqueur buying binge. We have almond, hazelnut, raspberry, chocolate mint, orange. I ought to toss some of this out, or give it away."

"I've had years like that." The judge lowered his big frame to a chair at the kitchen table. "Put some of the hazelnut stuff in mine."

"Whipped cream?"

"But of course."

A judge had fewer opportunities to socialize than did the members of the bar. They had to watch appearances, exhibit good behavior at all times, and avoid anything approaching political use of their office.

Lonely business, being a judge.

"Your drink, sir." Trent pushed a handsome little creation across the table and straddled the opposite chair. Hannah Stark appreciated a well-made hot chocolate.

But did she know how to let somebody appreciate her?

"To your health," Halverston said, taking a sip.

"And yours," Trent said, doing likewise with his. "What has you looking so moony? You miss Helen more on the holidays, don't you?"

"The first year was the hardest. The first Christmas,

the first anniversary of her death, the first Easter when
we didn't go to Deep Creek. I tried going by myself a
few weeks later, but it was a mistake."

"Does the grief fade at all?"

"It does," the judge said, staring at his drink. "At first
you don't want it to because that's scary and disloyal,
but then you begin to let it go, to hold on more to the
good things, and to realize your life is still before you,
whether you know what to do with it or not."

"When Sheila left"—dumped Trent and their daughter—"I felt that way. I was single again, but not quite,
not with Merle glued to my hip and depending on me for
every blessed thing."

"Sheila was determined to go, and you were doing
most of the parenting anyway."

"I was?"

"I've gone fishing with Mac several times since
Helen died. He doesn't say much, so one tends to recall
what few words he parts with, and he does catch a lot
of fish."

"I've had the pleasure," Trent said, though it had
been years, since right after the divorce in fact.

"There was a woman," the judge said, stirring his
drink slowly. "Way, way back in law school. She was
brilliant, Trent, a far more apt pupil than I was. She'd
worked her backside off to get through undergrad, and
was doing law school on determination and scholarships. I got to be editor of law review because she'd
gone over what I'd written and challenged me on it until
my article looked as brilliant as she was."

There was a woman… Did every man's list of
regrets start with that phrase? Did Hannah Stark's list

of regrets include a man? "An old flame? Did you keep in touch?"

"We were so in love." Halverston pushed his half-full mug away by a few inches. "We were of different faiths, and her family was very conservative, and choosing me would have meant losing all of their approval and support. They'd helped her as much as they could with school, and it would have been a hard choice."

"Different faiths wasn't an insurmountable problem, even thirty years ago." Though meddling family could be the wrecking ball that dealt a relationship its death blow.

"We had other problems. I was competitive as hell, much as I loved her, and she realized it."

"Most professional couples deal with the same thing. Sheila and I certainly did."

"Look how easily you got that resolved."

"I'm happy with this resolution." If lonely, and lately, horny.

"Professional jealousy wasn't the basis of all our problems, though it made splitting up easier. Maybe Louise made the right choice when she ended it with me."

"Louise?" Trent murmured, though he knew exactly which Louise.

"You'll put two and two together. Her Honor, Louise Merriman. We were a hot ticket for a one short, glorious year of law school."

"What happened?" And what flavor of liqueur would Hannah prefer in her hot chocolate?

"I'm still wondering that myself. We went off for our summer associate positions between second and third year, and we stayed in touch, but when I came back in the fall, no Louise. She'd transferred to a school several states away, citing money, but money wasn't the reason."

"In the intervening decades, you've never talked about this?" For all that they argued and briefed and pleaded, lawyers were not noted for their ability to just plain talk.

"I got a Fulbright to study comparative law in England. She started right off doing appellate work for one of the big DC firms. We grew apart, until we both ended up on the bench. She didn't marry until right before she ran for a judgeship, and I've always wondered if she was truly in love with her husband, or just lonely."

A man could be both in love and lonely.

"You were in love with Helen," Trent said, his hot chocolate growing lukewarm. "Any damned fool could see that."

"I was certainly infatuated, but wait until you're pushing fifty and some sweet young thing bats her eyes at you."

"I hope if that day comes and I'm still in a position to take advantage of it, I'll be as wise as you were and jump in with both feet." The judge was quiet, doubtless pondering loving and losing, as opposed to never loving at all. "You want a refill?"

"No thanks. I want a pep talk, or a lecture, or someone to tell me I'm not an old fool."

"You know better," Trent said, getting up and collecting both mugs. "You know you wouldn't trade those years with Helen for anything, and you're just gun-shy about trying for some years with Louise. How long has she been a widow? It's been a year now, at least."

"Closer to two. We lost our partners within weeks of each other."

"Then you're burning daylight, Daniel. Get on your horse and go get the girl before some other cowpoke stands up with her."

"What about you? I heard you on the phone with your new associate. She could do a lot worse."

Daniel was dodging Trent's last comment, because fools of any age could grow comfortable with their loneliness. Well, hell.

"I have a kid to think of, Judge, and that slows a lot of women down, or it should."

"You're burning daylight," Halverston said, his lips turning up. "Best saddle up now, before James beats you to the dance."

"Or Mac. He bears constant watching, you know."

"It will take special women for all three of you," the judge said, rising. "I could swear I've seen Hannah Stark somewhere before."

"I saw her first. Go chase your own dream."

"We're having lunch again next week. Louise and I."

"Kiss her cheek in public. James says it's a surefire way to charm any lady."

Halverston looked intrigued with the notion, and Trent sent him on his way twenty minutes later, with turkey and mashed potatoes to go with that advice. Sometime soon, Trent would take Hannah to lunch and see how surefire James's move really was.

Chapter 9

"I'VE HAD DEBBIE KEEP AN EYE ON HANNAH," MAC said behind the closed door of James's office. "Hannah has met with all of her clients, looked up all the relevant case law, memorized the facts of each party's situation."

"So she's ready," James said, wondering what a rare visit from Mac was really about. "Trent must be expecting no less, or he would have at least called from the courthouse."

"He's in a weeklong divorce trial," Mac said, his tone suggesting a bout of mononucleosis would be preferable. "He's having lunch with his client, scrambling to return phone calls from other clients, cleaning up as best he can from last week's trial, and he expects us to guard the ranch."

"You said Hannah's doing fine. I can take her to lunch today." She'd laugh at James again, something he'd found unnervingly and genuinely endearing.

"She won't eat. She tossed her danish on Tuesday, developed a migraine yesterday, and she's kept her door shut all morning today. The girl is probably off her feed and pacing her stall all night."

You could take the boy off the farm…

"You want me to tell Trent?"

"No," Mac said. "I want you to sit on your handsome fanny and let her go down in flames while her boss knows nothing and does nothing. She's got court tomorrow, James, her very first contested matters, and Trent has his head up his ass."

In the clouds, perhaps, and wasn't it about damned time?

"Once again," James said, getting to his feet and reaching for his coat, "we must conclude I got all the charm in the family."

"And Trent got the looks, which means I got the only complement of brains. Take my car, it's easer to find a space for if you're going to the courthouse."

He tossed James the keys and left, muttering something about brothers even the wolves would not have adopted.

"There ought to be a limit on domestic trials," James said. "Three days and they begin to stink, just like fish."

"But oh, the billable hours," Trent replied. "I do love an unhappily married doctor. What brings you to the courthouse?" Though it was good to see a friendly face—very good.

"Let's find a witness interview room."

In other words, James's agenda was personal, or sensitive, or something James wasn't about to let anybody overhear.

"How's the trial going?" James asked when they had the privacy of a small conference room.

"Just fine." Which meant for the opposition, it wasn't going fine at all. "Husband is parading witness after witness in to testify to his fine, upstanding character, his integrity, his fitness as a parent, and to Wife's utter self-absorption, her marginal parental fitness, and her general contemptibility."

James winced, his distaste for family law born of a sensitivity few would have guessed, though Mac was even worse. "Why isn't your client having apoplexy?"

"Because she knows we have Husband's driving record, with no less than three DUIs. We have a former receptionist in the medical office who was the object of Husband's sexual advances, and who was fired when her tolerance for those advances came to an end."

Hell hath no fury like a receptionist fed up with the boss.

"We also have witness testimony about Husband's evenings of grand rounds," Trent went on, "of the bars that is. Moreover, the children are prepared to tell the judge they've been putting up with weekends at Dad's through the trial because they're afraid of his temper, particularly when he's drinking. What they want, and what their attorney wants, is nothing less than supervised visits with Dad, neutral drop site to be determined."

That recitation should have been gleeful, not exhausted and marginally disgusted.

"Who's opposing counsel?"

"God bless him, Elvin Gregory." Not the good doctor's most shrewd choice. "I can only conclude Elvin hasn't bothered to read the report of the attorney for the children yet. The damned thing is thirty pages long, and Elvin would have to have read it over the weekend."

"So the physician will be healing himself," James concluded. "But, Brother, not all in your kingdom is going so well."

The uh-oh feeling could land on any parent—especially a working parent—faster than a judge could bring down his gavel.

Trent whipped out his phone. "The school hasn't called. They know if they can't reach me to call you or Mac."

"Another damsel is in distress, counselor. While you're here baiting your trap for bear, Hannah Stark is tearing her hair out back at Comedy Central. Am I right she's never appeared in court before on a contested matter?"

Well, shit. Such was the gravitational pull of a long trial that Trent had to mentally track down what day of the week it was.

"Her first docket is tomorrow. Damn it all to hell."

"We know you're shorthanded, but child support isn't something Mac or I can step in on very easily. Lee is down in DC doing depositions, Ann took vacation this week, and somebody needs to peel your girl off the ceiling or we'll have a disability claim on our hands. Any chance you'll wrap up this afternoon?"

"Hardly." Trent flipped his tie when he wanted to yank the damned thing off. "Husband will conclude his case this afternoon, and I might get through opening argument by four o'clock."

"From the looks of her, I'd say Hannah hasn't slept much this week. Debbie says she's got a migraine going as well."

"She's coming unglued." Trent should have seen this coming, should have known Hannah would never, ever ask for help when she knew he was nose down in a domestic trial.

"To the casual observer, she's a rock," James said. "To the trained eye of the connoisseur—meaning me, not you or Mac—she's in a flat panic, and she deserves more from us than to be left alone to paddle around in the deep end with the sharks."

"She's new, James, but she's not stupid, and the cases aren't complicated. I'm not sure how much help I could be to her." Though he could hold her hand, hold *her*.

James sat forward and lowered his voice, though the door was closed.

"There is no telling what bombs Matthews left unexploded in those files, Trent. The boy was just not right, and nobody was keeping a close eye on him those last few weeks. Margaret Jenson will play fair, but she'll play hardball if she has to."

"Mac was paying attention to Matthews. I should have been." Trent had seen Gerald at the courthouse though, and the guy looked twitchy as hell.

"Even you, oh Wonder Dad, can't be two places at once and have eyes in the back of your head. If Gerald's in court this week, you know he was entering his appearance weeks ago, because it takes that long to schedule cases in this benighted jurisdiction."

"You going back to the office?" Trent asked, not wanting to belabor the topic of Gerald Matthews.

"I'll grab something for lunch on the way and try to get Hannah to eat a bite or two."

"She's helpless to resist chocolate mousse. I'll waive my opening argument entirely and ask for an early recess so I can do some last-minute preparation for tomorrow."

"That's a different approach."

"No rule says you have to have an opening argument," Trent said. "I'll explain to the client we're keeping our cards close to our chest. She's a woman scorned, and she likes anything that reduces Husband's chances of standing upright or siring children when this is all over."

Which wasn't exactly cheering. A spouse that thoroughly scorned by her ex could turn around and scorn her lawyer just as enthusiastically.

"You love this?" James asked, tipping his chair back on two legs. "That miserable excuse for a husband is somebody's daddy too, you know."

For James of all people to raise that argument was interesting.

"If he'd acted more like a dad," Trent said, "and less like God's gift to lonely receptionists and Jack Daniel's shareholders, I might treat him more like a dad."

"I'll look after your nervous filly," James replied, "and you might mention to Mac you appreciate him keeping an eye on things."

"So he can thump on me and snarl something about Merle not bringing me up right?"

"Mac needs his jollies, maybe more than anybody."

James left, and Trent went in search of his client. Mrs. Williams was a statuesque brunette with good bones and a pretty face. She'd age well, and not lack for male appreciation while she did. Trent found her sipping a cola in the basement snack shop.

"Lucy, I hope you're happy with the morning's developments?" Trent slid onto a chair across from her at a table for two.

She jammed her straw into the ice of her drink, repeatedly. "I cannot wait to see his expression when Theresa walks into the courtroom tomorrow morning. That look will be worth putting up with fifteen years of his shit."

Lucy did not mince words, which wasn't prudent when judges and opposing counsel could walk in at any minute.

"Mustn't count our chickens, Lucy. Your former receptionist might not appear, and then our case is not as strong."

"She'll show up. She's no dummy, and she's probably angrier at him than I am."

Trent studied his client, and unease gathered in a low-down place he'd learned to listen to.

"What haven't you told me?" he asked, sitting back and regarding her with his best prosecutorial frown.

She gave the ice another hard jab. "Just that Theresa is about eight months pregnant with the child Doctor Williams told her to abort."

Silence sat between lawyer and client for about thirty seconds, while Trent heard James in his head, going on about the unknowable mind of Woman.

"I wish you'd told me this earlier," he said, humor warring with exasperation. "It changes the complexion of the case, so to speak, and means you'll likely get less child support."

"I'd get less anyway, but I'll make it up in alimony, right?"

"Alimony isn't supposed to be punishment." Though the equities had a way of creeping into a judge's view of the case, by back doors and indirections. "We might want to let your husband know what we have planned, Lucy. His settlement offer could be more than what the judge is supposed to give you, and though they have no patience for him now, the man is your children's father."

"And the father of Theresa's child, who is their half

sibling." She kept her voice down, but her tone was fierce. "*Doctor* Williams has been in that courtroom all week, his pretentious little black bag at his side, making me appear to be a cocktail-swilling cow who wants to bleed him dry while I hug his long-suffering children to my gin-soaked bosom rather than let them see their own father."

She banged on the table hard enough to make her drink jump. "I will *not* bargain with him, not when I put him through medical school. Not when I quit a good job to stay home with the children who never saw him. Not when I tolerated his rages when he did recall he had a family. Infidelity wasn't even the last straw, but a bastard child he hasn't bothered to inform himself of has destroyed any regard I ever had for him or his standing in the community."

Trent yanked at the knot of his tie, trying to see past his client's rage to the legal issues. Until the child was born, paternity was a coin toss, for one thing.

"Did you pay Theresa for her testimony?" Trent asked. "I want the truth, because the woman will be under oath once she's on the stand, and opposing counsel ought to ask."

"I did not."

"Thank God for that. In some ways, this makes my plans for the afternoon all that much more sensible." He outlined his intentions, couching the absence of an opening argument as if it were some clever ploy, when in fact, Trent often waived argument simply to save time and keep opposing counsel guessing.

Trent made it through cross-examination of Husband's last witnesses, drove straight back to the office, and picked up a wad of message slips when he sailed past the receptionist. He didn't let himself start sorting through the messages, didn't even stop at his own office, but rather, went directly to knock on Hannah's partially open door.

He got no response, so he peeked into her office. No Hannah, though an Act of God had apparently come through on hundred-mile-per-hour winds. Law books were scattered everywhere, fifteen feet of tape flowed from the calculator on her desk and cascaded onto the floor. Pink sticky notes were plastered to yellow legal pages, and message slips were sprinkled throughout.

The Cat in the Hat could not have made a finer mess. Three third-year law students studying for finals for a straight week could not have created such fuss and bother. Four hyperactive gorillas on crack with a law library between them could not—

He had been truly derelict, but where was his budding litigator?

Trent needed to dump his briefcase and jacket before he went in search of her, and traced a path to his own door, which was closed. When he was at court, that wasn't unusual. The associates would go in and help themselves to what they needed just the same.

He let himself into his office, closed the door, and loosened his infernal tie, but didn't get it entirely off.

Hannah Stark lay on his sofa, flat on her back, one arm flung over her head, lips slightly parted as she slept. A surprisingly long swatch of brunette hair wound down from her shoulder toward the carpet.

Good old barbarian lust warred with guilt and something else—protectiveness? *Tenderness?* She was pale, she had purple shadows under her eyes, and a pink sticky note had attached itself to the back of the hand that had drifted to the floor. An afghan was draped over her legs, and her shoes were off.

Trent put his briefcase down and hung up his coat and jacket. Still, she didn't stir.

He'd done this to her—he and his merry band of deadbeat dads.

He went to the kitchen and fixed her a cup of Earl Grey, stealing a sip on the way back to his office. When he'd again closed his office door, he didn't pause to consider his actions, didn't do a cost-benefit analysis, didn't consult company policy or weigh the pros and cons.

He settled at her hip on the sofa and waited a moment to see if she roused. She sighed and brought her hand down from above her head, but didn't waken.

Sleeping Beauty was out cold, and he was at least partly responsible. He slipped his arms around her, gently, gently, and kissed the princess in his office awake.

———

Hannah was finally warm, though her limbs had turned to lead, and as if some evil spell held her in thrall, she couldn't get her eyes open. Something smelled good, like sandalwood and shampoo, and something tasted like bergamot.

"You're awake."

Trent Knightley loomed over her as she lay on his sofa. She tried to move, but he was perched at her hip, trapping her under the afghan.

"You kissed me awake, and you're my boss."

Both facts made her happy. Trent had kissed her before, but then he'd made sure she'd had a chance to opt out.

"Two for two, though I seem to have misplaced my supervisory responsibilities."

"Maybe the kissing is more important." More special. She winnowed a hand through his hair, the silky warmth of it soothing her. Trent wasn't wearing a tie, meaning Hannah could also touch the pulse that beat at the base of his throat. She urged him forward until he folded down over her, his arms settling around her.

"Are you angry with me, Hannah?"

"I always kiss and cuddle the guys I'm peeved at," she said, stroking his hair. *I've missed you, I've missed you.* "I took it out on the shortbread stash. Mac said something about partner cookies."

"You're disappointed then," Trent said, heaving out a sigh that made his chest move against hers. "I'm out of practice, if you want the sad truth. Work with me a bit, Stark, and the next kiss will do more than just wake you up."

He sounded determined on that.

"You're laughing," he said, snuggling in closer. "I can feel it. Disappointed, and now laughing at a man's first attempt to play handsome prince in I don't know how many years. Where is your respect?"

"Where is my boss?" She purposely did not take the bait about his kiss, which hadn't been disappointing in the least.

"That fool." Trent sighed again, and Hannah suspected he did it to feel her breasts against his chest. "I am so sorry, because apparently this week has gone for you exactly as I didn't want it to. You've been abandoned with your first docket, with nobody to help."

To have this discussion while they embraced was cozy and somehow easy.

Also very odd.

"I assume you're here now to dispense reassurances with your apologies?" Hannah began to work at the tension at the base of his skull, kneading with her fingers.

"Apologies all around. Every night this week, I've gone home, done my chores, and impersonated Wonder Dad, and I've thought after I tuck Merle in: I'd better call Stark, see how she's holding up."

"I didn't get your calls."

"I didn't want to hover," he said, nuzzling her neck, which might be a prevarication or an attempt to distract her—or tickle her. "The phones work both ways, you know. You could have called, strictly to yell at me."

Most of Hannah's adolescence had been spent in places were her only phone access was the communal phone on the wall in the hallway. The phone as a source of comfort had never occurred to her.

"Would that have made your trial settle?" she asked.

"It would not."

"Then I'm keeping my powder dry." Let him be the one to stare at his phone, wishing, hoping, and praying it would ring.

"What you're doing to my neck will have my back leg twitching here directly, Stark."

"You've done the same for me, but, Trent?"

"You remembered my name, that's encouraging."

"I really am scared."

"We'll take it slowly," he said, and she knew he

was deliberately misunderstanding again—sort of. "As slowly as you need to."

Before she could smack him or tug on his hair, he was kissing her again, a gentle, sweet tease of his lips over hers, side to side, before he settled in and got serious.

He tasted faintly of bergamot as he cupped her head with his hand, threaded his fingers through her hair, and seamed her lips with his tongue.

Ah, such heat, and such skill. In one single kiss, Trent caressed Hannah's mouth with his, coaxed and tasted and made her feel dizzy, while she knew she was solidly supported by the couch and by his palm cradling her head.

"Enough." She managed to pull away half an inch to get out one word, but it stopped him, as she'd known it would.

"You weren't exactly scampering away," he said, resting his cheek on her forehead. "That wasn't nearly enough, but I can appreciate the value of a little anticipation. A little."

"There's two hundred pounds of male on top of me, sounding the mating call for all he's worth. How am I supposed to scamper anywhere?" *Not that she wanted to.*

"I weigh a little more than that." He kissed her forehead and nuzzled her ear.

"Because your ego weighs so much."

"When you kiss me like that, my ego swells, it becomes engorged—"

Hannah stopped him with her fingers over his lips. "It really has been a while for you, Trent, hasn't it?"

"No," he said, moving away enough to frown down

at her. He stroked her hair off her forehead while that single word registered in Hannah's brain: No, it hadn't been a while?

"It hasn't been a while. It has been *forever*. You make me—well, it's a novel experience, sounding the mating call with you."

"To me, not with me," she said, missing the feel of him over her. "None of this is preparing my cases for tomorrow's docket."

Trent dropped his forehead to hers. "Deliver me from single-minded women who aren't focused on the same thing I am. Don't tell James you were able to think of child support cases while I was pitching my best woo."

"Tell it to the Orioles. Let me up, now please." Lest she pitch some woo herself.

Trent lingered, inhaling through his nose, nuzzling Hannah's neck and making her insides go all fluttery while her IQ threatened to plummet into the single digits. She cadged a few more strokes of his hair, of the soft, silky abundance of it, until she knew if Trent didn't take himself away soon, her common sense would implode altogether.

"Off," she said, tugging gently on his hair. "Now."

He sat up, looking like some sort of barbarian prince with his hair in complete disarray. He also looked like he wanted to say something, so Hannah touched her fingers to his mouth again.

Such a deceptively soft pair of lips he had.

"I want to go over my docket with you, Trenton Knightley. I need to."

"Your docket. Right," he said, speaking the words against her hand. "Your wish is my to-do list, et cetera, but you'll drink your tea first."

He got off the couch, and Hannah's traitorous body let out a silent yelp of bereavement. "Where are you going?"

"To tell the secretary to straighten up the war zone now known as your office."

"But if she moves my—"

"It's twenty file folders, Hannah. She will assemble them in docket order, so they'll be ready for you tomorrow morning. Drink your tea before it gets cold, and give a man a minute to regain his tattered dignity."

Involuntarily, her gaze dropped to below his waist. His dignity was not tattered.

He shrugged into his suit coat, saluted with two fingers, and sauntered out, closing the door behind him. Hannah scrambled to a sitting position, a short nap having eased her headache.

Or perhaps Trent Knightley's hands in her hair had done that.

Hannah's bun had disintegrated, but without retrieving her purse and brush, she could do nothing about that. She sipped her tea, which was still wonderfully hot and fixed exactly as she liked it, with both cream and sugar.

Those kisses had been exactly as she liked them too. What lady wouldn't like being wakened by a handsome prince?

"I hadn't realized your hair is so long." Trent closed the door behind him, and Hannah was glad for the privacy. He'd rattled her thoroughly, though she'd been rattled since she set foot in her office Monday morning.

"I need to get it cut," she said, aiming a frown at the ends trailing over her arm. "It's a nuisance when it's down."

"It's beautiful," he said, settling in beside her. He'd brought a clipboard and a copy of the docket with him. "Now tell me about your cases, Stark. I will attempt to supervise you. I hope it makes you happy."

"It will make me relieved," she said, setting her mug down. At some point while she recited facts and cited cases, Trent's arm went around her shoulders, and his hand wandered around in little caresses and strokes and pats. His touch felt good, and only moderately distracting.

An hour later, Hannah's tea was gone, her headache was fading fast, and she still sat side by side with Trent on the couch.

"You know your cases cold," he pronounced. "You'll keep Margaret on her toes, and I'll check in on you if my divorce takes a recess."

"And yet I'm scared."

He gently pushed her head to his shoulder. "What can you possibly be scared of? You're a hundred times more prepared than Gerald ever was."

"What if I forget everything? What if the judge brings up some precedent I haven't even read? What if my clients don't show up because I told them the wrong time, and then bench warrants are issued for failure to appear? What if Gerald Matthews comes and sits in the back of the courtroom and laughs the whole time I'm trying to do my job? What if I'm so inexperienced I don't even know the right things to be worried about?"

Foster care left a woman with an overactive imagination for all the wrong things.

Trent said nothing, and to Hannah's horror, her breath hitched. If he'd only stop touching her, maybe she could find her composure and put together two-and-a-half coherent thoughts relating to something halfway—

Trent kissed her temple, which didn't help one freakin' bit.

"My head hurts, and I have damned c-cramps, and I can't think…" She had *not* just said that.

"Hush."

"I hate this." Or that either.

"You hate to feel overwhelmed. We all do, but give yourself credit, Hannah. You're taking on one hell of a challenge, and you've prepared well for it."

"Now you start with the boss talk. I'm scared out my feeble wits, and I'll never like going to court."

"You may not like it—even I dread court sometimes—but litigation will become routine, just part of the job, one of the things you do to earn your daily bread. The work is honorable work, and you can do a lot of good for a lot of people with the skills you have."

"The skills I hope I have."

They fell silent, Hannah trying to marshal her resolve to get up and leave the comfort of simply being near Trent.

"I probably shouldn't have been hitting on you," Trent said. "I am sorry, but you looked so adorable catnapping, and I am not entirely myself where you're concerned."

Finally, a shaft of real encouragement, because maybe the loss of balance wasn't exclusively Hannah's?

That helped a little. "I haven't decided to hit back, you know. Or to…"

"I know," he said, patting her hand, which still clutched a mangled tissue. "If you decide my overtures aren't welcome, that will absolutely be the end of it. I hope you know that."

"Good to hear it." Sort of.

"You'll be OK in court tomorrow, Stark?"

She looked at their joined hands and tried to recall why being entangled with the boss was a legendarily dumb idea.

"I'll manage. I always do." *Foster care strikes again*, though for the first time, Hannah regarded that enforced habit of resilience as something more than simple cussedness.

"If you're going utterly to pieces," Trent said, "ask Linker for a recess. You're a female. He'll let you go pee."

"The things they don't tell you in law school."

"Like how important a good night's sleep is," he said, giving her back her hand. "It's five o'clock, Hannah. Merle will want to know how court went for me today, and because I'm doing a multiday trial, I'm excused from cooking. You want to do carry-out with us?"

Just like that, reality reasserted itself.

This was why getting entangled with the boss was a complicated idea. Not because the boss would take advantage or morale would suffer in the department or Hannah wouldn't pull her share of the workload. Trent would never take advantage, he'd be the soul of discretion, and nobody had ever called Hannah Stark lazy.

But there was Grace. Always, for the foreseeable future, there would be Grace, and the need to protect Grace.

"I'll go home and crash," Hannah said, shifting forward on the seat. "I haven't been sleeping well, and for

me to sleep during the day, I'm either coming down with
something or exhausted or both."

"You look a little short of sleep. You should eat
with us some night when I've fired up the grill.
Lots of good food, and we eat off paper plates, so
no dishes."

"That does sound good." It sounded cozy and domestic and delicious. Hannah struggled to her feet and gave
herself a moment to find her balance.

"You OK?" Trent was on his feet beside her, his hand
on her elbow.

"Fine. Just wiped out. I'll get my briefcase and be on
my way."

"Will you do me a favor?"

This favor wouldn't involve any more kisses. "Ask."

"Leave the briefcase here tonight. I've been a lousy
boss this week, but I'm trying to make up for it. You're
ready, Hannah. You are. You'll do fine tomorrow, and
there's nothing in those files that you need to look at
one more time, or review yet again. You need to rest and
pamper yourself tonight. Take a hot bath, curl up with a
book, paint your toenails."

Be a princess? "I've never painted my toenails in
my life."

"So indulge yourself tonight. Ditch the briefcase."

Trent was winding up for a closing argument.
Apparently princes could be as obstinate as princesses.
"No briefcase."

"That's my lady. May I walk you to your car?"

"You may." Because he'd be obstinate about that too.
Hannah got her coat and purse, but Trent followed her to
her office and took them from her. He held her coat and

drew her hair carefully from the coat collar, then tucked her purse over her shoulder.

"If I were James, I could offer you my arm and make it look smooth."

"If you were James," Hannah said as they made for the parking lot, "you would have been dropping by my office three times a day, offering me your stash of trail mix and fretting over the new associate rather obviously."

"Did he bother you?" Four words, but they portended closed fists for James, depending on Hannah's answer. Kinda sweet, that.

"He was being sweet."

That kept Trent quiet until they reached Hannah's Prius.

"Some day, my dear, we must talk about reliable transportation. We can get a lot of snow out this way."

Hannah was fond of George, and so was Grace, which decided the matter. "I am not your dear." An objection for the record, nothing more. "But you are dear, and the car's half paid off."

She climbed into her chariot and left him standing in the parking lot, darkness falling around him, her briefcase locked in his tower.

Chapter 10

HANNAH EXPLAINED TO GRACE THAT MOM WAS scheduled to try her first contested matters the next day, and Grace responded by being as biddable and solicitous as she could be.

The Stark family was small, but its members were terrifically loyal to each other, and as Hannah drove to work Friday morning, she decided the best outcome of the day would be if Grace could be proud of her mother.

If Hannah could be proud of herself, and if Trent could be proud of his newest associate, whom he had kissed witless and held and kissed some more.

Hannah pulled into a twenty-four-hour drugstore to pick up over-the-counter cold and sore throat remedies. Going short of sleep, neglecting meals, and generally stressing about the docket, she'd managed to invite that might-be-getting-sick feeling for a visit. She'd get herself better too, though that would take the weekend and some rest to accomplish.

She was surprised to find Trent's sedan in the parking lot at such an early hour. She parked next to it, recalling the heated seats with something approaching lust.

To have tea or to skip tea? Having tea meant managing nature's call when Hannah had to be in court. Though a cup of tea would help wash down the pills she was about to swallow, which was the greater need.

Hannah forgot all about tea and pills when she saw

her office. Sitting on her desk in a thick crystal vase was a huge spray of yellow gladiolus. The color brightened the whole room, and Hannah had to drop into a guest chair, so pleased was she by the gesture. She was still beaming like an idiot—or a princess—when Trent wandered in holding a steaming mug and took the other chair.

"Flowers make me sad sometimes," he said, his tone contemplative.

"Sad?"

"Because their beauty is so fleeting. It's as if they offer it up, knowing that for the flower at least, as soon as the blossom opens, it begins to fade toward death. I know the biology of the flower is more interesting than that, but the uselessness, the futility of the beauty is so, I don't know—poignant? It reminds me of childhood, the fleeting beauty that has to die."

He held the steaming mug out to her.

"Thank you," Hannah said, "for the tea, the flowers, the philosophy."

The warmth of the mug in her hands comforted, while his words made her sad. Childhood was not always a time of even fleeting beauty.

"You got some sleep," Trent said, studying her. "Probably not enough, though."

"I'll catch up over the weekend." Hannah took a sip of hot tea, which was ambrosial. "The docket shouldn't go for more than half the day."

"Let's ride over together anyway. You can take my car back at lunch time, or have Gino come pick you up. Then too, you never know when Margaret will get a wild hare and try every case on the docket as a contested matter."

"Somehow the concepts of wild hares and Madam State don't quite mesh. These flowers are truly wonderful, Trent. Truly thoughtful."

"Merle likes flowers. Even Mac likes flowers, though that's a state secret. The Victorians thought the gladiolus stood for strength of character."

"I will need some strength of character today, won't I?" Not only for court.

"Stark, you have everything you need, not simply to endure this day, but to do a good job at it. I don't require constitutional arguments and brilliant interlocutory motions from you. I don't need you to be a hero or a martyr today. Just stumble through the docket as best you can. It's the hardest docket you will ever have to take. After today, you might come across more difficult cases, nastier opposing counsels, more miserable clients, but today is tougher than all that because you're going into it without anything but nerve to sustain you. The practice of law will get easier, I promise you."

He squeezed her hand, then stood.

"I'm supposed to meet my client a little early," he said. "I know you want to be in the bullpen before the crowd gathers, so let's pack up your files and charge the gates, shall we?"

His suggestion made all kinds of sense, because the twenty folders would not fit in Hannah's briefcase. Trent put most of them in the oversize attaché he used for court and escorted her to his car.

He popped a disc of Vera Winston playing Chopin ballades into the CD player on the way to court—music to brood by—and all too soon, they were in Courtroom Two, piling cases onto the counsel table in docket order.

"I can't do this for you," he said, "but I would if I could. Ask for a recess if you need one."

"Right." Because even princesses needed to pee.

The courtroom was filling up. Young men stood at the back in small groups, looking nervous or sullen. Young women arranged babies and diaper bags on the church pews, and counsel for the defendants were off in corners, chatting with clients.

"What?" Trent asked.

"I never wanted to practice family law. I still don't, but I need to conquer the courtroom, to make it mine. I see that now." Especially the family law courtroom. Hannah didn't like that revelation, hated it in fact, but it landed in her gut with the low-down, leaden conviction of a personal truth.

"You will be fine," Trent said, and Hannah wished in that moment, boss or no boss, courtroom or no courtroom, she could lean into him and feel his arms around her.

"I will," she said, wiggling her toes in her black high heels. "Go meet with your client. I'm not the only one with a courtroom to conquer."

"One last thing." He lowered his voice and leaned closer. "Gerald Matthews has a case today. I asked Margaret to put Gerald on first, in hopes he'll clear out and leave you free to represent your clients."

Hannah loved this man. Loved him for his protectiveness, for his innocent view of childhood, for his forethought and his flowers.

"I appreciate the warning."

Then Trent was gone, leaving Hannah with an upset stomach, an aching throat, and twenty cases to get through.

—⁓—

Hannah Stark was moving through her docket like a goddamned pro, and Trent couldn't recall when he'd been so proud of another adult. She used the strategies they'd discussed, objecting when she needed to and letting slide what would have been posturing and delay. She got good results for her clients and didn't get bogged down in petty sniping or judicial ass kissing.

On her first day in court, she was ten times the lawyer Gerald Matthews had been with two dozen dockets under his belt.

Trent sat in the back of Courtroom Two while his case took a twenty-minute recess to let the judge hear a domestic violence ex parte. Lucy was off on a smoke break, letting Trent catch a little of Hannah Stark in action.

She was already a very good attorney. She conducted herself like a lady and fought fair, but she fought hard without losing sight of the people she was fighting for. He resented the need to get back to his own case, but when fifteen minutes had gone by, he chose a break between cases and stood up, waiting until he could catch Hannah's eye.

Her expression was impassive and professional. When Trent winked at her, she scowled, much as Merle would have scowled had Trent started applauding at the wrong moment in the school play.

He gave her two thumbs-up and left, more proud of her than ever.

—⁓—

Hannah got through her cases.

She put up with the judge pulling the same

"empty your wallet" drill on some hapless fool she didn't represent.

She put up with Margaret objecting a few times just to try to derail Hannah's questioning.

She put up with the judge asking if she'd been out to the driving range yet.

She put up with Gerald Matthews snubbing her in front of God, opposing counsel, and everybody, and she'd put up with Trent lurking in the courtroom, probably to hide from his client.

Worse than all that were the feelings she put up with as she made her way to the snack bar in search of ice water with which to take more pills.

Hannah had hated doing that docket.

Hated it, loathed it, despised it. She was competent to manage more dockets, she knew that now, but she was competent to do a lot of things—muck stalls, scrub floors, change dirty diapers. Pick nits.

Any of those might be a better career choice for her. The judge didn't respect the people in his courtroom. The moms and dads didn't seem to respect each other, and many of them didn't even seem to care about their children. Worse, Hannah had a sinking premonition this callous and cavalier treatment between people wasn't limited to the courthouse's family law dockets.

"I wondered where you'd gotten off to." Trent Knightley filed into the lunch line behind her. "I'll buy you lunch, and you can tell me all about your morning."

He scanned the menu, and Hannah wanted to walk away. Except they'd carpooled in, a million years and twenty cases ago, and if she were smart, she'd spend the afternoon watching the brilliant Mr. Knightley demolish his client's marriage at a hefty hourly rate.

He ordered a burger, rare, while Hannah ordered soup and toast. Her throat was killing her, and she wouldn't have been surprised to find she was coming down with the flu, so badly did she ache.

When they found a table over by the windows, Trent held her chair for her, and Hannah wanted to howl at him to get lost. Outbursts of temper were never a good idea. She'd spent years learning that lesson, until she'd been threatened with medication and a diagnosis of explosive temper disorder as an adolescent.

"You don't look like a lady who just handled twenty cases in a row without once putting a foot wrong. I was impressed, Hannah. Really, truly impressed, though you seem a little worse for wear." He folded his bun over his meat, picked it up, and took a big old bite of rare protein.

Hannah looked at her soup and felt queasy. "You must be hungry."

"The food here is surprisingly good. They probably live in fear of being sued, come to think of it. You want a bite?" Trent gestured with his sandwich, munching happily away, like a raptor devouring his kill.

"No, thank you. My digestion's tentative right now."

He put a few potato chips on her plate.

"You'll be an old hand at this in another month. Ready for the tough cases just because they provide some variety. We should have some fun and games this afternoon with my divorce when the very pregnant former paramour and receptionist comes toddling in the door."

He bit into his pickle. If Hannah didn't eat something,

she'd never keep her meds down. She lifted her spoon, only to watch it go clattering back into the bowl.

"Hannah?" Trent put his half-eaten pickle down. "You feeling OK?"

"A little shaky. Low blood sugar, I suppose. If you'll excuse me, I forgot to heed nature's call at the morning recess, and it's catching up with me now."

The same tactic he'd told her to use with Judge Linker: tell him you have to pee. She got to the ladies' room sink just as the dry heaves started, then hung miserably for a moment, hoping they'd pass.

"Hard night?" A statuesque brunette regarded Hannah sympathetically over a tube of carmine lipstick.

"My first contested docket. My throat is killing me, I can't keep anything down when I do eat, and I'm so tired I could curl up right here on this ugly, cold tile floor."

None of which this woman wanted or needed to know.

"Come here," the brunette said, twisting the lipstick closed and waggling her fingers. "I'm a registered nurse, or I was a lifetime ago. Say ah."

Something in the woman's brisk assumption of compliance was reassuring, and Hannah obediently tilted her head and opened her mouth.

"My goodness," the lady said. "Nowadays, we're supposed to do a culture before we pronounce sentence, but that is a larruping case of strep if I ever saw one."

"I can't have strep," Hannah said, thinking of Grace.

"It's making the rounds early this year." The lady tossed her lipstick into a Gucci bag, then grasped Hannah's wrist. "Come with me, there's a doctor in the house, and damned if he isn't toting his medical bag with him. What's your name, honey?"

"Hannah Stark. Where is your doctor friend?"

"Lucy Williams, and His Highness will still be in the courtroom, hatching up evil plots with the desiccated limb of Satan he's retained to represent him."

Lucy lead Hannah through the double doors of a courtroom smaller than the one Hannah had spent her morning in. A tall, academic-looking man got to his feet while Elvin Gregory remained seated at the counsel table, a newspaper spread before him. The room was deserted otherwise, the judge and staff having apparently gone to lunch.

"Lucille." The tall man clutched an old-fashioned black medical bag as if it were a protective talisman.

"Don't get your knickers in a twist, Doc," Lucy said. "I brought you a case of strep. This is Hannah Stark, and she has a four-alarm sore throat. You're a doctor, so do your almighty thing, and I'll leave you in peace."

This doctor, whoever he was, did not appreciate Lucy's presumption. Hannah wasn't too keen on it herself.

"I'm sorry if it's a bother, Doctor," Hannah began, backing away from the couple who were now glaring at each other. "It isn't really urgent, and I didn't realize I'd be imposing."

"Oh, sure, let her suffer," Lucy said, gaze locked on the doctor. "Hypocritical oath, not Hippocratic, as I've long suspected. You have about as much compassion as a snake wrapped around a mouse."

The doctor glared at Lucy for a long moment, then let out his breath slowly, like a tire going flat.

"Hannah? I am Dr. Williams, and I would be remiss not to offer assistance if you're truly unwell."

He reached for her hand, and Hannah instinctively pulled back before she realized what he was about: doctors took pulses. She let him take her wrist and measure her pulse against the sweep hand of his Rolex.

He should shoo her off to the urgent care, but Lucille stood, arms crossed, apparently challenging him in a manner that required this display.

"You're a little fast," he said. "Let's sit you down."

Hannah took a seat on one of the courtroom benches, and the next thing she knew, she had a thermometer in her mouth while Dr. Williams asked her about onset of symptoms. He listened to her breathe, and finally looked at her throat.

And winced.

"You are a weapon of biological warfare in your present condition," he said. "I can't be one hundred percent sure you have strep—and a secondary sinus infection on the way—but I'm certain enough that I want you to take these right now." He handed Hannah two oblong pills that looked about the right size for a very sick Clydesdale.

"You need to rest," he went on, pouring a cup of water from the pitcher on the table. "The antibiotics can't do anything to help with viral infections, and as crummy as you're feeling, you need to know that opportunistic viruses love to come gate-crashing on the heels of bacterial infections."

He got out a notepad and started scribbling. "If you don't ease up for the next few days, you are setting yourself up for viral pneumonia and God knows what else."

Hannah nodded, the room bouncing peculiarly as she did.

"There's a drugstore across the street from the court-house," Dr. Williams said, tearing off three sheets from his notepad. "I want you to get these prescriptions filled right now, directly. Not after work, not tomorrow morning. They should give you some symptomatic relief by tonight. This time tomorrow, you won't be infectious, and your throat should be in much better shape."

"Thank you, Doctor," Hannah said, opening her purse. "What do I owe you?"

He considered a moment then patted her arm.

"You got my wife to speak to me for the first time in four months. We're even." He stood up, still wearing the same concerned, competent expression he'd worn as he'd examined her; then his gaze fell on Lucille, and his expression filled with…what? Dread? Reluctance?

While Hannah would have called Lucy's expression bittersweet.

"Thank you," Hannah said to Lucy. "Your doctor was a godsend."

"Yeah, I used to think so too." Lucy's tone was wistful, not the cutting lash she'd used to address him earlier.

"Hey, Godsend," Lucy said, rising and coming toward them. "What say you and I go have a cup of coffee? There are some things my lawyer hasn't told your lawyer, and they are things you'll want to know."

Dr. Williams glanced at Gregory, who shrugged noncommittally.

The couple left the courtroom as Hannah zipped her purse shut and prepared to follow them. She got as far as the door before Trent Knightley came barreling in, nearly knocking her off her feet.

"What in the hell happened to you?" He glared

down at her, speaking through clenched teeth. "You take off for the ladies' room, and you don't come back. I send Margaret after you, thinking you've fainted from stage fright or hypoglycemia or God knows what, and no Hannah. You're not in the courtroom, the lunchroom, the bathroom. Nowhere. Then I see my client breezing past me with her embittered spouse in tow, and I find you're the only person in here. What gives, Hannah?"

He took her arm in a grip that Hannah broke with a jerk.

"I'm a weapon of biological warfare. You better hope I don't breathe on you, Trent Knightley, lest you come down with strep, a sinus infection, and viral pneumonia."

"I beg your pardon?" He didn't try to touch her again, but his gaze roved over her, and Hannah had the sense his daughter was never going to get away with anything, not one thing, not even as a distinguished honor roll high school student.

Hannah sat, felled by the realization that Trent was worried for her. The tightening around his mouth and the light in his eyes only *looked* angry.

"Lucy was good enough to have her husband examine me. I did not know she was your client, and if the two of them talking ruins your fun and games, I do abjectly apologize. Now if you'll excuse me, I'm going to follow Dr. Williams's kind advice and get all three of these scripts filled."

Trent stood beside her, hands on his hips, brow knit. "Did you tell Lucy to settle?"

Spare me from litigators. "For God's sake, I didn't even know she was a party to a case, much less your client, until you came flapping in here breathing fire. Ask Mr. Gregory, he was here for the entire exchange."

Trent glanced up sharply, seeming to notice Elvin's presence for the first time.

"Knightley." Gregory nodded at him from across the room, then went right back to his newspaper.

Trent dug the heels of his hands into his eye sockets. "I'm sorry I barked at you. I was concerned."

Hannah said nothing as he lowered himself to the place beside her on the hard bench. He'd been not simply worried, he'd been frantic.

Which was puzzling.

"You want to sit with me at the counsel table this afternoon?" Trent asked.

Elvin Gregory snapped his newspaper closed and rose. He gave Trent a pointed look, then looked just as directly at Hannah.

"I have an errand to run over at the pharmacy while we're waiting for the judge to get back from lunch," he said. "Maybe Ms. Stark would let me take care of her business there too? I believe she has prescriptions to fill?" He gave the plural a lawyerly little emphasis.

"Thank you, Mr. Gregory," Hannah said. "That won't be necessary."

He looked from her to Trent. "Knightley, my little girl gets out of law school this spring, and I would hate to think any attorney who is himself the father of a little girl would ignore his employee's health just so she could watch him hash through one more damned domestic trial, especially when that same employee has come up to snuff overnight with the trash Matthews left on the child support docket."

With that, Gregory left the courtroom, giving Hannah a nod and sweeping past Trent without a glance.

"Likes his closing arguments, Elvin does," Trent said, sitting forward and propping his elbow on his knees. "I owe you an apology. How long have you been feeling bad?" He frowned at her over his shoulder, as if he could see her illness if he only peered at her hard enough.

Hannah often looked at Grace the same way.

"I was fine yesterday, just tired, but today—" Today she'd faced an enormous, writhing bucket of fears and insecurities. Princesses did that too, didn't they?

"Today you soldiered on because you had a docket to do, and I didn't even notice you were ailing. It's strep?"

"Unconfirmed, but both a doctor and a nurse pronounced it so."

"Don't say it's nobody's fault."

"You're thinking James and Mac will beat you for overworking me," Hannah said, wanting to touch Trent's hair. But she was infectious, and they were in public. Still, the urge to touch him was almost irresistible. To be touched by him.

"I'm probably the one who got you sick," he said. "In addition to running you ragged, I fended off a cold a week ago that's probably found a better home in you."

"You're immune to strep?"

"I'm the father of a school-age child. We're made of Toledo steel. Here." Trent fished his keys from his pocket. "Take the car, hit the drugstore, go directly to the office, and then home, Hannah. Get into your favorite jammies and cuddle up with a book. I've got your files, and I can have somebody take me back when I'm done here."

"You're sure?"

That he'd trust her with his lovely car meant something; that he'd spring her for the afternoon meant a whole lot more.

"I am positive," he said, putting the back of his hand on her forehead. "I do believe you're running a fever, just to make my guilt complete."

"I don't feel fevered."

Trent's hand slipped to the side of Hannah's face, and it was all she could do not to lean into his palm.

"Scat," he said, drawing her to her feet. He kissed her forehead and stepped back. "I think I have a settlement conference to attend, and I have you to thank for that."

"I didn't say anything. Honest."

"He's been sober since they split, and he's done inpatient hospital-based rehab, which had to be hard for a doctor. He's in counseling and anger management, and he's cut his practice way back. I begged that woman to at least let him know she'd entertain an offer," Trent said, looking puzzled. Then he focused on Hannah again. "If you need Monday off, just call me. We'll manage."

"I won't need Monday off, and thank you."

He tossed her the keys, and she left after stashing most of her files in his briefcase.

The car was a pleasure just to sit in, much less drive. Hannah cranked up the seat heater, hit the CD player, and turned the Chopin just as high.

The car was wonderful; Trent's concern for her—once he realized she was ill—had been wonderful; having found free medical treatment right at the courthouse was more wonderful still, if a bit weird.

But Hannah's morning had been awful, and when she

finally reached the safety of her office, she took fifteen minutes to stop crying. By then her throat hurt worse than ever.

—⁂—

"Mom?"

Hannah forced her eyes open, because she'd been shamelessly sleeping in for the second morning in a row. She rolled over to find Grace, still in her jammies, standing beside Hannah's bed, a favorite stuffed bear clutched by one worn paw.

"Good morning, sunshine. How long have you been up all by yourself?"

"I'm not all by myself. Wishes got up before me because he had to pee."

Hannah pushed away from her pillows, swung her feet over the side of the bed and into her slippers. Wishes wasn't the only one who had to pee.

"Did you and Wishes have breakfast?"

Grace bounced up onto the bed and scrambled into the place Hannah had vacated.

"Nice warm mommy-bed, huh, Wishes?" Grace dragged the covers over herself and her bear. "We had cereal, Mom, but Wishes ate most of mine."

"You are a rascal, Wishes Stark," Hannah said, shaking a finger at the bear. Two days on antibiotics and copious sleep had done wonders. She was creaky, but otherwise vastly improved from Friday morning. "What do you think of pancakes for breakfast today, though I'm not sure Wishes will have room for any."

"Probably not," Grace said, grinning. "When can I have a big bed like yours? Your bed is warmer than mine, and I could fit all my stuffed animals in a bed this big. I'd switch with you." She made that offer blinking earnestly at her mother.

"You will not charm me out of my bed," Hannah said, tousling her daughter's dark hair.

"Why do you do that to my hair? I don't do it to any of my stuffed animals, not even to Bronco."

"I do it because I think you're getting too grown-up for me to carry around everywhere, and because your pretty, silky hair is very handy—you were kind enough to put it on top of your head, after all—and because touching you is one way to say I love you."

Hannah stood and belted her old maroon velour bathrobe at her waist.

"Mrs. Bentley has hair on her lip," Grace said. "I didn't put my hair on my head, God did." She scooted down under the covers and sat her bear on the pillows. "God did something else too."

"He's a busy guy. What's He gotten up to now?"

"Look out the window," Grace said, eyes dancing. "I got a wish-can-true."

Hannah didn't bother correcting Grace's language— the term dated from Grace's early toddlerhood—but pulled the curtain aside.

"Oh, my gracious." Everything was blanketed in white, with more coming down in big, fluffy, this-means-business flakes. The fence posts across the lane sported six-inch caps of snow, and the trees were already heavily weighted too. "Perfect weather for making pancakes."

And thank God, Hannah had bought a tarp last week to put over the woodpile.

"Honey, you can stay in bed with Wishes for a while if you want, but I'm starting on breakfast, and then I have to finish the Weekly Rampage."

"I thought we did the rampage yesterday."

"Just the counters, floors, waste baskets, and kitty litter. I still have to do laundry, clean out the woodstove, and vacuum our bedrooms."

"I'll fold the socks."

"You always do such a good job of that," Hannah said. Matching and balling up the clean socks more often than not degenerated into a rolling game of sock-tag.

Though probably not today. As Hannah made her first cup of tea of the day—jasmine green tea, an extravagance made possible by regular employment— she admitted her energy level was still dragging. She opened the kitchen door to let out a fat, long-haired orange tomcat who'd been helping himself to leftover milk in the cereal bowl on the counter.

"Shameless varmint," Hannah muttered as she nudged him through the door, except the cat's front end stopped in mid-nudge, resulting in his back end making an undignified slide up Hannah's foot.

"Haven't you seen snow before?" Hannah bent to push the beast through the door. "And you call yourself a retired barn cat." As she straightened to close the door, she saw what had caught the cat's attention. A black sport utility vehicle had pulled into the short driveway in front of her house.

"Interesting." Though the sight of strangers in the driveway never cheered a kid raised in foster care, the State of Maryland probably wasn't providing child welfare workers sport utility vehicles these days.

Dadgummit thought the vehicle was interesting too, for he settled on his furry haunches and wrapped his tail around his paws with feline aplomb. Figures were emerging from the SUV. Trenton Knightley and a child about Grace's size looked around the property as they slammed their doors.

"I know this is where she lives, Daddy, because she said she had a cat whose head was wider than his behind the color of a pumpkin."

The child with the unusual syntax was female, based on her voice. The rest of her was swaddled in a snowsuit, scarf, mittens, and hood. Rosy cheeks were barely discernible.

Oh…dear. Oh dear, oh dear, oh dear. That child was *Merle*.

Grace would never biddably sleep through this, not that Hannah could conceive of misleading Trent or his daughter when they were on her very property. That realization made her anxious, even as she also admitted getting this encounter over with might be a small relief.

Or a large one.

Trent and his daughter came across the yard—no telling where a sidewalk might be under the snow—and Hannah barely had time to glance down at her ratty bathrobe and fuzzy slippers before the child climbed onto the porch.

"Hi! Is Grace here? I'm Merle, and it's time for the unicorns to play in the snow."

Hannah opened the door wider and tried not to stare at a child who had eyes the exact same color as her father's.

"Hello, Merle, and welcome. I'm Hannah. If you go

upstairs to the big bedroom at the back of the house, you can surprise Grace."

"Yippee!" Merle dashed across the kitchen, her snow-suit susurrating, boots clomping gleefully up the steps.

"Hello." Trent followed his daughter into the kitchen. "You have a daughter."

"A common condition, apparently. Can I get you a cup of tea?"

She wouldn't offer explanations or excuses, but it would be rude not to offer a hot drink.

"Tea would be nice."

Hannah filled the kettle at the sink rather than endure Trent's scrutiny.

"I'd heard this place was sold last year, and then Merle told me her new best friend lived here. We were headed to the tower road to go tobogganing, and Merle hasn't ever had a best friend before. She started wheedling…"

His voice trailed off as he glanced around Hannah's kitchen. Cupboard doors didn't quite hang plumb, the linoleum had seen better decades, the fridge was plastered with Grace's unicorn art. Hannah's personal space, worn and tattered around the edges, but as tidy and cozy as she could make it.

"You have a nice place. Comfy."

"It suits us," Hannah said as a damned blush crept up her neck. "Cream, honey, sugar?"

She opened the door to the refrigerator so she could turn her back on Trent again. Of all the kitchens on all the hillsides in all the valleys of western Maryland…

"Hannah?" He still stood by the door, regarding her curiously.

"Hmm?" She shut the fridge with her hip and met his

gaze over a pint of half and half—another blessing of regular employment.

"I'm glad we're neighbors, and I'm glad Merle has a friend."

Hannah got down a clean mug—this one sporting Eeyore—and the box of jasmine green tea bags. "Grace is very pleased to have a friend as well. She's tended to keep too much to herself."

Like her mother.

Trent didn't say that, though Hannah could hear him thinking it. He sat on the bench near the door and started unlacing his boots.

"Merle has been the same way. She's cordial to the kids at Pony Club, but they aren't buddies, not the way she seems to have buddied up with Grace. They share vivid imaginations."

"We don't have a TV," Hannah said, relaxing a little. People with kids sometimes sat in each other's kitchens drinking tea, though that hadn't happened to her in her kitchen.

Ever.

"Grace can occupy herself for hours in her art corner," she went on, "and she's been horse mad since she could skip around the living room and whinny."

"It's genetic, then. Merle has the same affliction."

Trent was down to his stocking feet, and when he rose to cross the kitchen, he seemed to Hannah larger than when he was in his three-piece suits at the office. Instead of tailored wool, he was in jeans and a plaid flannel shirt, with a black silk underlayer peeking through at his throat and cuffs.

The whistling teakettle saved Hannah from touching

any of those soft, masculine play clothes. "Where do you and Merle live?"

"About two miles farther south along the mountainside," Trent said, leaning back against the counter in exactly the same posture he leaned back against his desk. "I have a few acres, and we keep some horses. Grace is welcome to come play anytime."

"She'd like that." Hannah poured the boiling water into his mug. "She doesn't know a great deal about horses, though she loves them. I could afford a few lessons this past summer, and she thinks she knows a lot more than she does. You never said if you want sugar or honey, and I was about to make pancakes—I'm babbling."

"Hannah?"

She set the kettle down but didn't turn. Trent was right behind her, and yes, he was taller when she was shod in old slippers, though he still bore the same sandalwood and spice scent.

"It's OK," he said, slipping his arms around her waist and resting his cheek against her hair. "I'm protective of Merle too."

That's what Hannah had been feeling—that anxious, panicky, what-do-I-do, what-do-I-say feeling had been protectiveness.

"I am protective. Very, very, and the girls shouldn't catch us cuddling like this."

"Why not?" He didn't move, didn't step back, and the solid warmth of his embrace was absurdly precious here in Hannah's own kitchen.

"I haven't said anything to Grace about you. She's never seen me being affectionate with anybody but her. It won't make sense to her."

Trent wore thick wool socks. They'd be the definition of cozy, if Hannah were to borrow them.

"Then it's about time Grace learned she isn't the only one who thinks her mother is special." Trent kissed Hannah's cheek then stepped back. When Hannah turned, he was squirting honey into his tea as casually as if they'd been meeting in each other's kitchens for years. "Merle has to learn the same thing. She's protective of me too, you see, and while that's touching and charming and sweet, it isn't her job."

"Because you don't need protecting?"

"Not in the sense she thinks I do. What about you? Do you need protecting?"

He set the honey down and took a sip of his tea, sparing Hannah the need to answer.

She did not need protecting. She refused to consider whether she might crave a little of it anyhow.

"By God, that's good," Trent said. "We'll have to get some for the office. You said something about pancakes?"

Why did she suspect his "we" included not only his two brothers, but also Hannah?

"Pancakes, right. I'd best get dressed first, if you don't mind a few minutes of solitude?"

"I will enjoy my tea." He gestured with his mug, looking absolutely relaxed and at home in Hannah's kitchen. From upstairs, the sound of two little girls whooping with laughter came wafting down.

Hannah said nothing—how long had she waited to hear her daughter laughing like that with a friend?—but repaired to the bathroom off the kitchen and shuddered at the half-dressed, tired, smiling buffoon she saw in the mirror.

Chapter 11

"MOM HAS BEEN SICK," GRACE INFORMED HER BEAR, though he was a stuffed bear, so he wouldn't ever answer. "Even if she's willing to go outside, I can't let her catch cold. We might have time to make a snow bear."

A snow unicorn would be really cool, though it might take all afternoon so that would have to wait until Mom felt better.

"Hi, Grace!"

"Merle! What are you doing here?" First snow, then pancakes, and now Merle? A magic day, surely. The day Grace had started riding lessons had been magic too.

"We're going tobogganing up at the fire tower. I begged Dad to bring you with us."

Grace flipped the covers back, and Merle toed off her boots and climbed on the bed. "That's an old bear. Bet you've always had him."

"As long as I can remember, though his fur isn't loved off yet. Did your dad say yes?"

Merle's gloves and scarf came off next, a matched set decorated with white horses. "He's talking to your mom. She's pretty. He'll get her to say yes. Is this your bed?"

"Nope. C'mon. I'll show you my bedroom. Is your dad nice?"

Grace hopped out of bed and headed for the door as Merle gathered up her winter stuff and scrambled after her.

"Dad's nice, but he gets cranky sometimes when he

has a big trial. I make him take me for ice cream then. You forgot your bear."

Grace pulled the covers up over Wishes and left him propped against Mom's pillow.

"Mom's been sick. She can use a bear for a while. She's nice too. I think she can use a grown-up to visit with."

Merle tucked the blanket right up to Wishes's chin. "Grown-ups get lonely, and they don't have recess or lunch to play with friends. I'm not sure I want to be a grown-up, if all we do is work and do chores."

"Me either, but, Merle, can I ask you a question?" Merle opened the door, and the scent and heat of the woodstove came wafting into Mom's room.

"Ask me anything. I have questions for you too."

"I've never been tobogganing. What's it like?"

"C'mon," Merle said, whirling down the hallway, "I'll draw you a picture! Tobogganing with Dad is the best fun ever!"

Hannah was in her jeans and favorite sweater, teeth brushed and face washed, when somebody rapped on the door.

"You decent?"

"I am." She'd yet to subdue her hair, though. Decent and presentable were two different things.

"Here." Trent opened the door and held her mug out to her. "I zapped it in the microwave."

"Thanks." Hannah took the hot tea, but she had to open the door to do it.

"I could do that for you, you know." He filled up the

doorway with good-looking guy who did great things for his jeans.

"Drink my tea?"

"Brush your hair. I'm the dad to a seven-year-old girl. I won the intergalactic fast-braiding division at the last Dad Games." Trent plucked the brush from Hannah's hand and took her by the wrist. "You sit and sip your tea. Prepare to be impressed."

Hannah wanted to argue. She *should* argue. She was going to argue. Very soon.

She sat at the kitchen table and took a sip of her tea.

"One braid or two?"

"One," she said as he drew the brush through her hair. Three passes of the brush and her eyes grew heavy.

"You have such beautiful hair, and you don't wiggle the whole time."

"Did you just kiss my nape?"

"Don't disturb the master at his art," Trent said, kissing the side of her neck. "The girls are off hatching up unicorn conspiracies, and a little kitchen kissing never hurt anybody's Sunday morning. I take it you're feeling better?"

Trent was French braiding her hair, and it felt soooooo good. Upstairs, two pairs of little feet cantered down the hallway, accompanied by giggles and laughter.

Trent really was a dad. He sorted through the tangles patiently and didn't yank on Hannah's scalp, and yet there was a briskness to his approach too.

"I am feeling better. Miracle drugs." The sound of little-girl laughter from upstairs was surely among the most miraculous drugs every invented.

"Miracle sleep," he countered. "You got your first docket under your belt. You'll be hard to guard now."

"I did not enjoy it." Hannah had hated it, hated how it left her feeling, and nearly hated herself for doing it.

"It'll grow on you. Like me." Trent unwrapped an elastic from around the brush handle and secured her braid. "All done."

"My thanks." She patted the braid. She could not have done it better herself, not if she'd had all morning. "Now to pancakes."

"I have a suggestion," Trent said, hunkering down to meet her eyes.

"There are children one floor up." Happy children and probably some unicorns too.

"Ah, you are having Naughty Thoughts, then? I'm encouraged, but I'm trying to behave, because I'm your guest, and I want to be invited back."

Hannah brushed his hair back from his brow, because despite the docket from hell, there was happiness in her kitchen too. "What's your suggestion?"

"Let me take the girls out, and you enjoy peace and quiet here while we're gone. We can have pancakes for lunch."

Hannah had assumed if Grace went sledding, Hannah would come along to supervise, to watch, to parent.

To freeze her butt off, because moms did not have snowsuits, and to trudge her weary backside all over the mountain, likely pulling Grace's sled.

"You need the rest," Trent said, "and I will guard the girls with my life. You know I will."

He *would* guard the girls with his life. That was dad talk, not hyperbole. "You won't let them go too fast?"

"The hill isn't that steep, but it's nice and long. Trust me, Hannah. I'll bring her home safe and sound, worn-out and happy. Early bedtime is a definite possibility."

He wiggled his eyebrows, the wretch. The eyebrows of a pirate prince.

"Don't get stuck up there," Hannah said. "It's snowing, in case you haven't noticed. Don't let anybody get too cold, either."

Trent kissed her again, this time on the mouth. "Thank you. Trusting me with Grace means a lot to me."

He might have said more, but Hannah buried her nose against his neck. "Thank you." His hand stroked her braid the way he often ran his fingers down the length of his tie. "For not fussing me. I never told you about Grace."

"You would have. I might have guessed."

"How would you have known?"

"Moms have a quality to them, a solidness, a sense of humor. I don't know. It's in your touch, too, when you tidy up me up. You gave James the brush-off, and made him laugh about it. He was impressed and pleased with you."

Had Trent been jealous of a silly lunch flirtation? "I did?"

"He said something to Mac about it."

"James was pleased?"

"James is easily pleased when it comes to females." Trent shifted to stand at the bottom of the steps. "Girls!"

"Yes, Daddy?"

"What, Merle's dad?"

"If we're not going to get stuck up on the tower road until spring, you'd best bundle up. Grace's mom has said Grace can come with us, and then we'll come back here for pancakes."

Squeals of glee, and the thunder of little feet coming down the stairs.

"Can I, Mom? Can I really? Did you hear that, Bronco? Trailclimber is coming too."

Trent waded in and got boots and mittens and scarves on the appropriate wiggling child, while Hannah washed up the tea mugs and silently marveled at how easily Grace accepted Trent's presence. True, he was "Merle's dad," but Grace instinctively trusted him.

Trent and his charges trundled out the door a few minutes later, leaving a ringing silence in their wake.

Hannah looked around her kitchen, which seemed empty now, not quite so cozy. She took the Eeyore mug, got out the tea bags, put the kettle back on, and tried to decide if she felt like laughing or crying.

Or both.

———

Trent loaded two rosy-cheeked cherubs into the back of the SUV less than two hours later, then waited patiently for the unicorns to pile in as well—maybe they were miniature unicorns—before closing the door and heading back down the mountain.

Carefully. The snow hadn't stopped, and before too much longer, four-wheel drive would have to be augmented by chains unless the plows got busy.

"Thanks, Merle's dad," Grace said. "I had fun, and so did Bronco."

"Me and Trailclimber too," Merle chorused. "But my feet are froze, and my hands are froze."

"And my ears are froze," Grace chorused, "and my nose is froze—"

"And this dad is froze," Trent cut in. "Remind me

next year I said this year was the last year I'd tow you up the hill."

"He says that every year," Merle added. "Then we go home and have hot chocolate and watch a movie, except Dad tries to sneak out halfway through the movie and says he's just going to the potty."

"I do go to the potty."

"But then you disappear into your study or check your email or go do Dad stuff."

"I make my mom watch a full-length with me every Friday," Grace said. "She's too tired to sneak off then."

Their conversation drifted off into various techniques for managing unruly parents, while Trent eavesdropped shamelessly.

So Hannah Stark was a single mom, and a single mom who, like Trent, had full-time duty.

Of course she was. It was a big part of what had attracted him to her. Single parenting took nerves of steel, stamina, self-discipline, humor, and a host of strengths Hannah had in spades, and yet he hadn't put the whole picture together.

Grace was a delight. Her imagination was endless, and her sense of fun abundant. Her mother had put the manners on her too, though the child barely hid her curiosity about "Merle's dad."

James and Mac would be pleased.

Trent was pleased.

He saw to unswaddling the little girls when Hannah greeted them. Without thinking, he bent down and touched his lips to hers, provoking a chorus of squeals and admonitions to the unicorns to hide their eyes.

"Sorry," he muttered when Hannah handed him a

mug of hot chocolate a few minutes later. "That kiss just slipped out."

———

"You're forgiven," Hannah said quietly, though she felt as perplexed as Trent sounded. "I took a nap. Do you know how long it has been since I took a real, sleep-in-peace nap?"

"You need a pair of doting brothers. You also need weather stripping on that damned door."

Grace, who'd been reliving toboggan runs with Merle, sat up straighter at the table. "Merle's dad said damn."

Hannah snitched a bite of fluffy, warm pancake. *Get out of that one, Knightley.*

"That door lets in the north wind," Trent said. "Makes my bones cold."

"Drink your hot chocolate, Dad," Merle admonished. "How come grown-ups can drink theirs standing up and we have to sit at the table?"

"Because this way," Trent said, "if you get out of line, I can thump you without reaching across the table."

He did sit though, and he ate a mountain of pancakes, while the ladies consumed much smaller portions.

"We're going upstairs to play, Mom," Grace announced when the girls had been excused. "Come on, Bronco."

"Come on, Trailclimber."

"I feel like I should be listening for the sound of little hooves," Trent said, bringing his dishes to the sink. "Do you have any weather stripping?"

What did it mean when a guy asked about weather stripping, and Hannah found the question romantic?

"Does it come in a roll and has a sticky side? I think so. Look in the drawer under the microwave."

He weather-stripped the door, split a significant amount of wood, tightened up the lock plates on the doors so they'd close snugly without being slammed, hammered down a loose floor board near the wood-stove, sharpened every knife in Hannah's drawer, and generally acted like a man putting off leaving as long as he could.

"You shouldn't be doing all this," Hannah said when the afternoon was well advanced and even the pasture upstairs had gone quiet.

"Somebody ought to, and you're on injured reserve for now, Stark. Where's your screwdriver?"

"Same drawer. Why?"

"Your cupboard doors are hanging askew because the hinges need tightening."

Was that a metaphor for something? "Trent, I haven't heard a single plow go by. Aren't you worried about getting snowed in here?"

"Would that be such a bad thing?"

Hannah caught the ramifications of his seemingly innocent question. Surprise, suspicion, and a spreading, happy warmth came on its heels.

"You planned this?" she asked.

"I can still dig out and probably get home. It's only a couple of miles."

"That doesn't answer the question." No way she'd let a child get into that SUV on a probably.

"Yes, I hoped." He frowned at a particularly loose hinge, a man seemingly absorbed in a task. "I hoped if I piddled around enough with manly-man chores, you might realize it would be much safer—and more fun—if you invited me and Merle to a sleepover."

"A sleep—a *sleepover*?"

He could not be suggesting what she thought he was suggesting. Not this soon, not with the children underfoot, not—

Not that she'd object so very strenuously.

"I'll take the couch, Stark, and get up every few hours to feed the woodstove. The house will be all toasty when you wake up, and Grace will think you're the best mom in the whole world ever. So will the unicorns."

She should say no. No, thank you. Or no, not this soon. Or no, I need time to think this through.

"It's entirely up to you, Stark." He closed the cupboard, and the door was for once hanging straight. "Me, I'd like to snuggle with you, but I haven't made a secret of that."

"You are not spending the night in my bed with two little girls just down the hall, waiting to come gate-crashing at three a.m. with nightmares, accidents, bad dreams—"

He touched the handle of the screwdriver to her lips, the plastic warm from his grip. "I know the drill, and I agree with you. I don't want Merle thinking the day she meets a woman, I'm hopping into that woman's bed. Merle understands where babies come from."

Hannah pushed the screwdriver aside with one finger. "So does Grace."

So did Hannah.

"So do I," Trent said. "While I am enough of a Knightley to always have protection with me, what's in my wallet probably expired before you passed the bar."

A year could be a very long time, more than year, now. "I have a wallet too, Trenton Knightley." Though it held precious little besides a copy of her name change court order, her driver's license, one credit card, and a folded twenty.

"Our virtue is safe for now," Trent said. "Up to a point." He moved on to the next cupboard, which also wasn't quite plumb.

This proposed sleepover—had the term ever been so misused?—could have all manner of consequences.

"Tomorrow is Monday," Hannah said. "Seeing you in the office after this will be odd."

"Working with people you also have some sort of external relationship with takes getting used to, but I do it with Mac and James, and we manage pretty well. I like knowing my brothers have my back even at work, if you want the truth."

For Trent, work was not a place free from family, as it was for most people, but then, for most of recorded history, many people had worked where they and their families lived.

"How are you feeling, Stark?"

"A little washed out, but well enough. Why?"

"Because I am feeling pretty pleased with myself and my life," he said, closing the second cupboard door and facing her. "My daughter, who is shy to the point of reticence, has been playing with a friend for hours. I hope I've been useful to you in a domestic sense by puttering around your house, and I'm looking forward to homemade pizza and a full-length movie to finish off this very nice day."

"Homemade pizza and a full-length?" Movie. A full-length *movie*.

"I've got *It's a Wonderful Life* out in the car." Trent grasped Hannah's wrist and pulled her closer. "Invite me to a sleepover, Stark."

"I should not." Though she would not send them out onto unplowed roads. Her adoptive parents had been killed in an accident that involved snowy roads.

Trent kissed her cheek and spoke quietly, almost whispering. "Mac gave me the best recipe for dough. I love the feel of it, soft and pliant in my hands, warm, smooth, with lots of give." He palmed her breast gently.

"You're invited," she said, scooting away a little—only a little. "You and Merle are invited. So is Trailclimber."

"We accept. Now come here and let me hold you."

"None of that pizza-dough business." Hannah curled against him, and without her heels, the fit was different. She felt more diminutive, more domestic. She liked the fit just fine. Liked this fit just fine—too.

Trent pulled her close, close enough she could feel a nascent erection, but other than that, she treasured a comfortable, trusting embrace.

"What time does Grace go to bed on a school night?"

"We'll have at least a two-hour school delay tomorrow," Hannah said, nuzzling his throat. "She's had a big day today, and we have to factor in that the girls will likely not drop off straight to sleep."

"I've had a big day too. Nine?"

"Nine sounds good." Though to Hannah, nine o'clock also sounded many eternities in the future.

Hannah lay awake for a long time, pondering the developments of the day.

Or trying to. Her ability to analyze and process rationally had been obliterated by a slew of small moments that should have been meaningless.

Trent winking as he shaped pizza dough on a floured cutting board.

Merle and Grace, giggling and laughing and tearing around the house and *making noise*, like children were supposed to.

Trent, gently reminding Merle—and therefore Grace as well—to ask to be excused at the end of the meal.

Grace telling her mother to go read a book, because she and Merle would clean up the paper plates and napkins from dinner, and Trent leading Hannah out of the kitchen to enforce the children's proclamation.

Hannah hadn't seen most of the movie. Oh, she'd been sitting on the couch, sandwiched between Grace and Trent, with Merle on Trent's other side. The evening had been cozy, sweet, warm, and precious. So, so precious, to cuddle up, not only her and Grace with a cat or a few stuffed animals.

Trent was a wonderful dad. He had the knack of setting limits without scolding, of bringing humor to his interactions with the children without making them feel ridiculed. He was affectionate with his daughter, and he genuinely liked his own kid.

He included Hannah and Grace in his affection, and that—that—was what stalled Hannah's mental engines. She could brief cases; she could manage the logistics of single parenting; she could analyze her client's situations and the best strategy for representing them in court.

She had no frame of reference for this lovely, dear,

and confusing business of familiarity with another adult and his child.

Familial business, maybe.

Hannah had tried to stand emotionally outside of the day, to ignore the pang in her chest when Merle bellowed dibs on the bathroom at intermission, and Grace had tried to race her there instead.

Hannah had wanted to pretend the day had been simply pleasant, a break from routine. Except Trent would casually stroke a hand over her braid or loop an arm around her shoulders, and she'd melt inside and have all she could do not to curl into his warmth.

She rolled over and pushed aside the curtain to the window beside her bed. Moonlight illuminated the snow, making the nightscape beautiful and peaceful. The plows had gone by some time during the movie. Trent hadn't noticed, or if he had noticed, he hadn't said anything.

Neither had Hannah.

"I will have to oil your hinges."

Her door creaked closed, and Trent Knightley stood in her bedroom. He was dressed, while Hannah, nice and warm under her covers, was not.

"I thought we agreed the children are right down the hall, and we weren't going to jeopardize our virtue?" Hannah hiked herself up on her elbows as Trent began shedding clothes.

"The Vandal horde is fast asleep. I checked, and I won't overstay my welcome, Hannah, not in your bed, not in your house. Mooch over, before a guy freezes his parts off."

She hesitated for as long as it took to inspect him, the healthy adult male by moonlight.

"I don't know if I'm ready for this," she said, scooting across the mattress.

"I said we'd take it slow, and I meant that. Mostly, I am here for some adult conversation conducted without the hovering presence of a pair of nosy unicorns. Do you believe me?"

"No."

"That saves some time, then." Trent climbed in, threaded an arm under her neck, and pulled her close. "Ah, Stark, you feel good. You feel so very, very good." He let out a long, happy sigh.

"You feel different." Hannah gave herself points for honesty, then deducted them for lack of flirtatiousness.

To have a big, warm, naked man in her bed, all his planes and hollows and surfaces available for her exploration was novel. She'd seen Trent's lean, muscular strength gilded by moonlight for only a moment, but it had been a fascinating moment.

She took a sniff of his shoulder. "You showered."

"A cold shower. I had to do something while I waited for the natives to settle down. Touch me, Hannah Stark, or I'll find my own mischief to get into."

"Where?"

"Where? Oh, for the—"

Hannah felt him backing up and reconsidering.

"I am not your first guy."

What was that supposed to mean? The cozy sense of adventure Hannah had been nurturing shifted toward confusion, toward shame even.

"You are my first since Grace was born. Before that hardly bears mentioning."

He was quiet, and Hannah feared he'd soon get

out of her bed and dress, because in two short sentences, she had made the situation awkward. Trent wasn't here for adult conversation; he was here to romp and play, just as James had offered to romp and play with her.

Except Hannah hadn't been offered even audit privileges in the class on romping and playing.

When she thought Trent would push the covers aside and make excuses, his palm cradled her jaw. For a long moment, he traced her features with his fingers, and Hannah held still, lest he stop.

"So maybe I am your first," he said, brushing his thumb over her lips. "You've been around boys, I take it, but never been with a man."

"That says it as well as anything would. You know what you're doing, and I don't. I know the basics, but none of the—I know the basics."

His hands went still on her face.

Now he would leave. Now he'd decide she was too much work. Now he'd make some sweet, sad riposte, and she'd never know—

He shifted over her, so he blanketed her with his naked length.

"Then you have to help me not bungle this. I'm out of practice, Stark, and I've never had the moves some guys have—or say they have—but I'm a fast learner, and I'm fascinated by the subject."

"The subject?" She stroked his hair, then the bare, warm skin of his back and shoulders and all down the length of his muscled arms to his wrists.

"The subject is Hannah Stark, and how to make her crazy with pleasure."

"Crazy?" She curled a leg around the back of his thigh, marveling at the sheer elegance of his form.

"You mustn't scream," he said, and Hannah felt his teeth—*his teeth?*—scrape her earlobe. "Or only a little, quietly. We can't wake the girls or those damned equine chaperones. Feels good to cuss."

He bit her earlobe gently, then sucked.

"I won't scream." She shivered instead, and pressed up against him.

"I might." He stopped tormenting her earlobe and settled his weight more heavily on her. "Scream that is."

"That feels good," Hannah said, clutching his backside to pull him even closer. "I like it, I like feeling you on me."

"Damn, your nails. No, don't let go. I like it, I love it. God help me." He shut up and used his lips to explore her face, just as he'd done moments before with his fingertips. Featherlight, he grazed his mouth over her brows and cheeks, down the length of her nose.

"Stop teasing me," Hannah whispered. Along her stomach, the heavy ridge of his erection lay strange, arousing, and a little frightening.

He could hurt her.

But he wouldn't. She knew he wouldn't hurt her that way no matter how aroused he became, no matter how inexperienced she was, no matter what.

"Tease me back," he said, giving her a glancing taste of his mouth. "Bully me without mercy. Read me the Riot Act. Torment me until I'm begging."

She angled her head to kiss him, to stop his foolish words, except there had been a desperate quality to his tone, suggesting it wasn't all foolishness. She brushed her mouth over his, and he sighed against her cheek. When she repeated the movement, the kiss caught them and held them, and soon Trent was running his tongue over her lips.

He was asking her a question with his kiss, and Hannah realized she could ask as well. She traced his mouth slowly with her tongue, provoking a soft groan from him. She did it again, sliding her hands up his sides, and he hitched closer.

When she parted her lips, he shifted again, up and more over her, and Hannah had the sense of him filling her awareness entirely, blocking out everything except him, his warmth, his maleness, his caresses. His tongue explored gently, until Hannah's wrapped both legs around his flanks.

Trent broke off the kiss and rested his forehead against Hannah's. "I want to be inside you. I want to *come* inside you."

"We can't." She was on birth control pills, but pregnancy was only one of the many risks holding her back.

"We won't," he said, turning his head so his cheek was against her hair. "You can trust me on that, Hannah. I need a distraction."

He shifted off of her, and Hannah wanted to howl with the loss of him.

"Where are you going?" She heard the insecurity in her voice and hated it, but if he left her now—

"Not far," he said, rolling to his back. "Come here, and keep me warm." He caught her under the arms and pulled her over him so she straddled him.

Self-conscious and uncertain, Hannah folded down over his chest.

"You are shy," he said, burying his hands in her hair. "Let me see you, Hannah Stark. Let me admire you."

"That won't qualify as a distraction."

"I'll be the judge of that." He didn't hurry her, didn't manhandle her. He kept his touch on her back slow and easy, then settled his hands on either side of her hips. "I won't look if you don't want me to, Hannah, but I want to touch."

Her breasts. He wanted her to sit up and expose herself to the moonlight coming in the window, while he looked at her and touched her and made her crazy.

"Close your eyes," Hannah said.

Trent did, so she eased up off his chest, took his right hand, and settled it over her left breast.

"No peeking."

"No peeking," he said on a slow exhale. His expression was a study in concentration, but Hannah had to close her own eyes, the better to feel his fingers shaping her breast.

"Lovely," he whispered. "Beautiful, wondrous." He explored her carefully, tracing his palm over her peaked nipple, his touch so light Hannah barely felt it on her skin, but registered it low in her body. She took his other hand and put it on her right breast, and he slowly closed his grip on both.

"Tell me what you like, Hannah." He kept his eyes closed, thank God. "Tell me if you want more, if you need more."

She closed her hands over his rather than attempt words, and he increased the pressure on her nipples slightly until she sighed with the pleasure of it, and pushed into his hands.

"You like that." He curled up and rested his cheek on her breast. "I like it too."

Then he turned his head and settled his mouth over her nipple, and liking didn't come close to Hannah's reaction. Currents of need sparked through her where only longing had been before. She sank her hands into his hair and held him to her, wanting to move, not daring to. His free hand came down to settle on her backside while the other plied her breast.

"Trent…"

"Move on me," he said, lifting his hips against her then dropping back to the bed. "Let me feel you moving."

His hand on her backside urged her to shift her hips with him, and Hannah picked up the rhythm. To undulate against him helped, but it also made all those low, humming currents burn hotter and faster.

"I'm making a mess," she said, mortified at the dampness between them.

"You're aroused. I'm making you wet. Lovely, wet, hot female. Make me wet too." He pushed up against her and rocked the length of his erection over her sex.

Trent wrapped her tightly to him with an arm low across her back, and the pressure of their bodies moving together shifted something inside Hannah, made her dizzy and hot and incoherent with need.

Crazy. Beautifully, wonderfully crazy.

"Use me, Hannah." Trent arched up to get his mouth over hers. His tongue mimicked the rhythm of their bodies, and his hand settled over her breast, and Hannah could not have uttered an intelligible sentence to save her life. Something gathered deep inside her, something urgent and compelling. It made her cling and grind and clutch at him until pleasure coalesced inside her and stormed through her in cascades of novel and overwhelming sensation.

The shock left her helpless to do more than endure the cataclysm, to hold onto Trent and let the pleasure wash over her and through her, and over her again.

When it receded, she was panting on his chest, her body at once heavy and light, floating and anchored, her mind at peace. Then gradually, she became aware of Trent's hands moving on her back, the rhythm of his breathing beneath her.

His erection, still pressed against her.

"I'm sorry," she said, "I had to have hurt you. I didn't mean—" Embarrassment stole her words, and some of her wonder, though not all. This was the experience other women took for granted, the one they joked about in high school and demanded as their due in college.

"You were magnificent, Hannah."

"But you're still— You didn't—" She pressed her nose to his sternum, certain he could feel her blush. "What now?"

"I can come like this too."

By contrast, his orgasm was nearly soundless. He kept their bodies snug while he moved; the strokes were slow and measured, just a half-dozen easy thrusts against her belly, and Hannah felt damp warmth between them, then a long, soft sigh from Trent.

"That's it? That's all you get?"

"Hush." He gently pushed her head to his shoulder. "It's enough. More than enough."

She did not believe him, except his touch had shifted, become slower, more tender if that were possible, and it was all Hannah could do to keep her eyes open. She dozed, curled on his chest, his arms around her, and a sense of loveliness pervading her mind and body.

So that was an orgasm?

And then, *So that was almost making love?*

"I've put you to sleep," Trent said, a trace of humor in his voice. "Let's tidy up before we both drift off."

He was matter of fact about it, snatching a handful of tissues from the nightstand and swabbing at Hannah's belly. He was brisk with himself, scrubbing at his softening cock, and then at his stomach. This sort of competence—confidence, really—amazed Hannah, and gave her almost as great a sense of intimacy with him as what had gone before.

Almost.

And now, now, she wanted to hear his voice, to talk, to learn how a couple eased from such closeness to what came after.

But what to say?

"Cuddle up." Trent shifted Hannah so she lay along his side, her head on his shoulder. "Don't go silent on me yet, Stark. A man could use a few reassurances."

He caught her hand in his, brought it to his mouth, and kissed her knuckles before settling their joined hands over his heart.

"What kind of reassurances?"

"The sincere kind. You enjoyed yourself?"

"I have never enjoyed myself quite like that before," she said, turning her face to his shoulder. "I am dumbstruck."

"Never before? Never?"

She shook her head, unwilling to elaborate. Let him think his was a novel approach for her, a different position, whatever a more sophisticated woman might have meant by "never."

Trent hiked Hannah's leg across his thighs, giving her foot a warm squeeze. "Never?"

"You want to talk about this?" She huffed out a sigh, but to cuddle naked with him, warm and safe in his embrace, her body still humming with pleasure made her want to give him the truth.

"I seldom had my own room growing up," she said, "and in college there were roommates, and certain skills take absolute privacy to develop. I didn't date much, and then there was Grace."

He was quiet for a moment, probably trying to think of something to say to such a personal disclosure.

"Ah, Hannah, how you honor me."

Honor. Not flatter or please or trust, but honor encompassed all three, and even more.

"How will I face you in the office?" Hannah yawned and closed her eyes as she posed the question. The office seemed a million miles and five years away, at least. A different planet, where people wore clothes and bustled around on company business.

"With a smile, my dear. You will face me in the office with a nice, fat, satisfied smile."

Chapter 12

GERALD MATTHEWS UNTANGLED HIMSELF FROM GAIL Russo's flowered sheets and took himself off to the bathroom. He'd swung by after making the rounds, as he occasionally did, though Gail had been next to worthless. She didn't party, and she was upset he'd left the firm, upset he'd be out on his own, upset he hadn't told her he was moonlighting.

Stupid, upset, clinging bitch. She'd be a lot more upset if she'd known that before he'd left Hartman and Whiny, he'd helped himself to a peek at Hannah Stark's personnel file, and oh, my, who would have guessed, Hannah Stark had at least one dependent?

A surreptitious investigation of Hannah's purse— silly Hannah, leaving her office and her desk unlocked when she used the conference room—revealed a school picture in her wallet of a cute little girl with dark hair and Hannah's stubborn chin.

Pay dirt, in other words, given that Gerald knew which elementary school a kid living at Hannah's address would attend.

Gail would shoot around the room backward like a deflating balloon if she knew Gerald had snooped to that extent.

He could still hear Gail's sermonizing: "How could you just waltz out of Hartman without leaving me some way to explain this? I'm the head of HR, and you broke your employment contract. Do you know how that makes me look? What if the company decides to sue you for breach of contract?"

Whine, whine, whine.

But Gail's rant had given him an answer to a question that had bothered him—he wasn't being sued, *yet*. He'd slipped a conspiratorial arm around her shoulders when she'd passed along that tidbit.

"Hartman won't sue me. They don't have the resources right now, especially in Trent Knightley's department. He's up to his ass in alligators, and Hannah Stark won't be any kind of replacement for me."

Gail looked uncomfortable, so Gerald prodded her.

"You holding out on me, Gail?" She leaned into him, poor, dispirited little Gail. "You can tell me. I don't even work there anymore." Thank Almighty God.

"Hannah did fine on her first docket, Gerald, and Trent sent her home at noon with strep throat. I don't think she'll fall on her ass, if that's what you're hoping for."

"Of course she managed, Gail." He dropped his arm. "That was a light docket, Linker was in a decent mood, and Margaret cut fellow-bitch counsel a break on her first day. Just wait until the January dockets hit. I saw what was scheduled for then, and I don't envy Hannah Stark what awaits her between now and spring. What I want to know is do you have anything waiting for me?"

And her clothes had practically fallen off of her.

He'd given her a little of the rough stuff, but as usual, she'd acted like she didn't like it. Women were so predictable.

Now she was off to work, even though it had snowed

a foot, the courthouse was closed, and most of the office would be claiming they couldn't make it in until tomorrow. Gerald treated himself to a long, hot shower, then slung a towel around his hips and made his way to the fridge. Gail stocked his favorite brand of beer, or she heard about it.

He stood in her kitchen, dripping onto her hardwood floor, and saw a note propped beside the beer.

> *Gerald, the circumstances under which you've changed employment suggest for both our sakes we should minimize our contact for the foreseeable future. I hope you understand what I'm saying. Best of luck, Gail.*

He balled up the note, pitched it in the general direction of the trash, and cracked open a Sam Adams, chugging half of it.

He was being sued for breach of contract; that was what Gail was "saying." Part of him wanted to kick her over the county line—she was the head of HR for shit's sake; she should have been able to prevent this—and part of him was touched at the quaintness of her warning.

She'd had to have one last roll in the hay with him before she cut him loose, the pathetic little tramp. Gail was one woman whose attentions he wouldn't miss, always so damned nice, always so damned guilty. He'd hated that part of her.

But Gail's note clarified one thing for Gerald: he would take Hannah Stark—or Juliet Randall—down if it was his last act as a member of the bar. No one made a fool of him, least of all some wet-behind-the-ears ice bitch stepping into his shoes. Hannah Stark would leave the practice of law—at least—or get kicked out of it.

Helping himself to another swallow of cold beer, Gerald went back to the bedroom, got out his cell phone, and found Joan Smithson's number.

—∿∿—

Monday morning dawned brilliantly sunny and temperate. The opening of school was delayed two hours, and Trent admonished Hannah not to show up at the office before noon.

He helped her tidy up the couch where he'd ostensibly slept, and caught her hands in his as they folded a blanket up.

"You will come to the Christmas party with me, Stark."

Thus Hannah admitted to herself, whether she was ready for it or not, she was dating the boss.

"I will let you pick me up and drop me off, because we live only two miles apart, and I'm mindful of my carbon footprint."

"Right." He took the blanket from her. "We'll carpool."

His smile was wickedly pleased, and Hannah had been relieved to bundle him and Merle off while she and Grace were still in their pajamas. She turned to face her daughter, who looked a little perplexed.

"We had some fun this weekend, didn't we, Grace?"

"Lotsa fun. Did Merle's dad slip you the fish?"

"*What?*"

"Joey Hinlicky's older brother has girlfriends, and he's always fish-kissing them. Joey spies on him and then tells us about it. Larry Smithson said his brother does the same thing."

"Why would you think Merle's dad would kiss me like that?"

"We saw you on the couch, while we were doing the dishes," Grace said with a shrug. "He kissed you."

"He kissed my cheek."

"I like him, and I don't have a dad. If he were my dad, he'd be kissing you on the mouth and you'd be kissing him too. Can I have peanut butter toast?"

"Peanut butter toast sounds good." Much better than a discussion of French kissing.

"Are you going to marry Merle's dad?"

"I like him, Grace, and he kissed my cheek, but getting married is a big, big decision, and it wouldn't be just up to me."

"It would be up to me too?" Grace got out the bread and put two slices in the toaster.

At least Grace hadn't brought Bronco into the decision—yet.

"That decision would be up to Merle's dad and me, though we'd listen to what you and Merle had to say about it, but he has not asked me." Hannah got the peanut butter down and opened it.

"You could ask him. He's really nice."

"I won't ask him any time soon. He is nice, but we work together, and it's tough enough to be friends and work together."

Grace frowned, a knife full of peanut butter in her hand.

"That doesn't make sense, Mom. My job is going to school, and if I didn't make friends there, I wouldn't have any friends. I don't want you to be lonely. I have a friend now, and you should have one too. Do you want some toast?"

"Yes, please."

Hannah watched, bemused, while her daughter made them breakfast. This was a first, and had something to do with acquiring a friend and being around that friend and that friend's father.

The whole morning unfolded with the same sense of bemusement, as if Hannah were simultaneously in two different realities.

The inside Hannah had to stop herself from dwelling on the image of Trent Knightley, naked, gilded in moonlight, standing in her bedroom.

The outside Hannah made it in to the office by 11:00 a.m., tackled the next docket worth of cases, and was relieved to hear Trent had gone to a settlement conference at another law firm and wasn't expected back until late afternoon.

Relieved and disappointed, though how on earth was she to face him?

Hannah drove out to the jail after lunch, town having gotten less snow than the slopes and the sun making an effort to melt what hadn't been plowed away. Her client was Beauregard Jefferson Davis, IV, and he was serving five years for rape. Hannah's job was to get him an abatement of child support while he was incarcerated, or he'd just be put right back in jail for nonsupport when his sentence was over.

And again, she felt a duality inside, between the part of her that would do a good job for this client and the part of her that wished Grace's dad was serving at least five years if not more.

Wherever he was.

The county detention center, where sentences of up

to eighteen months could be served, was a long, low, red brick building with precious few windows. On one side, a concrete "courtyard" was fenced with chain link and razor wire. Floodlights would keep the whole area illuminated at night, and a couple of basketball hoops lent a surreal touch.

Hannah shut off her car, gathered her briefcase—but not her purse—locked the car, and headed for the main entrance. Her stomach protested more the closer she got to the building, as if her body sensed the misery the bricks and mortar kept confined.

Breathing as regularly as she could, Hannah identified herself to the duty officer behind the bulletproof glass. He made a copy of her driver's license, made sure her brief case held only files, noted something on a log of some sort, then made a phone call while Hannah waited.

"You can go down to interrogation, Ms. Stark. Straight along the hallway to room number seven, on your right. We'll bring Davis up in a few minutes."

Hannah waited for a heavy metal door to slide open beside her. She stepped through it, and the door slid shut. When the first door clanged closed, a second equally heavy door before her slowly slid open.

A symbolic airlock, so none of the jailed air mixed with the free air. How did Mac Knightley not only endure the criminal defense business, but thrive on it?

She proceeded down a hallway painted some incontinent color between gray and yellow. The corridor should have been cold, except it wasn't. Higher temperatures made the inmates more sluggish, according the Hannah's Criminal Procedure professor, and so jails were usually toasty places.

Hannah found room number seven, which contained a pair of folding chairs and a battered table, nothing else. She was deciding which chair to take when a sandy-haired man dressed in jail-orange overalls rapped on the doorjamb.

"Ms. Stark? I'm Gard Davis." His modest height did nothing to mask a powerful build—working out was one of the pastimes inmates were permitted. His eyes were light blue, and his face had an appealing masculinity.

Rapists were supposed to be as ugly on the outside as they were on the inside, but this man wasn't ugly, and when he spoke, his voice was as quietly attractive as the rest of him. He was also young, just barely into adulthood.

He held out his hand, and Hannah's nerves leaped as she forced herself to shake hands with him.

He smiled then, a mischievous, charming grin, confirming that Hannah had passed some sort of test. The smile was rife with humor, something else rapists weren't supposed to have.

"How do, ma'am. I'm Beauregard Jefferson Davis the Fourth, but my friends call me Gard. I am mighty glad to see you."

Hannah replied, exchanging civilities that seemed incongruous with the surroundings. "You're my only client here today. We can take our time. Shall we sit?" Good God, was she supposed to let him hold her chair?

Gard got them through the moment by waiting until Hannah took a seat, then taking the other chair. She busied herself fishing out his file and setting it on the table between them, all the while thinking he'd forced some woman to have intimacies she did not want, probably hurting her both physically and psychologically, possibly leaving her pregnant, diseased, and screwed up for life.

Davis regarded her patiently while she glanced over the notes in the file.

"I got an appeal pending," he said eventually. "It won't go anywhere."

Hannah took out her legal pad and pen, paltry weapons against the chaos inside her.

"Your wife paid the firm a good chunk of money to get you an abatement of child support, Mr. Davis. I don't need to know any more about the criminal matter than you want to tell me."

She wanted to know less than nothing about it, in fact.

He scrubbed a hand over his face. "You know I was convicted of second-degree rape," he said. "I'll be sent to the Division of Corrections after Friday, and serve five years, flat time. What you don't know is that my victim was thirteen years old."

Hannah involuntarily shut her eyes. His voice was slow, even, the measured recitation of a Southern Gentleman, but in her mind Hannah pictured Grace at thirteen, Merle…herself.

"Shit." Mr. Davis stood up, his chair scraping back. "Will you help me or not?"

Foster care had been a sort of prison. Some of the group homes were locked facilities, and Hannah had hated those the worst.

"I will do the very best I can to get you an abatement of your child support."

He sat. She'd passed yet another test.

"My victim was thirteen years old, but she told me

she was seventeen, and believe me, ma'am, she looked seventeen and she dressed seventeen. She also drove a car, because her daddy thought it was cute to let her play grown-up. We dated for a few months and screwed around some—she wasn't any virgin, and it wasn't anything exclusive.

"She knew I was separated from my wife and kids, and knew I'd rather be back with them. The day I told her my wife was letting me come home was the day she told her daddy I'd raped her. I was arrested that night, and I haven't seen my kids since, because now I am a pedophile. A goddamned child molester, whose picture will go on the Internet, and who will have to register with the police wherever I live—if I make it through my sentence."

Hannah was too stunned to write anything.

She knew the kind of thirteen-year-old he'd run into. Too tall and too pretty much too soon and way too sexually, they ran riot through the foster care system, ending up pregnant even in locked facilities.

I wanted to practice corporate law. Corporate law.

"You know what the worst part is?" Davis asked, sitting forward and staring at his hands. "The worst part is having to sit in all these sex-offender group therapy sessions, and listen to a bunch of sicko perverts talk about what they've done and what they want to do when they get out. I think the group leader is the sickest of them all, but he keeps telling the guys if they want a decent discharge summary, they have to disclose."

Numbness descended on Hannah, a blessed numbness that protected her from imagining what Davis had to hear if he was to be "rehabilitated" for a crime he hadn't known he was committing.

"I have a daughter, you know," Davis finished quietly.

"How old? You mentioned you have more than one child."

This man was a parent, a *dad*.

"I had a son when I was sixteen, my little girl is just two. Names are Beauregard Jefferson Davis the Fifth, and Annalisa Evangelina Davis. They're the best kids."

Hannah picked up her pen. "How old are you, Mr. Davis?"

"I have reached the ripe old age of nineteen, Ms. Stark, which means my son is three. I will likely be twenty-four years old when I get out, and by then the baby will be in school."

"Who has the children now?"

She clicked into interview-the-client mode, establishing that Mrs. Davis had the children and was living with her parents while her husband served out his sentence. She hadn't intended to sue him for child support, but the wheels had been put in motion by the State when she'd applied for medical assistance for her children.

And the arrearages were piling up.

Hannah could do nothing about the arrearages, except make the abatement retroactive to the day it was filed.

Her interview was concluded, but she wasn't satisfied. "Does your wife visit you?"

"Her parents would make her life hell if she tried. It's probably better she doesn't."

"If you wrote to your children, would she share that with them?"

"That dog won't hunt. The group leader, who does not deserve to be called a mental health professional, would just say I was in denial and failing to take responsibility for my addiction."

"Your addiction?"

"I'm a pedophile, remember? I've never laid an inappropriate hand on a child before or since, but I'm a pedophile."

"What if your wife agreed to write to you twice a year, send you pictures and update you on how the children were doing? You still get mail, don't you?"

"We do," he said, looking thoughtful. "They look through it for contraband, but we do get mail. Pictures of my own kids would likely get through."

"OK, so if you agree not to seek visitation while incarcerated, then maybe she'll send you pictures and updates on a regular basis."

He picked up Hannah's pen and scratched something on her yellow pad.

"That's my wife's work number. You probably have her home phone number, if her mom came with her when she hired you. They keep a close eye on her, but I think this number is still good."

Hannah sat back, when she knew she should be marching down the hallway toward the freedom side of that air lock. "Did you plead guilty to this rape?"

For the first time, he didn't meet her eyes.

"I sure did, and it is the sorriest mistake I ever made. My lawyer told me how pathetic Melissa would look on the witness stand, and how little chance I had of winning. He got me five years flat time, second degree, and I went for it."

"Didn't anybody testify they'd seen her driving a car?"

"My lawyer didn't produce witnesses, Ms. Stark. He didn't even interview any witnesses, and I am post-convicting the son of a bitch, and maybe I'll get me a new trial. That's what the appeal is about."

Mr. Davis was claiming he hadn't had the effective assistance of counsel at his trial, which wasn't likely to get him anywhere. Before he plead guilty, the judge would have asked him under oath and on the record if he was pleading guilty because he *was* guilty. The same judge would have asked if Davis had known he was giving up his right to subpoena and question witnesses— giving up all his trial rights by taking the plea bargain.

The same judge would have asked Davis if he were satisfied with the efforts of his attorney. Davis would have said yes all around, and that would be the end of his chances for appeal.

"Mr. Davis, who was your victim?" Hannah put the question neutrally. *Please, God, don't let it be someone I know. Don't let it be a young girl I shared a room with in some foster home when I was a teenager. Don't let it be a person.*

Just a name.

"Melissa Lewis," he said, matching her neutral tone.

Hannah didn't recognize the name. "What if she recanted her testimony?"

"She did not testify. She made a statement to a very sympathetic cop. If she recanted, she'd be charged with making false statements, which her daddy would not permit. He's some wheel at the Department of Defense, and he'd lose his security clearances, at least that's what Melissa told my wife. Besides, statutory rape is a matter of age, not a matter of consent."

"Your sentence can be modified. If Melissa's parents are raising her to be a lying, promiscuous little tramp and providing her wheels illegally, they are contributing to the condition of a minor, and for Melissa's sake, something needs to be done."

"You going into criminal law, Ms. Stark?" He eased back in his chair, a rebel boy grin on his face.

"No, I am not, but I know a very good criminal attorney, and I will discuss your appeal with him. If you don't hear from me before next Friday, assume your case is still scheduled for the morning docket. I'm on your call list, so give me a ring if you have any questions."

"I will see you Friday," he said, getting to his feet. "Assuming they remember to transport me."

Hannah stood and snapped her briefcase shut. "I have a question."

"Ask."

"How do I get out of here?"

His grin softened to a genuine smile. "You just go back the way you came and knock on the window. They let you out. One of the first stories you hear when you're locked up is about some lawyer who had to wait around at the door for hours for the duty officer to let him out. He sued the place for false imprisonment, so they man the door now. Thank you for coming, and thanks for taking my case."

He shook her hand again, and Hannah felt his eyes on her as she made her way back to the sliding doors that led to freedom.

She made it as far as her car before she began to cry.

"Hannah?" Trent shot his older brother a look of consternation, then carefully wrapped his arms around a very upset lady. "Honey, what's wrong?"

"He can't see his own ch-children," Hannah got out. "She lied to him, and now he's a pedophile, and I can't... *I hate this*."

The last was said in such low, miserable tones, even Mac's eyebrows rose. He passed Trent a monogrammed handkerchief, which Trent tucked into Hannah's hand.

"Just catch your breath. Take your time, and we'll sort it out."

"Don't use your daddy voice on me," she said, pulling away. She swiped at her cheeks, then balled up the hankie. "What are you two doing in the parking lot of the county jail?"

"My conference got cut short. I gave Mac a ride because his truck is in the shop. What has you so upset?"

"My client." She stared at the wrinkled hankie with the embroidered initials. "I shouldn't let it get to me, but he's serving a five-year sentence, in essence, for being too trusting."

"What are the facts?" Mac asked. "And leave your maternal instincts out of it." As Trent watched, under careful, dispassionate questioning, Hannah gradually regained her composure.

"And it's rape," she said. "I wasn't prepared to deal with rape, and then he's not even a rapist, except in the technical sense, and he never stood a chance. Do you know what the incidence of AIDS is in the incarcerated population?"

"What did you say the vic's name was?" Mac asked.

"Melissa Lewis. You know her?"

"She's somewhat infamous in the juvenile system and was picked up last month for soliciting an undercover cop. Her dad tried to bribe the cop, and the whole thing is awaiting trial."

"Can you do anything for Gard Davis?"

"You're asking me to?"

"I am. The system hasn't done right by him."

Mac frowned at her, and Mac's frowns were revered throughout the criminal community for their ability to loosen a perp's bowels. Then the corners of his lips turned up.

"The system surely has not done right by him. I will see what I can do, but for now, I have clients to interview and promises to keep. If you'll take Trent back to the office, it will save him having to read in the car until my boys are done with me."

"I don't fit in her car."

"So put your ego in the trunk," Mac said, turning to go. "That should leave you plenty of room."

A silence extended between Trent and his favorite associate counsel. He hated to see Hannah cry; he loved that she put that much heart into the job.

"I went for years without crying until I took this job," Hannah muttered. "Let's have our argument in the car with the heater going. You want me to drive?"

She gave him a look that suggested he'd just offered to dance on his head and spit nickels, then she passed him the keys. He got in, sliding the driver's seat back as far as it would go.

They tooled along in silence for a few minutes while the car heated up.

"What are we supposed to argue about?" Hannah asked.

"You'll tell me you never agreed to involve yourself with a criminal population, and family law is bad enough, but you draw the line at convicted rapists."

"He's not a rapist." She sounded tired and defeated and so sad.

"I'm sorry you're upset. Every job has the equivalent of rotten cases, bad decisions, aggravating opposing counsel. That isn't unique to the practice of law." Though a rotten day as a ditch digger probably never brought anybody to tears.

"I know. No job is perfect."

"I'd feel better if you'd argue," Trent said, trying for a bantering tone. "Maybe call me a few names? Threaten to quit?"

"I'll be all right." She stared out the window and remained silent, not offering another word all the way back to the office, until they were in the Hartman parking lot and Trent had turned off the engine.

"Why did Mac make that comment about my maternal instincts?" Hannah asked.

"I don't know. I told him I'd taken your daughter tobogganing with Merle, but nothing of any note about the weekend. Why?"

"You *told him* I have a daughter?"

She was staring straight ahead, and her tone was miserable.

"Him and James both. Is that a problem?"

She leaned her head back against the seat. "Make sure they know not to mention it to anybody. Get out your cell phone now, and make sure."

Trent considered the stubbornness in Hannah's words. "Is this something we can discuss?"

"Not now," she said. "Maybe someday, but for now, you have to trust me. The fewer people who know about Grace, the better."

"Are you in the witness protection program?" He'd come across three people who were, as if Damson County was on some top secret federal map of nice small towns.

"I won't be cross-examined, Trent. You either accept this or I start looking for a new job, but, no, I am not in any witness protection program."

Hannah's tone was implacable, brooking no argument, no discussion. Trent considered her profile, utterly calm, telling him nothing, and he recalled the night and the day he'd spent with her and her daughter.

He got out his cell phone.

All week, Hannah expected Trent to corner her, to start with the casual questioning, or perhaps even to engineer a confrontation.

Who was Grace's father?

What was his role in the child's life?

Why *didn't* Grace's father have a role in his child's life?

But Trent was the same as he'd been the first day Hannah worked at Hartman. Friendly, supportive, as helpful as he could be while in and out of the office. By Thursday, Hannah was as focused on her looming confrontation with Trent as she was on her upcoming docket.

He appeared in her doorway late Thursday afternoon, and Hannah had to admit she was relieved to see him.

"Come with me, Stark." He beckoned and backed toward his office. "Time for you to grill me on child support and paternity law."

Hannah grabbed her notebook and followed him. "Did your case settle?" she asked as Trent closed the door behind her.

"To hell with my case."

He wrapped his arms around her, and the next thing Hannah knew, he had her up against his desk, his mouth on hers.

"Missed you, Stark," he said against her lips. "I'm climbing the damned walls for want of you."

For a moment she was too stunned to react, then her arms were around him and she was kissing him back.

"Missed me too, huh?" He rested his forehead against hers. "I had to get that out of my system, had to remind myself. Hell, one single kiss won't do. I have to remind myself again."

He took his time, reminding *her* of the subtlety and pleasure to be had from a skillful man's use of his mouth for things other than opening arguments and cross-examination. Trent was playful and tender, then challenging, and Hannah's grip on him shifted from passive to exploratory to demanding.

"We will consummate our relationship on this damned desk if one of us doesn't show some sense," Trent growled.

That sobered Hannah, barely. "Not during business hours."

He kissed her again, a quick, give-me-strength smackeroo. "Mac would be proud of you. James would laugh his ass off."

"I'm serious." Hannah laid her cheek over his heart. "Not during business hours, not on company time. That crosses a line."

"It does," he said, easing back. "And you deserve better than a quickie on the desk."

"Do you want to hear about tomorrow's docket?" She smoothed her fingers over his hair, resisting the urge to retie his necktie. Nothing equine today, a simple swatch of blue-and-purple paisley.

"I do not want to hear about tomorrow's docket," he said, "but I will be a good sport and pretend I'm listening while you talk about it. The semierect penis creates in men the ability to appear to multitask. Don't be fooled."

"I have no idea what you're blathering about," she said, hopping off the desk. "But I will tell you about my cases."

"I'm talking about the ability to walk around this office the livelong week with a perpetual nascent erection, all the while impersonating the head of the domestic law department. You are to blame."

His expression held humor and disgruntlement, but something else too.

"You don't like being distracted," Hannah said.

Trent's brows rose. He crossed to the couch, sat and patted the place beside him.

"Distracted? Distracted is when I'm preparing for trial and Merle might be coming down with something. Distracted is when I'm worried about James or Mac, but as usual, they forget the use of the English language where I'm concerned. Distracted is trying one case while I'm in preparation for four other trials. What I'm suffering—and I use the word advisedly—is an annihilation of my ability to concentrate."

Hannah took a seat on the sofa a few inches away from him, knowing he was probably exaggerating, but pleased nonetheless. Despite the awkwardness at the jail, despite the even worse scene following that encounter, despite any worst-scenes-of-all to come, she was pleased.

"I've thought about you too." She did not kiss his cheek.

She didn't dare. Not when she could recall in vivid detail the sight of Trenton Knightley wearing nothing but moonlight, and not when he was likely sitting on a powder keg of questions regarding Grace.

"She's thought about me," Trent observed to the room in general. "I pour out my soul to her, and she's thought about me."

In truth, Hannah had worried about what she was *doing* with Trent. She'd missed him, in her bed, in her kitchen, in the office, all the while trying to convince herself if Trent pried regarding Grace's father, Hannah really, truly would look for another job.

It would break her heart, but she'd do it.

"You're pouting," she said, patting his hand. "I'm flattered."

He grabbed her fingers and brought her knuckles to his lips. "You should be flattered. I haven't been in this state since high school."

Hannah flipped open the next day's docket. "I haven't been in this state *ever*. May we talk about my cases now?"

"For nineteen minutes, yes, you may."

The clock read precisely 4:41 p.m.

Chapter 13

HANNAH WENT OVER THE DOCKET WITH TRENT, CASE by case, and for a guy who was supposedly only impersonating a lawyer, he paid close attention. His questions and suggestions were helpful, and Hannah realized that in only a week, her confidence and her competence had doubled.

"Are you looking forward to the Christmas party?" he asked when the last case had been briefed.

"I am. Grace is looking forward to having Merle over again too."

"Please thank your friend Eliza for doing double duty," Trent said. "I don't have a long list of babysitters, particularly when both Mac and James will attend the party with us."

"Eliza has sons. She's looking forward to a girls' night. Will you be at the courthouse tomorrow?"

"I might have an ex parte domestic violence hearing. My client isn't coming in until five thirty, so I'll walk you to your car now."

"You don't have to do that," Hannah said, rising. "I'm glad I caught you to go over my cases, though. I feel more prepared when I talk them through with you."

"And I feel better," Trent said, getting to his feet. "I'm supposed to know what you're up to, but the holiday season is typically busy for family law attorneys."

"Another reason to transfer to corporate," Hannah said, wrinkling her nose.

He gave her a silent, frowning perusal, then let his gaze travel out over the parking lot. "I'll let you go if I have to. I won't like it, but I'd rather have you working down the hall for James than hating your job with me."

His pronouncement eased a tension Hannah had stashed somewhere on her growing list of things to worry about.

"I wouldn't hate family law—" Hannah stopped herself. "I don't exactly hate it, but the charm of domestic relations law has thus far eluded me."

"Diplomatically put," Trent said as they crossed the hallway to Hannah's office. He held her coat for her, carried her briefcase, and opened doors for her.

"Why are you doing this? It's sweet of you, but bound to cause talk."

"I've walked both Lee and Ann to their cars when they get stuck here late. Mac and James do likewise. We were brought up not five miles from town, and in case you haven't noticed, Damson Valley isn't exactly the throbbing heart of modern civilization."

"So you're simply old-fashioned?" Hannah asked as she unlocked her car. She was old-fashioned enough herself to have parked under a streetlamp.

"I could tell you, yes, I'm old-fashioned, but if I'm honest, I will admit your safety matters to me very much, and I'm happy to have a few more minutes in your company."

He stood beside her car, the chilly breeze teasing at his hair. Hannah wanted badly to touch him, wanted to drag him back into the office now that it was after five.

Trenton Knightley deserved more than a quickie on the desk, and Hannah *wanted* more than that.

"I probably shouldn't say this," Trent went on.

"You'll think I've got a screw loose, but I want people to understand you're spoken for. I want James and Mac and every male looking out these windows to know the pretty redhead at Hartman is already leading Trent Knightley around by his…nose."

He'd surprised her. Not by admitting the attraction, but by admitting any vulnerability where she was concerned.

"I haven't said I'm spoken for," she replied, tossing her worldly goods into the backseat.

"No, you haven't." His breath puffed white in the evening air. "I'm saying I'm spoken for though."

Hannah leaned back against her little car, feeling as if she'd taken a blow to her middle. She expected questions and prying, and he offered her exclusivity, for however long their interest in each other lasted. Handed it to her in blunt, simple words, like a knight knelt before a princess, no ceremony, no rhetoric, but plenty of dignity and heart.

Hannah wanted what Trent offered, had craved it, and longed for it with him, all the while telling herself they would have nothing more than a friendship with benefits, or some damned useless baloney. The yearning made no sense—they didn't know each other well, hadn't even really made love, and were both too busy to spare a relationship much time and energy.

She could trust Trent, though. He wouldn't run away, he wouldn't walk away, he wouldn't leave at all unless she gave him several good reasons.

"You are a brave man. A lovely man, and if I had any experience with this sort of thing, I'd have a glib reply all polished and ready to lob over the net at you. I don't know what to say, Trent, except I believe you mean your words, and you make a gift of a precious sentiment I don't feel I've earned."

That was the ghost of foster care talking, the Hannah who'd been repeatedly welcomed only to be rejected a year or even months later. She'd lived those rejections and died some with each one, and couldn't ignore the legacy of caution they'd given her.

"The gift is you, Hannah." He looked like he'd say more, but Hannah stopped him by opening her car door.

"I'm looking forward to the Christmas party. Really looking forward to it."

She could be that honest.

A smile dawned in Trent's eyes, and Hannah had the sense he'd taken her meaning clearly. There might be more gifts exchanged on Saturday night than simply those warranted by the season, circumstances permitting.

"Good night, then." He took a step back. "I'll sustain myself on anticipation and imagination."

Trent watched Hannah drive off, telling himself she'd reacted well to a declaration made too early and in the wrong context. She hadn't laughed; she hadn't told him to take a number; she hadn't been coy or silly or any number of things that would have suggested his heart was dragging him in a foolish direction.

By the time Trent returned to his office, he had still not convinced himself he'd made the right move. When he wanted to ponder and consider and *lawyer* his exchange with Hannah, he instead had to deal with Mac, who was waiting in his office.

"Your truck still in the shop, MacKenzie?"

"Nope."

"You have a family law question?"

"I do not."

"You still dithering over what to get Merle for Christmas?"

"I am not."

"I have a client coming in five minutes, MacKenzie. We can play twenty questions until then, or you can tell me what you're doing in my office when you ought to be on your way home."

"You have Merle to come home to. Had I such a compelling motivation, I might not be here." Whatever was on Mac's mind, it had him rattled enough to admit, in a passing, sidewise Mac-understatement that he was lonely.

"You have my entire attention for another four and a half minutes."

"I like your Hannah. I respect her."

Trent hid his surprise, because Mac did not intrude into anybody's personal life without good cause— though she was *his* Hannah.

"Is there a but?"

"There's something," Mac said, turning the rhododendron ninety degrees, then rearranging the foliage so none of it was cramped by the window. "I usually make a little fuss over the new hires at the Christmas party, officially welcome anybody who's joined the company in the past year. Hannah is our most recent hire, so I looked up a few things."

"Things about Hannah?"

Mac nodded, and the unease in Trent's gut coalesced into an urge to strangle his older brother.

"I found no record of a Hannah Stark attending the University of Maryland in the past ten years."

UMD, where paintball and farm-team baseball qualified as dates. "Maybe she was married at the time. She has a child."

"About whom, we aren't supposed to say a word."

"Do you have something more on your mind, Mac?"

"Hannah Stark did attend law school."

Trent was not proud of the relief that admission engendered. "So she was married during undergraduate, and changed her name back when she divorced." Except she'd never mentioned a marriage, and Trent had good reason to believe she'd never been married.

"Maybe, but I did a quick search of the divorce records, and no divorce was granted to a party resuming use of the maiden name of Hannah Stark," Mac said, his tone level. "She's in good standing with the Maryland courts."

"Why are you telling me this?"

More to the point, why hadn't Trent allowed himself to do any of this digging?

Mac slid the rhodie half an inch closer to the end of the window ledge.

"Hannah's a lawyer, and a good one," Mac said. "My gut tells me she's also a good woman, but she has problems, Trent. The secrecy about the child, the lack of a past, the blanks on her employment application and human resources forms... They're troubling."

"You want me to grill her into admitting those problems?" A hypothetical question, because Trent wouldn't do it. If he attempted to turn inquisitional, Hannah would disappear from Hartman and Whitney, and from his life.

But not from his dreams.

Mac took a long, silent moment to study the rho-dodendron. It was a beautiful, thriving specimen, but Trent kept it in the office rather than have a toxic plant in his home.

"You'll do what you think is best," Mac said, "for you, for Merle, and even for Hannah and her daughter. I simply wanted you to know if James or I can do anything to help, we're here for you. And for Hannah and the child, if it comes to that."

He left, and Trent sat abruptly, hoping his damned five-thirty client no-showed. He'd had his dukes up, expecting Mac to lecture, warn and admonish—which Mac could do like a mother superior who'd forgotten her anxiety meds.

Trent hadn't expected Mac to offer help, though Mac's latest revelation only confirmed that Trent was falling in love with a woman in trouble.

And there was not one damned thing he was willing to do to stop himself.

―⁂―

Hannah got through her docket. By the time the last case concluded, half the lunch hour was gone, Hannah's stomach was growling, and the judge was barking at everyone except the deputies. Margaret finished the docket, packed up her files, and tromped past Hannah with a silent shake of her head, leaving Hannah alone in the courtroom, save for the bailiff.

And Trent Knightley.

"What are you doing here?" she asked as she shoved files into her briefcase.

"Ambushing you. I'll help you carry those to your car, but then I've got a shelter care hearing I need you to take because my benighted, damned domestic violence case got bumped to the afternoon docket."

The very words "shelter care hearing" still had the ability to scare Hannah. When the Department of Social Services thought a kid was at imminent risk of harm, and couldn't find another plan for keeping that child safe, they popped the child into foster care first and answered questions from a judge, the child's lawyer, and lawyers for the child's parents later—usually a day later, seldom more than a week later.

"I wasn't aware shelters would be part of my caseload," Hannah said evenly. Many a family law specialist never set foot in a foster care proceeding. Hannah had desperately hoped to get through her six months in family law purgatory among that number.

"Don't poker up on me now, Stark. All you have to do is consent to have the kid stay in foster care for thirty days while the Department sorts the situation out. It isn't complicated, but I can't be in two places at once."

A child was torn from everything and everyone he knew and loved, and *it wasn't complicated*?

"Have you read the petition, Trent?" Because even in an emergency child welfare situation, the Department of Social Services had to lay out the facts in writing for the judge and other parties.

"Not yet," he said, stuffing some of Hannah's files into his briefcase. "The social worker usually brings the paperwork to the hearing, which is scheduled for 1:30 p.m."

"If you haven't read the petition, and haven't met

with our client, how do you know we'll consent to thirty days of foster care?"

She put the question quietly, hoping Trent didn't hear the tremor in her voice.

He passed her the last file, which Hannah could barely wedge among the others in her briefcase.

"The local Department of Social Services is not in the habit of snatching children unless there's a strong suspicion of abuse or neglect, Hannah. I know these people, and they do a good job, contrary to what the newspaper sometimes implies."

Hannah knew *these people* too. "I want to do a good job as well, and until I meet with the child, I won't know whether the hearing is contested. Counsel for the parents might have something to say about it too."

Trent snapped his briefcase shut.

"Nobody expects brilliant advocacy at a shelter care hearing, Hannah. The cases pop up without any warning, the rules of evidence don't strictly apply, and all the judge can do is deny shelter or turn the child over to the Department for thirty days. It doesn't have to be a big deal."

A shelter care hearing should never be anything less than a big deal. Hannah had sat through numerous shelter care hearings, her own—when her placements disrupted—and several times as a forgotten observer when other cases had been bumped ahead of hers on a harried docket. Trent was right: they were usually handled efficiently, with little or no dispute as to the facts or the need for temporary placement.

And into foster care the child would go, which was a huge damned deal for the kid.

"If you're telling me you cannot do this," Trent said, "I'll juggle somehow. Patlack is reasonable about giving opposing counsel some scheduling leeway, and the judges are pretty understanding as well."

"Who's Patlack?"

"Brian Patlack represents the Department of Social Services. He's damned good, though not the most charming soul. He'll work with you if you're reasonable. Can you do this or not?"

Trent wasn't pushing, he was offering Hannah a choice, for which Hannah would never stop respecting him.

She could do it. She didn't want to, but now was not the time to disclose her history, or the fact that she'd supplied less than complete information on her employment application.

"I'll manage."

"That's my lady."

Trent toted files out to Hannah's car, bought her a bowl of soup for lunch, then disappeared to meet with his client and try to work out a settlement with opposing counsel in the domestic violence hearing.

Hannah tossed her soup away after half a bowl and nibbled the crackers, mostly to get her stomach to quit cussing at her.

The child support cases had shown her that she needed to face the family law dragon and at least twist its scaly green tail. Maybe she needed to chop off a head or two of the hydra in the foster care courtroom too.

If only she had a white charger to gallop around on.

Hannah made her way to Courtroom Four by one o'clock, and found the corridor deserted. No social worker, no Patlack, not even a bailiff or deputy to open the courtroom. At twenty-five minutes after one, a red-haired man in pointy-toed boots and a brown three-piece suit came striding around the corner.

"You from Hartman?"

Hannah stood. "I am."

To her consternation, he didn't offer a handshake but instead took a seat on the bench she'd just vacated and flipped open an alligator-finish briefcase.

"Hannah Stark," she said, "counsel for the alleged child in need of assistance."

Courthouse Cowboy began leafing through files. "Brian Patlack, attorney for DSS. The worker should be bringing your client, Tyrell Oliver, unless he's succumbed to a badly timed case of happy feet. We don't expect a contest from Mom, and Dad is, as we say, unavoidably detained." He pulled a slender file from the briefcase. "I'll let the judge know we need a few more minutes."

He strutted off to disappear behind the heavy wooden door that led to judges' chambers.

Bastard. It was 1:30 p.m., Hannah had been cooling her heels for half an hour, waiting for Patlack, his social worker, and Hannah's client to show up—along with the paperwork necessary to try the case.

And now Patlack was back in chambers, telling golf stories because his worker was late, and he hadn't even had the courtesy to ask Hannah if she had a position on the case.

A bailiff hurried by to unlock the courtroom, and a tall, painfully thin African American boy, accompanied by a short, well-fed, middle-aged Caucasian woman showed up shortly thereafter—at 1:35 p.m.

"Tyrell?" Hannah held out a hand, which—give the kid credit—he shook. "I'm Hannah Stark, and I'll be representing you in this hearing. May I talk with you for a minute before the hearing gets started?"

Tyrell shot a look at the woman beside him, but said nothing.

"You're his worker?" Hannah asked.

"I am," the lady said, not offering a name. "You're from Hartman?"

"Mr. Knightley couldn't get free of another emergency case," Hannah said. "Tyrell and I need a few minutes to talk. We'll use the courtroom for privacy."

The worker looked uncertain, but Hannah didn't wait around to hear that she'd best watch her client lest he bolt, or whatever helpful invective the woman might spew.

Hannah sat on the counsel table and eyed the young man who'd followed her into the courtroom. "What's the deal, Tyrell?"

"Dunno," Tyrell muttered, hands in the pockets of his slacks. His V-neck sweater proclaimed him a student of the local Catholic school.

"Look, Tyrell, the judge will come prancing in here any minute, and the Department will ask her to keep you in foster care for the next month *at least*. Unless you tell me something different, I will agree to that on your behalf. Gimme a clue: Where do you want to be?"

Tyrell shrugged.

He was having the bad day to end all bad days, so Hannah waited. The first shelter care hearing was always the worst, walloping a kid's life sideways, even if his very survival necessitated that disruption.

"Maybe with my grandpa. He'd take me in."

Tyrell had thrown Hannah a bone. She leaped on it. "Who's your grandpa, and where does he live?"

"Lucien Medley. He lives over on Mulberry. They got a phone."

Another bone—a phone number.

"We'll call him, but first tell me what's going on at home, Tyrell, and don't pretty it up. What you tell me stays between us unless you give me permission to share it with the Department."

Tyrell was silent a minute. Hannah watched the change in his eyes as disgust overcame a young gentleman's reticence.

"That idiot my mom took up with over the summer, Ray, he smacks her around. She has a black eye now from when he got mad last night, but she'll say she fell against the refrigerator by accident. It wasn't any accident, Miss Hannah."

From a child facing foster care, that was quite a speech.

"You call your grandpa." Hannah handed him her cell phone. "Tell him to get over to Courtroom Four on the double-quick, unless he wants to see you in foster care. I'm going to talk to your worker."

She left, and she did not warn him not to take off. She knew the look of a runner. Tyrell didn't have it, not in his eyes, not in his body language, and Tyrell wasn't about to leave his mother alone with Ray if he could help it.

Out in the hallway, Hannah stuck her hand out to the worker.

"Pleased to make your acquaintance…?"

"Betsy Niederland. And your name again?"

"Hannah Stark."

A vaguely concerned look came over Betsy's round face. "Do you think it's a good idea to leave him alone in there? He's pretty depressed, and his mom says he can be explosive at times. She says he's absolutely out of control, but the school doesn't have a problem with him. He usually makes honor roll, and last year he finished up on distinguished honor roll. We're looking to get him into a group home here in the county, eventually, and maybe start some family therapy down the line. We have a bed for him in a shelter in Baltimore for now." Betsy offered this mixture of facts, opinions, and wishes with a befuddled air.

"What about Ray?"

"Ray? Mom's boyfriend? Oh, I don't think he'd want to serve as a resource for Tyrell. Tyrell has quite a mouth on him when he gets a mind to cut loose. Ray says he loves the boy like a son, but he can't stand to see the way Tyrell treats his mother. He's a big boy, for only fourteen."

Tyrell was tall, but he was about as big as a matchstick. "Where's Dad?"

"Down at Maryland Corrections, serving a sentence for assault with intent to maim. Mom was the victim, and Tyrell is the one who called 911. If he hadn't, she might have bled to death."

Tyrell came to the door of the courtroom, a ghost of a smile on his face. He gave Hannah a barely perceptible nod and passed her the phone.

The cavalry was on its way.

"Is Mom coming to the hearing?" Hannah asked as Tyrell ghosted back into the courtroom.

"She should be," Betsy replied. "She was adamant that she didn't want a lawyer for herself, but she'll have to testify to Tyrell's out-of-control behaviors if you won't consent to shelter. I don't think that would be very good for the family, do you? For a mom to have to rat out her own son?"

The disturbing truth was that Betsy truly did care for this family. She'd nonetheless failed utterly to see the cause of Tyrell's "behaviors" and the danger to Mom.

But to answer Betsy's question, Hannah didn't want either family member to have to rat out the other.

"What about relatives, Betsy? Is there anybody who can take Tyrell in?"

"Neither Mom nor Dad identified any. I called Dad down at the prison, but he said the only family in the area is on Mom's side."

Betsy hadn't asked Tyrell. Hannah stifled a howl of frustration. Tyrell was nearly six feet tall and had already saved his mother's life once, but Betsy hadn't thought to ask him about relatives or a friend he might stay with.

Brian Patlack sauntered out from judge's chambers, sparing Hannah not even a glance. "Ready to go, Betsy?"

"We might want to wait a few more minutes," Betsy said. "Mom isn't here yet, and she's the one who can testify to Tyrell's out-of-control behaviors."

Patlack shot his cuffs. "Does Trent Knightley know you're contesting this case, Ms. Starch?"

"Stark. S-T-A-R-K. I neither know nor care what Trent Knightley's assessment of this case would be if he were here. I will ask the Department to at least put on testimony. What is it, exactly, that you think Mom will testify to?"

Hannah directed her comments to the social worker, behaving as dismissively toward Patlack as he had toward opposing counsel.

"Tyrell gets pretty mouthy," Betsy said, consulting her notes. "He uses the F-word, and he's been telling his mother he's thinking of running away."

Now Hannah did direct her words to Patlack.

"No threat of harm to the child there, at least not without some steps toward actually running. Is there a reason why you can't steer Mom to Juvenile Services if Tyrell is a child in need of supervision?"

"What else have you got, Betsy?" Patlack asked, ignoring Hannah's question.

"Mom says she's afraid Tyrell will get physical with her."

"Has he ever lost his temper like that in all his fourteen years?" Hannah asked.

"Not yet."

"Has Tyrell's mother chosen violent partners in the past?" Hannah pressed, and at that, Patlack seemed to start paying attention.

"Tyrell's dad, but you know about that. This guy Ray seems OK, if you don't mind a little machismo."

"What's Ray's last name?"

"Santiago."

Hannah swung a brittle smile on Brian Patlack.

"Let's wait another ten minutes for the mom," she said. "Your worker can call her to be sure she's on her way, and I'll hit the criminal case database. Give me a birth date, Betsy, and we'll see how Ray has been behaving lately."

Patlack swore succinctly and barked at the worker to

call Mom and tell her to get her ass over to the court-house. He turned a sardonic smile on Hannah.

"What have you got?"

"I have a kid who is sick of watching his mom get beat up, and a mom who won't tell her family what's going on. Grandpa is on his way over here to say he's willing to take Tyrell, and last I heard, relative place-ment is preferred to foster care under Maryland law."

Patlack offered a genuine hint of a smile. A stingy effort, but then, what would a steady diet of foster care cases do to somebody afflicted with a soft heart to start with?

"Betsy is not the brightest bulb in the chandelier of life. Did Knightley scope this out for you?"

Hannah regarded Patlack with a raised eyebrow of her own, mimicking his expression even as she knew the question was intended to deflect her from the weak-nesses in his case.

"What is it with you and Trent? He may be here any minute, but he really did have a domestic violence case that wasn't heard this morning. Do you truly want the taxpayer footing the bill for this kid to be in foster care when there's a relative willing to take him?"

Patlack straightened his tie, which sported an honest-to-Pete gold tie tack to go with his gold cuff links.

"You may be buying this kid's version of events, Ms. *Stark*, but my guess is Mom's story is the version that will fly with Judge Merriman. She takes a dim view of uppity teenagers."

"Go ahead and put Mom on the stand, then, Mr. Patlack. I will ask her, one by one, how she got all those fresh bruises, and I will ask especially about her black eye. Let's just agree her dear friend Ray will not be present in the courtroom when I do, or he'll no doubt beat the daylights out of her *again* because she isn't good enough at perjury to convince the judge."

"I fucking hate fucking loser cases."

Such a gentleman, but at least Tyrell hadn't overheard that language. "No one likes to lose, Mr. Patlack, and no one wants to see this family slip through the cracks. They need help, and your people can get it for them, but not if they swallow Mom's baloney. I know Tyrell is probably a handful at home, but he toes the line at school, and he has no delinquency record. Shelter the kid with Grandpa, order a family assessment to include Ray, and let Grandpa be the gatekeeper for visitation with Mom and Tyrell."

Hannah had his attention. She was offering him an uncontested hearing—a way to leave early on Friday—a solution to his way of thinking, so she plowed on.

"I'll agree to a statement of facts that there's been increasing tension in the home since Dad was put away, and tempers are running near the boiling point. I will agree Tyrell is moody and possibly at risk for self-injurious behaviors, and I will agree Mom cannot control him or make choices consistent with his best interests."

Patlack exchanged nods with Judge Linker, who ignored Hannah as he hustled by with his robe over his arm.

"Put it on the record, we'll go for it—if my worker can get Mom here. You understand the Department can't consent to placement with the grandparent, though. We don't know anything about this guy, except that he raised a woman who nearly got herself killed by her husband."

Got herself killed… Hannah set aside the need to shake Patlack until his lawyer bling went flying in all directions. *This is not a game.*

"If I recall the regulations," Hannah said through gritted teeth, "the Department is supposed to meet with all parties to discuss ways of keeping this case out of court. Based on my impression of Betsy, I'm guessing that meeting never took place."

"Now, Ms. Stark, no need to get touchy. All I'm saying is we don't know Grandpa, so we can't say the kid is any better off there. Maybe Betsy held a meeting, and Mom had a good reason for not letting us know how to get in touch with Gramps. If you had more experience with these kinds of cases, you might understand that the pleadings don't always reflect the entirety of the family's problems."

If she had more experience with these kinds of cases…

The statistics regarding the number of children abused in foster care should have been tattooed on Patlack's forehead.

Patlack was looking at her oddly, and Hannah realized he expected a reply.

"I'm off to the law library to research Mr. Santiago," she said, but her first stop was the ladies' room, where she spent a good three minutes largely failing to get her temper under control.

When she returned to the courtroom, she found Tyrell sitting beside an older African American man.

"Lucien Medley?"

"That would be me." The man rose and extended a hand. He was a mature version of Tyrell. Scholarly, wearing wire-frame glasses, and slender, but no longer afflicted with the rail-thin, emaciated look of an adolescent in the double grip of emotional problems and a growth spurt.

Hannah shook his hand and introduced herself. "Can you provide a home for Tyrell?"

"I can and I will. My daughter has made some sorry choices in the company she keeps, and that Ray Santiago is no fit influence on my grandson."

"We have another few minutes before the judge comes on the bench," Hannah said, turning to Tyrell. "Did Ray go by any aliases that you know of?"

Raymundo del Santiago, Raymond St. James, Raoul Sandia... Hannah stopped writing after five. "Is he illegal?" she asked.

"I dunno," Tyrell said. "He ought to be."

Another small smile, and a clear point of agreement between grandfather and grandson.

Hannah hurried off to the law library, passing a tall African American woman whose sunglasses didn't entirely hide one heck of a shiner.

The lady was still wearing her sunglasses when Patlack called the case by its docket number a few minutes later.

"This matter comes before Your Honor as a shelter care hearing," he went on, "and I believe the boy's mother agrees that thirty days of shelter care is necessary at this time. Tyrell is represented by the firm of Hartman and Whitney, and I will leave it to the Court to inquire regarding consent on behalf of the minor child."

The Honorable Louise Merriman was a mature, attractive brunette with a light of keen intelligence in her eyes. Hannah rose, thinking the judge managed to be both pretty and intimidating.

"Hannah Stark, Your Honor, and the firm of Hartman and Whitney on behalf of the respondent, Tyrell Oliver. We contest the Department's plan to place the child in a shelter care facility. Tyrell's grandfather, Lucien Medley, is here today and willing to provide a home for his grandson. Moreover, Your Honor, on Tyrell's behalf, I dispute that his behaviors are the exclusive cause of shelter, and would instead offer an agreed-upon statement of facts."

Hannah waited for the judge to say something, to ask for testimony, to ask for the statement of facts, anything. But the woman stared at Hannah as a silence took root in the courtroom.

"Counsel will please approach the bench," Judge Merriman said.

Hannah and Patlack came to stand directly before the judge, who turned on a white noise generator before she spoke. "Ms. Stark, have you been in practice long?"

Patlack made no effort to hide a smirk, clearly anticipating a trip to the judicial woodshed for Hannah.

"I started with Hartman last month, but it's not my first position out of law school." Temping counted as a position, sort of.

As the judge continued to study Hannah, Patlack's smirk faded.

"May I ask if you have family in the area, Ms. Stark?"

"No close family, ma'am."

"I see." The judge sat back and steepled her fingers against her lips. "For reasons which are not relevant to either of your cases, I cannot hear this as a contested matter. I propose that Tyrell be permitted, by virtue of a service agreement between his mother, his grandfather, and the Department, to visit his grandfather indefinitely. Call it temporary custody, whatever Mom will accept."

Patlack spoke first. "The worker would need a minute to determine if Mom is willing to sign such an agreement."

Hannah didn't object, because the agreement wouldn't be as binding as a court order, but it would give the Department plenty of ammunition to deal with Mom and Ray nonetheless.

"Domestic violence has to be addressed." Hannah passed a printout to Patlack. "Mom's current paramour has a rap sheet as long as your arm, with ample helpings of assault and battery, as well as disturbing the peace."

Patlack scanned the printout and handed it up to the judge—criminal history was public record, and easy enough to get before a judge in proceedings that did not strictly follow the rules of evidence.

"Child Protective Services is not in the business of finding homes for wayward mothers, Ms. Stark," Patlack said. "Domestic violence there might be, but we can't save everybody."

The judge looked at Hannah, apparently expecting a retort.

And Hannah had one ready. "This child has already seen his mother beaten nearly to death by one man, Mr. Patlack. How do you think he'll fare knowing Mom is living alone with another abuser in her life?"

"Judge, perhaps you have some ideas?" Patlack asked, the stinking soul of stinking humility.

"As it happens, I do. Your worker will negotiate the

service agreement with Mrs. Oliver before she leaves the courtroom, Mr. Patlack, and will include an immediate referral to the women's shelter, and I do mean immediate. I will have the sheriff's deputy accompany Mrs. Oliver to retrieve her effects from the home if necessary, and I'm sure your worker will discuss a domestic violence restraining order with her too."

The judge turned again to Hannah, her gaze searching, taking in Hannah's features one by one.

The attorneys returned to their respective tables. The judge turned off the white noise and signaled to the court reporter, who turned on the recording system.

"Tyrell, Mrs. Oliver," the judge said, "with the consent of both counsel, I'm continuing this case, which means the court takes no action on it today. Mr. Medley, my thanks for your attendance especially, because Tyrell will be staying with you for a time if matters go as planned. Mrs. Oliver, I anticipate a discussion between you and the social worker, and I suggest you take advantage of every service she can put at your disposal. We all need help at some point, though we're not all smart enough to ask for it."

After another pointed study of Hannah, the judge left the room before the bailiff could tell everybody to rise.

Chapter 14

TRENT HAD REALIZED LONG AGO THAT NOBODY LIKED shelter care hearings. They forced choices all around, on short notice for high stakes, with little warning. Even if the Department and the parents worked out some agreement at the last minute, the very fact that the case had been brought to court meant a child was in serious trouble.

When the Department made mistakes, children were plucked from all they knew, traumatized, and thrust into that situation every child is told is dangerous—that of relying on strangers.

If the judge denied shelter in the wrong case, the child remained in a dangerous situation, one often made worse by a parent's realization that the Department could take anybody's child at any time on the strength of little more than a few phone calls.

And yet, this shelter wasn't going according to the usual game plan. Hannah and Brian Patlack stood before the bench, consulting with Judge Merriman in voices too low to be overheard.

A printout of some form was thrust at the judge, probably somebody's criminal record.

More conferring, and then, after Louise Merriman had given Hannah about six visual once-overs, Hannah prowled back to the counsel table. Trent could practically see a long, feline tail twitching behind her and hear a low, menacing rumble coming from her side of the room.

And then, the case was continued, shelter neither granted nor denied, and the judge nearly scampered off the bench.

Trent hustled to the front of the room, lawyerly curiosity, pride in Hannah, and a niggle of foreboding hurrying his steps.

"Stark, can you explain to me what just went on in here?"

She gave him a look such as Merle conferred on stinkbugs. "My client is a little upset right now, Mr. Knightley."

The utter chill of her demeanor wasn't merely courtroom histrionics.

"My apologies to you and your client." Trent raised his voice a bit. "Brian, you'll join us in the hallway?"

Patlack, who probably considered himself king of the foster care proceedings, put his files into his briefcase and got to his feet.

"Mr. Medley," Hannah said, "if you'd sit with Tyrell for a minute, I'd appreciate it, and Ms. Niederland will need to meet with Mom for a bit."

Tyrell stared resolutely at the floor. Hannah touched him on the arm—not a pat, not a bid for eye contact, just a small moment of acknowledgment—then went out to the hallway.

"What was that bench conference about?" Trent asked.

Patlack jammed a hand into his trouser pockets and began jingling change.

"First, Judge Merriman asked if Ms. Stark grew up around here, then she asked if she had any family in the area. Damned if I know what it's about."

"It's as Brian said, Trent," Hannah added, still in her Counsel from the Coldest Circle of Hell persona. "The judge asked a few personal questions of me, then said she couldn't hear the case as a contested matter."

"It doesn't make sense." Neither did the way Hannah was acting.

Betsy Niederland came bustling out of the courtroom, a worker whom Trent had mentally consigned to the ranks of those hanging on until retirement.

"Mrs. Oliver will sign a service agreement giving the grandfather custody of Tyrell for the duration," Betsy said with the anxious eagerness of the perpetually overwhelmed. "She's agreed to go to a battered women's shelter for evaluation and counseling, and says it will be a lot easier to find work if she doesn't have to ride herd on Tyrell."

This was apparently Betsy's idea of a happily ever after.

"What about Tyrell?" Hannah snapped.

Betsy blinked at her. "Beg pardon?"

"What about my client? Will he have to change schools if he moves in with Grandpa, does he need help getting his things from Mom's house, is he on any medication that must be refilled immediately, or can Grandpa afford to wait a couple of weeks to get a copy of the signed agreement giving him custody?"

Betsy looked at her attorney, who was probably mentally overworking his already overworked store of profanity.

"I'm going to talk to my client," Hannah said.

"You don't have a client," Patlack replied, his tone smug, as if in this at least, he could exhibit his lawyer smarts. "The matter has been informally resolved, hence Tyrell has no right to representation. You can talk to the kid, but you'll have no attorney-client privilege."

Trent put a hand on Hannah's arm, because her gaze went from chilly to spare-me-from-lawyers-with-little-dicks arctic.

"The judge merely continued the case, she didn't dismiss it, Mr. Patlack," Hannah spat. "Until you file a motion to dismiss your petition, and that motion is ruled on in your favor, I most assuredly do have a client."

She whirled and marched into the courtroom, leaving a bewildered, over-accessorized suit where a fairly good, if obnoxious attorney had stood.

"Will Ms. Stark be handling any more of the DSS cases?" Patlack asked.

"Betsy needs her ass kicked," Trent said. "She doesn't do the follow-up, and if there was a relative right here in town ready to take the kid in, she should have tried that long before turning this into litigation."

"I'm all for kicking Betsy's ass," Patlack said, "and I'll tell her supervisor as much, but I'm not real keen on having my own backside booted across the courtroom."

He picked up his briefcase and trundled off, his backside doubtless headed for an early happy hour at a local watering hole frequented by attorneys, social workers, and cops.

Damson Valley was usually a friendly place, after all.

Trent took up a lean between portraits of two judges from a bygone era. One was the stern, Wrath of God type—he'd died of a pickled liver, according to bar association legend. The other had a twinkle in his eye and a Santa Claus beard. The name under that portrait was Hiram Alverston Knightley.

"My newest associate just took zealous advocacy

to new heights," Trent informed his great-great-grandfather. "I'd be pleased to find a ferocious litigator had joined the family law department, but I don't think she's a happy, ferocious litigator."

When she confronted Betsy after the hearing, Hannah had looked ready to chop the worker in tiny pieces and feed those pieces one by one to rabid dogs.

The unhappy litigator escorted her client from the courtroom, the older gentleman and the boy's mother with her.

"You have my card, Tyrell. Be the first foster kid ever to surprise his lawyer, and let me know how you're doing. The Department can bring another petition any time if things don't improve for you and your family."

Mrs. Oliver's head came up—the warning had been meant for her. The family departed, maybe sadder and wiser, maybe only more scared and angry. Hannah's expression remained unreadable, just as Judge Merriman's expression had been unreadable.

The two of them bore a resemblance, in fact, about the eyes and chin.

"You lawyered the hell out of this," Trent said. "I mean that as a sincere compliment. You did a better job for the child than I could have, than anybody could have. I think you might have found your niche, Stark."

Trent offered her a compliment, which seemed like a safe place to start unpacking the case.

"I traded insults with opposing counsel, sniped at his worker, compelled my client's mother to admit she's been assaulted by a guy who will not forget her inconvenient bout of honesty, likely flummoxed the judge entirely, and you're pleased with me?"

He was proud of her, also uneasy as hell. "Foster care cases are often a matter of no good options for the judge, Hannah. I know they aren't simple."

Nothing about family law was simple, but what worthwhile endeavor was simple or easy?

"Trent, I care that"—she snapped her fingers before his nose—"for the judge's crappy options. Those same options are the *child's* crappy outcomes, and that ought to be what matters to every person in that courtroom. I hate myself for the way I've handled this case, I hate the Department for nearly popping this child into some facility in Baltimore, and I just about hate you for assigning the case to me."

If she'd been crying, Trent might have attributed her reaction to the usual recoil of wading into child welfare waters, but she was still in the grip of something that went beyond advocating zealously within the bounds of the law.

Something fierce to the point of ugliness.

Trent picked up his briefcase in one hand and Hannah's in the other.

"We'll take my car," he said. "I don't know as you're in any shape to get behind the wheel and Gino can pick up your Prius easily enough when he and Debbie drop off the day's motions with the clerk's office."

Hannah shrugged into her coat before he could hold it for her, and when they got in his car, sat beside him silently. Something else was in the car with them, something to do with the child Grace, with the blanks on Hannah's employee forms, with her unlisted phone number.

"You really feel lousy for the way you handled that case, Hannah? You did a magnificent job."

She didn't answer for about two miles.

"I do feel lousy. I feel ugly. If that means I'm a real lawyer, then the legal profession should be ashamed of itself."

—–ᴡᴡ–—

Hannah drove home, feeling leaden and somehow ashamed. Trent had continued to give her odd looks for the balance of the day, but had walked her out to her car at five o'clock on the dot and reminded her he'd pick her up on Saturday to take her to the Christmas party.

To celebrate the season of brotherly love after the day she'd had felt obscene. Two of her clients had been locked up for nonsupport, but they'd deserved incarceration. They complained their exes didn't use the money for the children, withheld visits when the check was late, and didn't need the money.

After only two weeks, the excuses were a predictable litany.

Gerald Matthews had been a much better fit for the child support docket than Hannah would ever be.

A better fit for the practice of law generally. Hell, Matthews had gone out and cadged private cases in addition to what Hartman assigned him. Surely that proved the presence of the gene for the legal field?

As Hannah drove along the slushy mountain road between Eliza's and home, Grace started up with the questions every thirty seconds. "Mom…? Mom…? Mom…?" Stupid questions, idle questions, I-forget questions.

Grace was reacting to the distant, churning vibe Hannah gave off, using a child's tools to try to establish a sense of safety and normalcy at the end of a long, hard week.

"Mom?"

"Yes, Grace?"

"Do you have a headache?"

Yes, Hannah thought, and her name is Grace.

And then: *Forgive me, please. I didn't mean that.*

"No, not really. I feel like I could get one, though. Like when you're really tired and cold, and you know you need an extra blanket, but you lie there almost shivering because you're too tired to get out of bed and get one."

Sharing a bed with Trenton Knightley, Hannah had slept wonderfully—in another lifetime.

Grace's face puckered, suggesting the experience of shivery exhaustion wasn't one she could identify with, though she was trying.

"I think I know what your headaches are like, Mom."

"What do you think they're like?"

"It's like you can feel your heartbeat from behind your ear to behind your eyes, and it hurts a lot, even in your neck. It feels like half your head is mad at you."

Hannah looked over at the back of her daughter's head—Grace had addressed her comment to the darkened woods going by outside—and concern cut through the emotional detritus of the day.

"Your head hurts, doesn't it, Grace?"

Grace nodded twice, but refused to face her mother, even in the dim interior of the car.

"Does it hurt a lot?"

Another nod, just one.

"I'm glad you told me, Grace, because we can give

you some pills when we get home that will help you feel better, though maybe not all the way better."

A shuddery breath from the passenger's seat. "OK."

When they got home, Hannah shucked her coat, eased Grace's off as well, and led the child to the bathroom, the warmest room in the house.

"Have a seat," Hannah said, getting a bottle of pain killers from the medicine cabinet.

Grace perched on the closed potty lid, eyes downcast, so Hannah hunkered before her daughter.

"I'm giving you some grown-up medicine. This is a little tricky, so you have to listen to me. You listening?"

A nod, no eye contact.

"To take grown-up medicine, you take a swallow of water but you don't drink it down. Then you sneak one of these pills into your mouth. You swallow the pill and the water at the same time. It can take practice, but you have to do it twice. Got it?"

Another nod, and then Grace complied with the directions, not spilling a drop. When the second pill was down, Hannah took the cup from Grace and lifted a hand to brush Grace's bangs from her face.

Grace flinched, and Hannah's hand fell.

Hannah sat back against the cabinets and looked her daughter over as carefully as she could without forcing Grace to meet her eyes. "Honey, tell me what happened."

A single teardrop fell from Grace's chin and hit the back of the hand Hannah rested on Grace's knee.

"Sweetie, you have to tell me," Hannah said as calmly as she could, but brain tumors started with headaches, didn't they? The problem could be anything from simple fatigue to a fight with the guys at Eliza's, but for Grace to flinch like that...

All in one motion, Grace threw her arms around her mother's neck and hopped over to sit on her lap. Hannah lifted the child in her arms and sat with her on the closed potty lid. For a few minutes she rubbed Grace's back and let the child cry.

When Grace calmed, Hannah held a tissue to her nose.

"What's the matter, sweetie? You have an I-did-something-dumb day?"

It was one of their codes, and usually Grace would smile at the term.

"It was an accident," Grace said, cuddling in close.

"Tell your mom about this accident. I know you didn't wet your pants."

"It was a playground accident, like the lunch aides are always talking about. Do I have to go to the hospital?" Anxiety came through loud and clear, despite the fact that Grace was speaking barely above a whisper.

"Tell me what happened, and then we'll decide."

Though likely not. Hospitals had forms, and on those forms were spaces for a father's name. "Unknown" had done in the past, but Hannah lived in fear of the questions that could raise.

"Larry pushed me off the space station, and I hit my head on the way down. I think I have a boo-boo, but it hurts to touch it."

I will kill the little hoodlum. "If I am very careful, may I look at your boo-boo?"

Nod.

"Point to where it is."

Grace pointed from behind her right ear to her right temple.

"You have a boo-boo, my friend, a big old goose egg that has to hurt like heck. The pills you took should help. Could you stand to have an ice pack on it?"

"A little one."

When Hannah brought a bag of frozen peas into the bathroom a few minutes later, she inspected the bruise more carefully—one big, ugly mother of a bruise.

"Grace, when you hit your head, did you tell the playground aides?"

"No. I didn't want to get Larry in trouble, and I wasn't bleeding or anything. It just hurt a lot."

"Were you dizzy at all?"

"No."

"Did you have any trouble seeing or hearing after you hit your head?"

"No, Mom. Am I going to the hospital or what?"

"Or what. It's Friday night, and we'll do a full-length video, and by the time it's over, your head should feel much better. Sound like a plan?"

From beneath her frozen peas, Grace offered a hint of a smile. "Sounds like a plan, Mom."

"Grace, why are you calling me Mom instead of Mommy?"

"Because me and Merle decided we're done with the *E* stage. You know: mom-my, blank-ie, horse-y. We're too old for that anymore. It's baby stuff."

"Got it, Gracey."

Hannah sat through the zillionth viewing of *Mulan* without seeing or hearing a single scene. Did trying to keep Grace safe mean Grace had learned not to seek help from anyone? Would Grace suffer a concussion rather than involve a classmate in any kind of public incident? Was Grace learning not discretion and safety, but isolation and poor judgment?

All through the movie, Hannah wrestled mentally, finally deciding she and Grace had both had bad days, and the only sensible course was to go to bed and hope things looked more encouraging in the morning.

And they did. Grace was back to her usual self, minus the *E*'s, even going so far as to call Merle so they could whisper and giggle on the phone for twenty minutes about their upcoming night together.

Grace had never called a friend before—not even Henry Moser—and Hannah saw it as a positive milestone. Grace had also never helped her mother get ready for a date before, and her assistance was both sweet and exasperating.

"You should wear red lipstick. It will make Merle's dad think about kissing you."

"You think I want him kissing me?"

"Maybe not, but he can think about it."

Out of the mouths of babes…

They had big fun, with Hannah putting a little foundation, blusher, and eye shadow on Grace, and spritzing her with perfume, and Grace helping to brush out her mother's long hair.

Grace approved of Hannah's ensemble, a simple black dress that fell to below Hannah's knees in a tailored A-line. It flattered a feminine figure without clinging, and the V-neck allowed a hint of a peek of a possibility of cleavage. A necklace of coral beads provided a suitable accent, though Grace thought a reindeer pin would have been more appropriate.

Trent showed up in a damned tux, making Hannah's heart speed up, even as Merle went squealing up the stairs and Eliza looked on beaming.

"If Eddie showed up looking like that, bedtime would be six o'clock, and not just for the boys," Eliza observed.

Trent thanked Eliza for taking on both girls, and then they were off in his car, muted Rachmaninoff coming from the CD player.

"I need to stop by the office," Trent said. "I hope you don't mind?"

"Whatever for?" The last place, the very, very last place, Hannah wanted to be was that dratted office.

"Mac left his notes on his printer, and because he and James are handling the last-minute party details, I said I'd pick up the notes."

"Notes for what?"

"He gives a short State of the Company speech each year, welcomes the new hires, and acknowledges milestones. Mac is one for ceremony."

"A proceduralist. It goes with being in criminal practice." While Hannah was a former foster kid trying to impersonate a lawyer, with less and less success.

As Trent led her through the darkened offices, Hannah was grateful to Mac for the detour. Trent kept his hand in hers, and just that—just holding hands— had Hannah wishing they were headed for an intimate dinner for two and not to a brightly lit company party.

"In here," Trent said, unlocking Mac's office. He didn't turn on the lights. He crossed to the desk, which was illuminated from the streetlights in the parking lot.

"This office is more opulent than yours or James's,"

Hannah said, sinking into the sumptuous comfort of an overstuffed couch. "Almost ostentatious."

"Mac says the criminal element is impressed with displays of wealth, and James and I are for any self-indulgent gesture Mac wants to make." Trent had taken the seat behind the desk, and he looked good there—he looked good almost anywhere. "Moonlight becomes you, Hannah Stark."

"It's streetlight."

"It's an old song," Trent said, rising. "Moonlight becomes you, it goes with your hair…" He sang softly as he crossed the room, a true, rich baritone. As he came closer in the near darkness, Hannah's heart skipped a few beats, then went into dancing-bunny mode when he straddled her lap rather than take a seat beside her.

"I cannot keep my hands off you, Stark. I've hit my limit."

Then he had his lips on her too. His kiss started out slowly, with a sweet and savoring quality, and Hannah relaxed into the cushy leather sofa. Trent was above her and around her, enveloping her in his presence and a sandalwood scent as he deepened the kiss.

"We'll be late for the party," Hannah said, leaning her head back and glorying in the feel of Trent Knightley, big and warm and at long last in her arms.

"God, yes. We'll skip the damned party."

"Trenton Knightley, for shame."

They were alone, no kids on the premises, and Hannah abruptly became interested in having a party of their own. Yesterday's cases had only added to the questions Hannah wrestled with—about the profession, about family law, and about her role as an attorney—but she was very sure about her regard for Trent.

"I'm going to make love to you right here and now, Hannah Stark, unless you stop me. This isn't what I had planned." His thumb brushed over her nipple. "What I had planned is a detour to my house at the end of the evening. I can't wait. I don't want to wait. For Christmas, would somebody please give me back my dignity?"

She sank her hands into his hair. "You'll wait if I ask you to?"

His hand went still over her breast. "Of course."

Dignity could hop the next toboggan out of town. "I can't wait either."

Trent had been a damned saint all week long, keeping his hands to himself, his lips to himself, his *dick* to himself…except for the one kiss on Thursday.

One, single kiss to last a desperate man for days was a bad plan. Thursday was ages ago, and Trent was drowning in the need for more.

"I want you naked, Hannah Stark."

"In the *office*?"

He'd shocked her; he could see that even in the limited light, but she was also intrigued.

"Yes, in the office. It's deserted for once, and that couch is as luxurious as any bed I've slept in. We have time, privacy—privacy, Hannah, the single parent's Cave of Wonders—and God knows I'm motivated."

For the first time, Trent resented the burdens of raising a child. He should have farmed Merle out to her uncles, cleaned the damned house, and made love with Hannah in his own bed like a grown-up. Taken his time, set the mood, plied her with good wine and soft music…

Her brows drew down, and his heart sank.

"Lock the door, Trent."

Thank you, Santa Claus.

He locked the door, toed off his dress shoes, and started undoing his shirt studs. Just knowing she was watching him had him hard as the handle of a splitting ax, but from somewhere he found the strength to slow down.

"Help me, Stark, or I swear I'll be tearing buttons and ripping seams."

She eyed him up and down, then rose from the sofa and slipped off her shoes. When she came toward him, Trent saw both purpose and unwitting seduction in her walk.

He wasn't the only single parent willing to make a few compromises in the interests of starting the party early.

"Let me." She brushed his hands away, reached around him, and unhooked his cummerbund. Her scent, spicy, rich, and warm, bore a hint of cinnamon and holiday memories.

Had Mac left his notes in the darkened office on purpose? Mac was that good a brother.

Hannah undid Trent's cuff links, gliding her fingertips over the backs of his hands.

She untied his tie with a single tug and gave him a look suggesting any scrap of satin might find alternative uses as the evening progressed.

Next, she took out his remaining shirt studs and leaned in to sniff at his throat before putting the studs and cuff links in a pile of gold on Mac's desk.

Trent caught her from behind, putting her hands on the desk and leaning over her, letting her feel his arousal snug against her backside.

"I am dying here, Stark. At risk of embarrassing myself." He got a handful of her dress—silk, or something equally soft and luxurious—and slid it up her leg. She went still, and he shifted the dress higher.

"Jesus save me. Woman, you are wearing a garter belt."

Silk stockings, a little lacy black garter belt, and—Trent slid his hand up to the juncture of her thighs—"And nothing else."

For long, quiet minutes he explored her with his fingers. She braced herself on the desk; he braced himself on her and traced damp folds and soft flesh—more luscious softness. With his hands on her, he could bank his desire, let himself breathe in her scent, and revel in the soft texture of her hair against his cheek.

"I need to kiss you," he said, letting her dress fall back over her legs. "The couch or the desk?"

"Couch," she said, straightening up. "Soon."

She turned between him and the desk and slid her arms around his neck; then she paused.

Hannah was right to take a deliberate moment, because this single kiss was the beginning of something special. Trent waited, his hands resting on her hips, his mind full of that delicate swatch of black lace holding up silk stockings.

She leaned closer and touched her lips to his.

"More," he said when she drew back. She came closer again, and he shifted his grip so he had one hand buried in her unbound hair, preventing her from teasing him endlessly.

Trent kept his exploration of her mouth delicate, consistent with a sense of new beginnings and holiday wonder. He teased; he stroked and petted with his tongue until she was soft and pliant in his arms.

"Couch," Hannah said, curled against his chest. "I want to feel your weight and your skin and the way you breathe, and, I want to feel *you*."

She slipped her hand down to his erection, shaping and caressing him through the fabric. After she'd tormented him nearly to begging, she slid his shirt off his shoulders, unzipped his formal trousers, and reached into his briefs to free his erection. When she'd pushed his skivvies and pants past his hips, she took a step back.

His turn, finally, at long, long, hard last. His socks joined the growing pile of clothing strewn about Mac's office.

Trent lifted the hem of Hannah's dress, unwrapping the best Christmas present he could ever imagine. He took his time, raising the dress slowly, to her hips, her waist, over her chest, and then up, off her shoulders, revealing a lacy black bra complementing the garter belt and stockings.

Hannah Stark was amply endowed. She dressed to not call attention to it, but her breasts were barely contained by the bra. She unhooked the front fastening and shrugged the bra down her arms, leaving her clad in silk stockings and a garter belt.

That little shrug made her breasts gently sway. Had she done that on purpose? Trent kissed her again, delighting in the feel of her naked breasts against his chest, and while he kissed her, he walked her back until her knees hit the sofa and she went down.

"On your back, Hannah."

She looked uncertain, and her fingers drifted to her thigh.

"Leave the stockings on, please." Then Trent realized why Hannah hesitated. He found his wallet and passed her the condom.

"I want your hands on me," he said, standing so his erect cock was at her eye level.

Her mouth level.

She scooted to the edge of the sofa, spreading her thighs so Trent stood between her legs. Trent had to remind himself to breathe.

Please, please, please...

But he wouldn't ask her outright, because she'd told him she lacked experience, and the purpose of this shared moment wasn't to gratify his every whim, but rather, to gratify hers. He hoped they'd have years to explore whims and fancies and adventures and fantasies. Decades—

She leaned in and pressed her cheek to the underside of his erection, nuzzling the hair at the base of his shaft.

"Soft," she said, cupping his balls. "I'm not sure what to do."

"Indulge your curiosity. Please yourself, and you'll please me." He caressed her hair and tried to convey a sense of trust to her simply by waiting.

Delicately, she traced a finger up the underside of his cock, and Trent felt her touch right up his spine. She did it again, studying his face, then bent her head and used her tongue in the same motion.

He widened his stance, bracing himself against the pleasure. She was curious and careful but creative too, using her tongue all over him, and her fingers. When she began to suck gently on that spot right under the head of his cock, Trent let out a pent-up breath.

"Did I hurt you?" She drew back, concern in her eyes, while she continued to pet him and stroke him.

"You found a sweet spot. The sweetest spot."

Hannah held up the condom in its little foil square, and when he nodded, she unsheathed it and unrolled it down his length.

"How do you want me?" Trent put the question neutrally, while hoping her answer began with the words, "right now." He tormented himself further by kneeling to caress every soft, sweet part of her.

The slope and heft of her naked breasts, the soft skin of her throat, the curve of her shoulders, the puckered pink flesh of her nipples, and the long, silk-clad lengths of her legs.

She shifted back to lie on the couch, braced on her elbows.

"I want you like this." After taking one instant to wish he'd turned on a light, Trent came down over her.

She was supple, warm, and exquisite beneath him. She brought her knees up, and Trent said a quiet prayer of gratitude that he was entirely naked and could glory in the slide of silk stockings against his flesh.

The couch was luxuriously soft and plush, almost as soft as the skin on the underside of Hannah's breast.

"You're sensitive," he said, gliding his thumbnail over the fullness of her breast and feeling a shiver go through her.

"You make me want." Hannah's voice was soft, yearning in the darkness, and she tilted up against him in wordless entreaty.

"Soon," he said, closing his mouth over her nipple.

She arched up into him, and her fingers tightened in his hair.

She was beautifully responsive, soft and warm. He'd barely started to tease her with his lips and his mouth when she began undulating against him.

"Trent."

"Tell me." He lifted up enough to see her face and to brush her hair back off her forehead.

"I want you," she said, turning her face into his open palm, nuzzling his hand as her hips continued to move. "I want you inside me, this instant."

He wanted to be inside her, wanted it in more than just a physical sense. The moment bore all manner of gratifications, primary among them the knowledge that this wasn't a lonely moment with a woman whose face he'd forget all too easily. This wasn't rutting with a willing partner; this was making love.

Maybe for the first time in his life, he'd make love with a woman who was his match. Hannah didn't underestimate the challenges they faced; she didn't make promises she couldn't keep.

And she wanted him, *right now*.

Chapter 15

TRENT LEVERED UP ONTO STRAIGHT ARMS AND WAITED until Hannah went still. "Guide me home, Hannah."

She found him with her hand, curling her fingers around his shaft. Her touch was careful but firm as she seated the head of his cock against the opening to her body.

He pushed forward a scant inch, wanting to both plunder and savor. She groaned, her expression confirming it as the sound of relief.

"Don't go slowly. You're driving me crazy."

"Crazy is good."

He set up a slow, shallow rhythm because she was blessedly, wonderfully tight, and the feel of their joining was a heady pleasure.

"Trent." A catch her voice this time. She slid her fingers around his wrists, gripping tightly. "Oh, holy—Trent…"

While he moved in her slowly, her body convulsed around him—just like that. Tension he'd been ignoring—Will I please her? Will she let herself go with me?—uncoiled as she bowed up. Trent lowered himself to his forearms and held her as he moved with steady, deep thrusts even as the tremors shook her.

"Hark the happy holidays." She relaxed back against the cushions, and Trent went still.

"You OK?" He eased down to rest his cheek against her hair. "That one caught me off guard."

"I'm not OK." She pressed her mouth to his throat and sighed against his skin. "I am completely, utterly undone. Mistletoe not included."

"That's a start."

Trent used the aftermath to kiss Hannah, to pleasure his mouth with the taste and feel of her, then he started moving again. She was with him too. He could feel that as she counterpointed his rhythm and slid a hand down to anchor herself with a grip on the small of his back.

"Use your nails, Hannah," he said, scraping his teeth along her neck. "Hold me tight."

She sank her grip into his backside, and the pleasure of it radiated out from his center. A little sound of longing, not quite a groan, came from the back of her throat, and the urge to thrust harder clamored against his control.

Crazy is good. Crazy is damned good. Crazy is—

Her ankles locked at the small of his back when he cupped her backside to hold her more snugly.

"Holy… Trent… I can't… Not again, so soon…" She thrashed beneath him, and he abandoned all restraint to show her that she could again, so soon, and harder than ever.

His good intentions backfired as he felt a drawing up that signaled his own satisfaction was about to crest.

Hannah's free hand cruised along his chest, her thumb inadvertently gliding over his nipple, and the pleasurable shock of that caress sent him over the edge. While she keened quietly against his shoulder, he drove home, hard, repeatedly, shuddering over her for long, sweet moments.

The next thing Trent became aware of as he coasted

into a lovely, thrumming afterglow, was Hannah petting his butt.

"I'm squashing you," he managed.

"Don't you dare move." She patted him twice, a caricature of an admonitory spanking, then went back to stroking him gently.

"You OK?" He lifted up on his forearms but kept his cheek against hers.

"You expect conversation?" She pinched him, gently. "I will never be coherent again."

Had he forgotten the soul-deep pleasure of making love to a willing woman, or had it never been quite this lovely before? Hannah turned her face against his neck, her tongue tracing up toward his ear, tasting him.

He snuggled down closer, taking much of his weight on his arms, content to linger as long as she'd permit it.

"I'm losing you," she said a moment later.

"You'll never lose me, but some tissues would come in handy." He raised himself off her reluctantly and crossed the office to grab a handful of tissues from the box on the credenza. He dealt with himself and the condom first, being sure to fold it up inside a wad of tissues, then came back to sit at Hannah's side.

She brought her knees up, almost touching, and held out her hand, but Trent shook his head.

"Let me."

At her look of consternation, he parted her knees and treated himself to the privilege of admiring damp skin glistening darkly by streetlight. Hannah was up on her elbows, watching him as he looked his fill.

"You've been with boys. A gentleman tends to his lady."

She lay back on a sigh, passive again while he tossed the tissues aside and stroked his fingers over her creases and folds. While she permitted it, he teased through soft curls and felt his cock threatening to rally.

"I could keep you here all night," he said, brushing his thumb experimentally over this and that.

"I'd gladly stay," she said, spreading her legs a little wider. "I'm learning things."

Trent did treasure Hannah's intellect—too. "What sort of things?" He used a bit of pressure on this pass.

"You and this urge to talk." She sighed and closed her legs, trapping his hand. "We'll be late for the party."

"We just had the party," he said, making no move to retrieve his hand. "We won't be late." He kissed her to stop her from uttering more of this responsible, conscientious, mustn't-be-late talk.

When Hannah fell silent and Trent had kissed his fill, he nuzzled the slope of her breast. "Stark?"

"Hmm?" Her fingers winnowed through his hair, and his hand was still tucked between her legs, where he was more than content to leave it.

"This will sound trite, but before we start getting dressed and putting on our public selves again, I want you to know this was special. You are special. I don't think I've forgotten what I was missing. I think it was never like this before."

Hannah's hands went still, then cradled the back of Trent's head to hold him to her.

"You have such courage, putting your feelings into words so easily."

"It isn't easy," he said, levering up to meet her gaze.

"But what good are the sentiments if you hoard them up in your heart and never share them?"

"You still know they're your sentiments," she said, stroking his hair back. "That counts for something."

"Saying them counts for more." Trent sat up and let his gaze travel over Hannah slowly, memorizing the sight of her replete and nearly naked on the couch. "Will you really make me get back into that monkey suit and impersonate an upstanding member of the staff of Hartman and Whitney?"

"You're a partner, not merely a staff member, so yes, I will make you put your clothes on and do your part at the Christmas party. But, Trent?"

She opened her legs so he could have his hand, but he kept it right where it was.

"I haven't any frame of reference for what goes on between consenting adults," Hannah said. "I'm as igno-rant as the mother of a seven-year-old can be, but this was precious to me. Maybe what I'm trying to say is I trust you. I don't understand it, I'm not entirely comfort-able with it, but in this regard at least, I trust you."

From Hannah Stark, that admission was worthy of gilded wrapping paper and a satin bow. She'd used as many qualifiers as she could, nearly taking back the gift with all her disclaimers and caveats, but she'd said enough that Trent was reassured.

Reassured he was different from whatever and who-ever had been with her in the past. Reassured he was special, in some way, just as she was special to him.

———

A sense of newfound tenderness lingered for Hannah as she and Trent dressed each other. He knelt to help her put on her shoes, and Hannah wanted to go to her knees and wrap her arms around him.

His intimate attentions had been one revelation after another, and the education he'd offered Hannah had been more than simply erotic. She'd learned about being with the man, Trenton Knightley. Hannah knew all too well that sex needn't be tender, sweet, and overwhelmingly pleasurable, but Trent Knightley made it that way.

He made the whole evening special, as he took her coat from her shoulders, met her gaze from across the room when she waltzed with James, and put a hand on her back as he escorted her along the buffet.

When Mac led her onto the floor for a slow dance, Trent's expression became curious and watchful, but he contented himself with a glass of wine, reclaiming Hannah when the last bars of the music died away.

She liked it. Liked his protectiveness, and even the hints of possessiveness. When they left the party promptly at nine thirty, a light snow dusted the parking lot.

"You want me to get the car?" he asked. "Your shoes can't be suited to trudging across the tundra like Sasquatch."

"It's only starting," Hannah said, slipping her hand into his. "I can manage."

"I once knew an attorney the clients referred to as Sasquatch," he said, linking their fingers. "The poor woman had an unfortunate build to go with the moniker."

"Where did you run across her?"

Hannah's voice was even, but inside her, an arctic chill descended. Miss Wallingham, of Douglas County DSS fame, had been referred to as Sasquatch.

"This lady represented the Department of Social Services when I clerked over in Douglas County. Wallingford? Wallingham? I forget her name, but her handling of the foster care docket was particularly lugubrious."

Hannah's heart started a slow pounding in her chest, but she managed to keep walking. "I didn't know you clerked in Douglas County."

"I lived over there at the time. The longest two years of my life." He said it lightly, amused with his younger self, then unlocked the car and held the door for her.

A perfect gentleman.

Hannah took a seat, and when Trent turned the key in the ignition, the indicator light went on for the heater in her seat.

If Trent had clerked in Douglas County, he'd probably sat through many of the foster care dockets, possibly even the last hearing or two Hannah had endured.

This was not good. Hannah might have maneuvered through a relationship with Trent while carefully skirting the issue of Grace's father. She might have dealt with her growing distaste for family law, an area of practice Trent respected above all others.

She might even have reconciled herself to a sense of unease with litigation in general, though it spoke of bewilderment with the entire legal profession, a profession that bound Trent to his brothers emotionally, financially, and logistically.

Knowing that Trent might have had a front-row seat on some of the worst moments in Hannah's life, or as good as, pushed her anxiety needle into the red zone.

She clicked off the seat heater. She was already

sitting on a hot seat, and facing choices that could cost her Trent's respect, his intimate companionship, and possibly Grace's safety.

Louise Merriman was hearing a criminal docket, but it hardly took up much of her attention. She'd drawn a morning of plea bargains, and all she had to do was listen to the deal cut between the state's attorney and defense counsel and decide if she could agree to it.

Louise brought her attention back to the case before her. Her mind had been wandering—again—to the matter of Ms. Hannah Stark, age twenty-seven, place of birth the Douglas County Hospital, no apparent family. Hannah was a distraction Louise would have to resolve, just as she'd have to return Dan Halverston's now weekly phone call.

Louise had made a trip to the Douglas County judicial archives and shamelessly used her standing to quietly access records that were otherwise unavailable. That research had only added more proof to Louise's own strong hunches.

Very abruptly, her personal life required a great deal more consideration than Louise was used to giving it, and maybe it was about time.

"Mr. State's Attorney, has an agreement been reached in this case?"

Louise glanced at her file as she posed the question, noting charges of soliciting and possession of drug paraphernalia. Mr. Matthews's client was thin to the point of emaciation, nervous, and pretty in a used-up-too-soon way.

"Your Honor, the State suggests a sentence of ninety days on each count, to be served consecutively," the prosecutor said.

Consecutively? Six months of enforced sobriety from the defendant's drug or drugs of choice wouldn't hurt the woman, though incarceration wasn't likely to lead to recovery.

"Mr. Matthews, what evidence was taken from your client suggestive of paraphernalia?"

"A cigarette lighter, Your Honor." He hadn't stood to offer that information.

Come on, old girl. You wear this robe for a reason. "Mr. Matthews, how old is your client?"

Matthews rose this time and bent his head to confer with his client. "Nineteen, Your Honor."

"Does she have children?"

He bent his head again. "A son three years old."

"Does she have a place to stay if she's not incarcerated?"

Another whispered exchange. "She can stay with her sister, Your Honor."

Louise carried out the interrogation for a few more minutes, and each time, Matthews had to consult with his client before answering.

"Mr. Matthews, do you know anything about your client?" *Other than the amount of the retainer she paid you?*

Matthews's expression turned disgusted, though he was trying to maintain a veneer of courtroom demeanor.

"Your Honor, with all due respect, I was retained only a couple of weeks ago, and have had limited contact with my client. The circumstances of the case—"

Louise exercised a judge's prerogative and baldly interrupted.

"She was at the jail awaiting trial, Mr. Matthews, available to you essentially 24-7. Counsel will approach the bench."

She did not make it a request. The state's attorney had the decency to look uneasy.

"Mr. Matthews, please enlighten me as to how Ms. Charles has had the effective assistance of counsel, when all she's done is plead guilty to both charges—one of which is beyond ridiculous? She's prepared to accept consecutive, not concurrent sentences, when she has no previous convictions and not even a prior charge. What in the hell have you done for this kid?"

The state's attorney's eyes showed resignation. Louise ignored it.

"Your Honor," Matthews said, "the paraphernalia charge could get her six months alone."

"Where are your witnesses to testify that the woman smokes cigarettes? If I looked over the evidence reports, I'd probably find she had cigarettes in her purse at the time of arrest, wouldn't I?"

The state's attorney looked away now. Prudent of him, because Louise had every intention of denying at least one of the easy convictions Matthews always seemed to hand him.

"Mr. Matthews, did you do anything to help your client solve the real problems in her life? Can she read and write? Does she have a place to live? Is there a drug problem? Did you at least give her a referral for an addictions assessment? Have you done anything to prepare her defense?"

Matthews took a few huffy breaths, and Louise told herself she was getting too old for attorney histrionics. His hair was precisely parted, but greasy. His three-piece suit looked expensive, but the dress shirt he had on beneath it was wrinkled. One cuff lacked its cuff link, and dirt lay under the nail of one index finger.

"I am not a social worker, Your Honor," Matthews bit out. "I am not Ms. Charles's keeper. She has accepted the State's offer, and I have found her to be under no disability that would render her consent invalid."

Louise picked up a pen and tapped it against the family law article she took with her into every courtroom. Matthews's clients were invariably facing drug charges, or solicitation and prostitution, occasionally drunk and disorderly. There was a pattern of selling his clients out to the State that was too obvious to ignore. His incompetence helped the State's conviction rates, so the prosecutors weren't about to complain.

"Gentlemen, you may return to the counsel tables."

She gave Ms. Charles a stet on the solicitation charge, putting the charges untried on an inactive docket, and dropped the paraphernalia charge, then had a short, confidential discussion with Ms. Charles in chambers. The topic, couched entirely in hypotheticals, was the nature of the retainer paid to Mr. Matthews.

When Ms. Charles left, a dozen agency phone numbers clutched in her skinny mitts, Louise made another call. An attorney in her jurisdiction had a problem with substance abuse, and her duty as a judge and member of the bar was to see the attorney thoroughly investigated and offered assistance for his problem.

―――✦―――

Hannah's week was passing by in a fog. She prepared her cases for the Friday docket, and she made a proper maternal fuss over Grace's pair of skinned knees on Monday night. Tuesday night it was a scraped elbow.

By Wednesday morning, Hannah had to admit she was avoiding Trent.

Making love with him had been the fulfillment of more fantasies and dreams than Hannah had realized she invented. He'd been tender and passionate and caring and *hot*. Wickedly, wonderfully hot, and now he'd stepped closer to parts of Hannah's life she wanted to put firmly behind her.

She owed him the truth, but not at the cost of exposing Grace to risk. The only real choice was to send Trent on his way, which would be damned awkward when they worked together.

Also painful. Brutally painful. As would leaving the firm.

"Greetings, Stark." The man himself lounged in Hannah's doorway, arms crossed, his blue eyes traveling over her in a way that made her breath seize.

"Trent."

"You have a minute?"

"I do. Debbie has pretty much put this week's docket together, and I'm only nervous, not in a flat panic."

"But then," he said, lips quirking, "it's only Wednesday, right?"

Oh, how she loved that smile.

How she would miss that smile. "Right."

"I've come to complicate your day. But step into my parlor, where you won't hear your phone ring."

Hannah followed him across the hall. She'd avoided his office all week and hadn't even let herself walk by Mac's office.

"It's nothing major," Trent said, closing his door behind her then taking up his perch against his desk. "Just a marital separation agreement for a friend of one of James's friends, but it's a do-it-yourselfer."

"Meaning?" Hannah didn't sit down, didn't scoot up onto the desk to sit beside him, didn't even look at him. Couldn't bear to.

"Meaning it's full of holes, but I've gone over it and made notes. All I want you to do is arrange the sit-down with the client and talk her through them."

"You want me to tell her what she and her husband put together off the Internet is amateurish, full of problems, and she'd be better off hiring us for our zealous advocacy?" Hannah asked.

Trent pushed away from the bridge of his starship and came to stand beside her.

"I told myself you were busy," he said, studying her. "Told myself you weren't avoiding me, you weren't playing hot and cold. But something is bothering you, Stark, and I am not a mind reader."

His tone was not accusing, but it held something careful. A little puzzled, a little hurt. He hadn't touched her since he'd kissed her good night on Saturday evening.

Hannah faced a choice. She could tell him Saturday had been a mistake, and he'd retreat to the friendly, supportive position he'd occupied when she'd first come to work for him. It would be a caricature of that stance, but for her sake, and for the sake of his pride, he'd pull it off until she moved to a different department, or a different law firm.

To put Trent through that would kill her.

Somewhere along the way, she'd lost her heart to him, at least the small piece of her heart that wasn't entirely commanded by her daughter.

"Hannah?" His gaze held concern and a hint of vulnerability. "Are you trying to find a way to tell me I've blown it?"

"You haven't blown it. It's me."

Still he watched her, making no move to touch her.

Tell him. Tell him the truth. Tell him some part of the truth. This is Trent, and he cares about you, and you have to tell him...

"You didn't enjoy that shelter care hearing," he said. "I have wracked my brain, and that's the only other thing I can think of. Something about it undid you."

"Everything about it undid me."

Hannah's heart started to pound against her ribs, dread beating through her veins, while she gathered her courage and tried to speak normally. She could tell him this much and blame her inability to sustain a relationship with him on her past. In a sense, it would be the truth, but it was a truth she'd admitted to no one.

"You need to know that I was a... I was..."

Abruptly, her voice and her nerves failed her. An attorney dealt in words, she told herself, *so deal*, but hurt, despair, and sheer, miserable grief clogged her throat. She moved to the door, as far from him as she could get, intent on turning the lock or leaving, while the lump in her throat threatened to strangle her.

Just like Grace's father had tried to strangle her, to end her life, even as he'd planted a new life inside her.

Hannah stood at the door, clutching the doorknob behind her back.

"I was in foster care for much of twenty years—"

One sentence was all she could get out, pinned against the door, heart hammering, hating even the sound of the words that had been her unrelenting reality.

She tried again, holding up a hand when Trent took a step toward her.

"I was in foster care for most of the first twenty years of my life. I was adopted once, but my adoptive parents were killed in a car accident when I was three. Then it was one home after another, group homes, or foster homes, shelters in between. Therapist after useless therapist—"

Her lungs stopped working. She pushed words out anyway, the effort greater than pushing cinder blocks off of her heart.

"There was some neglect, but mostly I was passed around like a bag of garbage. I was in a lot of good homes too, but by then, I wasn't any good. You cannot make me go back to that, Trent. Not as a person, not as an attorney. I will not do it. I just can't. But Friday, you made me, and I let you. I let you do that to me."

She was crying now. She closed her eyes to block out the sight of his face, not wanting to see the bewilderment and dimming of his regard for her. She would become not Hannah to him, not his Stark, but a case, a casualty, and he would be kind, and that would kill her.

"I'm so sorry." He'd moved; his voice was rough, right near her ear, and then she was scooped up against his chest and carried to the sofa. "Hannah, I am so very, very sorry. I should have known, I should have seen, I'm sorry. Forgive me."

He held her, cradling her in his lap, and Hannah's tentative grasp on her dignity shattered. She wept openly, heartrending, uncontrolled sobbing that had little to do with a single hearing, and a lot to do with twenty years of being unheard in any meaningful sense.

"Go ahead and cry," Trent murmured. "You won't cry alone, Hannah. Not while I have breath in my body." He stroked her back; he passed her tissues; he petted her hair and whispered meaningless comforts to her while she gradually became quiet in his arms.

"I hate to cry. I hate this job for making me cry."

"You have every reason to cry." Trent's tone was fierce, but the way he rested his cheek against her hair was tender. "I never want to make you cry like this again, Stark."

When she shifted, trying to climb off his lap, he let her get only as far as the place beside him on the sofa, her hand trapped in his.

"There's more, isn't there?"

Hannah tossed a balled-up tissue into Trent's wastebasket. "There's always more."

"It has to do with Grace's father?" He was shifting into his lawyer mode, but maybe that wasn't entirely bad.

"Some of it. We don't have to talk about that now."

"I'm ready to hear whatever you're willing to tell me, Stark. Jesus, when I think of you having to deal with Patlack, and that skinny kid on Friday, and all those child support clients turning their backs on their progeny." He squeezed her hand.

God bless him for sparing Hannah an explanation

of the poor fit between her and family law. Oh, she'd manage well enough in a domestic relations courtroom if she had to.

But Trent's reaction told her she didn't have to. The relief of his acceptance was dizzying, even though it might also be temporary. He stayed beside her while Hannah's breathing calmed and her system tried to find its equilibrium.

"I'll help you locate your birth parents, if that's what you want," Trent said. "The private investigators we use are very good, Hannah. They find needles in haystacks for me all the time, and all it takes is a phone call to turn them loose."

Hannah had never once, not in her wildest imaginations, thought he might help her put her family back together. Never thought anybody *could* help.

"What if my mom died in detox last week? What if she had no idea who my dad was? What if he r-raped her?"

She'd said too much. Beside her, Trent's demeanor underwent a subtle change.

"If he did, we'll deal with it. But how on earth did you ever have the courage to have a child of your own, Hannah? Where did you find the strength?"

The question was logical under the circumstances, but Hannah hadn't seen it coming and couldn't quite muster the fortitude to answer it entirely.

"Grace was a gift. I never expected to be anybody's mother, but when the opportunity arose, I was determined my daughter would at least know her mother loved her and wanted her and didn't abandon her."

Trent raised their joined hands and kissed Hannah's knuckles.

"I will see about moving up the hire date for your replacement. You will not be forced to deal with domestic relations any longer than necessary."

Hannah was about to tell him not to be so hasty, that she could manage the next few months provided he was guarding her back, but a knock on the door stopped her.

Trent went to the door, opening it far enough that Hannah could see James on the other side, his expression serious.

They spoke quietly, then Trent opened the door farther.

"There's a social worker on line one for you, Hannah," Trent said. "Debbie recognized the exchange. The call is coming from one of the local elementary schools."

Hannah reached for the numbness any foster kid learned to conjure eventually, an indifference beyond panic. A social worker would contact Hannah in the middle of the day for one reason and only one.

She went to Trent's desk, waited for him to usher James out and close the door, then picked up the phone.

"Hannah Stark."

"Good afternoon, Ms. Stark, my name is Kelly Post, and I'm with the Child Protective Services unit of the Damson County Department of Social Services. I've just concluded an interview with your daughter Lucy, and need to speak with you personally at your earliest convenience."

The numbness evaporated into a choking dread. "Where did you interview my daughter?"

"We're at the Department's Child Services Center. If you can get away, I'd like to speak with you at our offices as soon as possible."

The worker's voice was clipped, detached, and professional, while Hannah wanted to scream and scream and scream.

Her daughter had gotten into a car with strangers and was even now in strange surroundings, being questioned and emotionally probed and perhaps even physically examined.

"I will be there in thirty minutes. If my daughter is to be physically examined, I want that done by her own licensed pediatrician. Is that understood?"

"We can talk more about that when we meet in person, Ms. Stark."

No guarantee, no bargaining, just the monolithic power of the State. DSS made the rules, enforced the rules, and bore few consequences for breaking the rules.

"Tell my daughter I'm on my way." Hannah hung up.

Trent watched her from the across the room, and she could no more have kept the phone call private from him than she could accept a career in family law.

"That was Social Services. They have Grace, and they want to talk to me."

"Wait here." He disappeared, coming back a few minutes later with Hannah's coat, purse, and briefcase.

"What did they say?" he asked as he held her coat.

"Just the usual. They have her, they need to talk to me in person. But if they took her into custody, they suspect either abuse or neglect, otherwise they would have talked to her at school and left it at that."

"You don't know that," Trent said, reaching for his coat. "Come on, the sooner we leave, the sooner we'll get there."

"I beg your pardon?"

"You are not dealing with those she-dragons alone, Stark, not after the day you've had. This is probably some simple misunderstanding, but I'm one of the few attorneys in this jurisdiction who's dealt with child welfare law in depth. I can clear up misunderstandings with the best of them. If that doesn't work, I'll start quoting them the Courts and Judicial Proceedings Article, COMAR, case law, local precedents from before Patlack's watch."

Trent had graduated from lawyer mode to gladiator mode, but all Hannah heard was, "You're not dealing with those she-dragons alone."

"Trent, I haven't been entirely honest with you."

"Worry about that later," he said, taking her by the elbow. "We can sort out your past when we're more certain of Grace's future. One thing I know for damned sure, you did not abuse or neglect your daughter."

The offer of support, the demand that Hannah allow his support, was too precious to quibble over. She got in his car and let him drive her downtown, but paused with him outside the drab brick office building that was Child Services.

"I changed my name," she said, wanting to tell him all of it.

"When?"

"When I was cut loose from foster care, I changed my name. They may not connect me with the Douglas County foster care case."

He scanned the building—a four-story tan brick box with a stingy allotment of narrow windows.

"The Department is inbred across county lines, particularly in this part of the state. You make the call whether to disclose your past or keep it to yourself. They aren't entitled to know everything about you, Hannah, contrary to what they sometimes think when they're in the middle of an investigation."

She let him escort her into the building and also let Trent be the one to approach the bulletproof glass and do the talking.

"Attorney Trenton Knightley is here with Ms. Hannah Stark. We have an appointment with Kelly Post."

Trent's voice was clipped, and apparently commanding, because the cipher behind the glass immediately picked up a phone.

"We'll wait by the window," Trent said, taking Hannah's arm. He led her past the usual gallery of pinched, anxious faces, and a few resigned, hopeless faces as well.

Did DSS have their children too?

"Ms. Stark, here to see CPS?" A woman who looked several years younger than Hannah stood at the interior door, scanning the lobby.

"There's a lawsuit right there," Trent muttered. "Blathering your business all over creation, for God's sake."

"Trent, they have Grace. Don't antagonize them." And they would demand to know who the child's father was in all likelihood.

"I'm Kelly Post," the woman said, extending a hand to Hannah. "Ms. Stark?"

"Hannah. And this is Trent Knightley."

The social worker extended a hand, her wary expression suggesting the "attorney" part had already been communicated to her. She led them to a small, nondescript conference room, closed the door, and took a few maddening minutes examining notes in silence.

"When can I see my daughter?" Hannah asked.

The worker looked up, her expression impossible to read. Was that the wrong question, or the only right question?

"She's down the hall in the playroom, and you can see her as soon as we're done, but what we have to discuss could be upsetting, and you may want some time to compose yourself before you see her."

Beside Hannah, Trent shifted back in his chair, but he held his peace. The subtle bracing of his body language was strategic, and Hannah was glad to have him beside her.

"I am assuming Mr. Knightley is here today in the capacity of your legal representative?"

"I am not," Trent said, surprising Hannah. "I am here in a supportive role only."

"Then I'm afraid I'll have to ask you to leave, sir," the social worker said. "Departmental investigations are confidential, and the matters they involve very sensitive."

Hannah cut in lest Trent lecture the little twit about having seen more departmental matters than she had in her entire filing cabinet.

"You do not have legal custody of my daughter yet. On her behalf, and on my own behalf, I will waive confidentiality and sign any necessary releases so Mr. Knightley can remain in the room at all times."

Trent settled. The social worker's brows rose, and then she shuffled papers.

"These are our standard releases," she said, sliding

two pieces of paper across the table. "If you'll sign one for yourself and one for your daughter, we can proceed."

Hannah complied, her mind going into a familiar form of split functioning. One part of her would play chess with this functionary who stood between Hannah and Grace, and another part of her was in a blithering, lunatic panic, praying as hard as she could.

Across the table, the social worker put the signed waivers into the file, and leveled a flat look at Hannah.

"What explanations do you have for the bruising and lacerations on your daughter?"

Chapter 16

TRENT'S ADRENALINE PUMPED, GETTING HIM READY FOR a knock-down, drag-out, steel-cage match against the forces of bureaucratic might represented by the tidy young woman across the table.

He kept his figurative powder dry, because Hannah was managing. He'd not have thought to simply waive confidentiality, but she had, even though it was her kid in the clutches of the authorities.

"Grace has two skinned knees from where she fell on the blacktop at recess," Hannah said slowly. "She has a fading bruise on the right side of her head from falling off the play station last week. She has both a bruise and a scrape on her elbow, from banging into a tree on the playground."

"Did she tell you how she fell off the play station?" Miss Post asked. "Head injuries can be very serious."

"Another child bumped her."

"Did she give you the child's name?"

"I don't recall. I'm not very familiar with the names of the other second graders."

The worker was writing quickly, not even looking up between questions. "What about the finger bruises on her arm?"

"I didn't know she had finger bruises on her arm. It's December, she's wearing long sleeves, and Grace is old enough to see to herself at bath time."

The worker let out a sigh that to Trent's ears was purely histrionic.

"Here's what we have, Hannah. Your child is cut and bruised, and your explanations are uncorroborated. The school can't vouch for how any of these injuries were received, and right now, we just don't know if this child is safe in your care."

Trent spoke up, unable to stand the theatrics. "What other explanations do you have?"

"What I am afraid we have is a very disturbed little girl." The worker closed the file and addressed herself to the manila folder. "When I asked her how she got the bruises—and I am not supposed to tell you this—she refused to cooperate. She said her mother warned her not to talk to strangers. I could not get a thing out of the child, which is not unusual in cases of familial abuse. Your daughter did tell me her guardian angel was going to have to talk to me if I didn't let her go back to class. Then she told me I wouldn't be allowed in the cloud pasture ever if I didn't listen to her."

Now the worker looked up at Hannah. "I am worried this kid is dissociating, and that the discipline she's subjected to at home is causing delusional episodes."

Before Trent could sputter out a response, Hannah spoke up.

"No one who knows her refers to her as Lucy, and you clearly didn't even check the school records to see that she goes by her middle name. You—who don't even know her name—will petition the court for permission to shelter her in foster care." Her voice was neutral, eerily so.

"You do know the law," the worker said, then she

seemed to come to some internal decision. "Look, Lucy is seven years old, and we have no protective services history on her at all. She's been in school for two years, and day care before that, and no one has reported anything prior to this. Whatever is going on, Hannah, we really do want to see it addressed."

Another theatrical little sigh, and this time her glance took in Trent as well.

"We know your history, Hannah, and if the supervisor learns I told you that, my job is gone." The worker's voice became apologetic. "We know you were a foster child, and some of the homes you were in were investigated for abuse or neglect, and we know from time to time, your foster parents said you had a problem with your temper."

Beside Trent, Hannah's fortitude was crumbling. He could feel it, could see it in her eyes, hear it in her voice.

That was the plan, of course. Kelly would be the good cop, the sympathetic ear, the empathetic face of an institution that could be cruel in the extreme. The supervisor would be the bad cop, and the roles weren't even planned or rehearsed.

"Can't you see your way to allowing Lucy to spend just a few weeks with a foster family?" Kelly asked. "We'll make sure she doesn't have to change schools, and I can probably get you two visits a week, though it will have to be supervised at the Department. All we need is some time to get therapy started for you and the child, do a family assessment, some drug testing... You want what's best for the child, don't you?"

It sounded so reasonable, so sympathetic, and to Trent, so twisted in a system where everybody was supposed to be presumed innocent until proven guilty.

"Aren't we overlooking something, Miss Post?" Trent asked.

"Sir?"

"Isn't it a requirement of the law that you either demonstrate that shelter was unavoidable to keep the child safe—and in the list of bumps and bruises on this girl, I don't hear anything besides normal childhood wear and tear—or you offer the parent a chance to make a voluntary placement first?"

Trent speared her with a look, informing her silently that he was happy to play endless rounds of Get the Social Worker.

"You have a point, Mr. Knightley," the worker said. "Why don't I get my supervisor in here so we can discuss the options?" She rose and left Trent sitting alone with Hannah, but before he could say anything, his cell rang.

Hannah got up and paced while he took the call.

"Mac says they've already scheduled this case for a hearing at nine thirty tomorrow morning before Judge Stevens. Patlack thought you should at least have the case heard by a judge who doesn't handle the child support docket."

"Sporting of him. You told your brothers what's going on?"

"I told Mac, and he'll fill James in."

Hannah would bristle at that, but she had no concept of the proper use of a family. None but what she and Grace had cobbled together in the last seven years.

Trent's thoughts were interrupted by the return of the social worker, accompanied by an older woman whose gray hair was in a thick braid coiled around her head. She wore glasses halfway down her nose, and from

Hannah's swift, indrawn breath, Trent concluded this supervisor was a ghost from Hannah's past.

"We meet again, Julie," the older woman said, her tone accusing.

"Candace, I believe you know Trent Knightley, and my name was changed by court order."

Candace neither greeted Trent nor looked at him. "Department regulations require that he leave, Julie. Now."

In the years since Trent had seen this woman in the Douglas County courtroom, she'd aged badly. She'd been a line worker, then, a lazy bully, but she'd known to dot her i's and cross her t's.

"Her name is Hannah, or Ms. Stark to you, Candace," Trent said. "Department regulations do not forbid her to waive confidentiality in writing, which she's done. Moreover, your worker concluded the initial interview, though to my mind, it was an oddly abbreviated attempt to get at the truth. Ms. Stark has also been told she may see her child only when you've concluded your interrogation, so if you have further questions, I suggest you ask them. Lucy, as you call her, is overdue for her after-school snack."

Candace lifted a penciled eyebrow at him, and Trent saw in her flat brown eyes the recollection of who he was and where their paths had crossed. Like most bullies, she made a tactical retreat in the face of substantial opposition.

"Let's not beat around the bush, then, *Hannah*." Candace put a fat file down on the table with a loud smack. "We will ask the court for permission to put your child in foster care tomorrow morning at nine thirty. She'll spend the night in foster care until then. You can consent or object at the hearing tomorrow, and we'll revisit placement in thirty days. It's up to you and your lawyer here if you want to make this more difficult than it has to be."

Trent folded his arms and regarded Candace down the length of his nose.

"If you had inquired of your subordinate here, Candace, you'd know I am not present in the capacity of counsel for Ms. Stark. I am here to support her and to offer my household as a temporary placement for the child. I do believe the Department is required to offer a parent the chance to make a voluntary placement before exerting its shelter care powers?"

"You?" Her jaw dropped, clearly taken aback by the quality of Hannah's reinforcements.

"Certainly. I know the Department can't vouch for the safety of the child in the home of a family law practitioner and officer of the court, but I think Ms. Stark is willing to take the risk, and we checked, Candace: you haven't filed any paperwork yet, you haven't actually sheltered the child as we speak. If the plan is acceptable to the Department, we'll gather up Grace and see you at nine thirty tomorrow."

"She does go by Grace?" The worker was frowning at her notes.

"Lucy Grace Stark," Hannah enunciated. "She prefers Grace. I am willing to place her with Mr. Knightley. His daughter is Grace's classmate and her friend."

Candace was frowning mightily, but the worker at least retained some professionalism.

"Why don't I have Ms. Stark execute a safety plan agreeing to leave the child with Mr. Knightley, and to not be alone with her between now and the hearing tomorrow?"

Candace nodded, but her glare was fixed on Hannah as the worker left the room.

"Look, Hannah. Parents who were abused as children often set up their own kids to be abused. I'm not saying you were the one who hurt Lucy, but somehow, you have failed to keep her safe, or that's the way it appears. We are not trying to hurt you. We're trying to keep your daughter safe. Don't fight us."

Hannah's voice was calm, the way a landscape appears calm before some fool sets off a land mine. "You know so little, Candace, and your ignorance is a greater threat to my child and every other kid out there than I could ever be on my worst day as a parent."

To Trent's relief, Hannah stopped there, but he could feel the emotions roiling in her.

"We're only trying to help you," Candace hissed. "And, Julie, I can do the math. I know when you got pregnant, and that you lied to us by omission about that. Don't lie to us anymore, or we can't help you."

She left before Trent could strangle her. When the door was closed, Hannah put her head in her hands.

"They want to help me get on a national registry of child abusers," she said. "My picture on the Internet, my license to practice law taken from me, my daughter taken from me. This is my worst nightmare. I had thought protecting Grace from her father was the most important priority. I lived in dread he'd find out about her, even assert a right to visitation or—God help me—custody. I don't even know where he is, but he has haunted me for seven years, when all along, the threat was from a different quarter."

In her posture, in her words, in her tone, she con-
veyed despair, and the insight that hit Trent nearly had
him in tears too.

"You were raped in a foster home."

———

Hannah nodded, but Trent saw what her admission cost
her in her brittle composure and tense silence. Was this
the rest of what she hadn't told him? Good God, how
much more could there be? He slipped an arm around
her shoulders.

"They don't have Grace yet, but that worker will be
back in here in a few minutes, so put on your competent-
mom face, and I'll soon have you out of here."

She nodded against his shoulder and sat up, expression composed.

The paperwork took only a few minutes after that,
but the worker had to warn Hannah to bring Grace to the
hearing and to pack a few days' worth of Grace's clothes
to bring along as well.

Through it all, Hannah remained composed, until the
worker stood to leave.

"May I see my daughter now?" Hannah asked.

Trent heard the tremor in her voice, and it nearly
broke his heart.

"You may. She's right down the hall."

The worker led Hannah from the room, but Trent
lingered, making a little production out of putting on his
coat and organizing his briefcase. When he was alone in
the room, he closed the door and opened the thick file
Candace had neglected to take with her.

Names of foster homes jumped out at him. He'd

clerked in Douglas County, and the names weren't entirely unfamiliar. He committed the names of the last family Hannah had lived with to memory, flipped the file closed, then got the hell out of the interview room.

The interrogation room.

—◆—

"If the Department thinks Grace is safe here for one night, why don't they just give Trent temporary custody of her and leave Hannah in peace? Why go forward with the hearing tomorrow at all?"

The question came from James, who was sitting on the floor beside the sofa in Trent's living room. Trent and Hannah had the sofa, and Mac was in a wing chair facing the sofa, while Merle and Grace had disappeared into Merle's room.

Mac fielded the question, which was fortunate, because Hannah had left her ability to form coherent sentences in the disinfectant-scented DSS playroom.

"They hadn't filed any paperwork yet," Mac said. "So Trent had them on the technicalities and had the clout to make a stink if they tried to dodge the rules for a single night. But they don't want the liability the next time somebody calls them and tells them Grace has unexplained bruising, so they're trying to get their hands on the kid through the hearing process."

"We keep me as a backup plan," Trent said. He gave Hannah's hand a squeeze, but to Hannah, he was admitting the possibility the Department's case would carry the day.

"If the judge gives them custody of Grace, they'd need to come look your house over," Hannah said, "do fingerprints, a background check. All that would take weeks while Grace is with strangers, and you'd have to complete foster parent training, too."

James stretched out his long legs. His thick gray socks were starting to unravel near the left little toe.

"What if you signed another one of those agreements?" he asked. "Said you'd do the counseling and the drug testing and the parenting classes and all that other bullshit. Would they give Grace back then?"

"It depends," Hannah said. "My guess is no, they'd wait to make sure I had at least three clean urines, to make sure the counseling was bearing some fruit, maybe even until I had completed parenting classes. They talk a good game about visitation increasing as you comply with their demands, but it all depends on the worker you get, and the supervisor he or she has. I'd really rather not trust Grace's well-being to the luck of the draw."

"It's enough to make you think twice about having kids," James said.

"We need to win tomorrow," Mac interjected, studying Hannah. "First, we need to win because Hannah did not abuse or neglect Grace. Second, we need to win because Hannah cannot be victimized again, not even by well-meaning social workers who honestly think they've spotted a protective services issue."

Hannah was grateful to Mac for the simplicity and power of his reasoning, but gratitude wouldn't keep Grace home.

"I just wish I could recall that kid's name," Hannah said, not for the first time.

"If I'm to represent you tomorrow, you need to

let me talk to Grace," Mac said. "I promise I'll be careful, Hannah."

"She doesn't know you," Hannah replied, staring at her hands and feeling again how a plan to protect a child had backfired, so Grace had few friends and fewer allies. "She won't rat out her classmates, no matter how careful you are."

They'd already tried talking to Merle, but every time Grace had been pushed, bumped into, or shoved off the equipment, she'd been alone, no witnesses available to incriminate the child responsible.

"What about having me talk to Grace?" Trent asked. "She knows me, and you can be there when I talk to her."

Hannah wanted to say no, to tell them to leave Grace alone, not to drag her into it, but it was Grace who faced foster care.

"He's good with kids," James said, patting Hannah's knee. "Merle vouches for him, and she's a tough critic."

Silence, while all three brothers waited for Hannah to give her consent.

"Be subtle," she said. "Don't put her on the spot."

"C'mon." Trent tugged her to her feet. "We'll tuck them in, and she won't even know I was in the room."

He was as good as his word, sitting on the edge of Merle's bed while Hannah leaned against the doorjamb.

"Good night, Daddy, sweet dreams, I love you." Merle reached up to hug him.

"Good night, Merle. Sweet dreams, and I love you." He gently hugged his daughter, then shifted to sit on the edge of Grace's bed.

"Got any extra hugs to give away?"

Grace held out her arms, wordlessly accepting his embrace, hugging him just as hard as Merle had.

"Good night, Grace, sweet dreams, and don't worry about tomorrow. Merle's Uncle Judge will be there, and her uncles too, and they are all in your corner."

"I'm not worried. Bronco will be there," Grace said, but her voice sounded small and uncertain.

"Speaking of certain guardian unicorns." Trent sat up and put a puzzled expression on his face. "I have a question I would like to ask Bronco, if you don't mind."

"What?"

"Where was he when you were having all these accidents at school? Let's see… You got pushed off the space station, knocked down on the blacktop, grabbed by the arm, and pushed into a tree. Maybe Bronco wasn't paying enough attention."

"Bronco isn't in charge of anybody but me," Grace said. "He can't help it if Larry isn't careful. Larry's guardian angel has to be in charge of him. 'Sides, I'm OK. It was no big deal."

"What's Larry's last name?"

"Smithson. He's in the other class."

"Do you think Larry's guardian angel was goofing off?"

"I don't know. Larry's usually OK, for a boy. When I had to leave class today to talk to Miss Kelly, he tried to smile at me like he knew it wasn't my fault I had to go to the office. Everyone else kind of looked away."

"Maybe Bronco can have a talk with Larry's guardian angel," Trent said, rising from the bed. "Tell him to pay more attention to his job."

"Maybe." Grace sighed a tired sigh, and her eyes

drifted closed. "Bronco said I wasn't supposed to worry about tomorrow. He said you grown-ups would work it out."

When Trent had finished with the good nights, Hannah closed the door to the bedroom and leaned against the wall of the hallway.

"I need more than the assurances of an imaginary winged unicorn," she said, letting Trent gather her in his arms.

"You have more. James and Mac will stay up all night strategizing, and Brian Patlack won't know what hit him."

Trent tugged her down the hallway by the wrist, while Hannah wanted to open the door and memorize the sight of her daughter sleeping peacefully, dreaming peaceful dreams.

Fifteen minutes later, Hannah was pacing the living room, feeling anything but peaceful.

"You were set up," Mac said. "Your kid comes home knocked from pillar to post, for the first time you can recall, all the injuries the work of this Larry, and then somebody calls protective services. Hannah, who would do this to you?"

"I don't know. Don't you think I'd tell you if I knew?"

"What about Grace's father, would he do this?"

Her gaze flew to Mac's, but she found no judgment there, merely an attorney trying to prepare a client for trial.

"I don't think he knows Grace exists."

"DSS will ask you about him. Family is a less restrictive placement than foster care, and they'll want to know who Grace's relatives are."

"I'll tell them I don't know. I'll tell them I was at a frat party and doing the whole football squad."

"So they'll add promiscuity and perhaps a sexual addiction to the things you need to have treated," Mac said. "Just who is her father?"

"Mac, back off," Trent interjected as Hannah came to a halt. She turned to look not at Trent, but at Mac.

"As he raped me, he wrapped his hands around my neck and squeezed. I passed out, so I can't recall every moment he was violating me. I had bruises on my throat for weeks, and wore turtlenecks in June to cover them up. I was just the weird foster kid—even for much of college. Nobody thought anything of it if I dressed a little funny. Social Services can have me involuntarily committed, MacKenzie, and I will not give up his name to them."

Mac's expression went blank, while Trent rose to put his arms around her.

"I'm sorry," Hannah said. "I can't think. I can't reason, not when Grace could be put into foster care."

"I found him," James said, charging into the room from Trent's study. "I used to date a gal who works in the media center at Grace's school, and she had a directory for the entire school, including Larry's class. I've got an address and a phone number. I've already left three messages."

"It's nine o'clock on a school night," Hannah said. "If Larry's family was going to answer, they would have picked up by now."

"I can send an off-duty cruiser," Mac said. "Half the guys in the judicial division of the sheriff's office had Trent represent them in support court."

"We are not intimidating a seven-year-old boy with illicit shows of force," Hannah said. "We play by the rules."

"Even if we lose by the rules?" James's voice was gentle, his expression troubled.

"We won't lose." Mac drew Hannah away from Trent by the wrist. "If we rule out Grace's dad, what about this day-care mom, Eliza? She would have seen the bruises, and might have been blamed for them if Grace didn't give us another explanation."

"Not Eliza," Hannah said. "She was in foster care with me, and the last thing she'd do is put another kid in foster care. She might deck me outright or read my beads at the top of her lungs, but she wouldn't sneak around."

"Should we have her at the hearing?" James asked. "She could testify that there's never been unexplained bruising before, that Hannah has a close and loving relationship with Grace, that Grace is very imaginative."

"It can't hurt," Mac said, "but that gets us no closer to a perp, assuming Larry didn't act on his own initiative."

The room filled with the unhappy quiet of a dead end.

"We don't have to prove anything," Trent reminded them all. "The State has to prove there is risk of substantial harm to Grace if she stays with Hannah. Bumps and bruises don't come close. Stevens has five kids. He won't be easily swayed."

"But nobody likes child abusers," Hannah said. "Nobody, and it's easier to label me than to get to the bottom of the real mystery. Grace wouldn't tell Kelly who was responsible when she had the chance, and if she gives him up now, it will look suspicious. We're screwed. We're totally, hopelessly screwed."

———

Mac and James eventually peeled off to their respective guest rooms, leaving Trent in the kitchen with Hannah.

"It's chamomile," he said, putting a steaming mug in front of her. "Drink it, and it might help you sleep."

"Nothing will help me sleep tonight." But she took a dutiful sip. Trent turned a chair around backward, straddled it, and reached across the table to her. When Hannah laced her fingers with his, he took a slow, deep breath.

"I am bringing this up now, Hannah, so you won't have to wrestle with one more burden. I was the clerk for the judge who closed your case. I was probably right there in the courtroom at your last hearing."

She bowed her head, but kept her hand in his.

"Hannah, were you ever going to tell me?"

When she raised her gaze to his, her cheeks glistened with tears. The phone call from DSS hadn't made her cry; the farce of an interview downtown hadn't made her cry; Mac's heavy-handed cross-examination hadn't made her cry.

"If it helps," she said, "I realized there might have been a connection only after the Christmas party, when you said you knew an attorney nicknamed Sasquatch. The only person I remember in detail from my hearings was Joe, the bailiff. Everybody else was just another stranger, and you weren't—"

"If I was observing your hearing, I was just another stranger, thanking God my parents had loved me and I'd never spent a day in foster care, while you spent nearly twenty years."

"Are you angry?"

Trent was six kinds of furious. "I am disappointed." He rubbed his thumb across her knuckles. "Because of decisions made years ago, a brutal rapist is probably on the loose and has likely offended again. You were thrust into motherhood without any support system at all, and I am bewildered. What did you think I'd do if you'd trusted me with the truth of your past?"

She rose and took her mug to the sink, then faced him, arms crossed over her middle.

"It isn't only you, Trent, it's the legal system. You love that system, you delight in it, and you are part of what makes it work as well as it does. That system is threatening my daughter with the same dubious experiences it inflicted on me. At the hearing tomorrow, I will have no meaningful chance to muster witnesses in my own defense, not even eight-year-old thugs. My constitutional right to privacy will be hung out like so much dirty linen, and my esteemed counsel—whom I cannot afford, by the way—will have had less than twenty-four hours to prepare my case. You tell me, Judge Knightley, why I should expect you to understand my perspective, much less respect it or me."

She went on, more softly. "You are devoted to a system that is very likely to take my daughter from the only person who loves her, and me from one of the few people I have been able to love, and yet, you ask me why I haven't shared twenty years of history with a man I've known less than two months."

She left the kitchen, silence ringing in her absence.

Trent sat for a long time, staring at nothing. At first he tried to tell himself Hannah Stark might have ended up dying in a trash barrel if it weren't for "his" system, but that was an excuse. She had a point: the legal system was not based on love, loyalty, or the healthy ties of a strong community. It was based on the need for something, anything, to serve when those ties disintegrated.

And were it not for his slippery lawyer tactics at DSS, he would not have learned where to start looking for Grace's father. If Hannah knew how Trent had come across the knowledge, would she be as disappointed in him as she was with the legal system?

Hannah fell into the only unoccupied bed on the second floor, an oversize king with a down comforter and flannel sheets. Sleep came for her, despite all her fears and anxieties.

Her last thought before drifting off was that she might never again spend a night under the same roof as her daughter. She tried to resign herself to that reality, because all of Mac's brilliance couldn't wipe out Hannah's record with Social Services, or relieve Grace of her loyalty to her imaginary friend or her steadfast silence regarding another child's meanness.

Hannah couldn't even cry. She was cried out and empty of everything except a gnawing pain.

Sometime later, she became aware of a presence beside her in the bed. Trent, of course. Even half-asleep, Hannah knew him by his scent. When his hand stole into hers, she rolled over and wrapped her arms around him, holding on tight.

Despite all their differences, despite mistrust and exhaustion and the looming tragedy of tomorrow's hearing, Trent held her just as tightly.

And she was comforted.

Chapter 17

"ALL RISE," THE BAILIFF CALLED. "THE CIRCUIT COURT for Damson County, sitting as a Juvenile Court, is now in session, the Honorable Paul Stevens presiding." The room shuffled to its feet; the judge took his place. "You may be seated."

Hannah shot one last look around the courtroom, and was surprised to see Judges Halverston and Merriman sitting on the respondent's side of the gallery. Eliza was there as well, with Henry beside her. Trent was in the next row up, Grace tucked against his side.

On the far side of the courtroom, no less than four social workers sat behind Brian Patlack and Kelly Post. Candace was among them, as was a second worker whom Hannah vaguely recalled from about ten years ago.

"Good morning, Your Honor," Patlack began, reciting the case number and explaining to the judge who was represented by whom. "Seeing the crowd gathered behind me, Your Honor, I'd preliminarily ask the court to invoke the rule excluding witnesses from the courtroom. This is supposed to be a confidential matter."

Stevens had the appearance of an aging warrior. Tall, a full head of white hair, and snapping blue eyes, he looked to Hannah like he didn't suffer fools.

"I see we are graced with the presence of two members of the bench," Stevens said. "Judge Halverston, Judge Merriman, good morning."

Curiouser and curiouser. What were Judges Halverston and Merriman doing in the courtroom, anyway? Trent shrugged, as if he'd read Hannah's mind, then Stevens addressed the courtroom.

"I'm not asking two distinguished judges to cool their heels in the hallway, Mr. Patlack, and if they stay, so do the rest of the camp followers and pot bangers, including that rogue's gallery from the Department behind you. Besides, the best decisions are made based on complete information, and kicking people out of the courtroom won't help us get to the bottom of this. It's the family's privacy at risk, and they're not asking me to serve as a judicial bouncer. Call your first witness, and if I deem it necessary, I'll excuse the junior contingent at a later time."

Stevens's tack was unusual, considering the young ages of the children, but Hannah could recall attending hearings as early as age four.

Patlack put Kelly Post on the witness stand and carefully laid out for the judge the number and extent of Grace's bruises, the child's reticence about discussing them, the school's inability to corroborate the parent's version of events, and the parent's long history of "troubled emotional adjustment" to various foster homes. Mac objected repeatedly, only to be reminded the rules of evidence were not strictly applied at shelter care hearings.

Mac opened his case by calling Eliza to the witness stand, leaving Henry squirming alone on the bench until Trent motioned for him to join Grace. Eliza testified to the length of time she'd known Hannah, and to the quality of the relationship she'd observed between Hannah and Grace. She also testified that Grace was an active child who played vigorously and had a vivid imagination.

Then it was Patlack's turn to cross-examine the witness.

"Ma'am, you said you've known Ms. Stark for about eleven years. Where did you meet?"

"We met at the Appalachian Hills Girls Home. We shared a room with two other girls."

"That would be a group home for foster children?"

Of course it would, Hannah fumed, and because the Department had all of Eliza's records too, the questioning followed a predictable course.

"Where did your paths cross again?"

"We were both moved to a shelter in Baltimore when the home was investigated for possible neglect, and then we were moved to separate foster homes here in the county, but we went to the same school."

"So it's more fair to say you're Ms. Stark's friend than her daughter's day-care mother, isn't it?"

"I am both."

"You're loyal to Ms. Stark, aren't you?"

"I am loyal to Grace as well, and would be the first to report potential harm to her."

"Except you didn't report it, did you? The child supposedly got off the bus after school, night after night, bruised and lacerated. She came to your home in this condition, and you never said a word to anybody."

Patlack went about systematically destroying Eliza's credibility and establishing that Eliza sent Grace home to Hannah, only to see the child with more scrapes and bruises the next day. He also established that Grace talked to a spotted unicorn—a spotted, *winged* unicorn,

Your Honor—that nobody else could see, and did not answer to her own name.

"She goes by her middle name, sir," Eliza said evenly. "To those who know and care about her, she is Grace."

Patlack shot an assessing look at the judge, and behind Hannah, Henry grew squirmier and squirmier.

Finally, cross-examination was over, and the judge aimed a frown at Mac. "Do you want me to interview the child?"

God, no. The awkwardness of a dozen judicial interviews rose up from Hannah's memory.

"He'll think she's nuts," Hannah whispered to Mac, "and allow the Department to put her in a psych ward. No, and that's final."

"Then the Department's version of matters will stand, Hannah," Mac said, "and you will lose your daughter."

Hannah's lungs seized, and her heart beat an aching dirge against her ribs, while the attorney for Grace— who'd spent an entire fifteen minutes with her client before the hearing—told the judge that a chamber interview with the child would not be necessary.

"If Miss Moser is through entertaining the court with her fabrications," Patlack said, "I'd like to move for a ruling. It appears the child has unexplained bruising, very troubling thought patterns, and a mother with a documented problem both controlling her temper and exercising sound judgment. If this"—he gestured to Eliza—"is the extent of Mother's case, then I'm afraid the court has no choice but to grant—"

Hannah's vision began to go black when a high, loud voice behind her sang out over the courtroom.

"Mr. Judge, that man is picking on my mom just the

way Larry picked on Grace. You better make it stop, Mr. Judge, because it's not nice!"

Henry Moser stood on the church pew, his chin quivering with indignation.

Patlack nonchalantly crossed his arms and addressed the judge, not even looking at the child.

"Your Honor, I ask that the unruly young man be excused from the courtroom. These matters are too sensitive for youthful ears, and I am surprised opposing counsel has as many children in the courtroom as he does."

Trent lunged over the rail to grab Mac by the back of the neck. He whispered fiercely in his brother's ear, and Hannah watched a slow smile spread over Mac's features.

"Your Honor," Mac said. "The unruly young man is my next witness."

The judge's frown faded. "Proceed, Mr. Knightley. We don't have all morning."

Eliza left the witness box and took a seat near Trent and Grace, indicating to Henry he should take the chair she'd vacated near the judge's bench.

The next move would have been to swear in the witness, but the judge intervened.

"Young man, what is your name?"

"Henry Moser, sir."

"How old are you?"

"Almost seven."

"When is your birthday?"

"May eighth."

"Let the record reflect it's mid-December, and the witness has accurately stated that by some algorithms, he is almost seven." The judge's expression was serious, but Hannah realized he'd made a judicial joke.

"May I call you Henry?"

"Sure. I mean, yes, Mr. Judge."

"Now, Henry, do you know the difference between what's real and what's make-believe?"

"Real is what's true, and make-believe is like Grace's silly unicorn."

The judge glanced at Grace to gauge her reaction, but when Hannah turned, her daughter was sitting calmly under Trent's arm.

"I'm glad we cleared that up," the judge said. "What about the difference between the truth and a lie?"

Henry's brow puckered and his legs began to swing. "A lie is when you make something up to tell somebody else because you don't want to tell the truth, but my mom would put me in time-out forever if I lied to you."

Even Patlack smiled at that response.

"This hearing today is very, very serious, Henry. Do you understand you must tell the truth, even if somebody would be mad at you for it?" Stevens asked. "You have to tell me the truth so I can decide what to do here."

"I understand." His six-year-old face was the picture of innocence as he sat in the too-big chair, his feet dangling several inches above the floor.

The judge nodded at Mac. "Your witness, Mr. Knightley, and you may lead the witness in the interests of judicial economy."

"Henry, you said something about Larry picking on Grace," Mac began. "Could you tell us who Larry is?"

"Larry Smithson. He's in second grade, but not in Grace's class, a year ahead of me. He was in second grade last year too, so he's the biggest kid in second grade. He acts like that's something great."

"Have you seen Larry picking on Grace?"

"You bet!" Henry darted a look at the judge. "First, he pushed her off the space station, and she landed on the ground. I was over at the swings when I saw that, and I was about to run to get the aide when Grace sat up and shook her head. She told me it was an accident, but it wasn't. I saw Larry look around before he did it, and none of the aides was...were watching him."

Patlack started whispering with Kelly Post.

"Did you see Larry pick on Grace any other times?" Mac asked.

"Just a couple, and Larry wasn't very nice. Once he pushed Grace down on the blacktop. She skinned her knees, but Larry didn't get in trouble. He bumped into her from behind, like he couldn't see where he was going, but I saw him look around first then too."

"Objection." Patlack was on his feet. "The witness may not give his opinion unless qualified as an expert."

"Overruled," Stevens said. "Henry, try to limit yourself to telling us what you saw with your own eyes. Proceed, Mr. Knightley."

"Henry, what other times did you see Larry picking on Grace?"

"He grabbed her by the arm and tried to pretend he was swinging her around, and he stomped on her foot, and he mashed her into a tree. That's all I saw. I'm going to stick with Grace on the playground now, and so will Merle, and it won't happen again."

"When did he stomp on her foot?"

"Yesterday."

The judge was watching Grace, probably to see if Henry was tailoring his story to her cues. When Hannah turned around to look, Grace was curled up in Trent's arms, her face against his shoulder.

"Judge?" Henry put the question quietly.

"Son?"

"We're making Grace cry, just like Larry did. Can we stop now?"

The judge rubbed a hand over his face and looked at Hannah for the first time.

"Ms. Stark, would you like to have your daughter removed from the courtroom while we finish this up?"

"We'll wait outside with the child."

The voice belonged to Louise Merriman, of all people, and Dan Halverston was standing with her. James scooped Grace up and joined the judicial procession leaving the courtroom.

Hannah could not comprehend why two sitting judges should offer to care for her child, and hoped they weren't simply trying to make it easier to hand Grace off to DSS at the close of the hearing.

"Hannah?" Mac laid a hand on her arm. "Is there anything else I should ask Henry?"

She scribbled a note, not trusting her voice.

Mac glanced at the note. "Henry, is Larry your friend?"

"Sorta. Larry doesn't have many friends because he's not very smart and he only knows one joke, about a parrot in a freezer. He's told it a million times. I feel kinda sorry for him, but he shouldn't have done what he did to Grace."

"A few more questions, then we'll be done. Have you ever met me or talked to me before today, Henry?"

"No, sir."

"Did anyone tell you that you might have to talk to the judge today?"

"No, sir." He shook his head for emphasis.

"Thank you, Henry. Now Mr. Patlack might have a few questions for you."

Patlack turned to the witness, expression stern.

"Mr. Moser, why aren't you in school today?"

"I'm sick," Henry said. "Wanna see?" He tilted his head back, stuck out his tongue, and let out a loud, long *ahhhhh*. "My brother had it last week, and I always get what he has. Mom was kind of mad that I had to stay home, but she really wanted to come today, and I promised I'd be good."

The adults in the courtroom were looking down or out the window, but Grace's champion wasn't done.

"Mom makes me drink lots of water when I'm sick, and pretty soon I'm going to have to wee-wee. Are we done yet?"

Patlack sat behind the counsel table. "Just one more question: Why were you paying such close attention to Grace? She isn't even related to you."

Henry shot a perplexed look at Patlack. "What has related got to do with anything? Mom says Grace is part of my family whether we're related or not, and Grace doesn't have anyone to stick up for her at school. Will you talk to Larry, or am I going to have to tell the principal on him?"

"No further questions, Your Honor."

"I have a few," the judge said. "But none that require Mr. Moser to delay the call of nature, and none that prevent me from dismissing the Department's petition with prejudice. Ms. Stark, you and your daughter are free to go. Mr. Patlack, I suggest your workers schedule an interview with this Larry fellow, in order that your investigation reach its appropriate conclusion and Ms. Stark and her daughter can henceforth be left in peace. Court is adjourned."

"All rise."

Hannah struggled to her feet, her knees so wobbly Mac's hand under her elbow was a necessary support. When she turned to him, no words formed. She hid her face against his shoulder until Trent was there, stuffing tissues into her hand and gently peeling her from his brother's arms.

"I have to thank Mac," Hannah said when Trent got her out to the hallway.

"You can thank him later, though I think he knows you're appreciative."

"Where's Grace? I have to talk to Grace. I don't want her to worry one instant longer than she has to."

"You wait here." Trent pushed open the door to a witness interview room. "I'll find Grace, and thank Mac and Eliza, and buy that boy a damned pony and season tickets to the Orioles and the Ravens."

"Two ponies," Hannah said, "and Redskins tickets."

They'd won. Thanks to Trent's brilliant notion to call Henry as a witness, Grace was safe, and they'd won.

Somebody had put Larry up to abusing Grace, though, and beneath Hannah's relief and joy lay a miserable knot of fear the judge's ruling hadn't addressed.

—◆◆◆—

"I need a name," Trent said to Eliza Moser. Eliza sat on a bench in the courtroom while Mac, of all people, explained the finer points of the morning's proceedings to young Henry.

"A name?"

"Who is Grace's father? I promise you, I will not use the information to contact him without Hannah's permission, not now, not ever. I have three possibilities in mind, all members of the last household where Hannah was in foster care, but you can save me a lot of time."

"Hannah should be the one to tell you." Eliza's eyes were teary as Mac lifted Henry up to his shoulders to peer over at the judge's desk in the now emptying courtroom.

"Hannah can't spell her own name right now, and in seven years, she hasn't been able to locate this guy."

"Why do you want to find him?"

"So Hannah will know where he is," Trent said. "The last thing she needs is to run into him at the toy store some fine day with Grace in tow. This haunts her, Eliza, and it will haunt her every day until that little girl turns eighteen, at least."

"God Almighty." Eliza offered a few more curses under her breath. "He was six-foot-two, a nineteen-year-old bodybuilding bully with a juvie record as long as your arm. His parents adored him, and Hannah's afraid he'll try to take Grace."

"Not while there's a Knightley brother standing to say otherwise," Trent assured her. "Hannah isn't alone anymore, Eliza, whether she's admitted it to herself or not, not in this."

Henry was now perched on Mac's hip, inspecting the reporter's recording equipment and the computer at the clerk's desk.

"You mean that," she said. "All three of you were here for her today, for her and for Grace."

She gave him a name, and better still, a date of birth and which high school the guy had attended. Trent thanked her and got out his cell phone.

Mac approached as Trent's call went through to the very best private investigators in captivity.

"When you're done with Miss Moser," Mac said, eyes dancing, "you'll want to know what Judge Halverston mentioned to me before the hearing started. I about wee-wee'd in my pants."

———※———

"Where are we going?" Hannah asked as Trent towed her along by the wrist.

"To get your family."

Hannah sensed a mystery, but held her peace until they stopped outside the door to judge's chambers.

"Hannah, does the name David Blackmun mean anything to you?"

She dragged back against his grip. If he'd struck her, she could not have been more stunned. "Less than nothing."

"Then you wouldn't be interested to know he's serving fifty years for armed robbery of a bank in West Virginia?"

"*What?*"

"He's in a maximum security prison several hours away, and won't be eligible for parole for probably twenty years. Violent offenders get the longest sentences."

"I looked all over Maryland," she said, sagging

against a wall. "I scoured the judicial databases. How did you find him?"

"I called our private investigators, and they nailed him in less than four minutes."

"I have to sit down." She was light-headed, and light-*hearted*. "He's really locked up?"

"Really and truly." Trent led her to a bench and sat beside her.

"I cannot take this in. First that hearing, now this. It's too much."

Trent stuffed some more tissues in her hand. He seemed to be doing that a lot lately.

"I'm done crying today. I won't be needing these."

"Keep them anyway."

"You don't know what this information means to me, Trent. It's the whole world, the universe, the eternal universe. My gratitude—"

He put a finger to her lips. "You and Grace deserve to know you're safe," he said. "Mac will wait for you both, and I'm sure Merle will expect to hear from her friend tonight. Grace is with Louise and Dan in chambers. I expect you to take the rest of the day off, Stark. You'll need the time to decompress, and I"—he rose, patting the hand clutching the tissues—"I'll need the time too. Now go in there and find Grace."

He kissed her soundly on the mouth and left.

Hannah rose, still a little unsteady and more than a little puzzled by Trent's behavior. Maybe he was concerned for his own daughter; maybe he was still troubled by the knowledge Hannah hadn't been honest with him. Maybe he was disappointed she'd failed to bring charges against Grace's father; maybe he was—

Her thoughts came to an abrupt halt as she made her way to Louise Merriman's judicial offices. There, behind the secretary's desk, was a four-foot-tall wall portrait of a white, winged unicorn with a sprinkling of silver spots across its hindquarters.

"I painted that when I was about fourteen," Louise Merriman said, emerging from her chambers. "It's kind of hokey now, but he was my personal totem. Unicorns are on the state seal of Scotland you know, and I'm mostly Scottish."

Hannah looked at the judge askance.

"I know your daughter"—Louise stumbled over the word—"I know Grace is partial to unicorns. I thought she might enjoy meeting this one."

Louise took a guest chair, the secretary having apparently abandoned her post, so Hannah took a seat as well.

"How do you know Grace likes unicorns?" Hannah asked.

"She told us, chattered away like a magpie about Bronco this and Henry that and Mommy the other. She has a lively mind and lovely manners." Louise smiled, though it struck Hannah as a sad smile.

"Thank you," Hannah said, but her curiosity got the better of her. "I appreciate your spending time with her, but Judge Merriman, what were you doing at the hearing this morning? The proceeding is normally confidential. I suppose Judge Halverston was showing up as some sort of judicial color guard out of respect for the Knightleys, but I can't for the life of me explain what you were doing there."

"For the life of you?" Louise looked at her hands, then peered at Hannah, her gaze so wistful Hannah wanted to pass the woman a tissue.

"Hannah, I don't know any other way to say this. I strongly suspect I am your natural mother, and that would make Dan Halverston your father. I would appreciate it, I would appreciate it very much if you would allow us a chance to get to know you."

Hannah heard the words and comprehended their meaning, but she struggled silently to grasp their significance.

"Why do you suspect this?" Her voice was calm, barely curious, but inside her emotions were rioting.

"You were born at the Douglas County hospital on the same day as my daughter, and there were no other girls born that day at that hospital. None born that week, for that matter. I abused a few judicial privileges and spent some time in the Douglas County court archives when we concluded our hearing last week. You look exactly like my little sister."

Louise rose and went to stand before the portrait, studying it as if she'd come across it in some gallery.

"You were initially adopted from the agency that placed my daughter. We have physical features in common, and you are a damned fine attorney. The personal characteristics you can dismiss as coincidence, but the date and place of your birth are facts."

Louise touched the tip of the unicorn's horn, which fairy tales imbued with healing properties.

"I hired the best private investigators money could buy, but there was no real Internet thirty years ago, no adoption registries even. The trail went cold before you were even a year old. I didn't know your adoptive name, your adoptive home, nothing. I would probably never have found you unless something turned up on the registries, especially because you changed your name again and went to so many different schools."

"You would not have found me. I wasn't on the registries. I was hiding from Grace's father."

Louise's shoulders drooped. Did the judge blame herself for every misery that had befallen Hannah?

"Does Judge Halverston know?" Hannah asked.

"He didn't know we had a child until I told him over the weekend, and told him my gut insisted the child was you. I've wondered, frequently, about red-haired girls who were the right age—once upon a time, I was a redhead—but this time, when I saw you, the hair stood up on my arms, and something physical hit me. I can't describe it, but I knew."

"Judge Halverston thought he recognized me too. This is so strange. Why did you give me up?"

Louise nodded as if she'd been expecting that one. "I was in law school, and so in love with your father. He's the only man I've ever loved that way, but we were of different faiths and very different backgrounds. He comes from old money, I do not. Back then, with our families, the differences were going to be a problem. I needed my family's help to finish law school, and he needed his father's support if he was to have the career he was meant to have. When I turned up pregnant, my parents gave me an ultimatum: I could have an abortion or be disowned."

"You kept me a secret from my father, and I've kept Grace a secret from hers, but how did you manage everything?" Hannah waved a hand, for an unwed mother had a great deal to contend with.

"I lied to my parents, of course. I transferred to a

different law school, bought a cheap ring, and told some tale about my husband being in the military overseas. My family simply didn't see me for an entire academic year. Dan never even knew I was pregnant."

"And then?"

"When my due date grew closer, I made the adoption arrangements, went about my classes, gave birth, and took three weeks off. I kept you with me for those three weeks, Hannah. I stayed up nights watching you sleep, but the days went by, I had no money for child care, and all too soon, the social worker came to pick you up. I started a trust for you with my first paycheck, though legally, I am nothing to you."

"What is my legal birth name?"

"Lucinda Gabriella Halverston."

God in heaven. The coincidences were piling up thick and fast. Hannah identified bewilderment, a little anger, and some joy in the emotions rocketing through her, but most of all, she was curious.

"How did you do it? How did you survive giving up your baby?"

"Not very well. I worked more hours than any new associate in the history of the profession. I avoided my family, I took ten years to start dating again, and when I did marry, I found a man who agreed not to have children. I didn't think I deserved children after giving you up, and Dan never had children either. You are an only child, Hannah."

Something tickled at the back of Hannah's mind as she listened to Louise's recitation. The woman had suffered, clearly, and was suffering still.

"Lilacs," Hannah said, smiling for no good reason. "You're wearing lilac perfume."

"I keep lilac potpourri in my office. I burn lilac candles at home," Louise said. "It's a soothing scent, and your father complimented me on it once. I've worn it ever since."

She smiled a shy, sidewise smile that, *holy God*, reminded Hannah of Grace.

"Well, Hannah, what do we do now?"

"Damned if I know. I am the last person to ask about how to be a family. I do know, though, that you have a granddaughter, and you would be within your rights to petition for visitation with her if you chose to."

Louise's eyebrows rose. "I may be a judge, Hannah, but that doesn't mean I want judges managing my personal affairs. Legally, I'm a stranger to that child. I'll keep my distance if that's what you want. I can't speak for Dan, but I can't imagine him learning how to be selfish and intrusive at this late date."

Hannah frowned at Judge…Louise…*at her mother*, and cast about for something she could honestly offer.

The silence stretched until it was broken by Grace's voice, high-pitched with happy excitement.

"This is soooo cool. The judge has a picture of Bronco in her office, and she painted it herself. Wait until I tell Merle!" Dan Halverston stood in the doorway to Louise's private office, Grace perched on his hip.

"Hannah." Dan Halverston's smile would have illuminated the infernal pit itself. "Your hearing went well."

When Hannah rose she found herself enveloped in a gentle bear hug.

"Mom, did you see Bronco's picture? Aunt Judge painted it herself when she wasn't much older than I am now. Well, maybe a little older, but it's *him*, Mom. Now I can show Merle exactly what he looks like."

Grace was beaming, the most beautiful sight under the sun. A happy child, safe and free to be amazed at the small and not so small glories around her.

She also wasn't wiggling to escape Halverston's arms and run to her mother.

"Thank you both for looking out for Grace today," Hannah said. "Things in the courtroom got a little peculiar." When she thought about how close she'd come to losing Grace, she abruptly dropped back into her chair. Halverston sat as well, shifting Grace to his lap.

"I want to sit with Aunt Judge," Grace said. She scrambled off Halverston's lap and climbed onto Louise's.

Hannah was struck anew at the resemblance. Two pretty smiles, both with dark eyes, perfect skin, and determined chins. The facial shape was the same, the tilt to the eyes, the line of the eyebrows.

"Why is Aunt Judge crying?" Grace asked, some irritation mixed with her bewilderment.

Hannah's voice was surprisingly steady.

"Aunt Judge is afraid, Grace, that because she sometimes couldn't cope very well when she was alone and overwhelmed, she might not be treated very nicely now. She is afraid we won't want to be her friends. I expect Uncle Judge is afraid of the same thing."

Grace scanned the three adults, her brows drawing down in a scowl.

"That's silly. Everybody has bad days, and I-did-something-dumb days. You tell me that all the time, Mom, and you don't throw me away on my bad days."

"That's right, Grace. And you don't throw me away on my bad days either. We wouldn't throw somebody away who was trying their hardest to do the best they could."

Louise set Grace down and gave her a push toward Hannah. Hannah's parents embraced, both of them in tears.

Hannah nudged Grace and whispered that they were going to find Mac and stop at the ice cream parlor on the way home, but she also paused to slip a note into an envelope and leave it on the secretary's desk.

Time enough later—the rest of their lives—to sort out this third miracle of the day. Grace needed an explanation, but she wouldn't be concerned with all the whys and wherefores yet. Grace was too busy accepting her grandparents on the strength of intuition alone, and her child's heart was more ruled by who needed loving than who felt deserving of being loved.

Chapter 18

HANNAH ANSWERED THE PHONE, SURPRISED AND NOT a little disappointed to hear James's voice instead of Trent's.

"How are my two favorite girls?"

"From what I hear, you have a different favorite girl about every four hours."

"That's because you listen to my brothers, who are just jealous. I wanted you to know DSS interviewed that kid Larry, and got exactly nothing out of him, except some guy threatened to strangle Larry's puppy if Larry didn't leave as many bruises on Grace as he could."

"Some guy?

"Larry couldn't even give a physical description. They talked on the phone."

"With a blocked number, no doubt. You've heard I acquired some relatives?"

James didn't even try to dodge. "It's all over the courthouse, though nobody is saying whether Stevens spilled the beans or Halverston or Merriman. My money's on Stevens. Do you know what this means?"

"I have no privacy?" Though Hannah did have family. The oddness of that was eclipsed only by the loveliness, for if Hannah had family, Grace did too.

"You're related to legal royalty, Hannah. Louise has a sister and a cousin on the federal bench, Dan's brother is on the Court of Special Appeals here in Maryland,

and his other brother teaches at Stanford Law. You've also got cousins practicing law, and there's a governor in the bunch somewhere too. I thought you should know before you came in to work tomorrow."

"Did Trent put you up to calling me?"

"No, sweetie, he did not."

"Since when do you call your prospective employee sweetie?"

"Since my brother had the great good sense to fall in love with you. I'd take your docket for you tomorrow, but I don't know the first thing about family law."

"And I wouldn't let you. Those are my clients."

James prosed on for a few more minutes, but Hannah barely heard him.

Had he said Trent was in love with her?

———

"Gerald, you gave it your best shot, but Social Services dropped the ball," Joan said. She kept her voice steady, her tone placatory, because the idiot butthead nutcase was doing the bad, hard stuff now, and it showed. The bones of Gerald's face were more prominent, going from handsome to feral. The light in his eyes wasn't merely arrogant, it was pure lunatic.

"Give it up, Gerald," she went on. "DSS won't go off half-cocked on another bunch of anonymous phone calls."

Gerald jittered around Joan's kitchen, his three-piece suit looking like some rumpled castoff Goodwill might have lent him for a rare job interview. Oh, how the mighty had turned mighty stupid.

"I got a fax from bar counsel, Joan, certified letter to

follow," Gerald snarled. "You know what that means? Hannah Stark has destroyed not only a decent job with cushy bennies, but the rest of my fucking legal career. If she hadn't been there to step into my shoes, the Knightley brothers would have been a lot more reasonable over a little moonlighting. Now they're taking me out."

He paused in this tirade, looming over her so spittle flew into her face when he spoke. Joan barely repressed the urge to gag as Gerald went on ranting.

"DSS didn't screw up, Joan. I did the research, I got into the confidential court files, and I laid a faultless trap. I didn't screw up, but your stupid nephew did. You said Larry was the biggest kid in second grade because he flunked a year. He apparently wasn't big enough to push around one bitch-lawyer's little brat. You said he'd get the job done."

Joan's temper rose, but she knew better than to let loose with Gerald in his current mood. He was too drugged up and too angry, taking chances no sane person would, for reasons no sane person would understand.

She sidled away and untangled the trailing twine of the dream catcher hanging in the kitchen window. No cops parked in the complex parking lot now, when she needed them—of course.

"Look, Gerald. Larry did what he could, given that he was scared to death. You did a low-down, rotten thing to an eight-year-old, especially when Larry has it tough enough without you turning him into some kind of playground enforcer. You never said you'd get ugly with him. If I find out you're leaning on him again, you will regret it."

Gerald went still.

"Joan Smithson," he said almost pleasantly, "are you threatening me?"

Yes, she was. Only a dumbass would have to ask.

People came and went in Joan's life, and her attitude had always been live and let live. Since Gerald had handled her DUI, she'd learned that she should have simply shown up in court in one of her Aunt Joan outfits and apologized for being an irresponsible idiot—which she absolutely had been. As a first offender with a clean record, she'd probably have been shown lenience.

"You're twice my size, Gerald. You have more education than everybody in my family put together, and you're a lawyer. The car you drive is worth more than my mama's mobile home. How could I possibly threaten you?"

He slicked his hand over hair that needed washing. "Damn right you're no match for me. Tell Larry he'd better keep that puppy inside. Where can I get some goodies?"

Gerald must have run out of that expensive cologne. He bore the subtle stench of old, nervous sweat, a stink common to the addict.

Boy was dumber than a puppy turd too.

"You go down to the convenience store on Eighth around seven this evening, and quietly ask the gal at the register if Leo's around. Browse for a few minutes while she makes a call where the security cameras won't see her, then Leo will meet you out back. He delivers the product, and one of his guys will meet you at your car and get the money from you. Don't screw with Leo, Gerald. It's his ball, his bat, and his rule book."

"You think that scares me?"

It damned well should. "Don't tell him I sent you, whatever you do."

"And have him think I rely on you for my connections? Not likely." Gerald left, one of his fancy shirttails hanging out behind.

Joan cracked a window, despite the cold, and watched him drive off. Before his Beemer had screeched around the corner, she dialed a number a friend had given her in case she ever needed legal representation again. As the receptionist asked to whom she could connect Joan, Joan waved at Gerald's disappearing taillights.

"Mr. Trenton Knightley, please."

—◆◆◆—

Hannah tried to focus on the morning's cases, but her mind refused to cooperate.

If Eliza had sent Henry to school yesterday, Grace would be in foster care.

If Patlack hadn't been so heavy-handed with Eliza on the witness stand, Grace would be in foster care.

If Judge Stevens hadn't raised five kids, Henry might not have been such a good witness, and Grace could be in foster care.

Something Judge Stevens had said kept going around in Hannah's head: the best decisions were the ones made based on complete information. When Hannah had made the decision to go to law school, then to sit for the bar, she hadn't had complete information. Nobody at the start of a career did.

Somebody had made an anonymous call to DSS, maybe several calls, and without knowing anything about that caller or his motives, the Department had charged off, determined to keep Grace safe from her mother.

This morning, with the child support cases, the judge wouldn't have complete information. He'd have a handful of facts, a few minutes to look them over, and then, boom, he could destroy lives or protect them with a few words.

Somehow, Hannah made it through her docket. Other attorneys gave her odd smiles, maybe because, as James had said, she was the local equivalent of legal royalty, maybe because she was the attorney whose kid DSS had tried and failed to snatch.

She returned the smiles automatically, wondering all the while who had called DSS, and why. After the last case concluded, Margaret wished her happy holidays then trundled off, leaving Hannah to pack up in the empty courtroom.

When her files were jammed into her briefcase, she considered her surroundings.

Lives were wrecked here. Yes, justice was done, sometimes, but more often, imperfect decisions were imposed by imperfect people on other imperfect people with far from perfect results.

"I hate you," Hannah said to the room. "I hate that my life was decided in rooms just like you. You're cold, utilitarian, and unfriendly. You're not very well informed. You smell like fear and mud."

"I hope you don't attribute those qualities to me," said a voice behind her.

Trenton Knightley, who had not called Hannah last night, no matter how hard she'd stared at the phone.

But then, she hadn't called him either. "I love

your scent," Hannah said. "You could never be cold or unfriendly without reason, but this place…" Sharp winter light slanted in the tall windows; a single small mitten lay on the front pew. "I can't do this, Trent."

She sat at the counsel table, more than post-docket crash knocking her off her feet.

Trent took the other chair, setting his double briefcase beside Hannah's overstuffed one.

"You're a good lawyer, Hannah. You can't throw seven years education and tons of ability out with the trash."

"I can't throw the rest of my life into the practice of law if it isn't right for me. I wanted to tame the courthouse dragons, I see that now, but they're not dragons. They're merely people trying their human best to manage impossible situations with tools that aren't always effective."

The room was silent, save for the wind rattling a back window. A bailiff came by and collected the water pitchers from the counsel tables.

"So you're leaving?" Trent asked when they were alone again. His tone was neutral, which hurt worse than if he'd made the question an accusation.

"I won't jump ship until you have a replacement," Hannah said. "I can impersonate a lawyer for a few more weeks." They would be long, hard weeks, even though making the decision to go gave her a sense of peace. "My parents might not understand."

"Families work through these things."

Hannah rose and took the child's mitten—grimy white with purple *X*'s and *O*'s stitched across the back—up to the judge's desk.

"You'll be busy over the holidays, won't you?" she asked. Foster care placements often fell apart during the week between Christmas and New Year's. Children who'd been promised a long overdue Christmas visit from Mom or Dad went to pieces when the visit never happened. Domestic violence on Christmas Eve was second only to the mayhem on Super Bowl Sunday.

"No busier than usual." Trent remained where he was, his big briefcase on the table before him.

Hannah didn't return to the counsel table, but took a seat on the front pew, which was about as cold and uncomfortable as a place to sit could be.

"Where does this leave us, Trent? I know you are unhappy because I don't like being a lawyer and you do. I suspect you're still angry because I didn't tell you about foster care or Grace's father, and those are serious problems. I'm sorry for my part in them, but if you can't be civil to me, then just admit it, and I'll give you as much space as I can."

He sat beside her when Hannah expected him to get up and walk away.

"It's not as simple as you not liking to be a lawyer," he said. "I've trained new attorneys before, and everyone goes through a period of disillusionment. Usually, I can be enough moral support that a balanced perspective results. In your case..."

"In my case?"

"How can we become more, become closer as people, when you've gone through what you have, and I have no intention of changing my job? I love what I do, Hannah. I go home every night knowing somebody's life is better because I was a good lawyer. Somebody gets to see more of their kids, even if they don't get custody. Somebody gets a lighter fine and has more money left to pay the bills. Somebody gets into rehab because I tell them their case requires it. The work I do matters to me."

"I'm listening," she said, pushing his hair back over his ear, possibly for the last time.

"I can't reconcile what I do with who you are, Hannah. How can I expect you to continue to work with a system that almost took your child?" He scrubbed a hand over his face. "You can't do it, Hannah. I know you that well, and you can't."

"So if I can't love your legal system, I can't love you?"

He stared at the empty judge's bench for a long moment, while Hannah marveled at what she'd just admitted to him.

Cross-examination was hell.

"Trent, I don't have any answers right now. I have a rattled daughter and an aching heart, also two parents who doubtless want a place in my life. I can't fall in love with the American system of justice, and I don't want to."

She went silent, drawing in a breath at what she'd almost said: *I don't want to fall out of love with you.*

But Trent could hear only the words she spoke aloud.

"You can transfer to corporate in the spring, Hannah, but it won't solve anything. Tee times can still drive dockets; some days attorneys are more interested in their gossip than their cases; and other days, the best judge can come down with a migraine. Sooner or later, if I'm what's keeping you tied to the practice of law, you will hate me. I could not abide that."

Maybe he was talking himself into dumping her,

or talking her into dumping him. Either way, Hannah didn't like the verdict.

"Trenton Knightley, you are deciding a lot of things based on incomplete information. I have said I won't leave you in the lurch, and I am not your former wife, to go merrily on my way when we hit some rough sailing. I am not close to many people, but I'm loyal as hell to the few people I have, and that, too, is a result of spending years in foster care."

He took her hand. "You need to know something."

She needed to know a lot of things, like how to pay the bills after she'd finished serving her sentence as a domestic relations attorney. Like how to mend a heart she'd thought couldn't ever break again, because she wasn't merely loyal to Trent Knightley, she was in love with the guy.

"Just tell me, Trent. As long as Grace is OK, I can cope." Having Trent's hand to hold helped too.

"Anonymous calls provoked the Department's attempt to shelter Grace," he said. "Yesterday afternoon, I got one of those anonymous calls from a woman who claimed that Gerald Matthews set you up with DSS. She gave me the times he'd called Child Protective Services, and described what he'd threatened that kid Larry with to get him to pick on Grace. I didn't ask for details beyond that, and she assured me Gerald wouldn't be bothering you again."

Hannah slid over so she could lean against Trent. "*Gerald* did this me? Did this to Grace?" Did this to the Knightleys too, and most especially to Trent. "That bastard."

"The story doesn't end there. Mac was listening to

the scanner last night, and a team of EMTs responded to a call from a convenience store downtown. Gerald was in the alley out behind the store, having suffered multiple contusions, as the saying goes. The EMTs did a routine drug test. It seems Gerald's family will put him into rehab somewhere on the West Coast, once he's out of the hospital." Trent's arm came around Hannah's shoulders. "You still OK?"

"Multiple contusions?"

"Several possible fractures, including the middle fingers of both hands, which Mac says is some kind of gang signature. The alley was dark, and Gerald never saw his attackers. Maybe there's bad karma in store for people who abuse their anonymous calling privileges."

Which Gerald had apparently done in spades. "Will he return to the practice of law?"

"No, Stark, he will never return to the practice of law. Your own dear mother threw him upon the mercy of the ethics folks at the state bar association. She learned he'd been, ah, bartering his legal services for retainers of a variety we won't mention in these hallowed halls. Hell hath no fury like the legal system when one of its own breaks bad."

Trent had called her Stark, and he'd kissed Hannah's temple.

She kissed his cheek. "This is the nicest Christmas present you could possibly have given me." And he'd already given her so many.

Trent held her hand when he walked her out to her car and waited while she stashed her briefcase in the backseat. He had afternoon cases, while Hannah did not.

"Are we OK, Trent?"

"What are you doing Christmas Day?"

Not a yes. "I'm stuffing wrapping paper into the woodstove, probably watching Rudolph and Garfield for the zillionth time. I should ask Louise and Dan if they have plans." She also needed to thank her mother for her judicial activism.

Maybe Hannah should call them Mom and Dad? Another lovely Christmas present, and yet, Hannah needed Trenton Knightley for Christmas too—for the rest of her life.

"Let's plan a playdate for the girls, and you and I will talk further. Don't worry, Stark. I'm loyal to the people I love too."

He kissed Hannah a right smacker on the mouth, there in the courthouse parking lot. He loved her, and he'd said so. The joy of that gift was infinite and scary and wonderful, and yet, as Hannah drove back to the office, she did worry.

⁓

"Disney Studios should be named in the will of every single parent," Trent said. "What are you having? I have Earl Grey, green tea with jasmine, hot chocolate, some orange and clove stuff that Mac's partial to, this blackberry hibiscus woo-woo concoction, and peppermint."

Hannah sat at his kitchen table in jeans and a green V-neck sweater, while Trent babbled about tea to stop himself from kissing her.

"Peppermint will do. What are the girls watching?"

For all he knew, they were watching *King Kong Versus Godzilla.*

"Yet another princess, I'm sure. Mac tried to get

Merle interested in *The Quiet Man*, but once the horse race was over, she fell asleep."

"Shouldn't you be in the office?" Hannah asked.

"Are you trying to get rid of me, Stark?" They'd spoken by phone every day since the Christmas break had started, but Hartman and Whitney had the damnable policy of giving the employees the week between Christmas and New Year's off. The accountant had come up with that bright idea, and it meant the partners manned the oars over the holidays.

"James and Mac say I should be with Merle over Christmas," Trent replied, "and they're right."

"They are. I'd have Merle over tomorrow, but Grace and I are going into the school to talk about a peer mediation session with the guidance counselors. Larry's mom asked for it."

The tea water began to boil, the kettle whistling as Trent got down two mugs—Pooh and Eeyore.

"You'll subject Grace to a confrontation?" he asked. "After what that little creep put her through? What do you hope to accomplish?"

He and Hannah needed to confront a few issues, such as the fact that she was walking away from a profession that desperately needed her skills. Trent couldn't help but see that as a step away from him too.

"I'll see if my daughter is interested in attempting nonviolent conflict resolution, Trent. It's a novel concept. Popped up after the ducking stool and trial by ordeal went out of fashion. It can also involve courtrooms and judges and juries. People need to solve their problems without bloodshed if they can, and most schools have peer mediation programs as a result. You don't like the idea?"

She thought advocacy *wasn't* her calling? Trent poured the boiling water in the mugs and nearly scalded his knuckles in the process.

"Don't be obtuse, but what will having two kids talk accomplish?" Trent asked.

"Here is what the counselor told me: the schools encourage kids to solve their own problems in a peer mediation format. Merle probably got the same raft of paperwork in her backpack on this stuff as Grace did."

Trent dunked two peppermint tea bags into the mugs, recalling something about school mediation, but what dad kept track of everything that came home in the grubby confines of the almighty backpack?

"Larry knows he's done something really, really wrong, and he feels bad about it," Hannah went on. "He and Grace will share a playground, possibly for the next several years. He wants to apologize, and he wants to explain to Grace that Gerald threatened to kill his dog if he didn't push her around."

"He more than pushed her around."

"And we know Gerald would have at least killed the boy's dog, don't we?"

For that alone, twenty years in jail was less than Gerald deserved—Gerald, whom Trent had hired.

"Grace wants to make sure Larry wasn't picking on her because of something she did," Hannah explained. "She wants to feel safe, and she wants to make sure Larry knows he caused a very big problem. I think Grace should tell the little booger off. She's too reticent, or she used to be. What is wrong with this happening with the assistance of a trained counselor?"

Trent stared at the two steaming teacups, the scent of peppermint wafting to his nose. "Nothing."

Was there a peer mediation program for lawyers whose views of the courthouse could not be more opposed?

"It's complete information, Trent. Two people who have different parts of a story fitting them together to solve a problem. Judge Stevens mentioned this at Grace's hearing, and I haven't been able to get it out of my head. It's basic to problem solving, and on my worst day, I will still admit the legal system tries to solve problems for people."

He squirted agave nectar into both mugs, though he didn't want Hannah throwing him a bone. The legal system was flawed, true, but every human system, from the family to the interstate highways, was flawed.

Hannah came up behind him and slipped her arms around his waist. "I don't want Grace to grow up the way I did, thinking she has to solve every problem on her own. I want her to know she can make friends and allies, that she doesn't have to face every battle as if it's single combat."

When had Hannah initiated an embrace? Trent tried to think back but was too befuddled by the pleasure of her breasts pressed against his back. He turned and wrapped his arms around her.

"You're not alone now, Stark. You have me. I can't accept that your law degree is so much effort and money wasted, though. You have a legal mind, you get the issues, you could fit in almost anywhere in the company, and when you do go to court—"

"When I go to court, I get the uh-oh feeling," Hannah

said. "I hate the uh-oh feeling, and you can't argue me past it. I get mad, cranky, and very oppositional when I'm trying to avoid the uh-oh feeling. I'd rather be smart and helpful, or smart and creative, or smart and—"

Insight clobbered Trent between one nibble on his chin and the next. Hannah wasn't afraid of messy problems. Her entire childhood had been one big messy problem, and she'd waded through it. Adulthood had presented more problems for her, and she'd dealt with those too. Lawyers solved problems, but not all lawyers solved problems in courtrooms.

He kissed the daylights out of her, sat her up on the counter, and kissed her some more.

"Can you watch the girls for a while?" Trent asked.

"Of course."

"I need to pop into the office, and then, Stark, we're having a sleepover."

"Bring home pizza," Hannah said, a slow smile illuminating her features. "Black olives and pepperonis are fine, but no dead fish."

"And no pineapple."

Trent did not kiss her again, lest he be late for an important, as yet unscheduled partner's meeting. He found James and Mac in the office kitchen, making popcorn and looking lonely.

"We're smart guys, right?" Trent said, tossing his jacket and briefcase on a table. "Good at coming up with creative solutions to life's hardest problems."

"So smart we're in here, while our loyal minions are all home, sleeping off excesses of fruitcake and wassail," Mac said. "Which you ought to be too."

"I have more important things to do." Trent got a

hand on each brother's nape and propelled them toward
the chairs at the nearest table. "I'm calling a meeting of
the partners, right now, and you two geniuses had better
be listening, because I have a proposal to make."

"Does Hannah know about this proposal?" James
asked, snagging the popcorn while Trent pushed
him along.

"No, but if you two like it, she'll know soon."

"You've heard of Alternative Dispute Resolution," Mac
said. "We've been sending parents to custody mediation for years, but now all the big firms are trying to
get in on the action. Mediation and collaborative law
are the family law faces of ADR, but in the criminal
arena, we're seeing victim-offender conferencing, and
in the corporate world, mediation and arbitration have
become standard contract clauses to head off litigation
wherever possible."

Mac and his opening arguments. Hannah looked
across the conference table to Trent for some clue
regarding the meeting's agenda, but his expression gave
away nothing.

"What has this to do with me?"

"District Court is clogged with petty squabbles
between neighbors," Mac went on. "Barking dogs,
encroaching tree limbs, and landlord-tenant disputes.
The judges would kill to have a civil mediation resource
available to sort out the cases truly in need of judicial attention."

"We think it's time we had a collaborative law
and ADR department," James said. "It's a market

opportunity, and the good old boys and girls practicing out here in God's country don't see it staring them in the face. We're willing to put some effort into being the first on the block to have this service, this resource, in as many areas of law as possible. We figure if we're good enough, the DC and Baltimore cases will come out here because we can be much cheaper and more responsive than anything available to them in the city."

Some of the firms Hannah had temped at had these capabilities—or some of them—but those were big companies with deep pockets.

While the Knightleys had big hearts.

For the first time in weeks, Hannah felt a fluttering of hope that her law school education might not have been the biggest mistake of her life. She again looked to Trent, but he was flipping his tie while Mac was still holding forth.

"The judges are meeting in January to decide which firm will get the bulk of their family mediation cases, and Trent says we already have the inside track, because he typically sends his associates to at least eighty hours of mediation training in their first year. Lee and Ann are both already up to speed, as is Trent."

"I have some of that training," Hannah said. "I took negotiation and arbitration in law school because it interested me, but they offered only the basic forty-hour mediation course."

"We've scheduled you for advanced mediation training in January," James said. "In case you're interested."

"Interested?" *Why wouldn't Trent look at her?*

"In the position," Mac said. "We could advertise, but you're a known quantity, you have excellent academic credentials, and we run a family business. So what do you think?"

"Of what?"

James smiled the way Grace would have smiled if Santa Claus had brought her a pony.

"We're offering you the newly created position of head of the Alternative Dispute Resolution Department, Hannah. You'll have to build your practice from the ground up, choose your staff carefully, and work long hours to make it profitable, but you were highly recommended for the position."

She studied at each brother in turn, the hope transmuting into dawning joy. "By whom was I recommended?"

"All three of us," Mac said. "And Bronco."

"If I take what you're offering, I'd leave Trent shorthanded," she said, hoping it would force Trent to *say something*. *To at least look at her.*

"You can work out the timing of this with him," Mac said, rising. "I'll get a revised version of the corporate organization chart together, and James can let Gail know we'll need new associates in corporate, family, and the newly created ADR Departments."

He left, clapping Trent hard on the shoulder on the way out, probably Mac's version of the happy dance.

"I'm not sure leaving you two unchaperoned is a good idea," James said. "Seems to me more like a *great* idea." He left as well, passing his hand over Hannah's hair as he went.

"Are we supposed to carry on like a pair of minks now?" Hannah asked. She hadn't accepted the position, a detail neither James nor Mac seemed concerned about.

Trent shifted to sit on the table beside Hannah's chair.

"I ran this by your folks, Hannah, and they thought it was a splendid idea. You can't try cases in front of Louise anyway, and nobody would have looked forward to opposing you, given your family connections."

She had folks now, and family connections. Merry Christmas and Happy New Year forever—but did she have Trent? "Was this about my family connections?"

"In a way, yes."

Hannah folded her arms and laid her head in Trent's lap. Sleepovers had made her cuddly. Next, the thought of cheesy shells would inspire her to purring.

"Honest reply, Counselor Knightley, but a little high-handed of you, cooking this up without telling me."

"I had to be sure it was truly a good idea, and not wishful thinking on my part. Mac said he'd been considering something similar, and James told me there's more money to be made in corporate arbitration than I ever dreamed of."

"Let's hope you're all right. I don't ever want to set foot in a courtroom again."

Silence settled as Trent smoothed Hannah's hair back over her shoulder. She wore it down now, the entire bun-and-barrettes drill having lost its appeal.

"What about a courthouse?" Trent asked quietly.

"Hmm?"

The rhythmic motion of his hand soothed Hannah's nerves, and tension she'd held inside for days unraveled. She wouldn't have to change jobs. She wouldn't have to leave the Knightleys' practice, and she wouldn't ever, ever have to litigate beyond the cases she'd handle for Trent over the next little while.

Neither would she have to worry that legal matters would come between her and Trent.

"I should be mad at you," she said, eyes drifting closed. "Letting me stew and worry and fret. What did you say about a courthouse?"

"I was hoping your allergy to courtrooms did not extend to the whole courthouse." His hand disappeared.

Hannah sat up and blinked. "What are you up to now, Trenton Knightley?"

"Let's talk about your schedule for the next few weeks. Your predecessor in my department was safely delivered of a slightly premature but healthy baby over the holidays. She expects to be back by the end of February. You willing to hang around family law that long?"

"Sure." Trent was holding out on her. Hannah could tell because he still wasn't meeting her gaze. Some of her anxiety crept back. "I guess that means I should be free to jump into this Alternative Dispute Resolution business by about March."

"March, it is. I think I can stand it that long."

"Stand what?" Hannah asked, her lawyer hackles coming up.

"Stand not being married to you, yet. While you still work for me, in a sense."

Yet…in a sense. Married. *Married?*

Hannah reared back in her chair. "Married, as in, married at the courthouse?"

"As in exactly that."

"You discussed this with my folks too, didn't you?" Her folks, who'd been all smiles and knowing glances when Hannah had had them over for dinner *last night*.

Trent didn't even look embarrassed. "I need reinforcements sometimes too, Stark, particularly when the stakes are the highest I've ever faced."

"You brought it up with the girls?"

"Not yet. Not with the unicorns, either—did I tell you I think Trailclimber is a mare? We should talk to the children together, if you agree. I'm pretty sure they've already drawn some conclusions of their own."

He was nervous, and Hannah hated that, but she had one more question.

"Did you tell your brothers you had marital plans for the head of the newly hatched Alternative Resolution Department?"

"They love you," Trent said. "Even Mac said I'd be a damned fool to let you and Grace slip through my fingers." He smiled, suggesting Mac had said a bit more than that.

"Well, then, no."

Trent hung his head, then nodded once before shoving off the table and turning to leave.

Hannah's voice stopped him, though she had to speak to his back.

"No, I will not wait until March to marry the man I love, the man who has saved my hopes and my heart. The man who has found a way to reconcile our philosophical differences without sacrificing our professional integrity. I will not wait until March"—Hannah took an unsteady breath—"to marry the man who is the father my daughter should have had, and the husband I dearly need and want. I can't wait that long. I need him too much. Right now."

Hannah was afraid Trent wouldn't turn around, terrified despite his words and his deeds, he'd walk right out that door, taking her heart with him. She'd been rejected before, rejected and rejected and rejected.

She went to him and wrapped her arms around his middle, pressing her cheek to his back. "Please, Trent?"

His arms closed around her, his embrace familiar and treasured. "They make you wait forty-eight hours for a license, and you have to pay cash."

"I have the cash. Race you to the car."

They were married at the county courthouse exactly fifty-two hours later. Attending as witnesses were the firm's two other partners, Judges Halverston and Merriman, both girls, and according to Grace, one smiling, spotted, winged white unicorn.

Read on for a sneak peek at the next book in the Sweetest Kisses series:

The First Kiss

A YEAR IN DIVORCE PURGATORY HAD TAUGHT VERA Waltham two lessons.

First lesson: When her ex acted like an idiot, she was allowed to be angry—she was getting good at it, in fact.

Second lesson: Vera could rely, absolutely and without hesitation, on her attorney's word. If Trent Knightley said somebody would soon be on her doorstep with a copy of the restraining order, that somebody was already headed her way.

Vera's emergency automotive repair service was a shakier bet.

"Ma'am, if this is the number where you can be reached, we'll call you back when we've located a mechanic in your immediate area."

"In my immediate area, you'll find cows, chickens, and the occasional fat groundhog. The truck is sitting in my garage."

"Then this isn't a *roadside* emergency?" The dispatcher clearly had raised small children, for she'd hit the balance between dismay and shaming smack on the nose.

"I'm stranded without wheels, nothing but open fields, bad weather, and my lawyer's phone number to comfort me. Please get somebody out to fix that tire, ASAP."

Vera was stranded in her own toasty kitchen, but what if Twy came home from school with a sore throat? Long walk to the urgent care in freezing temperatures, that's what, because bucolic Damson County boasted no rural taxi service.

"We'll do the best we can, ma'am. Please stay near your phone until a mechanic calls you back."

"Thanks. I'll do that."

The line went dead, which meant the next step was locating the truck's owner's manual. Vera was still nose down in a description of something called the spare brace assembly when wheels crunched on the crushed gravel of her driveway.

An SUV pulled up at the foot of her steps, and a man in a sheepskin jacket and cowboy hat got out.

Could be a mechanic. He was broad-shouldered, he drove a motorhead's sort of vehicle, and he wasn't wearing gloves.

A pianist noticed hands. His were holding a signature Hartman and Whitney navy blue folder. When he rapped on Vera's door, she undid all three dead bolts and opened it.

Not Trent Knightley, but a close resemblance suggested Vera beheld one of the brothers with whom he shared a law practice. Same blue, blue eyes; same lean, muscular height; same wavy hair, though this guy was blond rather than dark.

"Hello," she said, opening the door wider. "You're either from Hartman and Whitney, or you're the best dressed truck mechanic I've ever seen."

"James Knightley. Pleased to meet you." He stepped over the threshold, removed his hat, and hung it on the brass coatrack. "Trent asked me to bring you a copy of a restraining order. He said it was urgent."

"My thanks, Mr. Knightley." Vera closed the door behind him and shot the dead bolts, then extended her hand in anticipation of gaining possession of a copy of the court order.

Instead, Vera's hand was enveloped by a big male paw, one graced with calluses she would not have expected to find on a lawyer.

James Knightley had manners—also warm hands. When he'd tended to the civilities—firm grip, not out to prove anything—he passed her the blue folder.

Vera flipped it open, needing to see with her own eyes that he'd brought her the right court order.

"Was there a reason to get it certified?" she asked.

"The courthouse was on my way here. If you needed a certified copy, then nothing less would do."

Consideration and an eye for details were delightful qualities in any man.

As were warm hands and a mellow baritone voice.

"May I offer you a cup of tea, some hot chocolate? It's cold out, and this errand has brought you several miles from town." Vera offered out of basic good manners, but also because anger eventually burned itself out, while a front tire on her only serviceable vehicle was still slashed, and the intricacies of the spare brace assembly thingie had yet to reveal themselves to her.

Then too, James Knightley had something of his brother's reassuring air. Maybe lawyers took classes in how to be reassuring, the way a pianist took a master class in Brahms or Rachmaninoff.

As he unbuttoned his jacket, James glanced around

at the foyer's twelve-foot ceilings, the crown mold-
ing, the beveled glass in the windows on either side
of the foyer. Vera had the sense he did this not with a
mercenary eye—not pricing property in anticipation of
litigation—but rather with the slow, thorough appraisal
of the craftsman. Pine dowels in the cross beam, hand-
made stained glass insets for the oriel window—he
inspected these, the way Vera had to stop and listen
for a moment to any piano playing in any venue, however faintly.

"A cup of hot chocolate would hit the spot," he said,
shrugging out of his jacket. "Trent said you had a lovely
old house, and he did not lie."

That smile.

Good heavens, that smile. Trent Knightley was tall,
dark, and handsome, a charming and very intelligent
man whom Vera had happily flaunted in Donal's face,
but this James…

He left a subtly more masculine impression. Donal
would hate him on sight.

James's gaze held a warmth Trent's had lacked, at least
when aimed at Vera. His smile reached his eyes, eyes a
peculiarly dark shade of blue fringed with long lashes.

Vera had no business admiring a man's eyelashes, for
the love of St. Peter. Or his hands, or his voice.

"To the kitchen, then," she said, leading James
through the music room and into the back of the house.
"My favorite room in the house."

"I'd guess this place predates the Civil War. Did you
have a lot of work done?"

"I intend to raise my daughter here, so I had the house
fitted out exactly as I wanted it." Right down to the

security system, which had done her absolutely no good earlier that very afternoon.

"I have a renovated farmhouse of my own. Every night when I tool up my driveway, and she's sitting under the oaks waiting for me in all her drafty splendor, I am glad to call her mine."

A poet lawyer, who composed odes to his farmhouse. Different, indeed.

"But we're not so glad to pay the heating bills," Vera said as they reached the kitchen. The room was blessedly cozy because of the pellet stove sitting in one corner of the fireplace.

"Good Lord, this must be original." James ran a hand over the gray fieldstones of the hearth. "Five feet square at least, and these look like genuine buggy axles."

He fingered the pot swings on either side of the enormous fireplace, then draped his coat over the back of a chair.

"I don't know what they are," Vera said. "An old Mennonite gentleman came to point and parge, and he ended up doing a great deal more than that. I love that fireplace, but I also love the exposed chestnut logs and the flagstone floor. This time of year, I wear two pairs of wool socks twenty-four-seven. Have a seat."

James wandered around the kitchen a while longer, a man who apparently enjoyed touching things—the mantel, the cabinets, the marble counters, the drawer pulls of the antique breakfront that stored her mother's china. He caressed wood and stone as if he'd coax secrets from Vera's counters and chimney, while she wondered where he'd acquired his calluses.

"Whipped cream, Mr. Knightley?"

"Please, and a little nutmeg, if you have it."

"A connoisseur." And lo, lurking next to the oregano in Vera's spice rack was a canister of nutmeg, probably leftover from holiday baking. A connoisseur would appreciate fresh, homemade cookies, so she got down her cookie tin and peered inside. "We're in luck. My daughter has left us a few cookies."

Half a batch of homemade chocolate-chip pecan turtles remained, and they'd be scrumptious with hot chocolate.

"Don't bother putting them on a plate," James said. "I can dip into the jar, same as any other civilian. How long have you lived here?"

He could probably finish the entire batch without gaining an ounce, too, and keep up the small talk the entire time.

Which was...charming? A lifetime spent in practice rooms and concert halls didn't equip a woman with a ready ability to analyze men.

Sobering thought.

"I moved here with my daughter a little over a year ago," Vera said, putting a plain white mug of whole milk into the microwave. "Twyla will get off the school bus in about fifteen minutes, and if I'm going to walk to the foot of the lane, I'd better not linger over my hot chocolate."

A bit rude, offering the man a drink one minute and hustling him along the next. Anger could leave a woman that rattled, but Vera's guest didn't seem offended.

"Your lane has to be half a mile long, and it's not quite thirty degrees out with a mighty brisk breeze. Are you sure you want to walk that distance?"

"I'm sure I do not," she said, giving his hot chocolate

a final stir. "But somebody has broken into my garage. Today, I don't expect an eight-year-old to trudge that distance by herself." Though Twyla did, on the days when her mother wasn't feeling paranoid.

Angry, not paranoid. Rattled, anyway.

And mildly charmed.

Something in James's expression changed, became more focused. "Your garage was broken into? You mentioned a mechanic."

"One of my tires is flat. I've called the road service, but I'm off the beaten path, and finding somebody to put on the spare will take a while. I'm pretty sure I can figure it out. I've changed a tire or two."

Half a lifetime ago, on a vintage Bug, while one of her brothers had alternately coached her and laughed uproariously.

Now would be a good time for a guy with broad shoulders and competent hands to tell her that tires went flat for no reason all the time. Even brand-new tires that had cost a bundle to have put on and balanced.

When Vera had squirted whipped cream onto James's hot chocolate, he appropriated the nutmeg from her and did the honors, then spun the lazy Susan that held her spices and added a dash of cinnamon.

They worked in the same assembly line fashion on Vera's drink, the spices contributing a soothing note to the kitchen fragrances.

"Ladies first," James said, saluting with his mug.

Because James looked like he'd wait all winter, Vera took a sip of her drink.

Rich, interesting, sweet, and nourishing—an altogether lovely concoction in the middle of a dreadful day.

A small increment of Vera's upset slid away, or at least from her immediate grasp.

"Your vehicle was vandalized while your car sat in a garage that I'll presume you keep locked," James said, staring at his mug. "You suspect your ex is behind this?"

Lawyers, even hot chocolate–swilling lawyers with interesting blue eyes, were good at putting together facts.

Right now, that was a helpful quality.

"I'm fairly certain my ex is carrying a grudge," Vera said, "and fairly certain he stole my copy of the restraining order. Without it, if I call the cops, they might show up, but they won't do anything if they find Donal here. If I can wave the order at them, they might lock him up."

James helped himself to a paper towel and passed one to Vera, folding his up to use as a coaster on her butcher-block counter. He wasn't shy about sharing personal space, and he smelled good—piney, outdoorsy, and—best of all—not like Donal.

"Domestic relations law hasn't been my area for several years," he said, "but I think you have the gist of it. If you like, I can reach Trent on his cell and verify that."

"Please don't. I already feel like a ninny for calling him. He's newly married, isn't he?"

"Very, and he chose well this time."

James's tone suggested the first Mrs. Knightley had not enjoyed her brother-in-law's wholehearted approval, though her successor apparently did.

"I chose reasonably well the first time," Vera said, "not so well on the rebound."

"Whereas I have yet to choose. You make a mean hot chocolate, Mrs. Waltham." He touched his mug to Vera's, probably signaling an end to the self-disclosure session.

"Call me Vera, and have some cookies."

He took a bite of cookie, catching the crumbs in his hand. "What time did you say the bus came?"

"Any minute. Why?"

He put a set of keys on the counter. "We can take my car."

"That's not necessary." In truth, as charming as he was, as handsome as he was, the idea of getting into a vehicle with James left Vera uneasy. Donal was handsome and occasionally gruffly charming. He could also be a damned conniving snake with a bad temper.

"You take the car then." James slid the keys toward her. "It's colder than a well digger's…boots out there, and I have a niece who's seven—a pair of them, actually. This isn't weather a lady should have to face alone at the end of a long day."

Twyla bounced up the lane on colder days than this, and James had to know that—the Knightley family was local, after all. He'd passed Vera his keys for another reason, one having to do with her near panic at having no wheels, and ladies facing bad weather all on their own.

"I can put your spare on while you wait for the bus," he said, while the keys sat three inches from Vera's hand.

Until fifteen months ago, Vera had never lived on her own, ever. She'd given up leaning on a man, and so far, the results had been wonderful—when they weren't scary.

"I can't let you do that, James. It's too much trouble."

"It's no trouble at all to a guy who was tearing down

engines from little up. I like the smell of axle grease, and I haven't had homemade cookies since I don't know when. Scat," he said, taking her hand and slapping the keys into her palm. "If you leave now, you can have the seats nice and toasty by the time your daughter gets off the bus."

He brought his mug to the sink and rinsed it out, leaving it in the drain rack. The line of his back was long and lean in the vest of what looked like a very expensive three-piece suit.

What was Vera *doing*, ogling the man's back?

James Knightley washed his dishes, and for some reason, that reassured Vera he could be trusted to change a tire. Even so, she had to wonder what Trent Knightley had told his brother of her divorce. Attorney-client privilege was one thing, but James was both brother and law partner to Trent.

Men gossiped. Alexander had assured her they gossiped as much as women did, and Vera's first husband had not lied to her...all that often.

"The garage is this way," she said, leaving her hot chocolate unfinished. "You can take the cookies with you."

"They're good." He took one more and set the tin back up on top of the fridge with the casual ease of a tall man. "Trent recalls your cookies fondly."

Not a hint of innuendo in that line—not that innuendo would have been welcome.

"I'll drop a batch off the next time I'm in town," Vera said, turning on the garage lights. "Call it a wedding present. I think the temperature has fallen as the day has gone on."

"We're supposed to get a dump of snow later this

week and—Vera Waltham, I am in love. You own a 1964 Ford Falcon, and this blue is probably the original paint color. My, my, my. Does she run?"

Cars and houses were female to James Knightley. Would he also consider pianos female?

"Not at the moment. The Faithful Falcon needs a battery, among other things, but some fine day, I want to see my daughter behind that wheel. The car belonged to Alexander's grandmother, and he wanted Twyla to have it."

James left off perusing the old car and scowled at Vera's other vehicle, a late-model bright red Tundra, listing slightly.

"That's why nobody wants to come change your tire."

"What's why?"

"These pickups have the spare up under the bed," he said, opening the truck's driver's side door.

His movements and his voice were brisk, all male-in-anticipation-of-using-tools-and-getting-his-hands-dirty. "The mechanism for holding the spare in its brace always gets rusted, and to get the tire down, you have to thread this puppy here"—he rummaged under her backseat—"through a little doodad over the tag, and into a slot about"—he emerged holding the jack and a long metal rod—"the size of a pea, and then get it to work, despite the corrosion. I love me a sturdy truck, but the design of the spare brace assembly leaves something to be desired. Why are you looking at me like that?"

Like she'd heard no sweeter music that day than a man recounting the pleasures of intimate association with a truck? He cradled the jack assembly the way some violinists held their concert instruments.

"You reminded me of my oldest brother. I forget not all men are like Donal."

Some men dropped their afternoon plans, took time to get a court order certified, minded their manners, and rinsed out their dishes. Some men changed tires without being asked. Vera would never be in love again—Olga had an entire lecture about the pitfalls of romantic attraction—but Vera could appreciate a nice guy when one came to her door.

"I couldn't stop you from changing that tire if I tried, could I?"

"No. You could not. Trucks and I go way back, and I don't like this Donal character very much." James's gold cuff links had gone into a pocket, and he was already turning back his sleeves. "Don't you have a school bus to catch?"

He said it with a smile, with one of those charming, endearing smiles. Could he know that for Vera to even drive down the lane alone would take a bit of courage?

Fortunately, nobody embarked on a solo career at age seventeen without saving up some stores of courage.

"You're right. I have a bus to catch," Vera said. "You're sure this is OK?"

"Shoo," he replied, positioning the jack under the axle with his foot. "I may not be done by the time you get back, but I will put the hurt to the rest of those cookies before I go, if your daughter doesn't beat me to it."

Vera left him in her garage, cheerfully popping loose lug nuts. If she'd had to do that, she'd probably have been jumping up and down on the tire iron while calling on St. Jude, and still the blasted bolts would not have budged.

Kiss Me Hello

A Sweetest Kisses Novel

by Grace Burrowes

New York Times and *USA Today* Bestselling Author

Sidonie Lindstrom's hands and heart are full—she's been uprooted from the urban life she loves, she's grieving for her brother while raising her foster son Luis, and she's trying to find a job with meaning.

But her burdens feel lighter when she meets MacKenzie Peckham. Their attraction is powerful and unexpected. Life is perfect…until Sid learns that Mac hasn't been completely honest about his job. When problems arise with Luis's foster care situation, she must decide: Can she trust Mac again, when she has so much more to lose?

Praise for Grace Burrowes:

"Burrowes's great writing and ability to bring her characters to life with subtle power and authenticity enhance an emotionally charged romance." —*Kirkus*

"I love her style of writing and the stories she tells have depth and emotion that will capture your heart and mind." —*Night Owl Reviews*

For more Grace Burrowes, visit:

www.sourcebooks.com

A Little on the Wild Side

by Robin Kaye

———~~~———

A woman who gets what she wants...

Bianca Ferrari—ex-supermodel turned successful businesswoman—seems to have it all: beauty, brains, and a career she loves. And she did it all by herself through sheer force of will and ruthless determination. So when her life is suddenly turned upside down, it's hard for her to admit that going it alone may not be an option.

A man who knows what she needs...

Sexy, rugged, and down-to-earth, Trapper Kincaid has a knack for attracting all kinds of women—mostly the wrong kind. When he finds out that the exhaustingly independent and drop-dead gorgeous Bianca is in serious need of help, he knows he's the man for the job. But Bianca isn't going to make it easy...

———~~~———

Praise for Robin Kaye:

"Robin Kaye's writing style is a pleasure to read. It's fun and lively. Every single character comes to life." —*Books Like Breathing*

"Robin Kaye continues to write smart, witty, and quirky novels." —*Romancing the Book*

For more Robin Kaye, visit:

www.sourcebooks.com

One Mad Night

by Julia London

New York Times and *USA Today* Bestselling Author

Two Romantic Adventures

One winter's night a blizzard sweeps across the country, demonstrating that fate can change the course of lives in an instant…and fate has a sense of humor.

One Mad Night

Chelsea Crawford and Ian Rafferty are high-profile ad execs in cutthroat competition for a client. When a major winter storm puts New York City on lockdown, the two rivals have to make it through the night together.

The Bridesmaid

When the weather wreaks havoc with transportation systems, Kate Preston and Joe Firretti meet as they are both trying to rent the last car available… As Kate races to her best friend's wedding, and Joe races to a job interview, it looks like together is the only way they'll make it at all.

Praise for Julia London:

"London knows how to keep pages turning… winningly fresh and funny." —*Publishers Weekly*

For more Julia London, visit:

www.sourcebooks.com

Return to You

A Montgomery Brothers Novel

by Samantha Chase

New York Times and *USA Today* Bestselling Author

She will never forget their past...

He can't stop thinking about their future...

James Montgomery has achieved everything he'd hoped for in life...except marrying the girl of his dreams. After a terrible accident, Selena Ainsley left ten years ago. She took his heart with her, and she's never coming back. But it's becoming harder and harder for him to forget their precious time together, and James can't help but wonder what he would do if they could ever meet again.

What readers are saying about Samantha Chase:

"Samantha Chase really knows how to tell a story."

"Perfect romance! Love it, love it, love it!"

For more Samantha Chase, visit:

www.sourcebooks.com

The Deepest Night

by Kara Braden

—⁓—

When everything you love is on the line…

The Isles of Scilly off the coast of England are remote, windswept, and wild. They're the perfect place for Ray Powell to recuperate after the toughest Afghanistan mission the military contractor has ever run. Except instead of the peace and quiet he so desperately needs, he's faced with a beautiful American woman who instantly challenges his iron control.

It's best to proceed with caution…

Seeking her own safe haven, Michelle Cole is intrigued and flustered by the intensely compelling and irresistible man.

As their cautious friendship slowly builds into simmering attraction, their hearts and souls are about to be broken open— if they'll allow it.

—⁓—

"This smashing sequel shows that respectful communication is downright scorching… This sweet contemporary will appeal to romance fans who like their heroes powerful and smitten and their heroines capable and genuine." —*Publishers Weekly* Starred Review

"The characters and plot are well developed, and *The Deepest Night* can stand alone." —*Booklist*

For more Kara Braden, visit:

www.sourcebooks.com

Full Throttle

Black Knights Inc.

by Julie Ann Walker

New York Times and *USA Today* bestselling author

—◦◦◦—

Steady hands, cool head...

Carlos "Steady" Soto's nerves of steel have served him well at the covert government defense firm of Black Knights Inc. But nothing has prepared him for the emotional roller coaster of guarding the woman he once loved and lost.

Will all he's got be enough?

Abby Thompson is content to leave politics and international intrigue to her father—the president of the United States—until she's taken hostage half a world away, and she fears her father's policy of not negotiating with terrorists will be her death sentence. There's one glimmer of hope: the man whose heart she broke, but she can never tell him why...

As they race through the jungle in a bid for safety, the heat simmering between Steady and Abby could mean a second chance for them—*if* they make it out alive...

—◦◦◦—

Praise for Julie Ann Walker:

"Drama, danger, and sexual tension... Romantic suspense at its best." —*Night Owl Reviews*, 5 Stars, Reviewer Top Pick, *Born Wild*

For more Julie Ann Walker, visit:

www.sourcebooks.com